Mary Balogh grew up in Wales and now lives with husband Robert in Saskatchewan, Canada. She has written more than 100 historical novels and novellas, more than 30 of which have been *New York Times* bestsellers. They include the Slightly sestet (the Bedwyn saga), the Simply quartet, the Huxtable quintet, the Westcott series and the Survivors' Club series.

Visit Mary Balogh online:

www.marybalogh.com
www.facebook.com/AuthorMaryBalogh

Praise for Mary Balogh:

'One of the best!'
Julia Quinn

'Today's superstar heir to the marvelous legacy of Georgette Heyer (except a lot steamier)'
Susan Elizabeth Phillips

'Ms Balogh is a veritable treasure, a matchless storyteller who makes our hearts melt with delight'
Romantic Times

'Balogh is truly a find'
Publishers Weekly

'Balogh is the queen of spicy Regency-era romance, creating memorable characters in unforgettable stories'

By Mary Balogh

Mistress Couplet:
NO MAN'S MISTRESS
MORE THAN A MISTRESS

THE SECRET MISTRESS
(PREQUEL TO THE
MISTRESS COUPLET
SERIES)

Huxtables Series:
FIRST COMES MARRIAGE
THEN COMES SEDUCTION
AT LAST COMES LOVE
SEDUCING AN ANGEL
A SECRET AFFAIR

Simply Quartet:
SIMPLY UNFORGETTABLE
SIMPLY LOVE
SIMPLY MAGIC
SIMPLY PERFECT

Bedwyn Series:
ONE NIGHT FOR LOVE
A SUMMER TO REMEMBER
SLIGHTLY MARRIED
SLIGHTLY WICKED
SLIGHTLY SCANDALOUS
SLIGHTLY TEMPTED
SLIGHTLY SINFUL
SLIGHTLY DANGEROUS

Survivors' Club Series:
THE PROPOSAL
THE ARRANGEMENT
THE ESCAPE
ONLY ENCHANTING
ONLY A PROMISE
ONLY A KISS
ONLY BELOVED

The Westcott Series:
SOMEONE TO LOVE

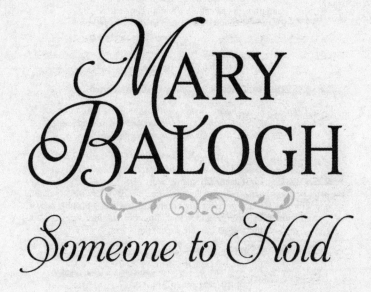

MARY BALOGH

Someone to Hold

piatkus

PIATKUS

First published in the US in 2017 by Berkley,
an imprint of Penguin Random House LLC
First published in Great Britain in 2017 by Piatkus

1 3 5 7 9 10 8 6 4 2

A CIP catalogue record for this book
is available from the British Library.

ISBN 978-0-349-41365-5

Printed and bound by CPI Group (UK) Ltd, Croydon, CR0 4YY

Papers used by Piatkus are from well-managed forests
and other responsible sources.

 MIX
Paper from
responsible sources
FSC® C104740
www.fsc.org

Piatkus
An imprint of
Little, Brown Book Group
Carmelite House
50 Victoria Embankment
London EC4Y 0DZ

An Hachette UK Company
www.hachette.co.uk

www.littlebrown.co.uk

The Westcott Family

(Characters from the family tree who appear in *Someone to Hold* are shown in bold print.)

Stephen Westcott m. Eleanor Coke
Earl of Riverdale (1704–1759)
(1698–1761)

Andrew Westcott m. Bertha Ames
(1726–1796)   (1736–1807)

David Westcott m. **Althea Radley**
(1756–1806)   (b. 1762)

Elizabeth m. Sir Desmond
Westcott   Overfield
(1779)   (1774–1809)

Alexander Westcott
Earl of Riverdale
(b. 1783)

George Westcott m. Eugenia Madson
Earl of Riverdale   (b. 1742)
(1724–1790)

Matilda Humphrey Westcott **Louise Westcott** m. John Archer **Mildred** m. Thomas Wayne
Westcott Earl of Riverdale   (b. 1770)   Duke of Netherby **Westcott**   Baron Molenor
(b. 1761) (1762–1812)   (1755–1809)   (b. 1773)   (b. 1769)

m. Alice Snow   m. **Viola Kingsley**   m. Ava Cobham
(1768–1789)   (b. 1772)   (1760–1790)

Boris   Peter   Ivan
Wayne   Wayne   Wayne
(b. 1796) (b. 1798) (b. 1799)

Jessica
Archer
(b. 1795)

Avery Archer
Duke of Netherby
(b. 1781)

Camille **Harry Westcott** **Abigail**
Westcott   (b. 1792)   **Westcott**
(b. 1790)   (b. 1794)

Anastasia Westcott   m.
(Anna Snow)
(b. 1787)

Someone to Hold

One

After several months of hiding away, wallowing in misery and denial, anger and shame, and any other negative emotion anyone cared to name, Camille Westcott finally took charge of her life on a sunny, blustery morning in July. At the grand age of twenty-two. She had not needed to take charge before the great catastrophe a few months before because she had been a lady—*Lady* Camille Westcott to be exact, eldest child of the Earl and Countess of Riverdale—and ladies did not have or need control over their own lives. Other people had that instead: parents, maids, nurses, governesses, chaperons, husbands, society at large—especially society at large with its myriad rules and expectations, most of them unwritten but nonetheless real on that account.

But she needed to assert herself now. She was no longer a lady. She was now simply *Miss* Westcott, and she was not even sure about the name. Was a bastard entitled to her father's name? Life yawned ahead of her as a frightening unknown. She had no idea what to expect of it. There were no more rules, no more expectations. There was no more society, no more place of belonging. If she did not take charge and *do* something, who would?

It was a rhetorical question, of course. She had not asked it aloud in anyone's hearing, but no one would have had a satisfactory answer to give her even if she had. So she was doing something about it herself. It was either that or cower in a dark corner somewhere for the rest of her natural-born days. She was no longer a lady, but she was, by God, a person. She was alive—she was breathing. She was *someone*.

Camille and Abigail, her younger sister, lived with their maternal grandmother in one of the imposing houses in the prestigious Royal Crescent in Bath. It stood atop a hill above the city, splendidly visible from miles around with its great sweeping inward curve of massive Georgian houses all joined into one, open parkland sloping downward before it. But the view worked both ways. From any front-facing window the inhabitants of the Crescent could gaze downward over the city and across the river to the buildings beyond and on out to the countryside and hills in the distance. It was surely one of the loveliest views in all England, and Camille had delighted in it as a child whenever her mother had brought her with her brother and sister on extended visits to their grandparents. It had lost much of its appeal, however, now that she was forced to live here in what felt very like exile and disgrace, though neither she nor Abigail had done anything to deserve either fate.

She waited on that sunny morning until her grandmother and sister had gone out, as they often did, to the

Pump Room down near Bath Abbey to join the promenade of the fashionable world. Not that the fashionable world was as impressive as it had once been in Bath's heyday. A large number of the inhabitants now were seniors, who liked the quiet gentility of life here in stately surroundings. Even the visitors tended to be older people who came to take the waters and imagine, rightly or wrongly, that their health was the better for imposing such a foul-tasting ordeal upon themselves. Some even submerged themselves to the neck in it, though that was now considered a little extreme and old-fashioned.

Abigail liked going to the Pump Room, for at the age of eighteen she craved outings and company, and apparently her exquisite youthful beauty was much admired, though she did not receive many invitations to private parties or even to more public entertainments. She was not, after all, quite respectable despite the fact that Grandmama was eminently so. Camille had always steadfastly refused to accompany them anywhere they might meet other people in a social setting. On the rare occasions when she did step out, usually with Abby, she did so with stealth, a veil draped over the brim of her bonnet and pulled down over her face, for more than anything else she feared being recognized.

Not today, however. And, she vowed to herself, never again. She was done with the old life, and if anyone recognized her and chose to give her the cut direct, then she would give it right back. It was time for a new life and new acquaintances. And if there were a few bumps to traverse in moving from one world to the other, well, then, she would deal with them.

After Grandmama and Abby had left, she dressed in

one of the more severe and conservative of her walking dresses, and donned a bonnet to match. She put on comfortable shoes, since the sort of dainty slippers she had always worn in the days when she traveled everywhere by carriage were useless now except to wear indoors. Finally taking up her gloves and reticule, she stepped out onto the cobbled street without waiting for a servant to open and hold the door for her and look askance at her lone state, perhaps even try to stop her or send a footman trailing after her. She stood outside for a few moments, assailed by a sudden terror bordering upon panic and wondering if perhaps after all she should scurry back inside to hide in darkness and safety. In her whole life she had rarely stepped beyond the confines of house or walled park unaccompanied by a family member or a servant, often both. But those days were over, even though Grandmama would doubtless argue the point. Camille squared her shoulders, lifted her chin, and strode off downhill in the general direction of Bath Abbey.

Her actual destination, however, was a house on Northumberland Place, near the Guildhall and the market and the Pulteney Bridge, which spanned the River Avon with grandiose elegance. It was a building indistinguishable from many of the other Georgian edifices with which the city abounded, solid yet pleasing to the eye and three stories high, not counting the basement and the attic, except that this one was actually three houses that had been made into one in order to accommodate an institution.

An orphanage, to be precise.

It was where Anna Snow, more recently Lady Anastasia Westcott, now the Duchess of Netherby, had spent her childhood. It was where she had taught for several years

after she grew up. It was from there that she had been summoned to London by a solicitor's letter. And it was in
London that their paths and their histories had converged,
Camille's and Anastasia's, the one to be elevated to heights
beyond her wildest imaginings, the other to be plunged to
depths lower than her worst nightmares.

Anastasia, also a daughter of the Earl of Riverdale,
had been consigned to the orphanage—by him—at a very
young age on the death of her mother. She had grown up
there, supported financially but quite ignorant of who she
was. She had not even known her real name. She had been
Anna Snow, Snow being her mother's maiden name—
though she had not realized that either. Camille, on the
other hand, born three years after Anastasia, had been
brought up to a life of privilege and wealth and entitlement with Harry and Abigail, her younger siblings. None
of them had known of Anastasia's existence. Well, Mama
had, but she had always assumed that the child Papa
secretly supported at an orphanage in Bath was the love
child of a mistress. It was only after his death several
months ago that the truth came out.

And what a catastrophic truth it was!

Alice Snow, Anastasia's mother, had been Papa's legitimate wife. They had married secretly in Bath, though
she had left him a year or so later when her health failed
and returned to her parents' home near Bristol, taking
their child with her. She had died sometime later of con-
sumption, but not until four months after Papa married
Mama in a bigamous marriage that had no legality. And
because the marriage was null and void, all issue of that
marriage was illegitimate. Harry had lost the title he had
so recently inherited, Mama had lost all social status and

had reverted to her maiden name—she now called herself Miss Kingsley and lived with her clergyman brother, Uncle Michael, at a country vicarage in Dorsetshire. Camille and Abigail were no longer *Lady* Camille and *Lady* Abigail. Everything that had been theirs had been stripped away. Cousin Alexander Westcott—he was actually a second cousin—had inherited the title and entailed property despite the fact that he had genuinely not wanted either, and Anastasia had inherited everything else. That *everything else* was the vast fortune Papa had amassed after his bigamous marriage to Mama. It also included Hinsford Manor, the country home in Hampshire where they had always lived when they were not in London, and Westcott House, their London residence.

Camille, Harry, Abigail, and their mother had been left with nothing.

As a final crushing blow, Camille had lost her fiancé. Viscount Uxbury had called upon her the very day they heard the news. But instead of offering the expected sympathy and support, and instead of sweeping her off to the altar, a special license waving from one hand, he had suggested that she send a notice to the papers announcing the ending of their betrothal so that she would not have to suffer the added shame of being cast off. Yes, a crushing blow indeed, though Camille never spoke of it. Just when it had seemed there could not possibly be any lower to sink or greater pain to be borne, there could be and there was, but the pain at least was something she could keep to herself.

So here she and Abigail were, living in Bath of all places on the charity of their grandmother, while Mama languished in Dorsetshire and Harry was in Portugal or

Spain as a junior officer with the 95th Foot Regiment, also known as the Rifles, fighting the forces of Napoleon Bonaparte. He could not have afforded the commission on his own, of course. Avery, Duke of Netherby, their stepcousin and Harry's guardian, had purchased it for him. Harry, to his credit, had refused to allow Avery to set him up in a more prestigious, and far more costly, cavalry regiment and had made it clear that he would not allow Avery to purchase any promotions for him either.

By what sort of irony had she ended up in the very place where Anastasia had grown up, Camille wondered, not for the first time, as she descended the hill. The orphanage had acted like a magnet ever since she came here, drawing her much against her will. She had walked past it a couple of times with Abigail and had finally— over Abby's protests—gone inside to introduce herself to the matron, Miss Ford, who had given her a tour of the institution while Abby remained outside without a chaperon. It had been both an ordeal and a relief, actually seeing the place, walking the floors Anastasia must have walked a thousand times and more. It was not the sort of horror of an institution one sometimes heard about. The building was spacious and clean. The adults who ran it looked well-groomed and cheerful. The children she saw were decently clad and nicely behaved and appeared to be well-fed. The majority of them, Miss Ford had explained, were adequately, even generously supported by a parent or family member even though most of those adults chose to remain anonymous. The others were supported by local benefactors.

One of those benefactors, Camille had been amazed to learn, though not of any specific child, was her own grandmother. For some reason of her own, she had recently called there and agreed to equip the schoolroom with a large bookcase and books to fill it. Why she had felt the need to do so, Camille did not know, any more than she understood her own compulsion to see the building and actually step inside it. Grandmama could surely feel no more kindly disposed toward Anastasia than she, Camille, did. Less so, in fact. Anastasia was at least Camille's half sister, perish the thought, but she was nothing to Grandmama apart from being the visible evidence of a marriage that had deprived her own daughter of the very identity that had apparently been hers for longer than twenty years. Goodness, Mama had been Viola Westcott, Countess of Riverdale, for all those years, though in fact the only one of those names to which she had had any legal claim was Viola.

Today Camille was going back to the orphanage alone. Anna Snow had been replaced by another teacher, but Miss Ford had mentioned in passing during that earlier visit that Miss Nunce might not remain there long. Camille had hinted with an impulsiveness that had both puzzled and alarmed her that she might be interested in filling the post herself, should the teacher resign. Perhaps Miss Ford had forgotten or not taken her seriously. Or perhaps she had judged Camille unsuited to the position. However it was, she had not informed Camille when Miss Nunce did indeed leave. It was quite by chance that Grandmama had seen the notice for a new teacher in yesterday's paper and had read it aloud to her granddaughters.

What on earth, Camille asked herself as she neared the bottom of the hill and turned in the direction of Northumberland Place, did she know about teaching? Specifically, what did she know about teaching a supposedly large group of children of all ages and abilities and both genders? She frowned, and a young couple approaching her along the pavement stepped smartly out of her way as though a fearful presence were bearing down upon them. Camille did not even notice.

Why on earth was she going to beg to be allowed to teach orphans in the very place where Anastasia had grown up and taught? She still disliked, resented, and—yes—even hated the former Anna Snow. It did not matter that she knew she was being unfair—after all, it was not Anastasia's fault that Papa had behaved so despicably, and she had suffered the consequences for twenty-five years before discovering the truth about herself. It did not matter either that Anastasia had attempted to embrace her newly discovered siblings as family and had offered more than once to share everything she had inherited with them and to allow her two half sisters to continue to live with their mama at Hinsford Manor, which now belonged to her. In fact, her generosity merely made it harder to like her. How dared she offer them a portion of what had always been theirs by right, as though she were doing them a great and gracious favor? Which in a sense she was.

It was a purely irrational hostility, of course, but raw emotions were not often reasonable. And Camille's emotions were still as raw as open wounds that had not even begun to heal.

So why exactly was she coming here? She stood on the pavement outside the main doors of the orphanage for a couple of minutes, debating the question just as though she had not already done so all yesterday and through a night of fitful sleep and long wakeful periods.

Was it just because she felt the need to *do* something with her life? But were there not other, more suitable things she could do instead? And if she must teach, were there not more respectable positions to which she might aspire? There were genteel girls' schools in Bath, and there were always people in search of well-bred governesses for their daughters. But her need to come here today had nothing really to do with any desire to teach, did it? It was . . . Well, what was it?

The need to step into Anna Snow's shoes to discover what they felt like? What an absolutely ghastly thought. But if she stood out here any longer, she would lose her courage and find herself trudging back uphill, lost and defeated and abject and every other horrid thing she could think of. Besides, standing here was decidedly uncomfortable. Though it was July and the sun was shining, it was still only morning and she was in the shade of the building. The street was acting as a type of funnel too for a brisk wind.

She stepped forward, lifted the heavy knocker away from the door, hesitated for only a moment, then let it fall. Perhaps she would be denied employment. What a huge relief that would be.

Joel Cunningham was feeling on top of the world when he got out of bed that morning. July sunshine poured into his rooms as soon as he pulled back the curtains from every window to let it in, filling them with light and warmth. But it was not just the perfect summer day that had lifted his mood. This morning he was taking the time to appreciate his home. His *rooms*—plural.

He had worked hard in the twelve years since he left the orphanage at the age of fifteen and taken up residence in one small room on the top floor of a house on Grove Street just west of the River Avon. He had taken employment at a butcher's shop while also attending art school. The anonymous benefactor who had paid his way at the orphanage throughout his childhood had paid the school fees too and covered the cost of basic school supplies, though for everything else he had been on his own. He had persevered at both school and employment while working on his painting whenever he could.

Often after paying his rent he had had to make the choice between eating and buying extra supplies, and eating had not always won. But those days were behind him. He had been sitting outside the Pump Room in the abbey yard one afternoon a few years ago, sketching a vagabond perched alone on a nearby bench and sharing a crust of bread with the pigeons. Sketching people he saw about him on the streets was something Joel loved doing, and something for which one of his art teachers had told him he had a genuine talent. He had been unaware of a gentleman sitting down next to him until the man spoke. The result of the ensuing conversation had been a commission to paint a portrait of the man's wife. Joel had been terrified of failing, but he had been pleased with the way the painting turned out. He had made no attempt to make the lady appear younger or lovelier than she was, but both husband and wife had seemed genuinely delighted with what they called the realism of the portrait. They had shown it to some friends and recommended him to others.

The result had been more such commissions and then

still more, until he was often fairly swamped by demands for his services and wished there were more hours in the day. He had been able to leave his employment two years ago and raise his fees. Recently he had raised them again, but no one yet had complained that he was overcharging. It had been time to begin looking for a studio in which to work. But last month the family that occupied the rest of the top floor of the house in which he had his room had given notice, and Joel had asked the landlord if he could rent the whole floor, which came fully furnished. He would have the luxury of a sizable studio in which to work as well as a living room, a bedchamber, a kitchen that doubled as a dining room, and a washroom. It seemed to him a true palace.

The family having moved out the morning before, last night he had celebrated his change in fortune by inviting five friends, all male, to come and share the meat pies he had bought from the butcher's shop, a cake from the bakery next to it, and a few bottles of wine. It had been a merry housewarming.

"You will be giving up the orphanage, I suppose," Marvin Silver, the bank clerk who lived on the middle floor, had said after toasting Joel's continued success.

"Teaching there, do you mean?" Joel had asked.

"You do not get paid, do you?" Marvin had said. "And it sounds as though you need all your time to keep up with what you *are* being paid for—quite handsomely, I have heard."

Joel volunteered his time two afternoons a week at the orphanage school, teaching art to those who wanted to do a little more than was being offered in the art classes provided by the regular teacher. Actually, *teach* was somewhat of a misnomer for what he did with those children. He thought of his role to be more in the nature of inspiring them to discover and express their individual artistic vision and talent. He used to look forward to those afternoons. They had not been so enjoyable lately, however, though that had nothing to do with the children or with his increasingly busy life beyond the orphanage walls.

"I'll always find the time to go there," he had assured Marvin, and one of the other fellows had slapped him with hearty good cheer on the back.

"And what of Mrs. Tull?" he had asked him, waggling his eyebrows. "Are you thinking of moving her in here to cook and clean for you among other things, Joel? As Mrs. Cunningham, perhaps? You can probably afford a wife."

Edwina Tull was a pretty and amiable widow, about eight years Joel's senior. She appeared to have been left comfortably well-off by her late husband, though in the three years Joel had known her he had come to suspect that she entertained other male friends apart from him and that she accepted gifts—monetary gifts—from them as she did from him. The fact that he was very possibly not her only male friend did not particularly bother him. Indeed, he was quite happy that there was never any suggestion of a commitment between them. She was respectable and affectionate and discreet, and she provided him with regular female companionship and lively conversation as well as good sex. He was satisfied with that. His heart, unfortunately, had long ago been given elsewhere, and he had not got it back yet even though the object of his devotion had recently married someone else.

"I am quite happy to enjoy my expanded living quarters alone for a while yet," he had said. "Besides, I believe Mrs. Tull is quite happy with her independence."

His friends had finished off the food and wine and stayed until after midnight. It had felt very good indeed to be able to entertain in his own rooms and actually have enough chairs for them all to sit on.

Now he strolled about his living and working quarters in the morning sunshine and reveled anew in the realization that all this space was his. He had come a long way in twelve years. He stood before the easel in the studio and gazed at the portrait he had been able to leave propped on it. Apart from a few small finishing touches, it was ready to be delivered. He was particularly pleased with it because it had given him problems. Mrs. Dance was a faded lady who had probably never been pretty. She was bland and amiable, and at the beginning he had asked himself how the devil he was going to paint her in such a way that both she and her husband would be satisfied. He had wrestled with the question for several weeks while he sketched her and talked with her and discovered that her amiability was warm and genuine and had been hard won—she had lost three of her seven children in infancy and another just before he finished school. Once Joel had erased the judgmental word *bland* as a descriptor, he came to see her as a genuinely lovely person and had had great pleasure painting her portrait. He hoped he had captured what he saw as the essence of her well enough that others would see it too.

But though his fingers itched to pick up his brush to make those finishing touches, he had to resist. He had made arrangements with Miss Ford to go to the orphanage school early today, since he had an appointment with another client this afternoon, which he had been unable to shift to a different time. But even the thought of going to school early could not dampen his mood, for he would have the schoolroom to himself and his small group today and, if he was fortunate, for the rest of the summer.

While Miss Nunce had taught at the orphanage school, Joel and his group had had to squeeze into a strictly calculated third of the schoolroom—she had actually measured it with a long tape borrowed from Roger, the porter, and marked it out with chalk. They had crowded in with their easels and all the other necessary paraphernalia of an art class while she conducted her lessons in the other two-thirds. Her reasoning had been that he had one-third of the total number of schoolchildren while she had two-thirds. The art equipment did not factor into her view. But last week, Miss Nunce had resigned in high dudgeon before she could be forcibly ejected.

Joel had not been there at the time, but he did not mourn her departure. It had not been beyond the woman to intrude upon his third of the room, stepping carefully over the chalk line so as not to smudge it, to give her verdict on the paintings in progress, and invariably it was a derogatory judgment. She was an opinionated, joyless woman who clearly despised all children, and orphans in particular. She appeared to have seen it as her personal mission to prepare them to be humble and servile and to know their place—that place being the bottom rung of the social ladder, or perhaps somewhat below the bottom rung. Sometimes he had thought she resented even having to teach them to read, write, and figure. She had done her utmost to quell dreams and aspirations and talent and imagination, all of which in her view were inappropriate to their parentless condition.

She had walked out after Mary Perkins went running to find Miss Ford to tell her that Miss Nunce was beating Jimmy Dale. When Miss Ford had arrived on the scene, Jimmy was standing in the corner, his back to the room, squirming from the pain of a sore bottom. Miss Nunce, it seemed, had discovered him reading one of the new books—unfortunately for him, one of the larger, heavier volumes—and actually chuckling over something within its pages. She had taken it from him, instructed him to stand and bend over his desk, and walloped him a dozen times with it before sending him to the corner to contemplate his sins. She had still been holding the book aloft and haranguing the class on the evils of the trivial use of one's time and of empty-minded levity when Miss Ford appeared. Seeing her, Miss Nunce had turned her triumphant glare upon the matron.

"And *this*," she had pronounced, "is what comes of allowing *books* in the schoolroom."

The books, together with a large bookcase to display them, had been donated a short while ago by a Mrs. Kingsley, a wealthy and prominent citizen of Bath. Miss Nunce had been quite vocal in her opposition at the time. Books, she had warned, would merely give the orphans ideas.

Miss Ford had crossed the room to Jimmy, turned him by the shoulders, and asked him why he had been reading in class. He had explained that his arithmetic exercise was finished and he had not wanted to sit idle. Sure enough, all his sums were completed and all were correct. She had sent him back to his seat after first removing her shawl and folding it several times into a square for him to sit on.

She had asked the day's monitors to take charge of the room and invited Miss Nunce to step outside, much to the disappointment of the children. Joel would have been disappointed too if he had been there. But then, the incident would not have happened if he had been there. No child at the orphanage was ever struck. It was one of Miss Ford's immutable rules.

Less than fifteen minutes later—the children and some of the staff in other parts of the building had heard the teacher's raised voice alternating with silences that probably indicated Miss Ford was speaking—Miss Nunce had stridden from the building with Roger a few steps behind her to lock the door, lest she change her mind.

Joel had rejoiced, not just because he had found it difficult to work with her, but because he cared for the children—all of them. He had been greatly relieved too, because Miss Nunce had succeeded Anna Snow, who had left a few months ago, and who had been everything she was not. Anna had brought sunshine to the schoolroom.

It was Anna whom he loved, though he tried doggedly to use the past tense whenever he considered his feelings for her. She was a married lady now. She was the Duchess of Netherby.

Two

✾

Soon after Joel arrived at the school, his art group—
children ranging in age from eight to thirteen—was
engrossed in the painting of a still-life grouping he had set
up on the table. They were using oils on canvas, a difficult
challenge for most of them. He walked quietly about the
room, observing their efforts while trying not to unnerve
any of them or break their concentration. It did not take
much to break Winifred Hamlin's, however. Her hand shot
suddenly into the air, and Joel sighed inwardly.

"Olga's teapot is smaller than her apple, Mr. Cunningham," she said without waiting for permission to speak—
so why the raised hand?

It was indeed. Olga's teapot had been painted with the
meticulous care one might expend on a miniature. Her
apple, on the other hand, was round and red and yellow
and green and shiny and exuberant—and huge. It actually

looked more appealing and appetizing than the original, which stood on the linen-draped table with the large teapot and a cup and saucer and a book.

"And so it is," he said, resting a hand on Winifred's shoulder. "When everyone has finished, we will ask her why that is. We will also ask Paul why the objects in his painting are in a straight line and not touching one another. And Richard will tell us why on his canvas the objects are seen from above, as though he were sitting at his easel on the ceiling. If you have finished, Winifred, you may clean your brushes and palette and put them away in the cupboard." He did not add that she should arrange them neatly. She did everything neatly.

In Winifred's painting, he saw, everything was in perfect proportion to everything else and positioned as the real objects were on the table. The table itself was absent, though. The objects dangled in space. He would ask her about that later.

There was a tap on the door and a few of the children turned their heads when it opened. Several did not, showing admirable concentration upon their work.

Miss Ford stepped into the room with a severe-looking young woman dressed stylishly but unappealingly from head to foot in fawn and brown. A new teacher? Already? Joel's heart sank. She looked as humorless as Miss Nunce, and he had been hoping for a respite even from a *good* teacher since it was the middle of the summer and most schools were closed until September. This one remained open only because it was on the children's living premises and kept them occupied and amused through the long, often hot days. At least, that was the philosophy behind keeping it going.

"Mr. Cunningham," Miss Ford said, "may I present Miss Westcott? She has applied for the teaching position, and we have mutually agreed upon a fortnight's trial."

All heads swung about.

Westcott? Joel's eyes sharpened upon the new teacher.

Miss Ford confirmed his suspicions. "Miss Westcott is the Duchess of Netherby's sister," she explained. "She is currently living in Bath with her grandmother, Mrs. Kingsley."

"*Half* sister," the woman corrected, giving the impression that as far as she was concerned, that was half a relationship too much. "How do you do, Mr. Cunningham?"

She was the elusive Miss Westcott, then, was she? Joel had seen the other one—the pretty one. Anna had been delighted when at the age of twenty-five she had at last discovered her family, but her half sisters had spurned her overtures of friendship and affection. To Anna's deep distress, they had removed themselves, first from London and then from their erstwhile home in the country to take up residence here in Bath. She had worried about them and had written to ask Joel if he could possibly discover their whereabouts and find out if all was well with them, as far as anything could be well when the very bottom had just fallen out of their world. He had discovered who their grandmother was and had seen her on a few occasions with the other sister, going into the Pump Room to join the fashionable set, who went there daily to take the waters and exchange gossip.

He had actually been introduced to the two of them at an evening party given by the very Mrs. Dance whose portrait was now standing on the easel in his new studio. She had invited him to attend and to bring some of his smaller paintings to show off to her guests in a kind attempt to help him acquire more clients. He had never set eyes upon the other granddaughter—until now. He had assumed she was a recluse. She was certainly the plainer of the two—and plainer than Anna as well. She also looked dour.

"How do you do, Miss Westcott?" he said.

She was tall and built on a generous scale, though her full figure was well proportioned and elegant. She had dark hair and fine blue eyes, a well-defined jaw and a stubborn-looking chin. Bold features prevented her from being pretty. She was not ugly, however. *Handsome* might be a good word to describe her. She looked like a woman born to command. She looked, in fact, like someone who had lived most of her life as *Lady* Camille Westcott, elder daughter of an earl.

He disliked her on sight. "I look forward to working with you."

"I have explained," Miss Ford said, "that you usually come here two afternoons a week, Mr. Cunningham."

Miss Westcott did exactly what Miss Nunce had often done, though there was no longer a chalk line across the room. She moved away from the door and wandered among the easels, looking at the paintings over the children's shoulders.

"Olga's teapot is smaller than her apple, miss," Winifred informed her.

Miss Westcott looked back at her with raised eyebrows, as though she could not believe the evidence of her own ears that a child had actually addressed her without being invited to do so. Then she glanced at the table where the still life had been set up, looked down at Olga's canvas, and took her time perusing it. Joel could feel his hackles rise. Miss Ford folded her hands at her waist.

"But the apple does look good enough to eat," Miss Westcott said, "or maybe even too good to eat. Perhaps Olga sees it as the most significant object on the table. Were you instructed to paint the objects as you see them or as you *feel* them?"

Irrationally, Joel felt even more annoyed. Was it possible that she *got* it, that she understood? Somehow he did not want that. He wanted to feel justified in disliking her. But was that just because she had been unkind to Anna? Or was it because she looked severe and humorless and he did not want her let loose upon the children here? Whatever had Miss Ford been thinking?

"Mr. Cunningham don't never tell us how to paint, miss," Richard Beynon told her. "He makes us work it out for ourselves. He tells us he can't teach us how to see things the way we want to paint them."

"Ah," she said. "Thank you. And that should be 'he *will* never tell us' or 'he won't *ever* tell us.' Have you ever heard the head-scratcher of the double negative actually making a positive?"

Richard's face brightened. "It does make you want to scratch your head, miss, doesn't it?" he said, grinning broadly.

Despite that exchange, she still looked severe and humorless when she returned to Miss Ford's side. She walked with an upright, unyielding bearing, as though she had been made to walk around as a child with a book balanced on her head.

"I beg your pardon, Mr. Cunningham, for interrupting

and thrown the paper on the fire. Not the orphanage school, Camille?"

After Camille had returned from that first visit to the orphanage, she had mentioned telling Miss Ford that she might be interested in the post if it ever became available. Her grandmother had been aghast.

"I have been there and spoken to Miss Ford," Camille said. "She has agreed to take me on as the new teacher." She did not add that the matron had been dubious about her qualifications and lack of experience and had finally agreed to give her a fortnight's trial, with no guarantee that she would offer permanent employment at the end of it.

Both her grandmother and Abigail argued and wheedled and cajoled and even shed tears for upward of half an hour after Camille had joined them in the drawing room.

"You do not need to work for a living, Camille," her grandmother argued. "I offered to make you both an allowance when you first came here, and you refused. Now I must insist that you accept, that you resume living in the manner to which you are accustomed. Your lives have changed, of course, but there is no reason in the world to believe they have been totally destroyed. Your mother was always held in the highest esteem as a Kingsley, and you and Abigail are impeccably well-bred, Camille. You are both young and accomplished and beautiful. You are my granddaughters. I am highly respected in Bath society and not without influence, you know. Your father's relatives have not turned their backs on you either. On the contrary, they have all written to you, some of them more than once.

There is every reason to believe you will both be able to make perfectly decent marriages, even if you must aim a little lower than the titled ranks of the nobility. Not only do you not need to work, Camille—you may actually do yourself real harm if you do. You may find that you will no longer be accepted for who you are."

"And who is that, Grandmama?" Camille asked. She was genuinely unable to answer the question for herself, though she had been asking it for a few months now. Her grandmother could not answer it either, it seemed, or perhaps she had realized the futility of arguing with the granddaughter she had always called stubborn even when Camille was a child. She got to her feet and left the room, shaking her head in clear frustration.

And of course she left Camille feeling guilty. Perhaps Grandmama was right. Perhaps their lives—hers and Abigail's—would settle into something resembling the way they had been if they effaced themselves and allowed family members to smooth the way for them to find a level of society where they would fit and husbands who would settle for their breeding and would not refine too much upon their birth. Perhaps Abby would be happy with that solution. Camille ought to be too. What was the alternative, after all?

But she could not settle for a pale shadow of her former existence. Good heavens, she had been Lady Camille Westcott, daughter of an earl. She had moved freely among the highest echelons of the *ton*. She had been betrothed to the very handsome, very eligible Viscount Uxbury. Oh no, she *would* not settle. She would rather teach in an orphanage school.

There was a loud silence in the room, she realized

suddenly, even though she was not alone. But the silence would not have been loud if she had been, would it?

"Cam," Abigail said, a soft cushion clasped to her bosom, "why the orphanage? Why does it hold such an attraction for you? I agree it is time we softened our attitude to Anastasia. I thought we both agreed to that after she and Avery called here on the way home from their wedding journey. I think we ought to write to her occasionally and somehow hold out an olive branch. She is, after all, Avery's wife and Jessica's sister-in-law and none of what has happened is her fault. She is part of the family whether we like it or not. But why your fascination with that horrid place where she grew up?"

Avery, the Duke of Netherby, was not strictly speaking a member of their family—of Papa's family, that was. Aunt Louise, Papa's sister, had married Avery's father, and they had had Jessica, an undoubted first cousin. Abigail and Jessica, who was one year younger than she, had always been the closest of friends and still wrote frequently to each other. She was not Abby's only correspondent, however. Letters flowed into the house in a steady stream, addressed to both of them. Once upon a time, in another lifetime, reading letters and replying to them at some length had been a regular part of Camille's day, as it was for any genteel lady. Now she read the letters but replied to none.

Her mother wrote of how busy she was at the vicarage, where she lived with Uncle Michael, and at the church and in the village. Her letters were full of cheerful news of a full, happy life. Camille could not bear to answer in a similar vein. Consequently she merely sent her love through Abby.

The rare letters from their brother were disappointingly short—but what was one to expect of a man, and a young one at that? They consisted of cheerful news of marching with his regiment all over Portugal and even into Spain, seeking out the elusive French while the elusive French sought them out. It really was a splendid game and a great lark. He was surrounded by loyal, amusing friends and colleagues and was having the time of his life. He was already next in line for promotion from ensign to lieutenant, and did not doubt it would happen before autumn, though he had to wait for a suitable vacancy.

Camille knew that officers acquired promotions far more quickly if they could afford to purchase them. Harry could not. She knew too how vacancies came about, and her stomach churned. Someone would have to die before Harry could be a lieutenant. Several someones, in fact, since the first to fill any vacancies were those who could purchase them. If Harry was close to being promoted anyway, men were dying in significant numbers. And that meant that at least occasionally the regiment caught up with the French, or the French caught up with it. And at least occasionally there were skirmishes, even pitched battles. Yet it was all such a lark, like a picnic. Camille could not bear to answer in the same light tone. She had Abby send her love.

And there were all the letters of which her grandmother had just reminded her from people who used to be her family and still were in a strictly technical sense. They were her father's family, including the Dowager Countess of Riverdale, Papa's mother; and Aunt Matilda, his unmarried sister. The dowager always seemed to Camille to be in robust health, though Aunt Matilda chose to believe otherwise and sometimes seemed determined to fuss and worry her into an early grave. Then there was Aunt Louise, the Dowager Duchess of Netherby, who liked to set herself up as family leader, though she was the middle of three sisters. And Cousin Jessica, her daughter, Abby's particular friend, Avery's half sister. And there had been letters from Aunt Mildred, the youngest of Papa's sisters, and Uncle Thomas—Lord and Lady Molenor. The only relatives who did not write, in fact, were their three sons, all of whom were still at school and wrote to no one except, apparently, their papa when they needed more money. All the others wrote with unrelenting cheerfulness of happy lives.

Even Cousin Alexander, the new Earl of Riverdale, had written one brief letter of courteous pleasantries and polite inquiry into their health and happiness. He had signed the letter merely *Cousin Alexander,* with no mention of the title that Harry had so recently lost to him. His mother, Cousin Althea Westcott, and his sister, Cousin Elizabeth, the widowed Lady Overfield, had also written kindly and cheerfully about nothing in particular.

Everyone wrote cheerfully. Nobody wrote any significant truth. As though denial could eliminate reality. As though tiptoeing about a disaster would leave it forever undisturbed. Camille sensed a great embarrassment in her erstwhile family. Not hostility or rejection, but just . . . awkwardness. She answered none of the letters. She sent her regards with Abby.

There were no letters from anyone outside the family. None from any of the myriad ladies who had once been her friends.

And none from Viscount Uxbury. Now, *there* was a surprise.

Abigail had abandoned her cushion and gone to stand at the window, looking out. The silence had stretched for rather a long time, Camille realized. Her sister had asked her why she was so fascinated with the place where Anastasia had grown up.

"I do not know, Abby," she said with a sigh. "I suppose there are various ways of coping with the sort of change our lives have undergone in the last few months. One can accept and move forward, trying to keep one's new life as similar to the old as it can possibly be. One can deny reality and carry on regardless. One can hide away and close one's mind to what has happened—which is what I have been doing until today. Or one can step out and explore the new reality, try to make sense of it, try to begin life again almost as though one had just been newly born, try to . . . Ah, I do not know how else to explain it. I only know that if I am not to go mad, I must *do* something. And somehow that involves going right back to the beginning or farther back than the beginning to what happened before I was even born. Why did he do it, Abby? Why did he marry Mama when he was already married to someone else?"

Abigail had turned from the window and was regarding her sister with troubled eyes. She offered no answer.

"But of course, it is obvious," Camille said. "In those days he was extravagant and impecunious and our grandfather was still alive and had cut off his funds but promised to restore them if he married advantageously. And Grandpapa Kingsley was eager to marry Mama to a future earl and offered a dowry with her hand that was irresistible. I suppose Papa must have faced a nasty dilemma when his first wife, his *real* wife, died and left him with Anastasia. What he did was heinous for everyone concerned, including the as-yet unborn—us. Had he admitted the truth then, perhaps he could have remarried Mama and they could have brought his daughter up as their own and we too would have been born within wedlock. How different all our lives would be now if he had only done that. Why did he not?"

"Perhaps there would have been legal difficulties if he had admitted to bigamy," Abigail said. "Would there have been? Is bigamy a crime? Would his title have protected him from punishment? Oh, I know nothing about such things. Perhaps he was just too embarrassed to admit the truth. But that is all history. We cannot change it by agonizing over it or imagining how different everything might have been. Why do you need to go to that orphanage, Cam? Are you trying to . . . *punish* yourself somehow for the fact that it was she who grew up there when strictly speaking it ought to have been us?"

Camille shrugged. "I cannot explain it even to myself more clearly than I already have," she said. "I just know I must try it, and I actually feel better since going there, even though I know I have upset you and Grandmama. I feel—invigorated."

"But how will you be able to teach?" Abigail asked. "Where will you begin? We had a governess, Cam. We never even went to school."

"Miss Ford gave me a copy of the course of studies I should use as a guideline," Camille said, "and she talked to me about it and about the children who attend the school. There are more than twenty of them, and they range in age from five to thirteen. I can do it." Actually the prospect terrified her—yes, and invigorated her too. She had not lied about that. "And the duties will be light for the next month or so. It is summer and I will be expected to do lots of recreational things with the children and take them out as often as I can."

"Oh, Cam," Abigail said.

"It does not seem like an oppressive place," Camille told her. "There is an art teacher who comes in two afternoons a week to teach those who are interested—Mr. Cunningham. He was there this morning, though that was apparently unusual. I looked at some of the children's paintings and I could see that he allows them to use their imaginations in interpreting a subject."

"Oh, I have met Mr. Cunningham," Abigail said, coming to sit down again. "He was at Mrs. Dance's the evening I went there with Grandmama. Remember? I believe he was painting Mrs. Dance's portrait. Perhaps he still is. He had brought a couple of completed portraits with him to show her guests, and they were exquisite. He has real talent. He was rather handsome too."

Camille was not sure she would say quite that of him. He was on the tall side—taller than she, anyway—and solidly built, though he had a decent, manly figure. His face was more pleasant than ravishingly good-looking, she had thought. His dark hair was cropped but not in any of the fashionable short styles, like the Brutus, for example. His eyes were dark and intelligent and he had a firm mouth and chin, all suggestive of a certain strength of character and will. His coat, she had noticed, though not ill fitting, was not fashionably formfitting either and had looked slightly shabby. His boots did not shine, not from lack of polish, she guessed, but from being scuffed with age. He was a man who seemed careless of his appearance, very different from the gentlemen with whom she had consorted until a few months ago. She would not have afforded him a second glance if she had passed him on the street—or even a first glance for that matter. But during the few minutes she had been forced into his company, she had been aware of a sort of restless energy and raw masculinity about him, and she had been slightly shocked at herself for noticing. It was not like her at all.

"I suppose," she said, arrested by a sudden thought, "if he has been teaching there awhile, he must know Anastasia."

Was that why she had sensed some hostility in his manner? Did he resent the fact that she was about to take Anastasia's place in the schoolroom? But of course he knew Anastasia—Miss Ford had introduced her to him as her sister, had she not? And she had corrected Miss Ford by saying she was Anastasia's *half* sister.

"Can I talk you out of going back there, Cam?" Abigail said. "Grandmama is going to take me to a concert at the Upper Assembly Rooms tomorrow evening. There are likely to be people there who do not attend the Pump Room in the early mornings. Come with us. Most people are polite to me. No one recoils in horror when they discover who I am. No one treats me like a leper. And not everyone in Bath is elderly. We will surely make a few friends close to us in age, given time and a little bit of effort. Perhaps even . . . Well . . ." She smiled and looked away.

But only Mrs. Dance of all Grandmama's supposed friends had invited Abby to her home. And there had been no sign yet of any younger ladies making friendly over-tures to her. And no sign whatsoever of any prospective beaux. Oh, poor Abby.

"You will not talk me out of going to school on Mon-day and every day thereafter, Abby," Camille said. "I want to go. I really do."

Abigail's eyes filled with tears. "Cam," she half whis-pered, "do you find yourself sometimes expecting to wake up to find this is all a horrid dream? Or at least *hoping* to wake up?"

"No longer." Camille got to her feet and sat beside her sister, gathering her into her arms as she did so. "Life has kicked us in the teeth, Abby, and I am about to kick back. Hard. I am going to teach at an orphanage school. *That* will show everyone."

Abigail almost choked over a sob that had turned to laughter. Camille laughed with her and felt cheerful for the first time in . . . how long? It felt like forever.

Three

❧

On Wednesday of the following week, Joel approached the school with lagging footsteps—like a reluctant schoolboy, he thought in disgust. The new teacher would be there—Anna's starchy, haughty half sister. He really did not look forward to sharing the schoolroom with her. Any hope that either she or Miss Ford had changed her mind since last week, though, was banished as soon as he opened the schoolroom door and found that she and the children were already in there, though it was surely not yet quite the end of the luncheon hour. He came to an abrupt halt on the threshold, his hand still grasping the doorknob. What the devil?

The easels for his class had already been set up with chairs pushed neatly in front of them. The art supplies were arranged in orderly fashion on the table. The easels took up a good two-thirds of the room. In the other third, the desks had been arranged in two lines and pushed together, nose to nose, to make one long table, which was strewn with a great tumble of . . . stuff. The children were clustered about it, looking flushed and animated and slightly untidy. Miss Westcott—was it really she?—was in their midst, issuing orders like an army sergeant, pointing with a wooden ruler from the stuff to various children and back again. All the pupils seemed to be jumping to her commands like eager recruits, even the older ones, who often liked to behave as though life was just too much of a bore to be bothered with. Two five-year-olds were bouncing up and down with uncontained exuberance.

She was wearing a severe brown dress, which was high to the neck and had long sleeves, though they were currently pushed up to her elbows. Her hair had been dressed with a severity to match the dress, but it had suffered disruption in the course of the day, and one lock hung down unheeded over her neck while other escapees appeared to have been shoved haphazardly back into her bun. Her cheeks and even her nose were a bit on the rosy and shiny side. There was a frown between her brows and her lips were set in a thin line when she was not issuing orders.

She looked up and caught sight of him.

"Good afternoon, Mr. Cunningham," she said, as though she were issuing a challenge. "I trust everything has been set up to your liking. Children, those budding artists among you may proceed to your class."

And his group, a few of whose members, he suspected, had opted for painting lessons merely to avoid whatever academic alternative the other side of the room was likely to offer, came meekly enough but surely without their usual enthusiasm.

"We went to the market this morning, Mr. Cunningham," Winifred Hamlin told him, "and looked at all the wares on all the stalls and we wrote down prices."

"But it was not as easy as it sounds, sir," Mary Perkins said, cutting in, "because some things are so much each, and other things are so much an ounce or a pound or half pound, and some things are so much a dozen or half dozen. We had to look carefully to see what the prices meant."

"The sweets lady gave us a toffee each," Jimmy Dale added, his voice high pitched with excitement.

Tommy Yarrow cut in. "And she wouldn't let Miss Westcott pay for them."

Mary giggled. "Miss Westcott said we had better promise to eat our luncheon when we got back here or she would be in trouble with Cook," she said.

"One lady give us some ribbon that was a bit frayed," Richard said, "and a man give us some beads that was cracked. Another lady wanted to give us a rotten cabbage, but Miss Westcott said thank you but no, thank you— because we must always be polite no matter what. The cobbler give us some bits of shoe leather he couldn't use. Miss Westcott brought some things from her house, and Nurse has let us have some pins and other stuff from her supplies that are a bit too old to use, and Cook give us some bent spoons and forks that she keeps for a rainy day."

"But she wants them back, Richard," Winifred reminded him.

"The verb *give* becomes *gave* in the past tense, Richard,"

Miss Westcott said severely from the other side of the room. "And some beads *were* cracked—plural."

"We are going to play shop tomorrow," Olga screeched above the general clamor.

Joel held up both hands, palms out, but to no avail.

"We are to take turns being shopkeeper," Winifred said, "two at a time. Everyone else will be a shopper with a list. And the shopkeepers will bring everything on the list and add up the total cost, and the shopper will have to work it out too to see if the two sums agree. And—"

"And the little ones who don't know their sums well yet will be paired with older ones who do," Mary added.

"Right," Joel said firmly. "It sounds as though the vendors at the market will need a quiet afternoon to recover from your visit. And you will need a quiet afternoon if you are not to murder my ears and your teacher's and if you are to get anything done that will astonish the art world with its brilliance. Sit down and we will discuss what you are going to paint today."

His eyes met Miss Westcott's as the children settled and a measure of peace and order descended upon the room. She looked thin lipped and belligerent, as though she were daring him to complain about the triviality of the morning's outing and the organized chaos of the schoolroom. But the thing was that it *was* organized. There was no question that she was in control of the children, excited as they were. And it struck him, reluctant as he was to admit it, that she had hit upon a brilliant way to conduct a mathematics lesson and a life lesson at the same time. The children thought it was all a game.

He had hoped so much for her to fail early and hard. That was nasty of him now that he came to think about it. And he knew suddenly of what she had been reminding him since last week. An Amazon. A woman warrior, devoid of any soft femininity. And, having thought of that unflattering comparison and convinced himself that it was quite apt, he felt better and turned his mind to his lesson.

Two hours passed, during which he was more or less absorbed in the artistic efforts of his pupils as they took on an imaginative project—the landscape or home of their dreams—after first discussing some possibilities. Reality did not have to prevail, he had assured them. If the grass in their dream landscape was pink, then so be it. He helped a few of them clarify their mental images and helped others mix the color or shade they wanted but could not produce for themselves. Inevitably, the grass outside Winifred's square box of a gray house was pink—the only concession she appeared to have made to the imagination. He taught Paul how to use brushstrokes to produce rough, cold water rather than the traditional smooth blue on the lake before his onion-shaped mansion.

And he noticed that tomorrow's shop organized itself on the desktops at the other side of the room and acquired cards in everyone's boldest and best handwriting announcing prices and the number or quantity of each item that price would buy. He noticed that the "cash" box acquired square cardboard "coins" upon which the value was written large—and neat. Tomorrow, Miss Westcott explained as though she were addressing a recalcitrant regiment, all the shoppers would be issued with a set amount of cardboard money to spend, and the rest of the coins would be left in the cash box so that the shopkeepers could give change. No one would be allowed to spend more money than he or she had. If they had bought too much, they would have to decide what to relinquish.

Joel wondered if any of his group wished they were minting square coins rather than painting their dreams, though none of them complained, and there was no discernible lack of concentration. On the whole their efforts showed greater artistry than usual.

He followed the painting session with the usual discussion after they had looked at one another's work. Then he supervised as they cleared up. It rather annoyed him that he watched more carefully than usual to make sure they returned the supplies only to the bottom two shelves of the storage cupboard and arranged them there in a neat, orderly fashion. Anna had forever scolded him for encouraging slovenliness in his pupils and for encroaching upon her shelves, and he had forever defended himself for the pleasure of annoying her further by talking of artistic liberty.

As soon as he had dismissed his group, they wandered over to the other third of the room, he noticed, instead of darting out to freedom as they would normally have done. By that time Miss Westcott had all the children sitting in a circle on the floor about her chair, cross-legged except for Monica, whose legs would not cross and lie flat like everyone else's but remained annoyingly elevated with knees up about her ears while she fought against losing her balance and being tipped backward to the floor. She was sitting on her heels at Miss Westcott's suggestion—Miss Nunce had insisted, without any success, that Monica persist in the cross-legged stance until she stopped being stubborn and did it properly. Miss Westcott had taken a book from the new bookcase and was reading from it in a strident voice that nevertheless seemed to have captured the attention of her audience.

Joel slipped out unnoticed. There was something he needed to do.

After three days in the schoolroom, Camille had come to the conclusion that she was the world's worst teacher.

She looked about the now-empty room with a grimace, ignoring the ingrained inner voice of her education, which warned that wrinkles would be the dire and inevitable result of frowns and grimaces and overbright smiles. That inner voice, which for so long had been her daily guide to genteel behavior, now annoyed her considerably. She would frown if she wanted to.

When she had arrived on Monday morning, the schoolroom had been neat and orderly, with straight rows of desks, a bare teacher's desk, neatly aligned books in the bookcase Grandmama had donated, easels stacked neatly at the far side of the room next to the window, and supplies arranged with almost military precision on the five deep, wide shelves of the storage cupboard. Yet now . . .

And there were no servants here to run about after her, picking up what she dropped, straightening what she had not bothered to tidy for herself. She was it. Actually, on this particular occasion, she and *that man* were it, but he had gone merrily on his way as soon as he had dismissed his class, leaving the easels where she had set them earlier out of the goodness of her heart. He had not even uttered any word of farewell. She almost wished he had not cleared away everything except the paintings and the easels. Then she would have had even more to complain of and might have thought the absolute worst of him, as he no doubt was thinking of her.

She had *hated* having him here, listening to everything she said, a witness to the chaos of the afternoon, to the untidiness, the lack of discipline, her appearance . . .

Her appearance.

Camille looked down at herself and would have grimaced again if she had not still been doing it. She had worn the most conservative of her dresses, as she had yesterday and Monday, but . . . her sleeves were still pushed up in a most unladylike fashion. She rolled them down to her wrists a few hours too late. The wrinkles from elbows to wrists might never iron out. And what on earth must her hair look like? The bun she had so ruthlessly fashioned this morning had been disintegrating ever since, and she had been impatiently shoving escaped strands of hair into it. She felt it now with both hands and realized that it must resemble a bundle of hay after a hurricane had blown across the field. And how long had that one strand been dangling down her neck?

And why did she care? He was only a man, after all, and recent experience had taught her that men were sorry, despicable creatures at best. He was also a rather shabby man—that coat and those boots! She did not care a fig what such a man thought of her. Or any man. She felt aggrieved, though, that he had left her alone to deal with the paintings and to put away the easels, though the disorder he had left behind was nothing compared to what she had created in her third of the room. The desktops were covered with . . . things ready for tomorrow's shop.

She had conceived the idea with the hope that the children would learn something practical they could apply to their future lives after they had left here and must provide for their own needs on what would probably be very little income—unless by some miracle they should discover themselves to be heirs or heiresses to a vast fortune, as their former teacher had done. Since that was as unlikely as their being hit by a shooting star, they needed to learn something about prices and quantities and choices and making money stretch. They needed to learn the difference between necessities and luxuries. They needed—

Oh dear, and she needed to learn it all too. She had been terrified and astonished at the market this morning. She had learned on her feet, only one step ahead of the children—in more ways than one. Tomorrow . . . Oh, she dreaded to think of tomorrow. Just look at all this mess. Perhaps she would not even come back tomorrow. Perhaps she would remain at Grandmama's for the rest of her natural life, buried beneath the covers of her bed.

But it was a thought unworthy of her new self. She squared her shoulders and strode over to the art side of the room to stand gazing at one of the paintings. This was where Paul Hubbard had been sitting. Paul's dream house, it seemed, was a purple onion overlooking a stormy lake with slate-gray water and whitecaps—it made Camille shiver. The landscape about it was bleak and gray, though the windows of the onion were bright with color and light and—surely—warmth. How had he created that impression? There was a strange sun or moon hanging in the black sky. Or *was* it a sun or moon? It was a colored orb, startlingly different from the landscape below, just as the windows and presumably the interior of the onion house were. It was . . . Was it by any chance meant to be Earth? Wherever were the onion and the stormy lake, then? She was frowning over the rather surreal painting and its meaning when the door opened abruptly behind her.

Mr. Cunningham had come back, clutching a bulging paper bag in one hand. Camille found herself wishing she had spent her time doing something about her hair and despised herself for thinking of her appearance before all else. He looked windblown and out of breath and . . . virile. What a horrid, shocking word. Where had that thought come from?

He held the bag aloft. "For your shop," he said. "I would suggest a ha'penny each but not three for a penny or fifteen for sixpence. I would limit each shopper to one item. Give them a brief lesson on scarcity and on supply and demand and anything else that seems appropriate. Nutrition, perhaps. If one shopper were to buy the lot, he—or she—would probably be spending the afternoon groaning in Nurse's room and being dosed with the unspeakable concoction she keeps on hand for stomach ailments."

Camille eyed the bag suspiciously, walked toward him, and took it. It contained brightly colored boiled sweets, one each for the children, she guessed.

"Who paid for these?" she asked. She could not have sounded less gracious if she had tried.

He grinned at her—and of course he had perfect teeth, which happened also to be white. Oh goodness, she thought crossly, she was going to have to revise her opinion of him and admit that Abby had been right in thinking him handsome.

"I swear they were not pinched," he said, raising his right hand, palm out, as though taking an oath. "A constable will not come bursting in here in the next couple of minutes to haul me off to jail and you too for being in possession of stolen goods."

"Every child will of course use one precious ha'penny to buy one of these tomorrow," she said, still cross. "How am I to teach them that the little money they have ought to be spent upon necessities?"

"Beads and ribbons and shoe leather?" He raised his eyebrows.

"Beans and carrots and beef," she said. "You are not the only one who teaches them to use their imagination, Mr. Cunningham."

"But how dull a life it would be," he said, "if there were never the occasional luxury or treat or extravagance."

"That is easy for you to say," she said. "You are a fashionable portrait painter, I have heard. You probably have pots of money and come from a moneyed background." Despite his shabby appearance. She had heard all about eccentric artists. "As do I. But I at least am trying to behave responsibly toward these children, who have nothing, not even, in many cases, an identity."

She turned rather jerkily to make space for the sweets on the desktops and found a square of paper upon which to write the price as well as the information that shoppers were limited to the purchase of one item apiece. She thought he had gone away until he spoke again and she realized that he was perched on one corner of the teacher's desk close by, one booted foot braced on the floor while the other swung idly. His arms were crossed over his chest.

"This was my home," he said quietly, "and the people here are my family. I grew up here, Miss Westcott, after being dropped off as a baby like so much unwanted rubbish. I have a name, which may or may not be my father's or my mother's. I had a decent upbringing here and never lacked for the necessities of life or for companionship and even affection. I was supported until I was fifteen by an anonymous benefactor, as most of the children here are. I left then, after employment and accommodation had been found for me. I also went to art school, since my benefactor was generous enough to pay the fees. The door here was not locked against me. Quite the contrary, in fact. But to all intents and purposes I was on my own to make my own way in life—with the full knowledge that though I will always call this place my home and the people here my family, in reality I am without home or family.

"We *orphans,* Miss Westcott, know all about necessities and the fine line between surviving and starving. We are not likely to spend the little money we can earn upon nothing but ribbons and beads and sweets. But we know too the value, the *necessity* of the occasional treat. We know that life is not all or always gray, that there is color too. And we know that we are as much entitled to some color in our lives as the wealthiest of the more privileged elements of society. We are people. Persons."

Camille set the card down against the bag of sweets. "You are angry," she said unnecessarily. And now she felt foolish. But she had had no way of knowing, had she? And she felt accused, despised, as though she had been looking down upon these children as inferiors and of no account. She had been trying to do just the opposite. She might have been one of them, instead of Anastasia.

"Yes," he said.

"I am not one of the wealthy and privileged," she told him.

"Neither," he said, "are you an orphan, Miss Westcott."

No. Only a bastard. She almost said it aloud. But he probably was one too. So surely were most of the children here—the offspring of two people who had not been married to each other. Why else would most of them have been brought here and supported in secret? He was telling her she could never understand. And perhaps he was right.

"You knew Anastasia not just as a fellow teacher, then," she said.

"We grew up together," he told her.

Somehow his words depressed her and made her feel even more of an outsider. But an outsider to what? "You were friends?"

"The best," he said. She had the feeling he was going to say more, but he did not continue.

She turned to look at him and thought unexpectedly of how different he was from Viscount Uxbury, to whom she would have been married by now if her father had not died when he had. Lord Uxbury was undeniably handsome, immaculately groomed, dignified, the epitome of gentility. No one would ever catch him perching on the edge of a desk, one foot swinging, his arms crossed, hands tucked under his armpits. No one would catch him with boots in which he could not see his own reflection. And no one would catch him with closely cropped hair that had not been styled in the newest fashion. It was strange, given the fact of his looks, that she had never really thought of Lord Uxbury as a *man,* only as the ideal husband for a lady of her rank and fortune. He had never kissed her, nor had she expected him to. She had never thought of the marriage bed except in the vaguest of ways as a duty that would be fulfilled when the time came. Yet she had thought of him as perfection itself, her perfect mate.

She looked at Mr. Cunningham's firm lips and chin and found herself thinking about kisses. Specifically *his* kisses. It was really quite alarming. His appearance offended her, yet it was perhaps the very absence of the veneer of gentility that made her so aware of his maleness. She was offended by that too, for there was something raw about it. A gentleman ought not to make a lady aware of his masculinity.

He was not a gentleman, though, was he? And she was not a lady. She looked into his eyes and found them gazing directly back into her own. They were very dark eyes, as were his eyebrows and his hair. Even his complexion had a slightly olive hue, suggestive of some foreign blood in his ancestry. Italian? Spanish? Greek? Mediterranean men were said to be passionate, were they not? And wherever had she heard such a shocking thing?

Passion was *vulgar.*

He had known Anastasia, had grown up here with her, had been her friend—her *best* friend. He had taught in this schoolroom with her. Had he perhaps loved her? How had he felt when she went away, when the great dream had become reality for her while he had remained behind— *with the full knowledge that though I will always call this place home and the people here my family, in reality I am without home or family.*

It disturbed her that he might have loved Anastasia. It almost hurt her. It reminded her of her own terrible loss.

"Why are you *here*?" he asked abruptly, breaking a rather lengthy silence. He sounded as though he was feeling offended about something too.

"Here at the orphanage school, do you mean?" she asked. He did not answer and she shrugged. "Why *not* here? I live in Bath with my grandmother, and I must do something. An idle existence is no longer appropriate to my station. And the salary, though a mere pittance, is at least all mine."

Her grandmother, true to her word, had insisted upon issuing a generous monthly allowance to both her and Abigail. It was larger than their father had given them. Camille had stuffed the money for this month into a little cubbyhole in the escritoire in her room, where she was determined it would remain. She had not accepted the quarter of a fortune Anastasia had offered, and she would not use what her grandmother gave, though of course she was accepting Grandmama's hospitality every day she stayed at the house in the Royal Crescent. She did not know quite why she would not accept the money, just as she did not quite know why she had come here as soon as she heard of an opening at the school. But at least the salary she earned by her own efforts would give her some money to spend.

It would give her some self-respect too, some sense of being in charge of her own life.

"If you object to my being here," she said, "you ought to have spoken up after I left last week. Perhaps Miss Ford would have written to cancel our agreement to a two-week trial."

He had been examining the boot on his swinging foot, perhaps noticing how disgracefully worn it was. But his eyes came snapping back to hers at her words.

"Why would I have an objection?" he asked her.

"Perhaps because I am not Anna Snow," she said.

She did not know where those words had come from. She was not . . . jealous, was she? How absurd. But the words had a noticeable effect. His foot was suddenly still, and they gazed steadily at each other for several uncomfortable moments.

"Do you hate her?" he asked.

"Do you love her?"

His eyes turned hard. "I could tell you to mind your own business," he said. "Instead, I will remind you that she is married and that it would be wrong of me to covet another man's wife."

But he had not denied it, she noticed.

"She married Avery, yes." She watched him closely. "Does her choice of husband rankle? He is so very . . . elegant. Almost effete. And oh so indolent." And somehow a bit dangerous, though she had never quite understood that impression she had always had of him. "And very rich. Have you met him?"

"Yes," he said. "I dined with them at the Royal York Hotel when they came through Bath shortly after their marriage. I believe Anna is happy. I believe the Duke of Netherby is too. Did you come here specifically to teach rather than to another school because of Anna? Out of curiosity perhaps to discover something about the sister you did not know you had until recently?"

"*Half* sister," she said. "I could tell you to mind your own business. Instead I will say that if I were curious about her, I would speak with her."

He got abruptly to his feet, crossed the room to remove the paintings from the easels and stand them against the wall, and began to fold and put away the easels while Camille watched him.

"But you have not done so, have you?" he said after a minute or two of more silence.

How did he know that? Did they communicate, he and Anastasia? Or had she told him when she was in Bath with Avery? "She is a duchess," she said, "and I am nobody. It would not be appropriate for me to speak with her." Her words sounded ridiculous as soon as she had spoken them, but they could not be recalled.

He set one folded easel against another and turned his head to look at her over his shoulder. "Self-pity is not an attractive trait, Miss Westcott," he said.

"Self-*pity*?" She lifted her chin and glared back at him. "I thought it was a case of facing reality, Mr. Cunningham."

"Then you thought wrong," he said. "It is self-pity, pure and simple. Anna would have opened her arms— would still do so—to welcome you as a sister, and never mind the *half* relationship. She would share her fortune with you and your brother and sister with the greatest gladness. But you would not condescend to have any dealings with someone who grew up in an orphanage, would you? And you would not be condescended to either. You would rather starve. Yet you seem to feel this need to step into her shoes to discover whether they will fit or pinch your toes."

She glared at him in shock and dislike, nostrils flared. "You presume to know a great deal about me, Mr. Cunningham," she said, "and about my dealings with Anastasia—or lack of dealings. She has obviously been remarkably loose-lipped." It was mortifying, to say the least, that he knew so much.

"I am her *family,*" he said. He grabbed another easel and folded it none too gently. "Family members confide in one another, especially when they are hurt or rejected by those to whom they have reached out in friendship. But I apologize for poking my nose in where it does not belong. You have every right to be annoyed. I will finish putting things away here. You must be wishing to be on your way home."

She was sorry he had apologized. The hurt remained and she did not want to forgive. *Self-pity is not an attractive trait.*

"What makes you think, Mr. Cunningham," she said to his back, "that I *want* to be attractive to you?"

He paused, the easel still in his hands, and turned his head again. At first he looked blank, and then he grinned slowly and something uncomfortable happened to her knees.

"I am quite sure it is the very last thing you wish to be," he said.

Or can be, his words seemed to imply. But he was perfectly correct. She did not want to be *attractive* to any man. The very idea! Least of all did she want to attract the art teacher with his slovenly appearance and wicked, insolent grin and his dark, bold eyes, which seemed to see through to the back of her skull and the depths of her soul. He somehow represented chaos, and her life had always been characterized by order.

And where had that got her, pray?

She turned, drew on her bonnet and gloves, took up her reticule, and cast one last despairing look at the mess she was leaving behind in the form of a pretend shop. He did not rush to open the door for her—but why should he? When she had opened it herself and was passing through it, however, his voice detained her.

"For what it is worth," he said, "I believe it was maybe a fortunate day for the children when you decided to come here, Miss Westcott. You are a gifted teacher. Your ideas for today and tomorrow are little short of brilliant. They teach a number of skills at a number of levels, yet the children believe they are having nothing but fun."

Camille did not look back. She did not thank him either—she was not even sure for a moment that he was not making fun of her. She closed the door quietly behind her and set off on the long, steep trek up to her grandmother's house. She felt a bit like weeping. But there were so many possible causes of such a strange feeling—she never wept, just as she never fainted—that she merely shrugged the whole thing off, pressed her lips together, and lengthened her stride.

She just hoped the predominant cause of the tears she was holding back was not self-pity. How dared he accuse her of that—just when she had stepped out of her misery to *do* something?

Had he loved Anastasia? Did he still?

It was absolutely *none* of her business. Or of any interest to her.

The very idea.

And so she thought of little else all the way home.

Four

✿

When Camille arrived home, hot and breathless and with a stitch in her side, her grandmother was in the drawing room sipping her tea while Abigail was on her feet, already pouring a cup for her sister and fairly bursting with news.

Camille sank onto a chair and slipped off her shoes and ignored the disgrace of her hair, even worse now after being flattened by her bonnet. Did anyone ever get used to that hill? And would she ever grow accustomed to being a workingwoman? Or would she die of exhaustion before she had a chance to find out? Well, she would *not* die of exhaustion, and that was all about it. That would be far too mean-spirited of her. It would be the ultimate defeat. She took the cup and saucer from Abigail with a word of thanks and waved away the plate of cake and scones.

"You ought to eat, Camille," her grandmother said. "You will be losing weight."

"Later perhaps, Grandmama," she said. "All I need now is a drink." And she could probably do with losing at least half a stone. It would be less weight to lug up the hill every afternoon.

"Oh, Cam, such wonderful news," Abigail said, sinking down onto the sofa and clasping a cushion to her bosom. "You will never guess."

"Probably not," Camille agreed after taking the first mouthful of hot tea and closing her eyes in sheer bliss. "But you will no doubt tell me."

"There was a letter from Aunt Louise this morning," her sister said. "The whole family is coming, Cam, to celebrate Grandmama Westcott's seventieth birthday. I had forgotten all about it."

"Here?" Camille stared at her in dismay. "*All* of them?"

"Here, yes," Abigail said. "To Bath. And yes, everyone except Aunt Mildred's three boys. It was Aunt Matilda's idea, as she believes it will be good for Grandmama to take a course of the waters for a week or so as a restorative to her health, though Grandmama never seems to be ailing except in our aunt's imagination, does she? But everyone likes the idea of coming anyway. The boys are going to a house party with friends from their school for a week or so, and Aunt Mildred apparently wrote Aunt Louise that she and Uncle Thomas will feel like fish out of water if they remain at home. So they are coming too. Aunt Louise says that Jessica is beside herself with excitement. The Reverend and Mrs. Snow are returning to their village near Bristol after spending about a month at Morland

Abbey, and Anastasia and Avery are going to accompany them and then come here for the celebrations."

"The Reverend and Mrs. Snow?" their grandmother asked.

"Anastasia's grandparents, Grandmama," Abigail explained. "Her mother's parents, remember? Anastasia and Avery went to visit them after their wedding before calling here."

"Ah, yes," Grandmama said. "Anastasia was called Anna Snow when you first encountered her, was she not?"

Camille's cup and saucer lay forgotten in her hand.

"Oh, and Aunt Louise invited Cousin Alexander," Abigail added, as though she had not already said more than enough, "and he and Cousin Elizabeth and their mama will be coming too. She has also written to Mama, but I do not expect she will come. Do you think she might?"

Why here? Camille was asking herself. Why to Bath of all places? She could not remember their grandmother ever having come here before or any suggestion having been made that she take the waters. And the whole family? Even Althea Westcott, whose husband had been only a cousin of Grandpapa Westcott's, and her children, Alexander and Elizabeth? They had been included, she supposed, because Alex was now the Earl of Riverdale. What was so very special about a seventieth birthday? But she had only to ask herself the question for the answer to be obvious. Grandmama's birthday was just an excuse to allow them all to descend en masse upon the lost members of the family in order to reel them back in. She ought perhaps to be as excited about it as Abby. But she was not yet ready to be reeled in. She was not sure she ever would be. They were her blood relatives, but they were divided from her now by a great gulf of a barrier. Was she the only one who could see it?

"No," she said, realizing that Abigail was anxiously awaiting an answer to her question. "I doubt Mama will come." Their mother was not related in any way to the Westcotts, even though for almost a quarter of a century she had borne their name and been apparently daughter-in-law, sister-in-law, aunt, or cousin to every one of them.

"You are not happy about their coming, Cam?" Abigail asked.

They had been kind and supportive from the start. Both Grandmama Westcott and Aunt Louise had offered them a home—even their mother. Mama had turned her back upon them, however, taking Camille and Abigail with her. Now they were coming to Bath. But could they not *see* that Mama had done the only possible thing? There was not a one of them who did not have a title— except for Cousin Althea, who nevertheless now had the distinction of being the Earl of Riverdale's mother. All of them were of impeccable lineage. All of them had regarded Anastasia with outrage when she had been shown into the salon at Avery's house on that most infamous of days. They would have continued to do so, even after knowing she was Papa's daughter, if she had also been his illegitimate daughter. They could not seem to see that that was exactly what Camille, Harry, and Abigail were. Viscount Uxbury had seen it in a heartbeat. So would the rest of the *ton* have done if they had been given the chance. There was no way back for them. It was illusory to think there might be. It was actually almost cruel of them to come and raise Abby's hopes.

But how could she, Camille, impose her own sense of alienation upon her sister? Who had made her God? "I am delighted for your sake," she said, forcing some warmth into her smile. "You have been missing Jessica in particular, have you not?"

"I miss Mama," Abigail said, looking so bleak suddenly that Camille felt as though the bottom had fallen out of her own stomach. But it was a momentary lapse on Abby's part, and she smiled brightly again. "I miss them all, not just Jessica, and it will be lovely to see them again and perhaps be included in some of the celebrations. Is it not wonderful that they have chosen Bath? Do you suppose it is at least partly because of us?" Her voice was wistful.

Clearly Camille had not fully understood the depth of her sister's suffering. Abby was almost always placid and cheerful. It was easy to assume that the change in their status and way of life had not affected her very deeply. After all, she had never been presented to polite society and therefore did not know the full extent of what she was missing. But *of course* she was suffering. She had in effect lost both Mama and Papa within the last year—and she was only eighteen. She had been disappointed when Papa's death had forced the postponement of the come-out Season she had been expecting this past spring, though she had never complained about it. Instead she had turned her thoughts to next spring and looked forward with great eagerness to her belated debut into society and the chance it would give her to be seen and wooed and wed by some gentleman of high estate. Those hopes and dreams had been cruelly dashed, and all she had to look forward to now were promenades in the Pump Room with their grandmother and the occasional concert and even less frequent invitation to a private home. And the faint chance that she would make a few young friends here eventually and perhaps, if she was very fortunate, find a respectable beau who would overlook the stigma of her birth. Was it any wonder she was so excited about the family's coming here?

"I do not know why they have chosen Bath," Camille said. "Perhaps they all agree with Aunt Matilda about Grandmama's health."

Grandmama Kingsley must have decided it was time to change the subject. "Elaine Dance told us at the concert the other evening that Mr. Cunningham was about to deliver her finished portrait," she said. "This morning she invited us to go and see it."

"It is amazing, Cam," Abigail said, brightening again. "I could not take my eyes off it. I wanted to gaze at it forever."

At a painting of *Mrs. Dance*?

"Elaine was not the prettiest of girls even when she was young," their grandmother said, "and she has let herself go in recent years and gained weight and a double chin as well as wrinkles and faded hair. And all of those things appear in the portrait. Nothing has been disguised. Her chins have not been reduced to one. Her hair has not been painted a darker or a glossier shade. And yet she looks . . . What is the word for which I am searching, Abigail?"

"Beautiful? Vibrant?" Abigail suggested. "He has painted her from the inside out, Cam, and she really is the kindest, most amiable of ladies. Mr. Cunningham has captured that, and it transcends her outer appearance. I have *no idea* how he did it."

"I sent off a note to him on our return," Grandmama said, "inviting him to call here tomorrow afternoon. I have portraits of your grandpapa and myself and of your mother a year before her wedding and of your uncle Michael and aunt Melanie—it was painted four years ago, not long before she died. I have none of any of my three grandchildren, however. I should like to commission Mr. Cunningham to paint the two of you, and perhaps Harry too when these wars are over and he comes home."

It was the final straw for Camille. Just a week ago today she had taken control of her own destiny, casting aside everything that was familiar from her past in order to forge a new life. Now Papa's family was about to descend upon them en masse, doubtless with the idea of somehow tucking them back into a life of gentility in some form. And Grandmama Kingsley was going to have them painted by Bath's most fashionable portrait painter and no doubt displayed in a prominent place for Bath society to come and admire. She doubted Bath society would be impressed.

She did not *want* any of it. She particularly did not want Mr. Cunningham painting her. She could not imagine anything more humiliating. And she was *not* being self-pitying. She wanted to be left alone to wrestle with her new life.

"Let him paint Abby," she said. "She is the beautiful one."

It was the wrong reason to give. "Oh, Cam," Abigail

cried, jumping to her feet and coming to sit on the arm of Camille's chair before wrapping both arms about her and resting a cheek against the top of her head. "You are beautiful too."

"I cannot have one of you painted without the other," their grandmother said. "And I have always thought you particularly handsome, Camille."

Unfortunately there were some bonds that could not be severed simply because one wished to be left alone. If Mr. Cunningham accepted the commission, she was going to have to sit very still for hours on end while he turned those dark, intense eyes on her and gazed upon all her imperfections and painted every one of them, just as he had apparently done with Mrs. Dance. Oh, it would be intolerable. She would be totally at his mercy. She would die.

No, she would not. She would sit stony faced for as long as it took and dare him to try painting her from the inside out, whatever *that* meant. He did not know anything about her inner self, and he never would know. She would see to that.

She felt as resentful toward Mr. Cunningham as if he had been the one to suggest painting her portrait.

Joel had received two letters from prospective customers that morning. One was from a Mr. Cox-Phillips, who lived up in the hills above Bath, where most of the houses were mansions inhabited by the very rich. Joel would have to hire a carriage to take him there, but he would write back later and suggest one day next week. The other letter was from Mrs. Kingsley, who wanted him to call this afternoon at half past four to discuss the painting of her two granddaughters. Anna's younger sisters, that was. Or her *half* sisters, to be precise. The younger of the two was the very pretty Miss Abigail Westcott, whom he had met briefly at Mrs. Dance's a few weeks ago. The other was the Amazon of the orphanage school. He wondered if she knew what fate awaited her. And he wondered if he wanted the task of painting her. Having to share a schoolroom with her two afternoons a week might be as much of her company as he could tolerate.

He would call upon Mrs. Kingsley, however, because there was one thing about the possible commission that attracted him. Most of the subjects of his portraits, as might be expected in Bath, were middle-aged or even elderly persons, none of whom were renowned for their beauty. He had even been a bit uneasy at first about agreeing to paint them, for he had feared he would disappoint the recipients and ruin his reputation even before he really had one. He would not paint vanity portraits, ones that would flatter the subject, and he always made that clear in advance. He would paint the person as he saw him or her. He had surprised himself by actually liking older subjects, who invariably had a depth of character developed through years of experience. He loved talking to people as he sketched them, watching their faces, observing their hands, their eyes, the language of their body and mind—and then deciding just how he was going to capture the essence of them on canvas. And he was pleased with the results so far.

However, he did sometimes long to paint someone young and lovely, and Miss Abigail Westcott was both. Unfortunately, he would not be able to paint her without also painting her sister. As he trudged uphill to keep the appointment, though, he was forced to admit that there was something about her that intrigued him at the same time as she irritated him. It would be an interesting challenge to try to capture on canvas the essence of Miss Camille Westcott, whom he had expected to be one of the world's worst teachers, while in reality it was altogether possible she was one of the best, and who seemed haughty yet had chosen to teach at an orphanage school. Perhaps she would have other surprises in store for him.

Mrs. Kingsley's house was almost in the middle of the Royal Crescent. He rapped the knocker against the door and was admitted into a spacious hall by a butler who made him uncomfortably aware of the shabbiness of his appearance with one sweeping head-to-toe glance before going off to see if Mrs. Kingsley was at home—as though he would not have been perfectly well aware of the fact if she were not. Besides, this was the precise time she had requested that he call.

A couple of minutes later he was escorted upstairs to the drawing room, where the lady of the house and the younger of her granddaughters awaited him. There was no sign of the elder, though she ought to be home from school by now. Mrs. Kingsley was on her feet, and with the practiced eye of an artist, Joel took in her slender, very upright figure, her elderly bejeweled hands clasped before her, her lined, handsome face, the half-gray, half-white hair coiled into an elegant chignon. She herself would be interesting to paint.

"Mr. Cunningham," she said.

"Ma'am." He inclined his head, first to her and then to the younger lady. "Miss Westcott."

"It is good of you to have come promptly on such short notice," Mrs. Kingsley said. "I realize you are a busy man. My granddaughter and I saw your portrait of Mrs. Dance yesterday morning and were enchanted by it."

"Thank you," he said. The granddaughter was smiling at him and nodding her agreement. She was as he remembered her, small and slender and dainty. She was fair-haired and blue-eyed and exquisitely pretty. She resembled Anna more than she did her full sister.

"You captured her kindly nature as well as her likeness, Mr. Cunningham," she said. "I would not have thought it possible to do that with just paint."

"Thank you," he said again. "A portrait is of a whole person, not just the outer appearance."

"But I really do not know how that can be done," she said.

She was even prettier when her face was flushed and animated, as it was now. The sight of her made him even more eager for the chance to paint her if the commission was indeed formally offered. But even as he was thinking it, the door opened behind him and Camille Westcott stepped into the room, seeming to bring arctic air in with her. He turned and inclined his head to her.

She was wearing yesterday's brown frock and yesterday's severe hairstyle, both tidy today but paradoxically even less appealing. She also had yesterday's severe, quelling look on her face.

"Miss Westcott," he said, "I trust your day went well? Did the children buy everything in sight?"

"Oh, many times over," she told him. "Morning and afternoon. At lunchtime the cook had to send an emissary to threaten dire consequences if the dining room tables were not fully occupied in two minutes or less. I spent my day preventing fights over groceries in the nick of time or breaking them up after they had started, and over bills too, for the shopkeeper's sum of what was owed for a transaction was quite often different from what the shopper was offering, and of course both insisted they were right. The shoppers argued with great ferocity, even when the shopkeeper was demanding *less* than he or she was offering."

Joel grinned. "It was a great success, then," he said. "I was sure it would be."

"When you were buying sweets in the market," she said, frowning at him, "you ought to have counted out the exact number for each child to purchase one. You actually bought three too many and caused no end of squabbling until Richard had the brilliant notion of taking them to three toddlers who do not attend school yet. He even insisted upon using three of his precious ha'pennies to buy them and so put all the other children to shame. As a result, they were less than delighted with him. So was I when he murdered the English language at least three times while being so kindhearted."

"Camille," her grandmother asked, "what is this about a shop?"

"You really do not want to know, Grandmama." She moved past Joel and took a seat. "It was just an ill-conceived lesson idea of mine."

Miss Camille Westcott, Joel thought, looked a great deal more handsome when she was ruffled. And a great deal more starchy and stubborn chinned and thin lipped too. Those children had probably not had more fun for a long time—or learned as much.

"Do sit down, Mr. Cunningham," Mrs. Kingsley said, indicating another chair. "I hope to persuade you to paint my two granddaughters, though I am well aware that your services are in high demand at present."

"It would be my pleasure, ma'am," he said. "Did you have a group portrait in mind or individual portraits?"

"My grandson is in the Peninsula with his regiment," she said. "If he were here, I would choose the group portrait of all three. As it is, I would prefer my granddaughters to be painted separately so that a portrait of Harry may be added after he comes home."

The grandson, Joel remembered from Anna's early letters, had lost his earl's title and fortune on the discovery of his illegitimacy and had fled England to fight in the wars. She had been very upset by it all. Her good fortune had been ill fortune for her brother and sisters, and she had not been as exuberantly happy as might have been expected when the dream of a lifetime had come true for her.

"I do not wish to sit for a portrait, Mr. Cunningham," the elder Miss Westcott informed him. "I will do so only to please my grandmother. But I do not want to hear any nonsense about capturing my essence, which is apparently what you did or tried to do with Mrs. Dance. You may paint what you see and be done with it."

"Cam," her younger sister said reproachfully.

"I am perfectly sure Mr. Cunningham knows what he is doing, Camille," her grandmother said.

Miss Westcott looked at him accusingly, as though he were the one arguing with her. He wondered what she had been like as Lady Camille Westcott, when almost everyone would have been her inferior and at her beck and call. She must have been a force to be reckoned with.

"I will sit for you, Mr. Cunningham," she said, "but I trust it will not be for hours at a time. How long *does* it take?"

"Let me explain something of the process," he said. "I talk with the people I am about to paint and observe them as I listen. I get to know them as well as I can. I make sketches while we talk and afterward. Finally, when I feel ready, I make a final sketch and then paint the portrait from that. It is a slow and time-consuming process. It cannot be pushed. Or varied. It is a little chaotic, perhaps, but it is the way I work."

Indeed, there was nothing orderly about the creative process. One could commit the time and the effort and discipline, but beyond that one had little control over the art that came pouring out from one's . . . soul? He was not sure that was the right word, but he had never been able to think of one that was more accurate, for his art did not seem to come from any conscious part of his mind.

Miss Westcott was looking very intently at him.

"Paint Abby first," she said. "You may observe me two afternoons a week in the schoolroom and get to know me that way. You may even present me with a written list of questions if you wish and I will answer all that I consider pertinent. I will allow you to discover all you can about me, but do not expect ever to *know* me, Mr. Cunningham. It is not possible, and I would not allow it if it were."

She understood, he realized in some surprise. She knew the difference between knowing *about* someone and actually *knowing* that person. She was beginning to intrigue him more than a little.

"Will you accept the commission, then, Mr. Cunningham?" Mrs. Kingsley asked him. "And begin with Abigail? I will have a room set aside here for your use. Perhaps we can agree to a schedule that will fit in with your other commitments. And to terms of a contract. I assume you would like something in writing, as I would."

"Yes to everything, ma'am," he said, glancing at the younger sister, who was flushed with seeming delight. For the first time it struck him that she would perhaps be more of a challenge than he had first thought. It would be a joy to paint youth and beauty, but it was not his way to paint only what he saw with his eyes. Was there any depth of character behind the lovely, eager young face of Miss Abigail Westcott, or was she too young to have acquired any? It would be his task to find out.

"Let us go down to the library to discuss details," Mrs. Kingsley said. "I will have some refreshments brought there."

But it was Camille Westcott who had the last word before they left the room. "Did you know that Anastasia is coming here?" she asked him.

He stopped in his tracks.

"She and Avery," she told him, "and all the rest of the Westcott family. They are coming to celebrate the seventieth birthday of the Dowager Countess of Riverdale, my other grandmother. You did not know, did you?"

"No," he said. No, he had not heard from Anna for more than a week. They did not write to each other as often as they had when she first left Bath. They remained close friends, but the fact that they were different genders complicated their relationship now that she was married. In addition, she was happy now and did not need his emotional support as she had at first. "No, I had not heard."

"I thought not." She half smiled at him. *Do you love her?* she had asked yesterday when he had asked her if she hated Anna. She was too intelligent not to have noticed that he had evaded answering the question. Just as she had not answered his.

Anna had rejected the only marriage offer he had made a few years ago, presumably because she did not love him. She had told him at the time that she thought of him as a brother. She had accepted Netherby's offer, presumably because she did love him and he felt nothing like a brother. It was as simple as that. He was not suffering from unrequited love. His life was full and active and really far happier than he had ever expected it would be. But he would rather she had not been coming back to Bath so soon after the last time.

"When do you think you will be able to start?" Mrs. Kingsley asked him as they descended the stairs.

Joel was striding back downhill half an hour later, hoping to reach level ground before the lowering clouds overhead decided to drop their rain upon him. He wondered what Anna would have to say when she knew he was painting her sisters' portraits. And what she thought of the fact that Camille was teaching at the school. Dash it, but he missed the long, almost daily letters they had exchanged when Anna had first left Bath.

Miss Camille Westcott was going to be difficult to paint. How was he to penetrate all that prickly hostility to discover the real person within, especially when she was determined that he would not succeed? It was altogether possible she would be his biggest artistic challenge yet. As he reached the bottom of the hill and strode briskly in the direction of Bath Abbey, the rain began to fall, not heavily, but in large drops that promised a downpour at any minute. He felt the first stirrings of the excitement a particularly intriguing commission always aroused in him. It did not happen often, but he loved it when it did. It made him feel more like an artist and less like a mere jobber—though he hoped he was never just that.

He ducked into the abbey just as the heavens opened, and took a seat in a back pew. He found that he was actually looking forward to sharing the schoolroom tomorrow. That had not happened since Anna left.

Five

✿

She was within a few hours of surviving her first week of teaching, Camille thought early the following afternoon. But could she do it all over again next week and the week after and so on? If, that was, she was kept on after her fortnight's trial. How did people manage to work for a living day in and day out all their lives? Well, she would find out. She might be sacked at the end of next week, but she would not quit on her own, and she would find something else to do if she was judged not fit to teach here. For if she had learned anything in the last week and a half, it was that when one had taken that first determined step out into the rest of one's life, one had to keep on striding forward—or retreat and be forever defeated.

She would not retreat.

She would *not* be defeated.

And that was that.

She had done a great deal of soul-searching last

evening after reading Aunt Louise's cheerful, affectionate letter, full of plans for what they would all do in Bath, and after listening to her grandmother and Abigail talk all evening about the myriad pleasures to which they could look forward. The arrival of such illustrious persons would set the whole of Bath society agog, Grandmama had predicted, and everyone would be eager to be a part of any entertainment at which they could be expected to appear. Camille and Abigail would at last be able to step out of the shadows in which they had been lurking to be acknowledged as part of the family.

Camille was not at all sure she wanted that to happen. She was not sure it ought to happen. She knew she was not ready to rely upon the influence of her family to draw her into a sort of life that could not possibly be more than a shadow of its former self. She did not know yet what she wanted or even who she was, but she was sure—at least, she thought she was—that she needed to stand on her own feet until she had discovered the answers. Would she ever discover them?

She had made a new decision before she lay down for the night. As a result, she had arisen at first light this morning to write a letter and make a few other preparations, and still be able to arrive early for school in order to have a word with Miss Ford. She had learned from a chance remark made during luncheon earlier in the week that the room that had been Anastasia's when she lived and taught here was still unoccupied. It seemed to be looked upon as some sort of shrine. And *this,* Camille could almost imagine visitors being told as they were shown around the building, was where the Duchess of Netherby once lived when she was known as plain Anna

Snow. Camille had asked this morning if she might move into the room and pay for her board out of her earnings. Miss Ford had looked at her with disconcerting intensity for several silent moments before asking if she had ever seen the room. Camille had not, and Miss Ford took her there.

It was shockingly small. Her dressing room at Hinsford Manor had surely been larger. The furnishings consisted of a narrow bed, an equally narrow chest of four drawers, a small table with an upright wooden chair, and a washstand with a bowl and pitcher upon it. There were three hooks affixed to the wall behind the door, a mirror on the door, and a small mat beside the bed.

Camille had swallowed hard, lest she make some inadvertent sound of distress, thought about changing her mind, and then, before she could, asked again if she could have the room. Miss Ford had said yes, and Camille had gone in search of the porter to ask if he could make arrangements to have the bag and portmanteau she had packed earlier fetched from the house at the Royal Crescent. She had also handed him the letter she had written to her grandmother and Abigail before leaving for school.

She had packed in the bags only what she considered the bare essentials for her new life, but even so she wondered if there would be space for everything in the room. The bags had arrived before luncheon, with a note in Abby's hand, though she had not had time to unpack yet or read the letter. Actually, she had been deliberately avoiding it.

Camille felt a bit sick to the stomach and was glad she had had no time to eat any luncheon. Even now she could change her mind if she wished, of course. Or tomorrow, or the day after. It was not as if she had done something irrevocable. Except she knew that if she admitted defeat on this one point, then she would soon be admitting it on every point.

She *would not* change her mind. If Anastasia had been able to live and work here, then so could she.

By the early afternoon, she was feeling exhausted and, as usual, untidy and inadequate. The children, in contrast, were as animated and as noisy as they had been all week. Did children ever speak at any volume lower than a shriek? Did they ever run out of energy?

And then the schoolroom door opened to admit Mr. Cunningham, and Camille felt that his arrival was the last straw. As if she did not have enough to think about without wondering what he thought of her as a teacher and as a person—and without knowing that he would be watching and listening, *as she had invited him to do,* so that he could paint that infernal portrait for Grandmama. She had even offered to answer any written questions with which he cared to present her. Surely he would not dare. She glared at him as though he had already done something to offend her—as he had. He had come.

He stopped on the threshold, as he had done two days ago, one hand on the doorknob, and gazed at the scene before him in open astonishment. As well he might.

"We are learning to *knit,* Mr. Cunningham," Jane Evans, one of the youngest and tiniest of the girls, screeched in her high, piping voice a moment before she started to wail, "Miss, I have dropped all my s-s-stitches."

Again? Was this the third or the fourth time? This had *not* been a good idea, Camille thought as she hurried to the rescue.

"So I see," the art master replied. "It is a hive of indus-try in here. The boys too?"

A typical male remark. Camille did not even dignify it with another glare. She was busy anyway, picking up stitches.

"In some countries, sir," Cyrus North informed him, "it is only the men and boys who knit, while the women and girls spin the wool. Miss Westcott told us so when Tommy said only girls knit and sew."

How else was she to have persuaded the boys not to mutiny?

"We are making a *rope,* sir," Olga Norton shrieked. Her segment of it was already a couple of inches long, she and a few of the other older girls having already learned to knit had considerable practice. They were both able and willing to be Camille's helpers in the gargantuan task of showing the boys and the younger girls how it was done and in rescuing them from almost constant difficul-ties and mishaps.

Paul Hubbard was darting after his ball of wool, which had dropped from his lap yet again to roll merrily across the floor, unwinding as it went.

"Ah, a rope. Yes, of course," Mr. Cunningham said cheerfully, proceeding all the way into the room and closing the door behind him. "In twenty different sections. Why did I not see at a glance? I feel compelled to ask, however. Why a rope?"

He was clearly enjoying himself—at her expense, Camille thought. It really was the maddest idea she had had yet.

A chorus of voices was raised in reply, and a score of

stitches were dropped and half a dozen wool balls rolled in pursuit of Paul's. It was only amazing, perhaps, that most of the children had stitches on their needles at all and that almost all had at least a small fringe of what looked roughly like knitted fabric hanging from them.

He was grinning. How dared he? He would be undermining her authority.

"We went on another outing this morning," Camille explained, silencing at least for a moment the clamor around her. "We walked over the bridge and along Great Pulteney Street to Sydney Gardens. Everyone was obedient to the command to walk in a line two by two, holding hands with a partner. Unfortunately, though, each pair chose a different speed and a different moment at which to hurry up or slow down or halt completely to observe something of interest. I was really more surprised than I can say when we arrived at the gardens to discover that everyone was present and accounted for even if a few were still straggling up from some distance away. And the same thing happened on our return to the school. I would not have been at all shocked to discover that I had lost a pupil or three on the way."

"Oh, not three, miss," Winifred informed her. "We were walking in twos, holding hands."

Only Winifred . . .

"A good observation, Winifred," Camille said. "Two pupils or four, then."

"Or you could have lost some of us in the maze, miss," Jimmy Dale added to a flurry of laughter. "We all went into it, sir, and we all got lost because we kept dashing about in a panic and listening to one another instead of working out a system, which is what Miss Westcott said afterward we ought to have done. She had to come in there herself to rescue the last four of us or we might still be there, and we would all have missed our luncheon and Cook would have been cross."

"Miss Westcott did not get lost herself in the maze?" Mr. Cunningham asked. He was still grinning, his arms crossed over his chest, and still clearly enjoying himself enormously. And he was looking more handsome than Camille wanted him to look. Whatever must he be thinking of her? Paul had retrieved his ball of wool and was chasing someone else's, causing the two lengths of wool to tangle together.

"She did get lost," Richard said, "but she found the four who was missing and brought them out by using a system. She was not in there more than ten minutes."

"Eleven," Winifred said.

"The four who *were* missing, Richard. Plural," Camille said. "We are knitting a rope, Mr. Cunningham, so that everyone can hold on to it whenever we go walking. As well as keeping everyone together and safe, it will teach cooperation. The older pupils will have to shorten their stride to accommodate the younger ones, and the brisk walkers will have to slow down a bit while the loiterers will have to keep a steady pace."

Mr. Cunningham was looking at her with laughing eyes, and Tommy announced that he had two more stitches on his needle than he had had when he started the row and asked if that was a good thing.

"Artists," Camille said firmly, "you will be delighted to know that it is time to go to your art lesson."

There was one faint cheer and a few protests that the pieces would never grow long enough to be crocheted together into a rope if they did not keep at their knitting. But within minutes the art class was in progress. Mr. Cunningham was teaching his group an actual skill today. He was demonstrating with charcoal on paper how to achieve perspective and depth. The accomplished knitters who remained on Camille's side of the room settled down with clacking needles to a steady rhythm, and the learners gradually mastered the art of knitting from one end of a row to the other with a regular tension and no stitches either added or dropped. Most followed her suggestion to unwind a length of wool before they actually needed it so that the ball would not be constantly jerked onto the floor to roll away. Within an hour Camille felt able to pick up a book and read aloud to a relatively tranquil room.

She was one step closer to surviving her first week.

And now she was fully and officially exhausted—with bags still to unpack upstairs. She was also still half convinced that she must be the world's worst teacher. But there was a certain feeling of triumph that she had done what she had set out to do. She had even gone one step further than she had originally planned. She was on her own. On Monday she would start her second week of teaching and perhaps do better.

Why, then, did she feel like bawling?

Jane, seemingly in unconscious sympathy, suddenly burst into noisy tears as one of her needles jerked free of the stitches and went somersaulting end over end over her desk to clatter onto the floor. Camille lowered the book with an inward sigh, but one of the older girls had already hurried to the child's rescue with helping hands and sooth-ing murmurs.

They were knitting a rope in more than twenty parts. Whatever had put such an insane idea into her head? It afforded Joel endless amusement for the rest of the after-noon. Would it not have been less costly, less trouble, and a good deal faster to buy one or, better yet, to ask Roger if there was a length lying around somewhere in the build-ing? She must have applied to Miss Ford to use some of the cash that was reserved for extra school supplies. Joel wondered if she realized it was Anna who had set up that fund quite recently and promised to replenish it whenever it ran low. Who, he wondered, was going to join all the pieces into one when they were finished? Had she thought that far ahead?

And why bright purple?

But perhaps, he thought as the afternoon wore on, it was actually a brilliant idea she had had, just as the shop had been. Knitting was a useful skill to have, for boys as well as for girls, but how could one persuade the boys and the reluctant girls to want to learn and keep at the task unless one could interest them in the production of some specific object? And how could one persuade the chil-dren, especially the older ones, to walk the streets of Bath clinging to a purple rope that would connect them together like an umbilical cord and make keeping an eye on them easier for their teacher unless one could give them a pro-prietary interest in the thing? How was one to devise a practical project on which all could work together regard-less of age and gender, and one on which the older and more experienced could help the younger and more halting? She was actually teaching far more than the basic skill itself. And the children were excited . . . about learning to *knit*.

His own group was attentive enough as he taught some of the tricks of creating depth and perspective. But when they proceeded to work on the exercise he set, they also listened to the story she was reading and an unusual peace descended on the schoolroom, broken only occasionally by a cry of anguish from one of the knitters. Each time that happened, one of the other children went quietly to the rescue so that Miss Westcott could continue with the story. The air of contentment in the room was especially extraordinary for a Friday afternoon in July.

She looked as forbidding and humorless as ever, Joel thought, observing her covertly as he kept an eye on his own group, offering quiet suggestions and comments as needed. She spoke like an army sergeant, even when reading aloud. She displayed none of the sparkle and warmth that had characterized Anna and made her so beloved in the schoolroom. The children ought to be as miserable as they had been under Miss Nunce's brief, unlamented reign. That they were not was a bit of a puzzle. *Miss Westcott* was a bit of a puzzle. She looked one thing, yet was another.

He had no idea how he was going to paint her portrait. If he painted her as he saw her, there would be no hint at all of the creative teacher who somehow appealed to children of varying ages and made them excited about learning. And no one looking at such a painting would guess that she was capable of a certain caustic sense of humor— *I would not have been at all shocked to discover that I had lost a pupil or three on the way.*

He wondered if it was going to be possible to get to know her well enough to paint a credible portrait. Would she allow him to get close enough? And did he really want to? Part of him resented the fact that though different from Anna in manner and methods, she was just as surely capturing the hearts of the children that he still thought of as Anna's. He resented the fact that when he glanced across the room, it was Anna's sister he saw and Anna's sister he heard. She lacked Anna's beauty and charm. And yet . . .

Most of all, perhaps, he resented the fact that he might just come to like Miss Camille Westcott. It seemed disloyal to Anna.

A number of the children, including six from his group, took their knitting with them when school was dismissed for the day. They were eager to complete the rope so that they could use it. They were voluntarily assigning themselves homework. Was the sun about to fall from the sky?

When Joel had tidied his side of the room and turned to take his leave of Miss Westcott, he saw that she was seated at one of the small desks, frowning in concentration over a length of knitting in her hands.

"A weak link in your rope?" he asked.

"Oh, it appears perfect," she said without looking up. "By some miracle there is the correct number of stitches on the needle. However, one was dropped about eight rows back, and one was acquired from an innocent loop two rows ago. I leave you to do the arithmetic."

"They cancel each other out," he said, grinning and strolling closer. The short length of knitted fabric looked considerably less than perfect. Some of the stitches had been very loosely knitted and resembled coarse lace, while others had been pulled tight and were all bunched together. The result was that the strip looked a bit like an arthritic snake. "You will turn a blind eye?"

"Certainly not," she said curtly as she afforded him one withering glance. "I shall make the corrections. Cedric Barnes is only five and he has done his best. However, he must have something to come back to that looks at least half decent or he might lose heart."

Joel raised his eyebrows as he watched her weave the dropped stitch up through the rows. He turned again to leave, but hesitated.

"You are not eager to go home?" he asked. "On a Friday afternoon?"

"I *am* home," she told him as she knitted along the row in order to drop the loop that ought not to be a stitch. She did not explain.

"Meaning?" he asked.

"I have moved in here," she told him. "It was too far to walk back and forth each day. I have taken the room that used to be Anastasia's."

He stared at the top of her head, transfixed with dislike and something that felt very like fury. What the devil was she up to? Was nothing sacred? Was she trying to step right into Anna's shoes and . . . obliterate her? And why did she persist in calling Anna *Anastasia,* even if it *was* her correct name?

"That room is rather small, is it not?" he said.

"It has a bed and a table and chair and enough storage space for those belongings I have brought here," she said. "It has a washstand and bowl and jug and hooks on the wall and a mirror on the back of the door. It was big enough for Anastasia. I daresay it will be big enough for me."

He folded his arms across his chest. "Why?" he asked, and wondered if he sounded as hostile as he felt.

"I have told you why." She had dropped the loop back to its original place and was pulling the knitting into shape about it. When he said nothing, she rolled up the ball of wool and pressed it firmly onto the ends of the needles before pinning the little name tag she had prepared to the knitting and taking it over to the cupboard, where she set it on a shelf with the others that had been left behind. "I do not have to explain myself to you."

"No," he agreed, "you do not." And it was a bit ridiculous of him to feel offended. Anna was long gone. She lived in a ducal mansion and was unlikely to need the room here ever again. He turned to leave.

"Anastasia found her family at the age of twenty-five," she said, fussing with the already tidy shelves of the cupboard, "and had to learn to adjust to relatives who were essentially strangers to her. I remember that when she first learned the truth about herself her instinct was to turn her back on the new reality and return here. I hoped with all my heart that she would do just that so that we could forget about her and carry on with our lives as we always had. That would not have been possible, of course, even if she had come back here. It would not have been possible for us or for her. The contents of a Pandora's box can never be stuffed back in once they have been released. I have to make the opposite adjustment. I have to learn not to belong to people who have always been my family. I have to learn to be an orphan. Not literally, perhaps, but to all intents and purposes."

"You are not an orphan in any sense of the word," he said harshly, irritated with her anew and wishing he had left when he had first intended to. "You have relatives on both sides and have always known them. You have a mother still living and a full sister and brother. You have a half sister who would love you if you would allow it. Yet you insist upon cutting yourself off from all of them as though they do not want you and moving to an *orphanage* as though you belong here."

"I know I do not belong," she said, "except in the sense that I teach here. I do not expect you to understand, Mr. Cunningham. You do not have the experience to understand what has happened to me, just as I do not have the experience to understand what has happened to you in the course of your life."

"That is where human empathy comes in," he said. "If we did not have it and cultivate it, Miss Westcott, we would not understand or sympathize with anyone, for we are all unique in our experience."

She turned her head toward him, her eyebrows raised, while the fingertips of one hand drummed on a shelf. "You are quite right, of course," she said. "Something catastrophic has happened to my life as I knew it, Mr. Cunningham. In the months since then I have wallowed in misery and denial and, yes, self-pity. You were quite right about that. I will not do it any longer. And I will not cling to relatives who would be kind but would possibly do me more harm than good, unintentional though it would be. I must discover for myself who I am and where I belong, and in order to do that I must put some distance between myself and them, for they would coddle me if I would allow it. *Some* distance, not a total one. I shall visit my grandmother and Abigail. I shall see my Westcott relatives when they come here, supposedly to celebrate a birthday. Did I tell you they are *all* coming, not just Anastasia and Avery? For Grandmama Westcott's seventieth birthday? But . . . I must and will learn to stand alone. I can do that better if I live here. Please do not let me keep you. You must be eager to go home."

He stood and stared at her for a few moments, irritated, disliking her. Not understanding her. Not wanting to understand. Dash it all. Why could her maternal grandmother not have lived in the wilds of Scotland? He had not needed any of this. He had needed to get over Anna with all the dignity he could muster and in his own good time.

"You had better come and have tea with me," he said abruptly, surprising himself. "Have you ever been to Sally Lunn's? You have not lived until you have tasted one of the delicacies named after her. They are famous."

Her lips thinned. "I have not yet been paid, Mr. Cunningham," she said.

Good God, was she penniless? He knew she had been cut off entirely by her father's will and that she had refused to share any of Anna's fortune. But . . . literally penniless?

"I have invited you to come and have tea with me, Miss Westcott," he said. "That means I will be paying the bill. Go and fetch your bonnet."

"If this is your way of gathering information about me so that you can paint a convincing portrait of me, Mr. Cunningham," she said before leaving the room ahead of him, "I would warn you that I will not make it easy for you. But if you *do* get to know me, please let me know what you discover. I have no idea who I am."

He stared after her for a few moments, half annoyed, half puzzled, and quite sure this was the last thing he wanted to be doing on a Friday afternoon. But despite himself, he found himself grinning before following her out of the room.

I have no idea who I am.

There was that dry sense of humor again—directed against herself.

Six

✿

Sally Lunn's tearoom, in the oldest house in Bath, was on the North Parade Passage, quite close to the abbey and the Pump Room. It was a tall, narrow building with a bow window jutting onto the street. Inside, it was tiny. The tables were crowded together, cheek by jowl, and all of them seemed to be occupied, as was very often the case. Joel did not come often—until fairly recently he had not been able to afford the extravagance—but he was recognized by a waitress, who smiled warmly at him and indicated a vacant table in the far corner.

Miss Westcott drew attention as they weaved their way between tables in order to reach it. The same thing had happened during their walk here, and he found it as uncomfortable now as he had then. Other patrons leaned out of her way to make more space for her to pass and watched her after she had gone by. It was not so much her appearance, Joel concluded, as the air of noble arrogance and entitlement with which she bore herself. It was inbred, he supposed, and quite unconscious, yet it did not manifest itself in the schoolroom. Outside, however, she expected people to move out of her way and to clear a path for her, but she acknowledged and thanked no one. Joel was intensely irritated as he murmured thanks for both of them and followed her to the table. He wished fervently he had not issued such an impulsive invitation.

She sat with her back to the wall, and he took the chair facing her across the small table. He ordered a pot of tea and two Sally Lunns from the suddenly flushed and flustered waitress. She actually bobbed a sort of curtsy as she left their table. Miss Westcott seemed unaware of her existence.

"I hope you are hungry," he said. "Though my guess is that you missed luncheon in order to purchase purple wool and needles to knit a rope in more than twenty segments."

"I am pleased that I amuse you, Mr. Cunningham," she said. "The shopkeeper had been stuck with the wool when the customer who ordered it took exception to the brightness of the color and bought gray instead. She offered it to me cheaply and I accepted, since I was using orphanage money."

Anna's money. It would be cruel to tell her that, though, just because he would like to take her down a peg or two.

"I expect the finished product will amuse half of Bath," he said. "And the children will tell the story behind it to anyone who stops to look or comment, and everyone will be charmed."

She stared at him, nostrils slightly flared, and he could see that she was not amused. "How does one get them to speak only when spoken to?" she asked abruptly. "And not to volunteer information until it has been solicited?"

"It is perfectly easy to do," he told her. "You have to make them feel small and worthless and oppressed. It helps if your name is Nunce and if you never do anything with them that is of the smallest interest to them."

She continued to stare, tight lipped. What an enigma she was. He had expected her to be at least as bad as Miss Nunce. Anyone looking at her now would expect it too. She was not pretty, he thought. But there was something about her firm jaw and chin, her straight nose, and her blue eyes fringed with dark lashes that made her more handsome than any of them and suggested both intelligence and firmness of character.

"You are an abject failure," he told her, grinning. "The children are not mute in your presence. And they are learning and enjoying themselves. They like you, a sure death knell to any chance of imposing rigid discipline."

"If that is true," she said, "that they like me, I mean, I have no idea why."

It was a surprise to him too. Perhaps children were able to see beyond the severity of outer appearance to . . . what?

"How do Mrs. Kingsley and your sister feel about your moving into the orphanage?" he asked to change the subject.

"I did not tell them," she said. "I packed my bags early this morning and wrote them a letter, and I left early to ask Miss Ford about the empty room. When she agreed to let me rent it, I asked Roger if someone could be sent to fetch my things and deliver the letter. Abby sent a reply with the man who brought my bags, but I have not yet had a chance to read it. I do not need to, however, to guess that she is upset. First our father died. Then our brother left to fight in the Peninsula. Then our mother went away to live with our uncle in Dorsetshire. Now I have moved out."

"She does not feel your compulsion to break away from all that is familiar in order to stand alone, then?" he asked.

"No," she said. "But I respect her right to reshape her life as she sees fit. All I ask is that my right to do the same be respected. Perhaps it is selfish of me to abandon and upset her and turn my back upon our grandmother's hospitality. It undoubtedly is, in fact. But sometimes we have no choice but to be selfish if we are to . . . survive. That is too extravagant a word, though I cannot think of a better."

"You feel threatened by the fact that your father's family has decided to come to Bath to celebrate a birthday?" he asked her.

"Not exactly threatened," she said, frowning as she gave his question some consideration. "Just . . . interfered with. As though I am incapable of working all this out on my own. As though I am just a . . ."

"Helpless woman?" he suggested.

"A *pampered* woman," she said. "As I am. Or as I always have been. It is strange how I never realized it until recently. I always thought of myself as strong and forceful."

"Perhaps you have always been right about yourself,"

he said. "It must have taken great strength to do what you have done this week when you really did not have to."

"Strength?" she said. "Or just stupidity? But Abby is beside herself with excitement that everyone is coming here. For her sake I must be glad too that they are determined to gather us back into the fold."

"Is that why they are coming?" he asked.

But their tea arrived at that moment and prevented her from answering. The teapot was large, the Sally Lunns enormous. Joel hefted the teapot and poured their tea, while Miss Westcott regarded her tea cake in some astonishment. It had been cut in half and toasted, and there were generous portions of butter and jam to spread on it.

"Oh, goodness me," she said. "I have just remembered that I missed breakfast as well as luncheon. *This* is one of the famous Sally Lunns?"

"And I expect you to eat every mouthful." He grinned at her.

She looked at him with some severity after taking a bite, chewing, and swallowing. "Do not think, Mr. Cunningham," she said, "that I do not know what you are up to and why you have brought me here and plied me with tea and . . . and *this*. And oh goodness, it is delicious. You think to get me talking about myself and my life so that you can paint me in such a way as to expose me to the world as I do not choose to be exposed."

"I do not paint nudes," he could not resist telling her, and her mouth, which had been open to take another bite, snapped shut. "Perhaps you merely looked weary and a bit lost, Miss Westcott, and I took pity on you and brought you here to revive you. Perhaps, having found myself sitting across the table from you, I make conversation because even a man who is not a gentleman does not invite a lady to tea and then gobble down his food without saying a word to her. He might leave her with the impression that the food was of more importance than she."

She looked hard at him before disposing of another mouthful. "The point is," she said, "that aristocratic families do not acknowledge their illegitimate offshoots, Mr. Cunningham. The aristocracy is all about the succession and property and position and fortune. Legitimacy is everything. If my father's family had known from the outset that he was not married to my mother and that we were therefore illegitimate, they would have ignored her and pretended we did not exist. It is what my mother did for more than twenty years with Anastasia, though she knew of her existence, and it is what the others would have done too if they had known. It is certainly what I would have done. When she was admitted to the salon at Avery's house, where we were all gathered a few months ago at the request of my brother's solicitor, everyone was outraged, and justifiably so. She was very clearly not one of us. I was more infuriated than anyone else."

"Why was that?" he asked while she spread butter and jam on the other half of her Sally Lunn. He hoped she would not suddenly realize again that she was doing what she had assured him she would not do—talking about herself, that was. But it was not just his portrait of her that made him want to hear more. He was fascinated to listen to the story of that day from her point of view. He had heard it from Anna's at the time in the long letter she had written him only hours afterward.

"I was the perfect lady," she told him. "By design. I was very conscious of who my father was and what was due to me as his daughter. From early childhood on I made every effort to do and be everything he would expect of Lady Camille Westcott. I was an obedient child and paid every attention to my nurse and my governess. I spoke and thought and behaved as a lady ought. I intended to grow up to be perfect. I intended to leave no room in my life for accident or catastrophe. I think I truly believed that I would never be exposed to trouble of any sort if I kept to the strict code of behavior set down for ladies of my class. There was never a rebellious bone in my body or a wayward thought in my mind. My world was narrow but utterly secure. It was a world that did not allow for a cheaply dressed woman of the lower classes being admitted into my presence and my family's and actually being invited to sit down in our midst. I was outraged when it happened."

Joel finished his tea cake and drank the rest of his tea without immediately responding. Good God, she must have been detestable, yet all in the name of what she had been brought up to consider right. But having aimed for perfection in the narrow world into which she had been born, she was finding the plight in which she now found herself bewildering, to say the least. He sat back in his chair and looked at her with renewed interest. Such a woman might be expected to be bitter and brittle. She, on the contrary, had neither crumbled nor raged against the injustice of it all—or, if she had, she was over it now. She had not wrapped herself in self-pity, despite the accusation he had made a couple of days ago. She was not interested in taking advantage of the imminent arrival of her family to try to claw her way back into some semblance of her old life.

Though maybe those words *some semblance* were the key. Perfection as she had known it was no longer possible for Camille Westcott, and she was not willing to settle for anything less. She must search for something wholly new instead. It was not easy to like the woman, but he felt a grudging sort of respect for her.

He amended his thought immediately, however, for when she was in the schoolroom, flushed and animated and in full military-sergeant mode and surrounded by organized chaos, he almost did like her. Indeed, he was almost attracted to that teacher self of hers. Perhaps because that self suggested some underlying passion. Now, that was a startling thought.

"You have a disconcerting way of looking at me so directly that I feel as though you could see right through into my soul, Mr. Cunningham," she said. "I suppose it is the artist in you. I would be obliged to you if you would stop."

He picked up the teapot and refilled both their cups. "Why do you think you were so single-mindedly devoted to duty and perfection?" he asked. "More than your sister, for example."

She hesitated as she stirred a spoonful of sugar into her tea. "I was my father's eldest child," she said. "I was not a son and was therefore not his heir. I suppose my birth was a disappointment to him. But I always thought that if I was the perfect lady he might at least be proud of me. I thought he might love me."

Good God. She did not seem the sort of woman who had ever in her life craved love. How shortsighted of him.

"And was he?" he asked. "And did he?"

She lifted her gaze to his and held it. In her eyes, easily

her loveliest feature, he detected some pain very deeply hidden behind a stern demeanor.

"He only ever loved himself," she said. "Everyone was aware of that. He was generally despised, even hated by people who were the victims of his selfishness. I longed to love him. I longed to be the one who would find the way to his heart and be his favorite. How foolish I was. I was not even his eldest child, was I? And Harry, his only son, was not his heir. Everything about my life was a lie and remained so until after his death. What I set as my primary goal in life was all a mirage in a vast, empty desert."

Impulsively, Joel reached a hand across the table to cover the back of hers as it rested on the tablecloth. He knew instantly that he had made a mistake, for he felt an instant connection with the woman who was Camille Westcott, and he really did not want any such thing. And he heard her suck in a sharp breath and felt her hand twitch, though she did not snatch it away. He did not withdraw his own immediately either.

"You must have been expecting that everything would change for the better after you married Viscount Uxbury," he said. "Did you love him?"

She drew her hand sharply away from his then. "Of course I did not love him," she said scornfully. "People of my class . . . People of the aristocracy do not marry for love, Mr. Cunningham, or even believe in such a vulgar concept as romantic passion. We . . . *They* marry for position and prestige and a continuation of bloodlines and security and the joining of fortunes and property. Viscount Uxbury was the perfect match for Lady Camille

Westcott, for he was a perfect gentleman just as she was a perfect lady. They matched in birth and fortune."

She was speaking of herself in the third person and in the past tense, he noticed.

"And he jilted you," he said, "when suddenly you and the match with you were no longer perfect."

"Of course," she said. "But he did not jilt me. He was the consummate gentleman to the end. He gave *me* a chance to jilt *him*."

"And so you did," he said.

"Yes," she said. "Of course."

He wondered if she believed it all—that she had not loved the man she was to marry, that what Uxbury had done was the understandable, correct thing, that even in breaking with her he had been the perfect gentleman. He wondered if she bore no grudge. He wondered how badly she had been hurt.

"I would wager you hate him," he said.

She stared at him tight lipped for several moments. "I would gladly string him up by his thumbs if I had the opportunity," she said.

He sat back in his chair and laughed at the unexpectedness of her reply. She frowned and her lips tightened further, if that was possible.

"You must have been quite delighted, then, with what happened to him," he said, "unless you would have preferred to mete out your own punishment."

There was another moment of silence, during which her expression did not change. "What happened to him?" she asked, and Joel realized that she did not know. No one had written to tell her. But then, who would have done so? He wondered if he ought to keep his mouth shut, but it was too late now.

"The Duke of Netherby knocked him senseless," he said.

"Avery?" She frowned. "You must be mistaken."

"I am not," he said. "Anna wrote to tell me about it."

She set her cup down on the saucer with a bit of a clatter, her hand not quite steady. "What was she told?" she asked. "I daresay she got it all wrong."

"Viscount Uxbury showed up at a ball to which he had not been invited," Joel said. "It was in Anna's honor and was being held at Netherby's home in London. Uxbury insulted Anna when she discovered who he was and refused to dance with him, and then he made some rude remarks about you, and Netherby and the new earl—Alexander, I believe his name is?—had him thrown out. The next day he challenged Netherby."

"To a *duel*?" She stared at him, clearly transfixed.

"Since he was the challenged, Netherby had the choice of weapons," Joel said. "He chose no weapons at all."

"Fists?" she said. "But it would have been a slaughter whatever weapon he chose."

"Netherby apparently did not specify fists," he said, "though that was what everyone concerned must have assumed he meant. The duel was fought early one morning in Hyde Park before a sizable crowd of gentlemen. Netherby put Uxbury down and out within a very short time and utterly humiliated him."

She looked suddenly scornful. "Well, now I know you are speaking nonsense," she said. "Who filled Anastasia's head with this drivel? Is she really so gullible? It was more likely the other way around. You have met Avery.

He is small of stature and slight of build and indolent of manner. He thinks of nothing but his gorgeous appearance and his snuffboxes and his quizzing glasses. I am only surprised he was not literally slaughtered—if, that is, the fight really did take place, which I seriously doubt. Viscount Uxbury is tall and solidly built and is reputed to be adept at all the manly sports, including fencing and boxing."

"Her cousin—Elizabeth, I believe—told Anna about the duel before it happened," Joel said. "Anna witnessed it for herself."

"Well, now I know that you are gullible too," she said, dismissing him with a withering glance. "Ladies never even know of these disgraceful and illegal meetings between gentlemen, Mr. Cunningham. It is quite inconceivable that any would actually attend one."

"Anna was not a lady until recently, though, you will recall," he said, "and will probably never be a very proper one. She went there at the appointed time and climbed a tree to watch. Her cousin went too. Your former fiancé was given a thorough drubbing, Miss Westcott. He was clad apparently in shirt and breeches and boots and had a supercilious smirk on his face and an offer of mercy on his lips if Netherby was prepared to grovel before him and apologize. Netherby declined the kind offer. He was clad only in breeches. Anna ought to have fallen out of her tree with shock, but she is made of stern stuff."

"You must think I was born yesterday, Mr. Cunningham," she said, "if you expect me to believe any of this."

"I wish I had been there to see it for myself," he said. "Apparently Uxbury struck a pose for the admiration of the spectators and pranced about on his booted feet and threw a number of lethal punches—or punches that would have been lethal if any of them had connected with their target."

Miss Westcott frowned again. "Was Avery badly hurt?"

"He knocked Uxbury to the ground with the sole of one bare foot to the side of his head," he said.

Her lips curled with scorn.

"And then, lest Uxbury and the spectators conclude that it was a chance blow and could not ever be repeated, he did it again with his other foot to the other side of the head after the viscount was back on his feet," Joel said. "When Uxbury chose to taunt him and say insulting things again about Anna and about you, Netherby launched himself into the air, planted both feet beneath Uxbury's chin, and knocked him down to stay. His body is apparently a dangerous weapon, Miss Westcott. He told Anna afterward that as a schoolboy he was trained in some Far Eastern martial arts by an elderly Chinese master."

She continued to stare at him, speechless, but Joel could see that she was beginning to believe him. He finished his tea, which was unfortunately almost cold.

"And Anastasia and Elizabeth and a large gathering of gentlemen witnessed Lord Uxbury's humiliation?" she asked.

"And the earl too," he told her. "He was Netherby's second."

"Alexander," she murmured. She sat back in her chair. "And it was done to avenge me as well as Anastasia?"

"Primarily you, I believe," Joel said, though he was not at all sure that was strictly true. Netherby had, after all, married Anna that same day. "According to Anna, everyone gathered there, almost to a man, was delighted that Netherby had even been prepared to fight what all expected to be a losing battle for your honor. Everyone was more than delighted that he avenged what Uxbury had done to you. He was never a perfect gentleman, Miss Westcott. He would always have been unworthy of you. You had a narrow and fortunate escape from him."

Tears sprang to her eyes, Joel was alarmed to see, and both hands came up to cover her mouth. He was suddenly aware of their surroundings again, of the murmur of voices behind him. He hoped she was not about to weep in full view of all the people crammed into the tearoom. His alarm increased when her shoulders shook. But it was not sobs that escaped her as she lowered her hands, but laughter—great peals of it.

"Oh," she said on a gasp, "I *wish* I had been there too. Oh, *lucky* Anastasia and Elizabeth. He was knocked out by two bare feet to his chin?"

"Out cold," he said.

"Were Anastasia and Elizabeth caught?" she asked.

"No," he said, "but Anna confessed."

"To Avery?" Her laughter subsided and she grimaced. "That was unwise. He would not have liked it."

"He married her an hour after," he said.

She looked at him, her eyes brimming with laughter again. Joel sat gazing at her, wondering how much attention she was drawing from the other occupants of the room. But, however much it was, she seemed unaware of it. He gazed back at her, more than a bit shaken, for she looked like a different woman when she laughed. She looked young and vivid and . . .

What was the word his mind was searching for? Gorgeous? She was hardly that.

Stunning.

That was it. She looked stunning, and he was feeling a bit stunned. She made prettiness seem bland.

Her laughter quickly died, however. "You must have gathered enough information about me to paint a dozen pictures," she said, sounding suddenly cross. "I wish you would paint that infernal portrait and be done with it."

"So that you can be rid of me?" he said. "Alas, you would not be that even if I were ready to paint you tonight. We would still be sharing the schoolroom two afternoons each week. But I am not ready. The more I learn of you, the more I realize I do not know you at all. And, by your own admission, you do not know yourself either."

She got abruptly to her feet, all chilly formality again. "The Sally Lunn was delicious," she said, "and the tea was hot and strong, as I like it. Thank you for bringing me here, Mr. Cunningham. It was good of you. But it is time to return . . . home. I have some unpacking to do and a letter to read."

All of which might fill half an hour if she dawdled. Unless, that was, the bags she had spoken of were actually a couple of hefty trunks. It was altogether possible, he supposed.

She swept from the tearoom ahead of him, seemingly unaware again of the eyes that followed her and of the people who leaned out of her way as she passed them. She stood on the pavement waiting for him while he paid the bill.

"We are going the same way," he said when she would have taken her leave of him and set out alone. "I have to cross the Pulteney Bridge to get home."

She nodded curtly and set off at a brisk pace. But after

a minute, she spoke. "All our talk has been of me," she said as he fell into step beside her, "as, no doubt, you intended. But what of you, Mr. Cunningham? Do you resent my moving into the room that was Anastasia's?"

The question took him by surprise, though he *had* resented it. "Why should I?" he asked her. "She no longer needs it."

"I believe you love her," she said. "I think that unlike me, you do believe in romantic love. Am I right?"

"That I believe in love?" he said. "Yes, I do. That I love Anna? Wrong tense, Miss Westcott. She is a married lady and I respect the bonds of marriage. And perhaps it was never romantic love I felt for her anyway. She assured me the only time I asked her to marry me, a few years ago, that the love we felt for each other was like that of siblings. Neither of us had a family of our own, but we grew up here together and were virtually inseparable. I daresay she was right. And I am very glad now she did not marry me. I would have been tangled up with what happened to her recently, and I would have hated that."

"Yet you could have lived a life of luxury as her husband," she said.

"Living in luxury is not everything," he said.

"How do you know that," she asked him, "unless you have tried it?"

"Do you miss it?" he asked her.

She considered her answer as they crossed the abbey yard and made their way parallel to the river toward Northumberland Place. "Yes," she said. "I would be lying if I said I did not. Oh, I know what you are probably about to say. I could continue to live in luxury with my grandmother. And I know I could be independently wealthy if

I agreed to allow Anastasia to share one-quarter of her fortune with me. I do not expect you to understand why I cannot accept either. I am not sure I understand it myself."

But strangely, he was beginning to. "I think it is because you agree with me, Miss Westcott," he said, "that living in luxury is not everything. And I think it is because the men in your life have been singularly cruel to you."

"Men?" she asked.

"Your father," he said. "Your betrothed."

"It is fortunate, then, in the case of my former betrothed," she said, turning her face away, "that I do not believe in love. I might have had my heart broken if I did."

She kept her face averted for the rest of the way, as though she found everything on the other side of her fascinating to behold. And Joel realized something else about Miss Camille Westcott. She *had* had her heart broken—by a man she had thought perfect, when in reality he was a cad of the first order, just as her father had been. It was only amazing she was still on her feet and not raving somewhere in an insane asylum.

They took their leave of each other when they came to the end of Northumberland Place, though she still did not look fully at him before turning to walk with firm steps toward the orphanage. Joel watched her go, half expecting she would lift a hand to wipe a tear from her cheek. She did not do so. Perhaps she felt his eyes on her back.

By God, he thought, she was a fascinating person. She was going to take some knowing, some understanding. For the first time in a long while he began to doubt his artistic abilities. How would he ever get her right? And what would he do if he never could? Paint her anyway?

. . . if you do get to know me, please let me know what you discover. I have no idea who I am.

He smiled to himself at the remembered words as she turned in at the orphanage doors and he went on his way. He had invited Edgar Stephens to share a meal with him tonight, and he was to do the cooking. And he had promised to call upon Edwina later. Yet all he really wanted to do, he realized, was shut himself up in his studio, grab paper and charcoal, and start sketching before some of his fleeting impressions of Miss Camille Westcott were no longer retrievable from that part of his memory that produced some of his best work.

Seven

❀

If Camille ever heard anyone claiming to have cried herself to sleep, she would call that person a liar. How could one possibly fall asleep when one's chest was sore from sobbing and one's pillow was uncomfortably damp, not to mention hot, when one's nose was blocked, and when one was so far sunk in the depths of misery that the notion of self-pity did not even begin to encompass it? And when one knew what a perfect fright one was going to look in the morning with swollen eyelids and lips, red nose, and blotchy complexion?

She did *not* cry herself to sleep. But she did cry and had to lie on her bed with a handkerchief half stuffed into her mouth, lest she wake everyone in the building. She tried to remember the last time she had wept, and could not recall any such occasion since she was seven and had saved her meager allowance for two whole months until she could purchase a fine linen man's handkerchief. She had then spent hours and days painstakingly embroidering the initial of her father's title—R for Riverdale—across one corner with *I love you, Papa,* beneath, the whole message decorated with flowery twirls and curlicues and a few little flower heads thrown in. It was the first time she had given him a birthday present all her own. He had glanced at it on the great day, thanked her, and put it into his pocket.

His lack of enthusiasm had been deflating enough when she had hoped, even expected, pleasure, astonishment, pride, paeons of praise, warm hugs, effusive thanks, and eternal love to pour out of him. How silly a seven-year-old child could be. And how vulnerable. A few days later she had gone into her father's study on some now-forgotten errand and had seen the handkerchief crumpled up on his desk. When she had gone to fold it neatly, she had discovered that it had been used to clean his pen and was liberally stained with ink that would never wash out. She had dashed upstairs—she had been taught that a lady never dashed anywhere—squeezed between her bed and the wall in the nursery room she shared with Abigail and cried and cried until she retched dry heaves, though she would not tell anyone what had made her so unhappy.

One would have expected her to have learned her lesson from that episode. But it seemed she had not. She could remember persuading herself at the time that her embroidery stitches must have been poorly executed, and she had worked hard and tirelessly to improve her skills.

She did not even know precisely why she wept now. The room was tiny and the bed narrow and none too soft and she ought to have waited until Monday because she did not know what she was going to do with herself all

day tomorrow and Sunday. But surely none of those facts
would have reduced her to tears for the first time in fifteen
years. She had upset Abby and Grandmama by coming
here. But it was not that either. She had muddled through
a week of teaching and had no idea how she was going to
get through another—and another. It was not that either,
though.

Admit the truth, Camille.

She cried because her heart had been broken—though
that was not strictly true either. Her heart had not been
involved in her betrothal. She had not been in love with
Viscount Uxbury. It was just that he had seemed perfect—
the perfect gentleman, the perfect suitor: wellborn, elegant, wealthy, mature, steady, serious minded, morally
upright . . . She could go on and on. It had not hurt either
that he was tall and well built and handsome, though she
had not been drawn to him for those trivial facts alone.
There had been nothing trivial about Lady Camille Westcott's opinions and actions. He had seemed perfect. He
had seemed—though she had never consciously thought
it—everything she would have liked her father to be. He
was reliable, the very Rock of Gibraltar. The whole of
her future had been built upon that rock.

And he had let her down. Oh, not so much in forcing
an end to their betrothal. She had understood the reason
for that, though his rejection had taken her by surprise
and hurt her. No, it was what had happened afterward,
what she had learned only today. He had said something
about her after going uninvited to a ball in Anastasia's
honor, something so insulting that Avery and Alexander
had had him removed from the house. He had said shameful things about her during his duel with Avery too, in

the hearing of what was undoubtedly a large crowd of gentlemen, not to mention Elizabeth and Anastasia.

It had been shockingly unkind of him. Oh, and far more than unkind. It had been cruel. And it seemed so out of character for the man she had thought him to be. Hearing of it had shattered the last of her illusions about the perfect gentleman and aristocrat with whom she had expected to spend the rest of her life. It had, in fact—yes, it was not too inaccurate a phrase. . . . It had broken her heart. One did not have to be in love with a man to have one's heart broken. Perhaps it was because Viscount Uxbury now somehow represented the whole of her life as it had been, though she had not known it at the time. It had all been built not upon rock, but upon sand. And, like even the most carefully built sand castle, it had crumbled and fallen.

She had laughed with genuine glee when she heard the story of Uxbury's humiliation at Avery's hands—or rather at Avery's *feet*. It had felt very good to know that after insulting her he had been made to look a fool before his peers. She was only human, after all. But while she had been walking back from Sally Lunn's with Mr. Cunningham, the misery of it all had come close to overwhelming her, and she had felt her heart fracture. Her father and Viscount Uxbury were very different from each other—yet much the same after all. Could she ever trust anyone again? Was she as entirely alone in this world as she felt?

Was everyone essentially alone?

Oh yes, there was a great deal of self-pity in her misery. And she hated that. *Hated* it.

She slept eventually after washing her face and turning

her pillow and straightening and smoothing out the bed-covers, though it was a fitful slumber punctuated by brief wakeful starts during which she struggled to remember where she was. After she woke up in the morning and washed and dressed, she was faced again with the question of what she was going to do with herself all day. She did not even know—she had not asked—if she was entitled to go to the dining room for breakfast. She considered walking up to the Royal Crescent to explain herself in person to her grandmother and Abby, but there was a light drizzle falling from a leaden sky, she could see through her window, and it looked blustery and cheerless out there. Besides, what more could she say than what she had written? She would see them next week and the family too when they arrived. She would not refuse to see any of them. That would be churlish.

She rearranged her belongings in the drawers and on the hooks—there was just enough room if she kept her toiletries crowded onto the washstand and put her book and writing things on the table. She set her empty bags by the door. She would ask Roger if there was some storage space where she could keep them. And there, that had taken all of twenty minutes, maybe less.

She fetched a pile of books from the schoolroom and spent a while going through them and deciding which would be most suitable to read aloud next week. It was a bit of a tricky decision, as the stories would need to appeal to both boys and girls and to children of all ages. Yet last week she had chosen quite randomly, and everything she read had been well received. She was probably overpreparing. But what else was she to do? She made a written list of what she wanted to teach next week—it was a formidably long list—and spent some time racking her brain for ideas on how to go about it. Her mind remained stubbornly blank. This past week she had taught with almost no preparation or forethought, yet everything had proceeded reasonably well, if a little chaotically. But how could she risk using the same method next week?

She frowned in thought at a sudden memory. *What exactly had he said yesterday? You are an abject failure. The children are not mute in your presence. And they are learning and enjoying themselves and liking you.* He had been grinning when he said it—something a gentleman would never do—and looking disturbingly handsome and attractive in the process. Oh, and virile too. *Attractive?* That was a word not usually in her vocabulary. *Virile* never was. They were somehow not genteel words. They were a little vulgar. She really did not want to think of any man as attractive—or virile. But he had been telling her that she was *not* a failure while apparently saying she was.

Camille sighed aloud. Oh, this was all hopelessly complicated, and it was still not even the middle of the morning. Goodness, she ought to have gone for breakfast. Surely her rent included meals. Her room was seeming smaller and more dreary with every passing moment. It was time to step out and explore her new home. Or *was* it her home? Did the fact that she was renting a room entitle her to wander about the whole building at will? But she could not remain confined to this space one moment longer. It would seem too much like cowering, and she had done that for too long at Grandmama's. She was now the newly invented, newly confident Camille Westcott, was she not?

No one looked aghast as she strolled about. No one went running for Miss Ford. The home hummed with the sounds of young voices and laughter and a few wails of indignation or distress. It was a large building—three sizable three-story homes knocked into one—and had retained much of the elegance the individual houses must have had when first built. It was also pleasingly decorated with light paintwork and curtains pulled back from the windows and bright cushions that lent an air of general cheerfulness. This was no gloomy institution, as she had realized during the tour Miss Ford had given her soon after her arrival in Bath.

The living accommodations consisted of cozy dormitories on the upper floors for five or six children, and each had an accompanying living room with chairs and tables and cushions and a few playthings. The idea was to give each group of children some sense of home and family, Camille supposed. And each group had its own set of housemothers, who offered them as close a sense of family as was possible under the circumstances. It was the housemothers who cared for the children all day and night when they were not at school, and supervised their play and took them for walks on nonschool days. There were a few smaller rooms on the ground floor, presumably for visitors, in addition to the schoolroom and dining room. A few children played quietly together now in one of them. Most, however, were congregated in the large common room or playroom, it being too wet for them to go outside into the walled garden at the back to play. Altogether it was not an entirely unpleasant home situation for the forty or so children who lived here.

Camille nodded at the housemothers who were supervising there and hovered uncertainly in the doorway. But three of her younger pupils wanted to introduce her to their family of rag dolls, and then two others, a boy and a girl, wanted her to see the tower they had built of wooden cubes Roger had carved and painted for them. Two boys were knitting under the eagle eye of Winifred Hamlin, who was working on her own strip too, already about eighteen inches long and seemingly without a flaw. The boys called Camille over to show her how much progress they had made since yesterday.

There were two infants in separate cots. One, a baby of perhaps four or five months, was playing happily with his toes and waving his arms in excitement whenever an adult or one of the children bent over him to tickle his chin and talk baby talk to him. The other, maybe a month or two older, lay on her back and sobbed quietly and refused to be entertained or consoled.

"She has been here only a week," one of the house-mothers explained when Camille drew closer. "She will settle down soon."

"Perhaps," Camille suggested, "she wants to be held."

"Oh, I do not doubt it." The young woman laughed, not unkindly, as she bent down to smooth a hand over the child's downy head and murmur something soothing. "But we cannot give all our attention to one child when everyone is clamoring for it."

Everyone was not, as it happened. Most of the children seemed perfectly happy with one another's company. However, the staff was definitely busy. They were cheerful too, as Camille had noticed before. But even so . . .

"May I pick her up?" she asked. Had the child been crying lustily, she might have been less concerned. But there was a bleak hopelessness to the soft sounds she made. "I have nothing much else to do and feel a bit useless."

"Certainly, Miss Westcott," the housemother said. "That would be good of you. But you must not feel obliged."

"What is her name?" Camille asked.

"Sarah," the woman told her.

Camille had never had much to do with babies—or with children at all—until this past week. She had grown up expecting to be a mother, of course. It would be one of her duties to present her husband with sons for the succession and daughters to marry into other influential families. But being a mother when one was a lady of the *ton* did not necessarily involve one in looking after the children or comforting them or entertaining them. There were nurses and governesses to do that.

There was a blanket folded over the foot of the cot. The room was not cold despite the dreariness of the weather outside, but a baby needed coziness. Or so Camille imagined. She spread the blanket over the lower half of the mattress, moved the baby gingerly onto it, wrapped it tightly about her like a cocoon, and lifted her into her arms. The child continued to wail softly, and Camille, acting purely from instinct—good heavens, she knew *nothing*—held her against her shoulder and rubbed a hand over her back, murmuring soothing words against her head.

"Everything will work out for the best, Sarah," she said. Foolish words. How could it? Did anything ever work out for the best? She kissed one soft cheek and felt somehow as though her stomach or her heart had turned over. The crying stopped after a while as Camille took a turn about the room, weaving in and out of groups of children, and then stepped out into the quieter corridor beyond. The bundle in her arms grew warmer until she realized the child was sleeping. And now she felt a bit like crying herself. Again? Was she going to turn into a watering pot?

No, not that. Definitely, certainly not that. The very idea!

She returned to the playroom and sat in a deep armchair in one corner, holding the sleeping baby close in her arms. The children around her were all occupied with some activity. The housemothers were busy. Two little girls leaned over the sides of the other baby's cot, making him gurgle and laugh. Everyone appeared clean and reasonably tidy. It was, Camille thought, a happy enough place, or at least a place that was no more miserable than many family homes, even those of the rich.

"You see, the trouble is that children can become overattached if they are held too much," one of the other housemothers said, stooping down on her haunches in front of Camille's chair and smiling tenderly at the sleeping baby. She was Hannah, Camille recalled, apple cheeked, bright eyed, sturdy, pretty in a wholesome, quite unsophisticated way. "We are taught that when we are being trained. But we are also taught that they need love and approval and dry nappies and hands that do not stick to everything they touch. It is not an easy job. Nurse says it is a bit like walking a tightrope every working day of our lives. We are thankful for your help, though you must not ever feel obliged to offer it. I thought when I first saw you that you were very different from your sister, but I think maybe I was wrong. Miss Snow—the Duchess of Netherby—was much loved here."

The nurse was a senior member of staff in charge of all the health needs of the children.

Camille nodded and smiled—at least, it was either a smile or a grimace. She was not sure which. No one had expected to like her? Did that mean they did anyway? Or at least that Hannah did? She lifted Sarah a little higher in her arms when Hannah had gone away and gazed into her sleeping face.

"Sir," someone called in an eager voice, "come and see our tower."

And there he was, standing in the doorway, looking his usual semishabby self, with a genial expression on his face, glancing about him, though he appeared not to have noticed Camille sitting quietly in her corner. Mr. Cunningham. He looked perfectly at home, even though he was the only adult male present. But of course he would feel at home. He had grown up here with Anastasia as his best friend and had then fallen in love with her and wanted to marry her. He still loved her, Camille suspected. But was that any reason to dislike him? Did she have any reason to dislike Anastasia?

He crossed the room, ruffling the hair of a little boy as he passed, and stooped down on his haunches to admire the wooden tower. He was clutching what looked like a sketchbook and a stick of charcoal in one hand. And Camille recalled some of the words he had spoken yesterday—*Uxbury insulted Anna when she discovered who he was and refused to dance with him . . .*

. . . when she discovered who he was . . . Viscount Uxbury, that was, the man who had been betrothed to Camille but had spurned her after learning the truth about her birth. Anastasia had refused to dance with him *because he had hurt her half sister*? Her, Camille?

Mr. Cunningham set his book down in order to help

construct battlements about the top of the tower—until the little boy whose hair he had ruffled came along and knocked the whole thing down with one swipe of his arm and a giggle. There were cries of outrage from the children who had built it, and Mr. Cunningham stood up, roaring ferociously, grabbed the child, tossed him at the ceiling, and caught him on the way down. The little boy shrieked with fright and glee and then helped Mr. Cunningham and the other two gather up the fallen bricks and start again.

Other children claimed his attention and he spent some time with each group before exchanging a few words with one of the older housemothers. He had brought the cook some fresh eggs from the market, Camille heard him say, and had wrangled an invitation to stay for luncheon.

"But you don't need an invitation, Joel," the woman told him. "You know that. Not to come home."

He laughed and sat down on a chair, his back half turned to Camille—he still had not seen her—and began to draw something in his sketchbook. The baby in his cradle, perhaps—he now had both feet clutched in his hands and was rocking from side to side, jabbering happily to himself. Or perhaps the girls engrossed in their game with the rag dolls. Or perhaps six-year-old Caroline Williams, one of the younger children at the school, who appeared to be reading aloud to an old doll from a large book, sounding out the words and following them along the page with one forefinger. Camille knew that in fact she had difficulty reading, something that was going to have to be addressed in the coming week.

The baby in her arms gave a hiccup of a sob and Camille looked down as one little hand waved in the air and came to rest against her bosom and clutch the fabric of her dress, even though the child did not wake. And then she did. She twitched, opened her eyes, gazed solemnly up at Camille, and . . . smiled a broad, bright, toothless smile. It felt like one of life's random and unearned gifts, Camille thought, smiling back, smitten with unexpected happiness. It was a totally unfamiliar feeling. She had never cultivated happiness—or unhappiness for that matter.

They were interrupted by Hannah, who had come to take the baby to change her nappy before feeding her. "The children have been sent to wash their hands before luncheon," she told Camille. "You will be wanting to go and eat too, Miss Westcott. I think Sarah has taken to you. She will soon settle here. They all do."

Mr. Cunningham was standing close by when Camille got to her feet. He had seen her at last and appeared to be waiting to go into the dining room with her. "*Madonna and Child,* do you think?" he asked her, holding up his sketchbook, its topmost page facing toward her, so that she could see what he had been drawing. "Or is that too popish a title for your liking?"

It was a charcoal sketch of a woman seated on a low chair, a baby, swaddled in a blanket, asleep in her arms. The drawing was rough, but it suggested a strong emotional connection between the child and the woman, who was gazing down at it, something like adoration on her face. The child was unmistakably Sarah, and the woman, Camille realized with a jolt, was herself, though not as she had ever seen herself in any mirror.

"But you did not even see me when you came in," she protested. "And you were sitting almost with your back to me while you sketched."

"Oh, I saw you, Miss Westcott," he said. "And like any self-respecting teacher, I have eyes in the back of my head."

She did not have a chance against him, Camille thought, not quite understanding what she meant. Within just a few minutes and with only paper and charcoal, he had reproduced exactly how she had been feeling as she held that child. Almost honored. Almost tearful. Almost maternal. Almost adoring. She looked at him, a little disturbed. And she wished, suddenly cross, that he was not handsome. Not that he was *handsome* exactly, only good-looking. What she really wished was that he was not *attractive*. Because he was, and she did not like it one bit. She was not accustomed to characterizing men according to their physical appeal. Though it was not all physical with him, was it?

"Shall we go for luncheon?" he asked, indicating the door. They were the last two left in the room.

"May I have the sketch?" she asked him.

"Madonna and Child?" he said.

"May I?"

He detached it from the book and held it out to her, holding her eyes as she took it from him.

"Thank you," she said.

"It is not a crime, you know," he said, "to love a child."

Joel had left Edwina's house earlier than usual last night despite her sleepy protests. He was working on a painting, he had told her, and was burning up on the inside with the need to get back to it before his vision dimmed. He had not even been lying, though he had felt a bit as though he were, for the arrangement with Mrs. Kingsley had been that he would start with her younger granddaughter next week and leave the elder until later, perhaps even the autumn.

He had been up until dawn, working by candlelight, capturing her laughter-full face and then her averted, tear-streaked profile—two sides of the same coin. But, unlike a coin, she had more than two sides. How many more he did not yet know.

He had snatched a few hours of sleep but had got up earlier than he intended, restless and impatient with the two portraits he must finish before getting too deeply involved in the new project. He ate his breakfast standing up and, gazing at one of the portraits on his easel, trying to feel the excitement of a character almost captured in paint with only a few slight tweaks remaining to be done. Then he sat down and wrote to inform Mr. Cox-Phillips that he would call on him on Tuesday. He did not really want to go at all. He wanted to finish the outstanding projects and then concentrate upon the two portraits that had captured his interest far more than he had expected. But it would not do to turn down the possibility of another commission out of hand. Who knew when they would dry up altogether and leave him without further income?

He had intended to settle to the painting after sealing the letter, but his mind was churning with myriad thoughts and he owed the subject of the portrait better than that. Perhaps later. Perhaps he was just tired. He had had maybe an hour of sleep at Edwina's, maybe two here after dawn. Finally he stopped pretending to himself, though he still did not admit his motive. He went to the orphanage, picking up some fresh eggs at the market on the way.

There was nothing so very remarkable about his visit, after all. He often went there unannounced, to chat with the staff that had been there for much of his life and to play with the children. They were his family.

And if he went at least partly to see how Camille Westcott was coping with her first full day there, then it was hardly surprising, for she was a work colleague, and she was Anna's sister. And he was to paint her portrait even if her sister's was to come first.

The garden was deserted, of course, since the drizzle was still coming down and making July feel more like April. He made his way to the playroom—and saw her immediately, even though it was almost overflowing with busy children and their adult supervisors and she was sitting quietly in a corner. Would she never cease to amaze him? She was holding a sleeping baby. If he was not mistaken, it was the one who had been discovered on the front step early one morning a week or so ago with one thousand pounds in banknotes tucked beneath the blanket in which the child was wrapped—a staggeringly immense fortune in money with a scrap of paper on which were written the words *Sarah Smith. Look after her.*

Joel played with several of the children, but all the time he was aware of the woman and baby in the corner. He had brought a sketch pad with him, as he usually did, though he did not often make use of it. He was always more of a participant than an observer here. But this time was different, and finally he could resist no longer. He sat down to sketch. He did not even have to look at them while he worked. He marveled that he had seen yet another aspect of Camille Westcott he would never have suspected. Her whole posture of relaxed stillness and her apartness in the corner of the room spoke of maternal love.

Of course she was unaware of it. She frowned when she saw the sketch after Hannah had taken the baby from her. He had seen the moment when she recognized herself and stiffened with displeasure and perhaps denial. Her lips had thinned when he told her there was no crime in loving a child. Yet she had asked him for the sketch, which he had wanted to add to the portfolio of her he had started early this morning. He gave it to her reluctantly and wondered if she would burn it or hang it in her room or hide it at the bottom of a drawer.

They sat at the staff table in the dining room with the nurse and Miss Ford, but they lingered there after the other two had left.

"Have you ever discovered anything of your parentage, Mr. Cunningham?" she asked him.

"No," he said.

"Do you ever wish you could?" she asked.

He considered the question—not that he had not done so a hundred or a thousand times before, but he had ambivalent feelings about it. "Perhaps I would regret it if I ever did ever find out," he said. "Perhaps they were not pleasant people. Perhaps they came from unpleasant families. It is only human, however, to yearn for answers."

"Do you suppose Anastasia has regretted finding out?" she asked him.

"I believe she did for a while," he said. "But she would not have met and married the Duke of Netherby if she had remained Anna Snow, orphan teacher of orphan children in provincial Bath. And that would have been something of a tragedy, for she is happy with him. She has also discovered maternal grandparents who did not after all abandon her. And she has a paternal grandmother and aunts and cousins who have opened their hearts to her and drawn her into a larger family. On the whole, I do not believe she has many regrets."

"On the whole?" She was gazing into her teacup, which was suspended between the saucer and her mouth.

"Her new life has brought some unhappiness too," he said. "She has been quite firmly rejected by the very family members she most yearns to love. And what makes it worse for her is that she knows she has brought a catastrophic sort of misery to those people but has not been allowed to make any sort of amends."

"Are you trying to make me feel guilty, Mr. Cunningham?" she asked him.

"You asked the question," he reminded her. "Ought I to have given the answer with sugar added to disguise some of the bitterness? *Do* you feel guilty?"

"I am tired of this conversation, Mr. Cunningham," she said.

"And I am tired of being *Mr. Cunningham*," he said. "My name is Joel."

"I have been brought up to address everyone outside my inner family circle with the proper courtesy," she told him.

"You would probably have called your husband *Uxbury* all his life if you had married him," he said.

"Probably," she agreed. "What I was brought up to does not amount to the snap of my fingers now, though, does it? I am Camille." She set her cup down on the saucer, still half full. "I see that the rain has stopped. I need to get out of here. Would you care for a walk?"

With her? She irritated him more than half the time, intrigued him for much of the rest of it. He did not believe he liked her. He certainly did not want to spend Saturday afternoon prowling the streets of Bath with her. He had better things to do, not least the completion of a portrait so that he could get on with hers and her sister's.

"Very well," he found himself saying nevertheless as he got to his feet.

Eight

❧

It was chilly and blustery, but at least it was not raining. Camille set the direction and strode off toward the river, Mr. Cunningham—*Joel*—at her side. He was not talking, and she felt no inclination to carry on a conversation. She could not explain to herself why she had wanted him with her, but she was pleased with herself about one thing. She had never before suggested to a man that he take a walk with her. She had never called any man outside her family by his first name either. Not that she had called Mr. Cunningham by his yet.

"Joel," she said, and was surprised to realize she had spoken out loud.

"Camille," he answered.

And no man outside her family had ever called her by *her* first name—not even Viscount Uxbury after they were betrothed. But instead of feeling uncomfortable, she felt—freed. She was no longer bound by the old rules. She could set her own. She had wanted company, and she had got it by her own efforts.

They crossed the Pulteney Bridge and walked onward to the wide, stately stretch of Great Pulteney Street. She had no destination in mind, only the need to walk, to breathe in fresh air, to—

"I believe we are being rained upon again," he said, interrupting her thoughts when they were less than half-way along the street.

And, bother, he was right. It was a very light drizzle, but the clouds did not look promising, Camille had to admit. Anyway, one could get just as wet in drizzle as in a steady rain if one remained out in it long enough.

She looked up and down both sides of the street, but it was residential. There was nowhere to shelter, and really only Sydney Gardens ahead of them, not a good place to head for in the rain. "I suppose we had better turn back," she said.

But she did not want to go home yet. She ought to have known better than to change her place of abode on a Friday with a weekend looming ahead. The trouble was that she had no experience with being impulsive and spontaneous—or with making her own decisions. She was about to suggest Sally Lunn's again for a cup of tea, though it was farther away than the orphanage, but she remembered that she had no money. Double bother! The drizzle was steady now.

"I live on this side of the bridge," he said.

"You had better hurry home, then," she said, "and I will do the same. It is not very far."

At that moment the drizzle turned to rain. She would

get soaked, Camille thought in dismay—and this would teach her to venture out without an umbrella. She was just not accustomed to going places on foot. He caught her by the hand before she could move and turned them back in the direction from which they had come.

"Hurry," he said, and they half trotted, half galloped back along Great Pulteney Street. He was still holding her hand when he turned onto another street before they reached the bridge, and they dashed along that too, heads down, and . . . laughing helplessly.

They were both breathless when he stopped outside one of the houses and let go of her hand long enough to fumble in his pocket for a bunch of keys, with one of which he unlocked the door. He flung it open, grabbed her hand again, and hauled her inside in such a way that they collided in the doorway, shoulder to shoulder. He released her again in order to shut the door with a bang, plunging them into the semidarkness of an entry hall. They were still laughing—until they were not. It was not a particularly small hallway, but it seemed very secluded and very quiet in contrast to the outdoors, and being here felt very improper. Of course, she ought to have kept going straight when he turned the corner.

"It was closer than the orphanage," he said, shrugging.

"This is where you live?" she asked—as though he would have the key to someone else's house.

"On the top floor," he said, indicating the rather steep staircase ahead of them.

He had not invited her up there in so many words, but they could not stand forever in the hall when it had not looked as if the rain would stop anytime soon. Camille climbed the stairs, and he came after her. It looked and sounded as though the house was deserted. How could silence be so loud? And so accusing?

"Does anyone else live here?" she asked.

"Two friends of mine," he said. "Both single men, one on the ground floor and one on the first. I am closest to heaven, or so I console myself when I forget something and have to climb all the way back up to get it."

Two men. Three altogether, counting him. This, Camille thought, was very improper indeed. Lady Camille West-cott would have had a fit of the vapors . . . except that she had never been the vaporish sort. And she would not have been out walking alone with him anyway to be caught in the rain, and even if she had been, she would not have allowed her hand to be grabbed and her person to be hauled at an inelegant dash along the street to be made into a public and vulgar spectacle for anyone who happened to witness it. The experience would certainly not have rendered her helpless with laughter.

But Lady Camille Westcott did not exist any longer. And, oh, the shared laughter had felt good.

She had to wait at the top of the stairs while he moved past her and unlocked another door. There was a narrower entry hall beyond it, no doubt just a simple corridor when the building had been all one house. Three doors opened off it, one on either side and one straight ahead. The one to her right was shut. The door straight ahead was open to show a spacious living room—she could see a sofa and chair in there and a big window that was letting in light despite the clouds and rain. The door to her left was also open, and Camille could see that it was a bedchamber. A largish bed, roughly made up, dominated the space and made her aware suddenly that his rooms were as deserted and as quiet as the rest of the house. She doubted he kept a manservant or housekeeper.

"This is all yours?" she asked him.

"I rent the whole floor, yes," he said. "I had just the bedchamber for twelve years, but last week the family who occupied the rest of the floor moved out and I was able to rent it all. I still have not recovered from the novelty of having all this space to myself. It makes me feel very affluent."

"The bedchamber," she said, "is a bit bigger than my room at the orphanage." Though not by very much. And it had been his home for twelve years. Before that he had, presumably, shared a dormitory with four or five other boys at the orphanage. Her thoughts touched upon the size of Hinsford Manor, where she had grown up, and veered away again. But really, how vastly different their experiences of life had been.

"It was my sleeping area, my living room, and my studio," he said. "It was where I stored my paintings and supplies. There was barely room for me."

They stood side by side just beyond the doorway, gazing in. He must have felt the awkwardness of it just as she did. They both turned away rather hastily.

"And now you paint in that room?" she asked, nodding to the room ahead. "There is plenty of light."

"No." He indicated the closed door. "My studio is in there. It is the most prized of my new rooms. My private domain. Let me take your bonnet and pelisse and hang them up to dry. I'll light the fire in the kitchen range and put the kettle on for tea. Come and sit at the table while you wait."

He hung her things on hooks in the hallway and she

followed him into the living room and through another
door into the kitchen and dining area. He tossed his damp
coat onto an arm of the sofa in passing and pulled on a
jacket that had been thrown over the back of it. The jacket
was even shabbier and more shapeless than his coat and
gave him a comfortable, domesticated look that somehow
emphasized his virility and made her even more aware
that she was alone with a man in his home in an empty
house two stories above the street.

He busied himself getting a fire started and filling the
kettle from a pitcher of water in the corner while Camille
sat at the dining table and watched him. He spooned some
tea from a caddy into a large teapot and took two mis-
matched cups and saucers from one cupboard and a bottle
of milk and a sugar bowl from another. He found a couple
of spoons in a drawer.

"You drank your tea without milk yesterday and at
luncheon earlier," he said. "Do you prefer it that way?"

"Yes," she said. "I will take a little sugar, though, please."

He poured a few drops of milk into one of the cups
and brought the sugar bowl to the table. He hesitated a
moment and sat down on the chair adjacent to hers. It was
going to be a while yet before the kettle boiled. He was
as uncomfortable as she, Camille thought. This was very
different from being at Sally Lunn's.

"Do people come here to have their portraits painted?"
she asked him.

"No," he said. "It was impossible until this past week.
There simply was not enough room. There is now, but my
general policy will not change. My studio is my private
place."

It was the second time he had said that. Was he warding off any request she might make to see his paintings?

"Does anyone come here at all?" she asked.

"The fellows on the two floors below have entertained me in the past," he said, "as well as a few other friends of mine. I was finally able to return the compliment and invite them all here last week, the day after I moved in, for a sort of housewarming."

"All men?" she asked. "No women?"

"No women," he said.

"I am the first, then?"

Silence, she realized again, was not always really silent. It acted as a sort of echo chamber for unconsidered words that had just been uttered. And it had a pulse and made a dull, thudding sound. Or perhaps that was her own heartbeat she could hear.

"You are the first, Camille," he said with a slight and slightly crooked smile. "Because of the rain," he added. He gave her name its proper French pronunciation—*eel* at the end instead of *ill,* as her family tended to do. She liked the sound of her name on his lips.

Their eyes met and held, and Camille found herself wondering foolishly if other gentlemen of her acquaintance were as masculine as he was and she had just not noticed. Was Viscount Uxbury—? But no, he most certainly was not, despite a handsome face and a splendid physique. She would have noticed. Good heavens, she had been going to *marry* him, yet she had never felt even a frisson of . . . desire for him. Was that what she felt for Mr. Cunningham—Joel—then? Or was she merely still breathless from that run followed by the climb up the stairs?

"I suppose," she said, "you planned to be busy painting this afternoon. But instead you agreed to come walking with me when I might have guessed that the rain would come back."

"I have a portrait to finish off," he said. "Two of them, actually. They are both near completion. But there is no particular hurry."

"And then it will be our turn?" she asked. "Abigail's and mine? Do you ever run out of work? Is the possibility a bit frightening?" In the past she had never really thought of being without money.

"It has not happened yet," he said, "and I do try to keep a little by me for that rainy day everyone warns of. Sometimes I wish there was more time to paint for my own pleasure, though. There will probably be another commission next week, though I do not know how many portraits it will involve."

"Next week?" she said.

"On Tuesday," he said, "I have agreed to call upon a Mr. Cox-Phillips. He lives some distance outside Bath up in the hills where most of the houses are mansions. I daresay he is very wealthy and can well afford my fee."

"Cox-Phillips?" She frowned in thought. "Do you know him?"

"No," he said, "but he must know me or at least have heard of me. My fame must be spreading." He grinned at her and got up to check the kettle, though it was clearly not boiling yet. "Do *you* know him?"

"I know who he is," she said, "or, at least, I suppose he must be the man I am thinking of. He was somebody important in the government a number of years ago, an acquaintance of my uncle, the late Duke of Netherby. I remember my aunt Louise talking about him. She used to describe him as curmudgeonly. He has some family connection to Viscount Uxbury."

"Curmudgeonly?" Joel said, sitting down again. "That does not bode well for me. He may not like being told he must wait for a few months until I have time to paint for him."

"You must play the part of temperamental artist," she said, "and pit your will against his."

"Who says it would be playing a part?" he asked her, grinning again. "If he cuts up nasty, I shall just refuse whatever commission he has in mind. Perhaps I will not even go up there."

"The word *curmudgeonly* has frightened you off?" she asked him. "But your curiosity will surely outweigh your fear. I hope so, anyway. I want to hear all about your visit when you come to school on Wednesday, assuming, that is, that you survive the ordeal."

He gazed at her without answering, and his fingers drummed a light tattoo on the table. "I need my sketch pad," he said. "You should do that more often, Camille."

"Do what?" She could feel her cheeks grow warm at the intentness of his gaze.

"Smile," he said. "With a certain degree of mischief in your eyes. The expression transforms you. Or perhaps it is just another facet of your character I have not seen before. I left my sketchbook at the orphanage, alas, though I do have others in the studio."

"Mischief?"

"Of course you are not doing it any longer," he said. "I ought not to have drawn your attention to it."

"The kettle is boiling," she said, and she pressed both

palms to her cheeks when he got up and turned his back. But the thing was that she really had been smiling and joking and rather enjoying the image of him confronting Lord Uxbury's crotchety relative, his knees knocking with fright but his artistic temperament coming to his rescue. And now she was probably blushing. She watched him pour the boiling water into the teapot and cover it with a cozy to keep the tea hot while it steeped. She had never seen a man make tea. He did not look effeminate doing it, though, despite the fact that the cozy had daisies embroidered all over it. Quite the opposite, in fact. "Mischief is for children, Mr. Cu— Joel."

"And for adults who are willing to relax and simply be happy," he said, turning to lean back against the counter, his arms crossed over his chest.

"You think I am not willing?" she asked him.

"Are you?"

"Ladies are not brought up to cultivate happiness," she said. 'There are more important things."

"Are there?"

She frowned. "What is happiness?" she asked. "How does one achieve it, Joel?"

He did not immediately answer. Their eyes locked and neither looked away. Camille swallowed as he pushed away from the counter and came toward her. He set one hand on the table beside hers and the other on the back of her chair. He drew breath as though to say something, but then leaned over her instead and kissed her.

Somehow she had known it was coming, yet when it happened she was so surprised, so shocked, that she sat there and did nothing to prevent it. It did not last long— probably no more than a few seconds. But during those seconds she became aware that his lips were slightly parted over her own and that there was heat in them and in his breath against her cheek. She was startlingly aware of the male smell of him and of a tingling awareness and yearning and . . . desire that were shockingly physical.

And then he drew back his head, and his eyes, darker and more intense than usual, gazed into hers, their expression inscrutable.

Camille spoke before he could. "That is how one achieves happiness?" she asked. Goodness, she had just been *kissed*. On the lips. She could not remember ever being kissed there before, not even by her mother. If she had been, it was so long ago that memory of it had faded into the dim, distant past.

"Not necessarily happiness itself." He straightened up. "But sometimes a kiss is at least pleasurable. Sometimes it is not."

"I am sorry I have disappointed you," she said, all instinctive haughtiness. "But I have never been kissed before. I have no idea how to go about it."

"I was not saying it was not a pleasure to kiss you, Camille," he said. "But I certainly did not intend to do it, and it ought not to have happened. I brought you in here out of the rain, but it was unconsidered and unwise. Even a man who is not a gentleman understands, you see, that he ought not to bring a virtuous woman to his rooms, and that if he does for some compelling reason—like a heavy rain—then he should not take advantage of her by kissing her."

"I do not feel taken advantage of," she said. Perhaps she ought, but she did not. It had happened, and on the whole she was not sorry. It was another new experience to add to all the others of the last few months, and she knew she would relive those few seconds for days to come, perhaps longer. Was that very pathetic of her?

He stood where he was for a few moments longer, his expression inscrutable, before turning away to pour their tea. He brought their cups and saucers to the table and set down the one without milk before her. He sat down while she stirred in a spoonful of sugar.

"Your betrothed never kissed you?" he asked. "Was not that a bit odd?"

Ought she to have been kissed merely because she was engaged to be married? But that was not what her betrothal had been all about. "I did not believe so," she said.

"Would you have gone through life unkissed?" he asked her.

"Probably," she said.

"But you would surely have wanted children," he said. "He would have wished for heirs, would he not?"

"Of course," she said. "And we would both have done our duty. But do we have to speak on this topic? I find it extremely uncomfortable." She stirred her tea again.

He was not going to let the matter drop, though. "What I find strange," he said, "is that there is a class of people to whom marriage and marital relations are quite impersonal, devoid of real feeling or any sort of passion. Or happiness."

"I wanted to be perfect," she reminded him, though there was something very arid in the word in contrast to the *real feeling* and the *passion* and the *happiness* of which he had spoken. She found her hand was trembling when she tried to lift her cup.

"Camille," he said, and she could feel his eyes very

intent on her though she did not look up at him. "What happened to you must surely have been the very best thing that could possibly have happened."

She lurched to her feet, sending her chair clattering backward to the floor, and hurried into the living room, where she turned blindly right instead of left and came up against the living room window instead of the hallway, where she might have grabbed her pelisse and bonnet and hurried away from there, rain or no rain. She came to a stop, hugging her arms about herself and gazing out into pelting rain without really seeing it.

"Camille." His voice came from just behind her.

"I suppose you disliked me even before you met me," she said. "She wrote and told you all about me, did she— Anastasia? And you disliked me when we met—I saw it in your face when Miss Ford introduced us. And I know you resented my walking into the schoolroom and look-ing at your pupils' paintings. Since then you have seen how poorly I teach and control my class, and you resent the fact that I am now living in *her* room at the orphanage. I have not liked you very well either, *Mr. Cunningham,* but I have not been cruel to you. You may have a poor opinion of the life of privilege in which I grew up, but at least I was taught decent manners."

"Camille," he said, "I had no intention whatsoever of being cruel. I daresay my words were poorly chosen."

She laughed harshly—and heard, appalled, what sounded more like a sob than laughter. "Oh really?" she said. "And what words were those?"

"You were headed for a life of cold propriety and duty," he said. "You surely cannot believe now that you would have been happy with Viscount Uxbury."

"You do not understand, do you?" she said, looking downward and seeing the rain actually bouncing off the road. "I did not expect happiness. Or want it. I did not expect unhappiness either. My feelings were never in question or in turmoil until a few months ago. Now there is nothing but turmoil. And unhappiness. Misery. Self-pity, if you will—that is what you called it earlier this week. Is this better than what I had? Seriously, Joel? Is it better?"

She turned as she spoke and glared at him when she realized he was so close behind her.

"You would have married a man who publicly and maliciously insulted your name as soon as he learned something about you that offended him even though you were in no way to blame," he said. "How would he have treated you if you had already been married?"

She had been trying for several months not to ask herself that question. "I will never know, will I?" she said.

"No," he said, "but you can make an educated and doubtless accurate guess."

She hugged herself more tightly. "Yet you still think I deserve what happened to me," she said.

He frowned. "That," he said, "is not what I said. It is certainly not what I meant. Sometimes good can come out of disaster. You had schooled yourself all your life not to feel emotion. You believed that that is what perfect ladies do. Perhaps you were right. But if it is indeed so, then perfect ladies are surely to be pitied." "My mother is a perfect lady," she said. And because he did not immediately answer, the words echoed in her head. Was that all her mother had ever been? The empty shell of a perfect lady? Camille had always wanted to emulate her unshakable poise and dignity. Her mother had never been at the mercy of emotion. She was never vividly happy or wretchedly unhappy. She had been a model of perfection to her elder daughter. Only now did Camille ask herself what had lain beneath that disciplined exterior. Only now did she wonder if it had been a misery bordering upon despair, for Mama had been married to Papa for almost a quarter of a century before she knew that she had never been married at all, and Papa must have been wretchedly hard to live with as a husband.

"Do you miss her?" he asked softly.

Abby did. She had said so a few days ago. Did she, Camille, miss her too? "I am not sure I know who she is any more than I know who I am," she said, and felt dizzy at the truth of the words she spoke. Oh, how could what was happening to her be the best thing that could possibly have happened? She reached out one hand to pat his shabby jacket, just below the shoulder. "Will you hold me, please? I need someone to hold me." She would have been appalled, surely, if she had stopped to listen to her own words of weakness. They went against everything she had always been and everything she was trying to be now.

He took a hasty step forward, wrapped his arms tightly about her, and drew her hard against him. She turned her head to rest her cheek on his shoulder and leaned on him—in every way it was possible to lean. And it seemed to her that he was all solid strength and dependability and the perfect height—taller than she but not towering over her. He was warm and he smelled good, not of an expensive cologne, but of basic cleanliness and masculinity. He rested his head against hers and held her as she needed to be held. He did not try to kiss her again, and she did not feel any of the desire she had felt in the kitchen a short while ago. Instead she felt comforted from the topmost hair on her head to her toenails. And gradually she felt a nameless yearning, something with which she had no previous experience, though not the physical one she had felt earlier.

"Why did Anastasia not fall in love with you?" she asked into his shoulder.

He took his time about answering. "Foolish of her, was it not?" he said.

"Yes," she said, and thought about the man Anastasia had married. She could not imagine asking Avery to hold her. And she certainly could not imagine his doing so like this. For one thing, he was small and slight of build and would not feel so comforting. For another, there was no discernible warmth in him. Some things really were a mystery. Why *had* Anastasia fallen in love with him rather than with Joel? It had nothing to do with the fact that Avery was wealthy, for so had Anastasia been when she married him. Avery was a duke, of course, whereas Joel was a portrait painter who wore shabby coats and felt affluent because he could afford to rent the whole of the top floor of a house in Bath. But it was not that either. Camille was convinced of it. Much as she would like to think ill of Anastasia, she could not deny that it was very clear her half sister loved Avery with all her being.

She drew reluctantly free of his arms. "I am sorry," she said. "No, I mean, thank you. I was experiencing a moment of weakness. It will not happen again."

"I thought perhaps it was only orphans who sometimes long to be held," he said. "It had not occurred to me that people who grew up with both parents might sometimes feel a similar craving."

"That baby I was holding earlier—Sarah," she said. "Before I picked her up, she was crying with the hopeless conviction that no one was ever going to hold her again. She hurt my heart."

"But you held her," he said.

"What was I to do?" she asked rhetorically. "What was I to do, Joel?"

He did not answer her because of course there *was* no answer. "Our tea will be getting cold," he said.

"I think I had better go home," she said. "You were quite right earlier. This was a mistake, and I apologize for forcing you into accompanying me on my walk and then leaving you with little option but to bring me here."

"The rain is heavier than it was when we arrived," he said. But he did not try to dissuade her from leaving. "I have an umbrella, a large man-sized one. We can huddle under it together."

"I would rather go alone," she said.

He nodded and went to fetch her pelisse and bonnet, which were still a bit damp. She was half splashing along the street a few minutes later, the umbrella he had insisted she bring with her keeping her dry, though she could hear the rain drumming upon it. She had been kissed and she had been hugged this afternoon, both new experiences. She had also begged to be held and had surrendered to the comfort another human being had offered, even if only for a minute or so. Now she felt a bit like crying—yet again.

She would not do it, of course. She had cried last night, and that had been more than enough to last her for another fifteen years or so at least. But she must not put herself again in the position of needing to be held by Mr. Joel Cunningham, who believed that the disaster she had met with earlier this year was the best thing that could have happened to her. She certainly would give him no further opportunity to kiss her—or herself further opportunity to invite his kiss. For she would certainly not put all the blame, or even most of it, upon his shoulders.

She wished she did not have to encounter him again next week in the schoolroom, where she would have to behave as though nothing had happened between them. Not that much had. Oh, somehow, sometime she was going to get through all this, this . . . whatever it was and come out on the other side. But what would that other side look like?

She tilted the umbrella to shield her face from the driving rain and hurried onward.

Nine

❧

Joel kept himself busy on Sunday and Monday. He finished one of his portraits on Sunday and went up to the Royal Crescent on Monday to begin sketching and talking to Abigail Westcott. Her portrait was going to be a pleasure to work on and a bit of a challenge too, for almost as soon as she started to talk he could sense a vulnerability behind her prettiness and sweetness and a carefully guarded sadness. It would take him some time and skill to know her thoroughly.

But while he kept himself occupied, his mind was in turmoil. *Why in thunder had he kissed Camille?* She had asked him how one achieved happiness, and like a gauche boy with only one thing on his mind, he had acted as though there could be only one possible answer. The thing was, he had taken himself as much by surprise as he had her. And then, as though that were not bad enough, he had proceeded to hurt her horribly with that ill-advised remark about the great disaster of her life having been the best thing that could possibly have happened to her.

He had not even enjoyed his evening with Edwina on Sunday. Indeed, he had returned home early without even having gone to bed with her.

He spent Monday afternoon and evening sketching Camille from memory—laughing in the rain, sitting at his kitchen table looking just kissed, standing at his living room window, arms wrapped defensively about herself, gazing sightlessly down at the street. He did not want to be obsessed with painting her yet. He wanted to be able to focus upon her sister. But perhaps it was not painting her that was obsessing him.

He was actually glad on Tuesday to have something to distract him. He hired a carriage and went to call upon Mr. Cox-Phillips. The house was somewhere between a manor and a mansion in size, stately in design, and set within spacious and well-tended gardens, commanding a wide and panoramic view over the city below and the surrounding country for miles around. Joel, having instructed the coachman to wait for him, hoping he would not be too long, as the bill would be running ever higher, nevertheless took a few moments to admire the house and the garden and view before knocking upon the door.

He was kept waiting for all of ten minutes in the entry hall, being stared at by a collection of stern marble busts with sightless eyes while the elderly butler inevitably went to see if his master was at home. Joel was admitted eventually to a high-ceilinged library. Every wall was filled with books from floor to ceiling wherever there was not either a window or a door or fireplace. A large oak desk dominated one corner of the room. On the other side an imposing leather sofa faced a marble fireplace in which a fire burned despite the summer heat outdoors. Matching leather wing chairs flanked it.

In one of the chairs and almost swallowed up by it, his knees covered by a woolen blanket, a silver-knobbed cane grasped in one of his gnarled hands, sat a fierce-eyed, beetle-browed gentleman who looked to be at least a hundred years old. His eyes watched Joel cross the room until he came to a stop beside the sofa. Another man, almost equally ancient and presumably some sort of valet, stood behind the gentleman's chair and also watched Joel's approach.

"Mr. Cox-Phillips?" Joel said.

"And who else am I likely to be?" the gentleman asked, the beetle brows snapping together in a frown. "Come and stand here, young man." He thumped his cane on the carpet before his feet. "Orville, open the damned curtains. I can hardly see my hand in front of my face."

Both Joel and the valet did as they were told. Joel found himself standing in a shaft of sunlight a few feet from the old man's chair, while its occupant took his time looking him up and down and studying his face. The lengthy inspection made Joel wonder, with an inward chuckle, who was going to be painting whom.

"It was the Italian after all, then, was it?" the old man said abruptly. It did not sound like the sort of question that demanded an answer.

"I beg your pardon, sir?" Joel regarded him politely.

"The Italian," the old man said impatiently. "The painter who thought his swarthy looks and accent that charmed the ladies and foreign names all ending in vowels would hide the fact that what talent he had would not have filled a thimble."

"I am afraid," Joel said, "I am not understanding you, sir. I do not know the man to whom you refer."

"I refer, young man," the old gent told him, "to your father."

Joel stood rooted to the spot.

"I suppose," the old man said, "they did not tell you a thing."

"They?" Joel felt a little as though he were looking through a dark tunnel, which was strange when he was standing in sunlight.

"Those people at that institution where you grew up," the old man said. "It would be a wonder if they did not. Very few people can hold their tongues, even when they have been sworn to secrecy. Especially then."

Joel wished he had been invited to sit down or at least to stand in shadow. There was a dull buzzing in his ears. "Do you mean, sir," he asked, "that you know who my father was—or is? And my mother?"

"It would be strange if I did not know her," Cox-Phillips said, "when she was my own niece, my only sister's girl, and more trouble to her mother than she was worth. Dead the lot of them are now. Never hope to live to be eighty-five, young man. Everybody who has ever meant a thing to you ends up dying, and the only ones left are the sycophants and vultures who think that because they share a few drops of your blood they are therefore entitled to your money when you die. Well, they are not going to have mine, not while I am alive to have a say in the matter, which I will have this afternoon when my lawyer arrives here."

Most of what he said passed Joel by. His mind was grappling with only one thing. "My mother was your niece?" he asked. "She is dead? And my father?"

"She would never tell her mother who he was," the old man said. "Stubborn as a mule, that girl was. She would only tell who he was *not*—and that was every likely and unlikely male her mother could think of, including the Italian, though how she ever got her tongue around his name to say it aloud I do not know. My sister sent the girl away for her confinement and paid a pretty penny for her care for six months too, but the girl died anyway in child-bed. The baby—you—survived, more was the pity. It would have been better for all concerned, you included, if you had died with her. Nothing would do for it but my sister had to bring you back here despite everything I had to say to the contrary. Her daughter got her stubbornness from her. She knew she could not bring you to this house to live and explain away to all who would have been sure to ask, and strange if they had not. She ought to have left you where you were. She took you instead to that orphanage and paid for your keep there. She even paid for that art school you wanted to go to, even though I told her she had feathers for a brain. I guessed then, though, that it must have been the Italian. Where else would you have got the cork-brained notion that you could make a decent living painting? They probably tried to make you see better sense at the orphanage."

"My . . . grandmother lives here with you?" Joel asked.

"Are you not listening, young man?" Cox-Phillips said sharply. "She died seven, eight years ago. How long has it been, Orville?"

"Mrs. Cunningham passed eight years ago, sir," the valet said.

"*Passed,*" the old man said in some disgust. "She *died*. Caught a chill, developed a fever, and was dead within a week. I expected that she would leave what she had to you, but she left it to me instead." He peered up at Joel and suddenly looked even more irritated. "Why the devil are you standing there, young man, forcing me to look up at you? Sit, sit."

Joel seated himself on the edge of the sofa and drew a few deep breaths. "And my father?" he asked. "The Italian artist?"

"*Artist.*" The old man snorted contemptuously. "In his own imagination only. He disappeared in a hurry. I daresay my niece told him her glad tidings and he took fright and flight in quick succession, never to be heard from again, and good riddance. I daresay he is dead too. I cannot say I care one way or the other."

"You are my great-uncle, then," Joel said rather obviously. His ears were still buzzing—so, it seemed, was the whole of his head. His grandmother had been Mrs. Cunningham. That had presumably been his mother's name too.

"You are doing well enough for yourself, or so I hear," the old man said. "A fool and his money can always be parted when someone offers to immortalize him in paint, of course. I suppose you flatter those who pay you well enough and make them appear twenty years younger than they are and many times better-looking than they have ever been."

"I study my subjects with great care and sketch them in numerous ways before I paint them," Joel told him. "I aim for accuracy of looks and a revelation of character in the finished portrait. It is a long, painstaking process and one I do with integrity."

"Touched you on the raw, have I?" the old man asked.

"You have," Joel admitted. He was not going to deny the fact. It seemed incredible to him that after twenty-seven years he had just been told who he was *by his own great-uncle,* yet the conversation had moved on to his art as though such a sudden, earth-shattering revelation could be of no importance whatsoever to him. Why had he been summoned here?

It was as though Cox-Phillips read his thought. "You expected, I suppose, that I was bringing you here to have you paint me," he said.

"I did, sir," Joel said, though his great-uncle had not *brought* him here, had he? The hired carriage was presumably still waiting outside, the bill growing higher with every passing minute. "I certainly did not expect that I was coming here to discover my identity. My grandmother never came to see me."

"Oh, she contrived numerous times to see you," the old man said with a dismissive wave of his free hand. "I told her she was a fool every time she went. She was always upset for days afterward."

But she had never made herself known to him. She upset herself by seeing him from afar, but never considered how a child who grew up knowing nothing about his birth or his family might feel. The loneliness, the sense of abandonment, the feeling of worthlessness, the total absence of roots . . . But it was not the time to think about any of that. It was never time. Such thoughts only spiraled downward into darkness. One had to deal with reality in one's everyday life and find daily blessings for which to be thankful.

But if he could have had just one hug from his grand-mother . . . It would not have been enough, though, would it? It was better that she had never revealed herself. Perhaps.

"I do not want myself painted," his great-uncle told him, "especially if you could not be persuaded to flatter me. There would not be enough time anyway if you do all that studying and sketching before you even lay paint to canvas. In a week or two's time I expect to be dead."

The valet made an involuntary motion with one hand, a wordless protest on his lips.

"You need not worry, Orville," his master said. "You will be well enough set up for the rest of your life, as you know, and you will not have me to bother about any longer. I am dying, young man. My physician is a fool. All physicians are in my experience, but this time he has got it right. I am not quite at my last gasp, but I am not far off it, and if you think I am looking for sympathy, you are a fool too. When you are eighty-five and every last morsel of your health has deserted you and almost every-one you have ever known is dead, then it is time to be done with the whole business."

"I am sorry you are unwell, sir," Joel said.

"What difference does it make to you?" Cox-Phillips asked, and then he alarmed both Joel and his valet by cackling with laughter and then coughing until it seemed doubtful he was going to be able to draw his next breath. He did, however. "Actually, young man, it will make a great deal of difference to you."

Joel gazed at him with a frown. He was not a likable old fellow and perhaps never had been, but he was, it seemed, the only surviving link with Joel's mother and grandmother, whose name he bore. This man was his great-uncle. It was too dizzying a truth to be digested fully. Yet it seemed there was very little time in which to digest it at all. He was about to lose the only living relative he would probably ever know, yet he had found him just minutes ago.

"I have four surviving relatives," the old man said, "of whom you are one even though you are a bastard. The other three never showed the slightest interest in me until I turned eighty. A man of eighty with no wife or children or grandchildren or brothers and sisters of his own becomes a person of great interest to those clinging to the outer branches of his family tree. Such people begin to wonder what will happen to his belongings and his money when he dies, which is almost bound to be soon or sooner. And with interest comes a deep fondness for the old relative and an anxious concern for his health. It is all balderdash, of course. They can go hang for all I care."

Was one of the three relatives to whom the old man referred Viscount Uxbury?

"I am going to leave everything to you, young man," Cox-Phillips said. "It will be written into my new will this afternoon, and I shall have enough people to attest to the soundness of my mind and the absence of coercion that even the cleverest solicitor will find it impossible to overturn my final wishes."

Joel was on his feet then without any consciousness of

having stood up. "Oh no, sir," he said. "That is preposterous. I do not even know you. You do not know me. I have no claim upon you and have no wish for any. You have shown no interest in me for twenty-seven years. Why should you show some now?"

The old man clasped both hands over the head of his stick and lowered his chin onto them. "By God, Orville," he said, "I think he means it. What do you think?"

"I believe he does, sir," the valet agreed.

"Of course I mean it," Joel said. "I have no wish whatsoever, sir, to cut out your legitimate relatives from a share in whatever you have to leave them. If you intend to ignore them out of spite, I will not have you use me as your instrument. I want no part of your fortune."

"You think it *is* a fortune?" Cox-Phillips asked.

"I neither know nor care," Joel assured him. "What I do know is that I have had no part of you or of my grandmother all the years of my life and that I want no part of your possessions now. Do you believe that would be compensation enough? Do you believe that I will remember you more kindly if you buy my gratitude and affection? I detect no sort of fond sentiment in you at coming face-to-face with me at last, only a confirmation of what you have suspected all these years, that my father was—or is—an Italian painter whom you despised. You would not have brought me here at all today, I now realize, if you had not conceived this devilish idea of using me to play a trick on your relatives. I will have no part of it. Good day to you, sir."

He turned and strode from the room. With every step across the carpet he expected to be called back, but he was not. He found his way downstairs and across the hall past the blindly staring busts and out onto the terrace, where the hired carriage awaited him.

"Back to Bath," he said curtly as he pulled open the door and seated himself inside.

Fury gave place to a racing mental confusion that could not be brought into any semblance of order as the carriage conveyed him back down to the city. His mother had died giving birth to him in secret. Good God, he did not even know her first name or anything about her except that she had conceived him outside wedlock and had stubbornly and steadfastly refused to name his father. His grandmother had taken him to the orphanage and made sure he had everything he needed, even an art education after he was fifteen, but had withheld herself. She had looked at him from afar but had given him no opportunity to look upon her and know that there was someone in this world to whom he belonged. His father was, presumably, an artist of Italian nationality who had been in Bath painting. It seemed to have been his own looks, Joel thought, that had convinced Cox-Phillips—*his great-uncle*—that it was so. He did not know the man's name, however, or whether he was alive or dead.

He paid off the carriage outside his rooms but did not go inside. There would not be enough space in there or enough air. He struck off on foot along the street with no particular destination in mind.

Caroline Williams had been attending school for a year and had somehow got away with pretending she could read. She liked to choose books Camille had read to the class and recite them from memory, but sometimes her memory was defective. Somehow or other the teaching methods that had worked with other children had not worked for her. Camille had pondered the problem until something that might help had suggested itself on Sunday when she was in the playroom holding Sarah again. Caroline had been reading a story to her doll—not the one written in the book, however, but one she was making up with considerable imagination and coherence as she went.

Now Camille was sitting at one of the small pupils' desks. The rest of the children had been dismissed for the day, but Caroline had been invited to stay and tell one of her own stories to her teacher, who had written it down word for word in large, bold print, leaving a blank space in the center of each of the four pages. Caroline, intrigued by the fact that it was her very own story, was reading it back to Camille, her finger identifying each word. And it seemed that she really was reading.

"You wrote *went* here, miss," she said, looking up, "when really she *ran*."

"My mistake," Camille told her, though it had been a deliberate one. And Caroline had passed the test, as she did again with the other three deliberate errors.

"Excellent, Caroline," Camille told her. "Now you can read your own story as well as other people's when you want to. Can you guess what the spaces are for?"

The child shook her head.

"The most interesting books have pictures, do they not?" Camille said. "You can choose your favorite parts of your story and draw your own pictures."

The little girl's eyes lit up.

But the door opened at that moment, and Camille

turned her head in some annoyance to see which child had come back to interrupt them and for what purpose. It was not a child, however. It was Joel Cunningham, who looked into the room, stepped inside when he saw she was there, and then came to an abrupt halt when he saw she was not alone.

"I beg your pardon," he said. "Carry on."

"You will miss your tea if I keep you here any longer," she said to Caroline as she got to her feet. "Do you wish to take your story with you to read and illustrate? Or shall we keep it safe on a shelf here until tomorrow?"

Caroline wanted to take it to read to her doll. And she would draw the pictures while her doll watched. She gave Joel a wide, bright smile as he opened the door to let her out, her story clutched to her chest.

"I am trying to coax her to read," Camille explained when he closed the door again. "She has been having some difficulty, and I have been trying out an idea."

"It looks as if you may have had some success," he said. "She seemed very eager to take that story with her. In my day we would have done anything on earth to avoid having to take schoolwork beyond this room."

Camille was feeling horribly self-conscious. She had not seen him since Saturday, when she had gone dashing along rainy streets hand in hand with him, laughing for no reason except that she was enjoying herself—and ending up alone in his rooms with him. And if that was not shocking enough, she had allowed him to kiss her and—perhaps worse—she had asked him to hold her. She had been plagued by the memories ever since and had dreaded coming face-to-face with him again.

"What are you doing here?" she asked, clasping her

hands tightly at her waist and straightening her shoulders. She could hear the severity in her voice.

"I came to see if you were still in the schoolroom," he told her, running his fingers through his hair, a futile gesture since it was so short. There was something intense, almost wild, about his eyes, she noticed, and the way he was holding himself, as though there were a whole ball of energy coiled up inside him ready to burst loose.

"What is it?" she asked.

"I went to call on Cox-Phillips this morning," he said. "He had nothing by way of work to offer me. He is eighty-five and at death's door."

"That is rather harsh." Camille frowned.

"On the authority of his physician," he said. "He expects to be dead within a week or two. He is setting his house in order, so to speak. His lawyer was going to see him this afternoon about his will."

"I am sorry it was a wasted journey," she said. "But why did he invite you up there if he did not wish to hire your services as a painter? Why did he not stop you from going if he suddenly found himself too ill to see you?"

"Oh, he saw me right enough," he told her. "He even had his valet pull back the curtains so that he could have enough light for a closer look." He laughed suddenly and Camille raised her eyebrows. "He was going to change his will this afternoon to cut out the three relatives who are expecting to inherit. I am guessing Viscount Uxbury is one of their number."

"Oh," she said. "He will not like that. But what does this have to do with you?"

"Not here." He turned sharply away. "Come out with me."

Where? She almost asked the question aloud. But it was obvious he was deeply disturbed about something and had turned to her of all people. She hesitated for only the merest moment.

"Wait here," she said, "while I fetch my bonnet."

Ten

Joel grasped Camille's hand without conscious thought when they left the building and strode along the street with her. He had only one purpose in mind—to go home. It was only as they crossed the bridge that he wondered at last why he had turned to Camille Westcott of all people. Marvin Silver or Edgar Stephens would surely be home soon, and they were good friends as well as neighbors. Edwina was probably at her house. She was both friend and lover. And failing any of those three, why not Miss Ford?

But it was for the end of the school day and Camille he had waited as he paced the streets of Bath for what must have been hours. She would listen to him. She would understand. She knew what it was like to have one's life turned upside down. And now he was taking her home with him, even after what had happened there the last time, was he? His pace slackened.

"I ought not to take you to my rooms," he said. "Would you prefer that we keep walking?"

"No." She was frowning. "Something has upset you. I will go home with you."

"Thank you," he said.

A few minutes later he was leaning against the closed door of his rooms while Camille hung up her bonnet and shawl. It seemed days rather than hours since he had left here this morning. She went ahead of him into the living room and turned to look at him, waiting for him to speak first.

He slumped onto one of the chairs without considering how ill-mannered he was being, set his elbows on his knees, and held his head in both hands.

"Cox-Phillips is my great-uncle," he said. "It was his sister, my grandmother, who took me to the orphanage after her daughter, my mother, died giving birth to me. She was unmarried, of course—her name was Cunningham. My grandmother was extremely good to me. She paid handsomely for my keep until I was fifteen, and then, when she heard of my longing to go to art school, she paid my fees there. She loved me dearly too. She watched me from afar a number of times down the years and was so deeply affected each time that she suffered low spirits for days afterward."

"Joel—" she said, but he could not stop now that he had started.

"She could not let me see her, of course," he said. "She could not call at the orphanage and reveal herself to me. I might have climbed up onto the rooftop and yelled out the information for all of Bath to hear. Or someone might have seen her come and go and asked awkward questions.

She could love me from afar and lavish money on me to show how much she cared, but she could not risk contamination by any personal contact. Something might have rubbed off on her and proved fatal to her health or her reputation. I was, after all, the bastard child of a fallen woman who just happened to be her daughter and apparently of an Italian artist of questionable talent who lived in Bath for long enough to turn the daughter's head and get her with child before fleeing, lest he be forced into doing the honorable thing and marrying her and making me respectable."

"Joel—" she said.

"Do you know what I was doing today between the time the carriage brought me back and the time I came to the schoolroom?" he asked, looking up at her. He did not wait for her to hazard a guess. "I wandered the streets, mentally squirming and clawing at myself as though to be rid of an itch. I felt—I *feel* as though I must be covered with lice and fleas and bed bugs and other vermin. Or perhaps the contaminating dirt is all inside me and I can never be rid of it. That must be it, I think, for I will never be anything but a bastard to be shunned by all respectable folk, will I?"

Good God, where was all this coming from?

"Joel," she said in her sergeant's voice, "stop it. Right this minute."

He looked blankly up at her and realized suddenly that he was sitting while she was still standing in the middle of the room. He leapt to his feet. "Yes, ma'am," he said, and made her a mock salute. "I feel as though I am teetering on the edge of a vast universe and am about to tumble off into the endless blackness of empty space. And how is *that* for hyperbole, madam schoolmistress? I ought not to have brought you here. I ought not to have kept you standing while I have been sitting. You will think I am no gentleman and how very right you will be. And I ought not to be spouting all this pathetic nonsense into your ear. We scarcely know each other, after all. I assure you I am not usually this—"

"Joel," she said. "Stop."

And this time he did stop while she frowned at him and then took a few steps toward him. If he had not been fearing that at any moment he might faint, or fall off the edge of the universe, and if his teeth had not been chattering, he might have guessed her intent. But her hands were against his chest and then on his shoulders and then her arms were about his neck before he could do so, and by then it was too late not to take advantage of the comfort she offered. His arms went about her like iron bands and pressed her to him as though only by holding her could he keep himself upright and in one piece. He could feel the heat and the blessed life of her pressed to him from shoulders to knees. Her head was on his shoulder, her face turned in against his neck, her breath warm against his skin. He buried his face in her hair and felt almost safe.

Will you hold me, please? I need someone to hold me, she had said to him here on almost this very spot a few days ago. Now it was he making the same wordless plea.

Why exactly was he feeling so upset? He had always known that someone had handed him over to the orphanage, that whoever it was had chosen not to keep him, that in all probability that meant he was illegitimate, the unwanted product of an illicit union, something shameful that must be hidden away and denied for the rest of a lifetime. Yes, *something*—almost as though he were inanimate and therefore without real identity or feelings. A bastard. He had always known, but he had never given it a great deal of thought. It was just the way things were and would always be. There was no point in brooding about it. Having learned now, though, the name and identity of the woman who had abandoned him and her relationship to him—she had been his *grandmother*—and knowing how she had gazed on him in secret and been upset for days afterward without ever being upset enough to come and hug him, everything in him had erupted in pain. For now it was all *real*. And that man, his greatuncle, had insulted what little dignity he had, wanting to use him in order to wreak vengeance upon legitimate relatives who he believed had neglected him.

Joel knew all about neglect. He did not necessarily approve of vengeance, however, especially when he had been appointed as the avenging agent. Just like an inanimate *thing* again.

She used a sweet-smelling soap, something subtly but not overpoweringly floral. He could smell it in her hair. She was not slender, as her sister was and as Edwina was—and as Anna was. But her body was beautifully proportioned and voluptuously endowed. She was warm and nurturing and very feminine—despite the fact that on first acquaintance she had made him think of warrior Amazons, and despite the fact that she had just spoken to him in a voice of which an army sergeant might be proud.

They could not stand clasped thus together forever, he realized after a while, more was the pity. He sighed and moved his head as she raised her own, and they gazed at each other without speaking. She kept her femininity very well hidden most of the time, but her defenses were down at the moment. She was warm and yielding in his arms, and her eyes were smoky beneath slightly drooped eyelids.

He kissed her, openmouthed and needy, and tightened his hold on her again. He pressed his tongue to her closed lips and they parted to allow him to stroke the warm, moist flesh behind them. She shivered and opened her mouth and his tongue plunged into the heat within. He felt himself harden into the beginnings of arousal as his hands moved over her with a need that was somehow turning sexual. But . . . she was offering comfort because he was bewildered and suffering. How could be take advantage of that generosity of spirit? He could not, of course. Reluctantly he loosened his hold on her and took a step back.

"I am so sorry," he said. "That was inappropriate. Forgive me, please. And I have not even invited you to sit down."

"I am sorry too," she said as she moved away from him to sit on the sofa. "I am sorry it has been so upsetting to you to have learned that your grandmother supported you but did not openly acknowledge you. It is the way the world works, though. It would have been stranger if she *had* made herself known to you. She had feelings for you despite everything, however, and she did do her best for you."

"Much good her tender sensibilities did me," he said. "And her best."

"Well, they did." She had herself firmly in hand again

and looked like the stern, proper lady with whom he was more familiar. She sat with rigidly correct posture and a frown between her brows—she frowned rather often. "The orphanage is a good one. So, I assume, was the art school. You are a talented artist, but would you be doing as well as you are now if you had not gone there? She paid your fees. Could you have gone otherwise? Or would you have spent your life chopping meat at a butcher's shop while your talent withered away undeveloped and unused? She could not show her affection openly. It is just not done in polite society for bastards to be openly acknowledged. And that is exactly what you are, Joel. Just as it is exactly what I am. Neither of us is to blame. It just *is*. Your grandmother did what she could regardless to see that you had all the necessities of life in a good home as you grew up and to help make your dream come true when you were old enough to leave."

"All the necessities." He stood with his hands at his back, looking down at her. He did not want to hear excuses for his grandmother. He wanted to feel angry and aggrieved, and he wanted someone to feel aggrieved for him. "Everything except love."

"So, would you rather not know what you learned today?" she asked him, her expression stern. "Would you prefer to have gone through life not even sure that your name was rightfully your own? Do you wish you had not gone to that house today?"

He thought about it. "I suppose not," he said grudgingly. "But what have I learned, Camille, beyond the very barest facts? My mother would never say who my father was. Cox-Phillips concluded he was the Italian painter solely on the evidence of my looks and the fact that I paint. I do not know anything about my mother and next to nothing about my grandmother. My great-uncle is the curmudgeon you said he used to be. I have no wish to know anything about his other three relatives, who are presumably mine too. And I do not imagine they would be delighted to know anything about their long-lost relative, an orphanage bastard, either."

"Mr. Cox-Phillips invited you to call on him, then, just in order to tell you the truth about yourself before he dies?" she asked him.

He stared at her. Had he not told her? No, he supposed he had not. "He wanted to write me into his will this afternoon," he said. "He wanted to leave me everything. Just to spite those other three. I said no, absolutely not. I was not going to have him use me in such a way."

She stared back at him.

"I suppose I am glad to have learned something of my identity at last," he said. "But my mother and grandmother are dead, and if my father is still living I have no way of tracing him. As for my mother's uncle, he has apparently known for twenty-seven years where I am and has shown no interest in making himself known to me. I have done very well without him and can continue to do so for a week or two longer until he dies."

"Oh, Joel." She sighed and relaxed into a woman again. She leaned back on the sofa. "You are hurting very badly. And you are trying to harden yourself against the pain and even deny it is there. You will feel a great deal better if you admit it."

"And this is a pearl of wisdom from someone who knows?" he said.

Color flooded her cheeks and he was immediately

contrite. Was he now going to lash out at the very person
he had sought out for comfort? She had given it with
unstinting generosity. "Yes, that is exactly right," she said.
"It feels a bit shameful to be suffering, does it not? As
though one must have done something to deserve it. Or
as if one were admitting to some weakness of character
at being unable to shake off the hurt. But hiding it can
turn one to marble with nothing but hollowness inside—
and an unacknowledged pain. Do you believe Mr. Cox-
Phillips was exaggerating when he told you he had only
a week or two left to live?"

"No," he said. "It was clearly what his physician had
told him and what he believed. And he looks far from
well. He is eighty-five years old and looks a hundred. He
is tired of living. He has outlasted everyone who has ever
meant anything to him and probably everything too."

"Did he try to persuade you not to leave?" she asked.
"Did he ask you to visit again?"

"No to both questions," he said. "He invited me out
there purely on a rather malicious whim, Camille. I
refused to play a part in his game when he had probably
expected that I would leap at the chance of inheriting
whatever fortune he has. That was the end of the matter.
There was no grand sentiment on either side when he told
me who I was. He did not clasp me to his bosom as his
long-lost grand-nephew. But then, I was never lost, was
I? Only unclaimed, unwanted baggage. He made not the
smallest pretense of feeling for me any of the sentiment
he claimed his sister felt. Yes, it was a bit upsetting to
learn the truth about myself so abruptly and unexpectedly
and dispassionately. I cannot deny it. My head and every

emotion were in a whirl after I had left him. I know I wandered the streets here for hours, though I would not be able to tell you exactly where I went. When I burst in upon you, I behaved like a madman and dragged you here when it was probably the last thing you wanted to do after a day of teaching. But you are wrong when you say I am still hurting. I am not, and I have you to thank for that. You have been kindness itself. I will not keep you any longer, though. I will walk you back home."

"Joel, you are speaking absolute nonsense." The grim schoolmistress had returned to confront him from the sofa. "You are going to have to go back. You must realize that."

"Back?" he said. "Up there? To Cox-Phillips's, do you mean? Absolutely not. For what purpose? I have nothing more to say to him and I am of no further use as far as he is concerned. He will have to find someone else to whom to leave his money if he really hates his relatives so much. That is his concern, not mine. Let me walk you home." Edgar and Marvin would be back from work soon and it might be more difficult then to smuggle her out unseen.

She did not move, and now she was the Amazon as well as the schoolmistress. She really was a disconcerting female. "He is your last surviving link with your mother," she said. "While he is alive he can tell you more, but it does not sound as if he will be alive for long. Did he tell you her name?"

He looked at her with open hostility before turning away to stare out through the window. She was not going to let this thing go, was she? He might have known it. "Cunningham," he said.

He heard her cluck her tongue. "Her *first* name," she said.

"What does it matter?" he asked her. "A boy does not call his mother by her first name anyway."

"But he knows it," she said. "And you have never called her anything else either, have you? There was never anyone to call Mama."

No. He was surprised by the shaft of pain that knifed through him. There never had been. Perhaps that was one of the worst things about growing up an orphan. There was no Mama—or Papa either. And by God, there was going to be no self-pity. No more of it, anyway. Already, after a few hours of wallowing in it, he was sick of it.

"Was she dark haired and dark eyed like you?" she asked. "Or was she blond and blue eyed, perhaps? Or—"

"If she had had dark coloring," he said, "Cox-Phillips would not have been so sure that it was the Italian who fathered me."

"What was *his* name?" she asked.

"Something long and unpronounceable that ended in vowels," he said. "He does not remember it. He probably never tried to learn it. To a man like Cox-Phillips all foreigners are inferior beings to be despised."

"Did your mother see you before she died?" she asked. "Was she the one who named you Joel? Why that particular name?"

He turned on her, angry now, even though he owed her everything but anger. "Do you imagine," he asked her, "that that crusty old man in his mansion up on the hill would know the answers to such questions? Do you imagine he cares? Do you imagine I care?"

"Yes to the last question," she said. "I think you do care or that you will care—perhaps when it is too late to get any answers at all. Just a couple of weeks ago I believe I would have said that nothing could be worse than what had happened to me—and to Abigail and Harry. But something could, I realize now. If our mother had known early on that she was not legally married, she might have left my father, and it is altogether possible we might have ended up at an orphanage, perhaps even three separate ones, and been told nothing about ourselves except our names. Perhaps not even those. Our father was not a good man. I understand now that he was incapable of loving me no matter how hard I tried. He loved only himself. But at least I know who he was. I knew and I know my mother and my brother and sister. I know who I am. I do not yet know who I will become because my circumstances have changed so drastically, but I know where I came from, and I think I realize now fully for the first time how important that is." She paused. "I am sorry your suffering has made this clear to me."

He gazed at her for a few moments, realizing that she had just come to a sort of epiphany of her own. She was all haughty aristocrat and stern schoolmistress and stubborn Amazon and . . . Camille. He went striding off without a word to his studio, where he grabbed a sketchbook and a piece of charcoal and went back into the living room to sit on the chair from which he had risen a few minutes ago. Without looking at her he drew the swift, rough outline of a woman with slightly untidy hair and a look of passionate intensity on her face. It was what he thought of as the Camille part of her.

"Is this always your answer to something you do not wish to talk about?" she asked. "Is this your escape from reality?"

He kept on sketching for a while. "Perhaps," he said, "it is my way of marshaling my thoughts. Perhaps it is my escape *into* reality. Or perhaps it is my way of filling in time until you allow me to walk you home."

"You think you want to be rid of me," she said, seemingly uncowed by the petty insult. "But it is your own troubling thoughts of which you want to be rid. You know you will forever regret it if you do not go back."

"Do you realize how incredibly fascinating you are, Camille?" he asked. And how irritating?

"Nonsense," she said. "I have never cultivated either beauty or charm, much less womanly wiles. I have cultivated only the will to do what I believe to be right in all circumstances."

He glanced up at her and smiled. She was looking prunish. "You will realize your own fascination," he said, "after I have painted you."

"Then your painting will be worthless," she told him. "I thought you refused to flatter your subjects. Why would you make an exception of me?"

He continued looking at her for a few moments so that he would get her eyebrows right. They would look rather too heavy on most women, but they were actually just right with her dark hair and strong features. He had not noticed that before. Strangely, he was not always an observant person when he looked merely with his eyes. He often did not see people clearly unless and until he started to sketch and paint them and draw upon what his intuition had sensed about them.

"You of all people will not be painted with flattery," he assured her before looking back down at his sketch. "You will be painted as who you are when all the poses and defenses and masks have been stripped away."

But would he ever know her completely? Or understand her fully? One never did, did one? One never knew even oneself to the deepest depths. How could one be expected to know another human being, then? It was an uncomfortable realization when he prided himself upon understanding the subjects of his portraits.

"I am horribly alarmed," she told him curtly without looking alarmed at all. "You are very adroit at changing a subject."

"Was there one to change?" he asked, smiling at her again.

"You have to go back," she said. "You have to talk to Mr. Cox-Phillips and find out all you can about yourself. You will forever regret it if you do not. It is true that your grandmother treated you badly, Joel, but it is equally true that she treated you very well. It is all a matter of perspective. You must find out more so that you can understand better. You must find out all you can about your mother. Had she lived, everything might have been different. Perhaps she is someone you need to love even though you will never know her in person. At least you can find out all you can."

"Sentimental drivel," he said. "He would conclude I had changed my mind about being in his will and had come crawling back there to ingratiate myself with him. He would assume avarice had caught up with me."

"Then tell him he is wrong," she said. "You must go. I shall go with you."

Joel set aside his sketch pad—he could not get her stubborn chin right anyway without making her look like a caricature—and leaned back in the chair. He crossed his arms over his chest and rested one booted ankle across the other knee. He ought to have gone to Edwina. Or to Miss Ford. Or come back here to brood alone. His first impression of Miss Camille Westcott had been the right one. She was overbearing and obnoxious.

"To hold my hand, I suppose," he said. "To prod me forward with a sharp finger at my back. To prompt me with the questions I need to ask. To scold the old man if he makes me cry."

Her lips virtually disappeared. She sat up straight and was doing the perfect-posture thing again. Her spine presumably did not need the support of the back of the sofa. It was made of steel.

"I thought to offer moral support," she said. "You clearly do not need it. Just as I do not need your escort back to the orphanage, Mr. Cunningham. I daresay I will not be accosted more than four or five times as I walk alone, and doubtless my screams will bring gentlemen running to my rescue. You will do as you please with regards to Mr. Cox-Phillips. I have learned that you are stubborn to a fault. It does not matter to me the snap of my fingers what you do."

She got to her feet and Joel jumped to his. He was between her and the hallway, so she stood where she was, holding his gaze, her jaw like granite. The Amazon in a belligerent mood. If she had had a spear in her hand . . .

"I made some soup yesterday," he said. "I ate some last night and did not poison myself. Let me warm it up.

I bought some bread at the bakery early this morning too. Stay and eat with me."

"To hold your hand?" she asked.

"I need one hand to hold the bowl and the other to spoon up the soup," he told her. "I apologize for what I said. You have been remarkably kind in coming here and listening to my ravings. Alas, I have repaid your goodness with bad temper. Stay? Please?"

It had been a purely impulsive invitation. Whatever would they talk about if she agreed? And what were the chances that Edgar or Marvin would knock on his door for some reason or other? Or that one or both of them would see or hear her leave later? But he did not want to be alone yet.

What if the soup had thickened to such a degree that it would need to be chiseled with a sharp-edged knife? He was not the world's best cook.

"What kind of soup?" she asked.

Eleven

❧

A hired carriage was awaiting Camille when school was dismissed for the day on Thursday. Joel jumped out when she appeared and handed her inside. She raised her eyebrows at the chipped, faded exterior, the shabby, slightly ripped seats inside, and the somewhat stale smell, which even the open windows could not quite dispel. But she did not say anything. At least it appeared reasonably clean. She had not looked too closely at the horses.

"You did not change your mind, then?" she asked as he seated himself beside her.

"Oh, I did," he said. "An hour ago. And two hours before that, and half an hour before that, and so on back to the night before last. This time I changed my mind in favor of going."

He both looked and sounded cheerful, but she was not deceived. He had agreed before she left his rooms two days ago that he would go back to Mr. Cox-Phillips's house and had told her with grudging good grace that she might accompany him if she wished. He had suggested that they go today after school.

"And did you write to inform him you were coming?" she asked as the carriage jerked into motion and gave Camille a foretaste of how ineffective the springs were going to be.

"No," he said. "Why should I give him advance warning? And it is not as though he is going anywhere, is it? Except to his grave."

She turned her head to glance reproachfully at him. He was looking suddenly grim and a bit pale, his head half turned toward the window next to him. She drew breath to speak, but he looked as if he wished to be left alone with his thoughts, and she had no wish to turn into a scold.

Something had happened to her on Tuesday. She would not go so far as to say she had fallen in love. She did not believe in such a thing. But she had gone to his rooms of her own free will, and she had listened to him and moved into his arms to comfort him. And she had kissed him. Yes, she had. It had been an active thing on her part, not just something she had allowed. And she had felt his man's hard body and his arms and his lips and mouth and tongue, and she had been . . . Yes, she had. There was no point in denying it. She had been disappointed when he had stopped abruptly and apologized. She would have liked to explore the experience a little more deeply.

She was not in love, but she had felt more like a woman since Tuesday. Which begged the question—what had she felt like before? He was extremely good-looking, she had decided, and powerfully attractive, whatever that meant, and she had responded to him as a woman. She still did, though she was puzzled too. She had neither the language nor the experience to explain to herself just what she meant. Perhaps it was merely that she cared.

It had been the middle of the evening and growing dusk by the time she returned home, and he had insisted upon accompanying her. The soup, thick with vegetables and a little beef, had been very good, the bread crisp and fresh. After eating they had taken their tea back into the living room, where they had talked and talked until the fading light beyond the window had caught their attention. He had been sketching her much of the time, though he had not shown her anything.

Afterward she had not even remembered everything they had talked about. She did know they had spoken of their childhoods, of books they had both read, of Sarah, with whom Camille spent some time each day. He had told her of his love for landscape painting, even though he believed his real talent was for painting portraits, and she had watched his face as he spoke of gazing at a scene, not sketching it as he would with a human subject, but somehow becoming a part of it until he felt it from the inside and could finally paint it. Painting for him, she had realized then, was neither a hobby nor just a way of earning a living. It was a passion and a compulsion. In a certain sense it was who he was. She envied him. She had never been passionate about anything in her life. She had never allowed herself to be. She had deliberately shunned any excess of feeling as ungenteel. It was almost as though she had feared passion and where it might lead her.

He did not like life to be too easy, Camille concluded. He liked the challenge of living it and pushing its boundaries instead of just existing and surviving. Perhaps that was one reason why he had not shown the smallest interest in the fortune he might have inherited from his great-uncle. Money would make his life a great deal easier—money always did—but he was not interested. How many people would voluntarily refuse a fortune, and have absolutely no hesitation about doing it?

Her own question arrested her. *She* would and had indeed done so. Anna had offered a quarter of all their father had left her, a vast fortune, and Camille had refused.

The carriage left Bath and struggled up the hill beyond. She turned her head toward Joel. "I had a letter this morning," she told him. "Well, two actually, but Abby writes every day."

"Yes, she told me that just this morning. I was there, working on her portrait," he said, turning away from the window to look back at her. "It is astonishing. Whatever does she find to write about? Do you reply?"

"Ladies are brought up to write letters," she told him. "She tells me everything about her day. Today her letter was full of her session with you yesterday, among other things. And yes, I answer. Of course I do. She is my sister. I write every evening and tell her about my day."

"And tomorrow," he said, "your letter will be full of this journey with me?"

"Yes," she said, "and of the progress of the purple rope

and of the noticeable improvement in Caroline's reading skills and of the ten minutes I was able to spend with Sarah before luncheon, counting her toes and kissing each of them in turn and drawing two whole smiles from her."

He gazed at her to the point of discomfort. Not that the carriage ride was comfortable even without that gaze. She would not be surprised if it jarred all her teeth loose.

"You had *two* letters today?" he finally asked.

"The other one was from my mother," she told him. "She wrote directly to me at the school. She has only ever written to both Abby and me in the past, but Abby had told her I was living at the orphanage. She is concerned about me. But she did not write to scold me or tell me how foolish I have been or how unkind to Abby and Grandmama. She understands and she honors my decision."

Camille had been surprised about that and more than a little touched. She had not expected it—or the letter. She had not even wanted a letter of her very own from her mother—until she had seen it. And ever since reading it she had felt, oh, a jumble of emotions. Resentment was still one of them. Mama had gone away to the comfort of Uncle Michael, but also away from her own daughters.

"Why did she not stay here with you and her mother?" Joel asked.

"It was at least partly for our sakes," she told him. "She thought life here would be intolerable for us, or more so than it was going to be anyway, if everywhere we went we had to be introduced as the daughters of *Miss* Viola Kingsley."

"Everywhere you went," he said. "But you did not go

anywhere, did you? You were a recluse until you went to the orphanage to teach."

"How do you know that?" she asked, frowning at him.

"I never saw you," he said. "I saw your sister a few times and was introduced to her at Mrs. Dance's soiree. The first time I saw you was in the schoolroom when Miss Ford brought you there. *Would* your mother's staying have made life more difficult for you?"

"I do not know." She shrugged. "But Abby has missed her."

"And you?" he asked.

"I do not know," she said again, and it was her turn to look out through the window on her side of the carriage in order to discourage further conversation—though she was the one who had brought up the subject. It was actually a good thing she had read her mother's letter early this morning before school. She had been unable to weep over it—she had had a class of children to face. *Would* it have made a difference if Mama had stayed? Abby was only eighteen, little more than a child. And as for Camille herself . . . Well, sometimes she felt as though she had been cast into outer darkness. She had felt when she came to Bath that there could not possibly be anything more to lose. But there was. Her mother had gone away.

The carriage was making a sharp turn between two stone gateposts and then proceeding along a winding driveway until a modestly sized mansion appeared to the right, a panoramic view downward opened up to the left, and a carefully laid-out, well-tended garden stretched out on either side of them.

"This is it," Joel said unnecessarily.

He helped Camille alight, instructed the coachman to

wait, and approached the steps to rap the knocker against the front door. He was looking grim again, and she knew he would rather be anywhere else on earth. She could not feel sorry, though, that she had goaded him into coming. She really believed he would be forever sorry if he did not. Of course, Mr. Cox-Phillips might refuse to see him or to answer any questions if he did admit them. But at least Joel would be able to console himself in the future with the knowledge that he had done everything he could.

An elderly butler admitted them to a hall cluttered with marble busts surely designed to make any chance visitor uncomfortable enough to flee. They all had empty eye sockets but stared anyway. Camille stared right back after the butler had gone off to see if his master was receiving. He had looked as though he might be on the verge of refusing even to check until his eyes had alit upon Camille, and without conscious thought she had reverted to a familiar role and had become Lady Camille Westcott without uttering a word. He had inclined his head deferentially and gone on his way.

"He may have been instructed to toss me out if I should ever have the effrontery to return," Joel said with a grin that did not quite compensate for the tense look on his face.

"Then it is a good thing I came too," she said. "I have my uses. I do not for one moment believe these marble busts are either marble or authentic. If they came from Italy or Greece or anywhere other than some inferior workshop in England, I would be very surprised."

"We concur in that," he agreed.

The butler returned and invited them to follow him.

They were admitted to a library, one that lived up to its name. As far as she could see from a single glance, there was not a space on the walls that was not taken up with bookshelves, and there was surely not a space left on those shelves for even one more book. The room was in semidarkness, heavy curtains having been drawn across the windows, perhaps to preserve the books or perhaps to protect the old man's eyes from bright sunlight.

There were three people already in the room, apart from the butler, who withdrew after admitting them and closed the door behind him. There was what appeared to be a very old, wizened man in the chair by the fireplace—the fire was lit even though the air was stifling. He even had a heavy blanket covering him from the waist down and a tasseled nightcap on his head. Behind his chair stood a soberly clad individual, every line of whose body told Camille that he could be nothing else but a valet.

The third occupant of the room was silhouetted against the fireplace so that until he moved he appeared only as a tall, broad-shouldered, well-formed man dressed in the very height of London fashion. When he did move, in order to take a few steps away from the fire and toward the door, he revealed himself also to be an extremely handsome man—with a haughty, condescending expression on his face.

"That is quite far enough, fellow," he said, looking Joel over from head to toe with insolent contempt and the aid of a quizzing glass. "I can see the butler ought to have known better than to come asking if he might admit you when my cousin is not well enough to make an informed decision. I shall be having a word with the servants about allowing in every riffraff petitioner who thinks to take

advantage of Mr. Cox-Phillips's advanced age and frail
health. Fortunately for him, such persons will have to get
past me in the future now that I am here to protect him.
You may take yourself off with the . . . lady." He turned
dismissive eyes upon Camille, who had remained behind
Joel, half hidden in shadow.

She felt close to fainting, though not from the heat of
the room. The training of years kept her from doing anything so missish or from otherwise humiliating herself.
"How do you do, Lord Uxbury?" she said, stepping out
of the shadows and looking him steadily in the eye.

He dropped his quizzing glass on its ribbon, and his
eyes fairly started from his head. It was a brief setback.
He recovered within moments, and a sneer replaced his
look of shock. "Well, upon my word, if it is not *Miss*
Westcott," he said, emphasizing her title, or, rather, her
lack thereof, and subjecting her to a sweeping head-to-toe
perusal.

She had last seen him at Westcott House in London
on the afternoon of the day she learned the truth about
her father and his bigamous marriage to her mother. She
had received him and told him what she had just learned,
expecting that he would be full of concern for her plight
and determination to bring forward their wedding. That
had been shortsighted of her, of course, for he was as
much a stickler for social correctness as she and it would
have been out of the question for him to marry a bastard.
He had taken a hasty leave and written to her almost
immediately suggesting that she send a notice to the
morning papers, breaking off their betrothal.

Now he looked both familiar and . . . alien. As though

he were someone from another long-ago lifetime, which, in a sense, he was. She had never before seen that look of contempt on his face directed at her. She had never witnessed him being spiteful. But she recalled that he had openly insulted her in her absence at Avery's ball and again in Hyde Park during the duel. And she recalled with intense satisfaction that Avery, who must be a full head shorter than he and surely at least a couple of stone lighter, had knocked him down and out with his bare feet.

"I beg your pardon . . . Viscount Uxbury, is it?" Joel said. "But my business is with Mr. Cox-Phillips. When I spoke with him a couple of days ago, he seemed perfectly capable of speaking for himself and of personally asking me to leave if he so desires."

Camille looked at him in some surprise. He was not quite as tall as the viscount, and he did not have such a splendid physique or as obviously handsome a face. Indeed, he looked even more shabby than usual in contrast to the splendor of Lord Uxbury's Bond Street tailoring. But he looked suddenly very solid and immovable. And he looked in no way cowed at having been called a fellow and a riffraff petitioner. He spoke with quiet, firm courtesy.

"If this is not the first time you have come to pester my cousin," the viscount said, "then it is a very good thing I came when I did. And Miss Westcott is not fit company for anyone in this house or any other respectable dwelling."

"You have come back, then, have you?" the elderly gentleman said from beside the fire. "You have changed your mind, have you?"

"I have not, sir," Joel assured him. "I have come on a different matter."

"Do not distress yourself, Cousin," the viscount said, his manner transformed into something altogether more soothing and deferential. "I shall escort this fellow and his . . . doxy out to—"

"I *will* distress myself, goddamn it, Uxbury," the old man said irritably, "if you continue treating me as though I had more than just one foot in the grave. How dare you treat me as if I have an imbecile mind, and not more than half an hour after you set foot in my house? Uninvited, I might add. Go and find yourself a guest room to stay in for a few nights if you must stay while you still have first choice. I daresay the other two claimants to my fortune are springing their horses in the hope of getting here as fast as they can."

"I will see this fellow and his woman out before I do so, Cousin," Viscount Uxbury said. "Your physician would not wish you to—"

"My physician," the old gentleman said, one of his hands closing about the knob of a cane by his side and banging it feebly on the floor, "would not want me to be plagued to death a few days earlier than I will be popping off anyway by relatives who pretend to believe that they have my best interests at heart. And I pay a butler to show guests in and out. I believe I pay him handsomely. Do I, Orville?"

"You do, sir," his valet assured him.

"Out." Mr. Cox-Phillips raised his cane a few inches from the floor and waved it in the viscount's direction. "And you two, come forward and have a seat."

Joel and Camille stood aside to let Viscount Uxbury pass. He looked haughtily and with considerable venom from one to the other of them as he did so, and Camille could not resist expressing some spite of her own.

"I hope you did not take any permanent harm from the kick you took to the chin, Lord Uxbury," she said.

His jaw hardened, and he strode from the room. Camille met Joel's eyes briefly, and it was possible she saw the hint of a smile there. But then he gestured toward the heavy sofa that faced the fireplace adjacent to Mr. Cox-Phillips's chair. She went and sat down, and Joel took his place beside her.

"May I present Miss Camille Westcott, a friend and colleague who was kind enough to accompany me here today, sir?" Joel said.

The gentleman's eyes turned upon Camille and examined her closely from beneath bushy eyebrows. "I do not have an imbecile mind, young lady, despite my age and infirmity," he said. "You were once betrothed to that relative of mine, I recall. Riverdale's daughter, I believe—the late Riverdale."

"That is correct, sir," she said. "I broke off the engagement after it was discovered that my father was already married when he wed my mother and that my sister and brother and I were therefore illegitimate."

"Hmm," he said. "That was the reason, was it? It was unsporting of Uxbury to call you a doxy just now, though I am not surprised. A nasty little weasel of a child, he was, I remember. Not that I saw him often. I took pains not to. Families tend to be pestilential collections of people who just happen to share some blood, but mine was always worse than most. Or do all people think that? What is your connection to Cunningham? The word *colleague* is meaningless without an explanation."

"I teach school at the orphanage where he grew up," she explained. "He volunteers his services as a teacher there too. I offered to accompany him here when he decided to return."

"You convinced him, did you," he said, "that he was an idiot to turn down the chance of inheriting the bulk of my fortune just because of a bit of pride?"

"I did no such thing, sir," she said.

"And yet," he said, "you could have had a splendid revenge upon Uxbury by talking your colleague into doing him out of what he thinks to inherit." His nightcap had slipped down almost over one of his eyes, and his hand had slid off the head of the cane, which fell to the carpet. "Orville, rearrange those damned cushions behind me. Where are they?"

The valet plumped up the cushions behind and to both sides of the old gentleman, moved him gently back against them, straightened his nightcap, tucked the blanket more securely about his waist, and picked up his cane.

"I came back," Joel said when the valet had resumed his place behind the chair, "to find out more about my mother and my grandmother, sir. And there has been no mention of my grandfather. But perhaps you are not feeling well enough—"

"A worthless waste of space and air," Mr. Cox-Phillips said. "Henry Cunningham inherited a tidy sum of money and sat on it for the rest of his life without either enjoying it or investing it—or spending any of it on my sister or my niece. An amiable idiot who came to stay here for a week soon after his marriage and left here almost twenty years later in his coffin. I was happy to spend much of that time in London."

"Henry," Joel said. "And what was my grandmother's name, sir? And my mother's?"

"My sister was Mary," the old man said. "My niece was Dorinda. She must have been named by her idiot of a father. Who else would have named a poor girl Dorinda?"

"What can you tell me about her?" Joel asked. "What did she look like?"

"Not anything like you, young man," Mr. Cox-Phillips assured him gruffly. "She was small and blond and blue eyed and pretty and as silly as girls come. She led my sister a merry dance before she took after that foreign painter fellow, but the dance became less merry when he disappeared off the face of the earth and she started growing plump and denying everything under the stars that could be denied. When denials were no longer of any use, she swore to her mother that he was not the one, but she would not say who was. If it was not the painter, though, then there must have been another Italian in Bath. There is no mistaking your lineage."

"You do not remember his name?" Joel asked.

"I never made the smallest effort either to learn it or to memorize it," the old man said, pausing for a few moments while his breath rasped in and out. "Why should I? He was beneath my notice. He ought to have been beneath my niece's notice too, but he was a handsome devil and she was too like her father—nothing much in her brain to hold her ears apart." His eyes fluttered closed and his head drooped back against the cushions while he caught his breath again.

"We must leave you to rest, sir," Joel said, getting to his feet.

The old gentleman's eyes opened. "It was a good thing for you," he said irritably, "that you turned up here so soon after Uxbury. I doubtless would not have allowed you in otherwise. You made yourself perfectly clear a few days ago and I have no reason to feel kindly toward you."

"Then I must be thankful that my timing was so good," Joel said. "I will not trouble you further, sir. Thank you for telling me what you have about my mother and grandparents."

The eyes had closed again. But Mr. Cox-Phillips spoke once more. "Orville," he said, "have someone go into my sister's room and find that miniature she always kept beside her bed. I daresay it is still there. I do not know where else it would be. Have it given to Mr. Cunningham on his way out. I will be glad to be rid of it."

The valet took a few steps forward and pulled on the bell rope beside the mantel.

"A miniature?" Joel asked.

"Of my niece," the old man said without opening his eyes.

Camille got to her feet and turned to leave. The poor man looked very tired and very ill. But Joel stood frowning down at him.

"Who painted it, sir?" he asked.

"Ah." There was a rumble from the chair, which Camille realized was a laugh. "You may blame—or thank—your grandmother that you exist, young man. She took Dorinda to him. He was Italian and handsome and spoke in that silly accent Italians tend to affect, and it seemed to follow that he must therefore be an artist of superior talent. He painted her."

He clearly had nothing more to say. After regarding him for a few moments longer, Joel looked blankly at Camille and walked beside her from the room and down the stairs. They waited silently in the hall until the butler came and handed a small cloth-bound bundle to Joel before opening the door for them.

The carriage had waited.

Twelve

Joel slid the package down the side of the seat next to the window. It had been called a miniature, but it felt a bit larger than that to him. He would wait to unwrap it until he was alone.

Henry and Mary Cunningham.

Dorinda Cunningham.

Three strangers. All dead. They did not feel like people who were in any way connected to him, though he shared their name and their blood. Would his mother seem more real when he looked at her likeness? Or less so? Would he sense his father's hand in the composition and the brushstrokes? Would he see from her face that she had been looking into his father's, and what she had felt doing so? He felt sick with apprehension at the thought of unwrapping the package. He almost wished the portrait did not exist or that Cox-Phillips had not remembered it.

The carriage lurched into motion and he recalled that

he was not the only one whose emotions had been aroused during this visit. Camille had come here with him after a full day of teaching to offer moral support, only to find herself horribly insulted by the man she had once been close to marrying.

"I am so sorry," he said.

"About Viscount Uxbury calling me a doxy?" she said. "About his saying that I was not fit to be in that house? Why would *you* be sorry? You did not say it. Nor did you drag me here."

"Despite the old saying about sticks and stones," he said, "words *do* hurt. And you once held him in high enough esteem to agree to marry him."

"I always thought that above all else he was a gentleman," she said. "It hurts to know I was so wrong. And it always hurts to be accused of being something one is not. Yet I cannot help remembering that when Anastasia was admitted to Avery's salon and offered a seat, I was outraged because she was not fit to be in that house with respectable people, among whose number I counted myself. Sometimes other people's words become uncomfortable mirrors in which we gaze upon ourselves."

"I must repeat what I have said before," he said. "That man is altogether unworthy of you, Camille. He is a thoroughly nasty customer, and you had a fortunate escape from him. What I was really apologizing for, however, was my own negligence in not smashing that aristocratic nose of his and blackening both his eyes. I ought to have done that much for you—and rammed his teeth down his throat. I have been put to shame by the Duke of Netherby."

"What Avery did was quite splendid in its context,"

she said, reaching up for the worn leather strap as the carriage rattled out of the driveway and onto the road. "According to your account, he had been challenged to a duel, and honor as well as pride dictated that he accept. Today's context was different. Both of you were guests of a dying man, and in his presence in his home. It would have been inappropriate to come to blows with Viscount Uxbury or even to engage in heated words. He did not behave like a gentleman. You did. You behaved with dignity and restraint, and for that, I thank you."

"You had the last word, though," he said, grinning at the memory, "by hoping he had recovered from the kick to his chin."

"I lied." She smiled suddenly, a bright, mischievous expression. "I did not hope any such thing. But I did want him to know that I know."

"Well, I am sorry any of it happened," he said. "It was poor thanks for your kindness in accompanying me here."

"I suppose," she said, "it was punishment for forcing my company upon you. I am not sorry I came, however. Mr. Cox-Phillips is very ill indeed, is he not?"

"Yes," he agreed, and was assailed by a wholly unexpected wave of near panic. His mother and his grandparents were dead, and his great-uncle, his last link with them, was dying. There could be no doubt about that.

"Will you go back yet again?" she asked.

Part of him wanted to do it right now, to lean forward and knock urgently on the front panel and instruct the coachman to turn around.

"Very probably not," he said. "There are more questions I would like to ask. Anecdotal questions. I would like to hear stories about his boyhood with his sister, my grandmother, about the arrival of my grandfather in the household, about the infancy and childhood of my mother. He must have stories to tell, must he not? But I doubt he would be willing to tell them even if he were fit and well. Why should he, after all? He does not know me. I am merely the bastard son of a niece for whom he does not appear to have felt much fondness. Anyway, he is neither fit nor well and would not even have told me as much as he did today if he had not been annoyed by the high-handed behavior of his kinsman. Besides, Uxbury has clearly come to stay, and the old man seems to believe that the other two claimants to his property and fortune will not be far behind him. I have no desire whatsoever to confront any of them."

"Even though they are your relatives too?" she said.

"Exactly because of that," he admitted. "I am not proud that Uxbury is somehow connected to me. I do not even know how and am not much interested in learning."

"But I do wish circumstances had permitted you to smash his nose and blacken both his eyes and ram his teeth down his throat," she added.

He grinned, remembering how at Sally Lunn's she had wished she could string the man up by his thumbs. She chuckled, perhaps remembering the same thing, and then they were holding hands and almost doubled up with laughter. He did not know why they were quite so amused except that it had been a miserable and emotionally charged visit in a number of ways, and life had a way of reasserting itself in face of insult and sickness and imminent death.

"Thank you for coming with me, Camille," he said when he could, and he squeezed her hand, which was still in his, and laced their fingers.

"I have been fearing that I ought not to have talked you into it," she said. "It was really none of my business."

"I learned the names of my mother and her parents," he said. "It is not a great deal, but even that much knowledge gives me more identity."

"And you have the painting," she said

"Yes, I have that," he agreed. "But I am afraid to look at it."

She tipped her head to one side as she gazed at him and frowned in thought for a few moments. "I believe I would be too in your place," she said. "You will look at it when you are ready."

"It is not just that the painting is of my mother," he said. "It is also that it was painted by my father. Or by the man who was supposedly my father."

"They must have been in company together a good deal when he was painting her portrait," she said. "She would have been gazing at him and he at her for hours on end. It is perfectly understandable that they fell in love."

"He did not love her, though, did he?" he said, and closed his eyes for a few moments. "There is no point in trying to romanticize what happened between them. He ran away as soon as he learned their affair had had consequences—me. I am not the product of a grand passion between ill-fated lovers who died of broken hearts after being plucked asunder. It was all far more mundane. Lust pure and simple, I would guess. And cowardice."

"You do not know all the facts," she said.

"No, I do not," he admitted. Would he know better when he saw the painting? Would he sense whether there had been love—in the eyes of his mother, in the brushstrokes of his father? Probably not. What had happened between those two had died with them, and that was the way it ought to be. Perhaps. Except that he was left to wonder. "I do know something about the son they produced, however. I would never abandon a woman I had impregnated. Or our child."

They traveled the rest of the way in silence, their hands still joined, their shoulders touching as the carriage swayed and bounced over the road. When they arrived back at the orphanage, he opened the door and jumped down to the pavement before turning to help her alight.

"Thank you for coming," he said again.

"Go back again," she told him, but she did not offer to accompany him this time or press the point. She hurried inside and closed the door.

After school one day earlier in the week, when the children were all outside playing or otherwise occupied elsewhere and the playroom was empty, Camille had sat down at the old neglected pianoforte, which had been pushed off into one corner, and played softly to herself. She had never been more than a tolerably skilled musician, but playing the pianoforte was a necessary accomplishment for a properly brought-up young lady and she had persevered. She had been missing playing as well as embroidering and watercolor painting—all strictly according to the rules set down by her governess. Sometimes she wished she could go back and relive her girlhood with more of a questioning, even rebellious spirit, but it could not be done. Going back was never possible, and there was no point in wallowing in regrets for what might have been.

When she had looked up from the pianoforte after a few minutes, it was to the discovery that three children had crept into the room unnoticed and were standing perfectly still, watching her. They would go about their play soon enough, she had thought after smiling vaguely at them and turning her attention to another remembered piece, but after that there were two more children watching her, as well as the original three and one of the housemothers. The next time she looked up, she was forced to the startled conclusion that there must surely not be a child left in the garden or any other part of the building. The playroom was as full as she had ever seen it.

She had switched to playing some folk songs that everyone knew—everyone in her old world, anyway, but apparently not in the new. She had picked out a few of the simplest tunes and taught the melody and the words of the first verses. The girls had soon been singing along with her while the boys looked warily at one another and held their peace while at the same time holding their ground.

Music in the form of folk songs and simple hymns and a few rounds had become a part of the school curriculum from that day, and Camille had soon been scheming for a way to bring in the boys. She had done it by brushing up on her knowledge of sailors' working chants and explaining them as exclusively male music. Indeed, for a while she banned the girls from singing them, something that proved highly successful when the girls burned with resentment and the boys preened themselves and sang loudly and lustily and not necessarily musically.

It was not singing she was teaching early on the Friday afternoon after the visit to Mr. Cox-Phillips's house, however. It was dancing. It had all started during the morning, when Camille had unveiled the purple knitted rope, whose various parts she had stayed up late the night before weaving together into one. It could not be unveiled, of course, without being put to immediate use. They had gone out as far as Bath Abbey, where Camille had given a brief lecture on the architecture of the church before leading the way to the Roman baths just a few yards from the abbey and below the Pump Room. Both the expedition and the rope had been an enormous success, the latter having drawn amused attention from several passersby. Not one child had either lagged behind or surged ahead without the others, and an occasional head count had satisfied Camille each time that she still had the correct number of children.

Their return to the school had been delayed by the presence in the abbey yard of some musicians—first a flautist, whom the children found enthralling mainly, Camille suspected, because watching and listening to him shortened the school day, and then by a troop of energetic dancers, who performed the steps of several vigorous and intricate country dances to the accompaniment of the flute and a violin. The children had been genuinely enchanted by them, and it would have been nothing short of cruel to drag them away before the performance came to an end.

On the way back to school a few of the older children had recalled the time when a former teacher had taught dancing. Miss Snow had not continued the lessons—*the Duchess of Netherby,* Winifred Hamlin had interrupted the speaker to remind him—because she could not sing the music and teach the steps at the same time. And Miss Nunce had not because . . . well, *because.*

If they wished to learn to dance, Camille had said rashly, then she would teach them. And had they noticed that in the troupe they had just watched there were exactly as many men dancers as women? One of the recently hired housemothers had even admitted to some skill at the pianoforte and might be persuaded to play while their teacher taught the steps. Her offer had been met with such enthusiasm—a public cheer in the middle of the street that would have scandalized Lady Camille Westcott even without the conspicuous addition of the purple rope—that she had decided to waste no time but to begin immediately after luncheon. Ursula Trask, the housemother in question, had agreed to play for them, though she had warned that her fingers were rusty and might well hit as many wrong notes as right.

It was only when she was already hot and bothered and disheveled and barking out instructions as she tried to teach the steps of the Roger de Coverley, however, that Camille recalled this was one of the days for art instruction. It was amazing she had forgotten when she had thought of little else but Joel Cunningham and their journey up into the hills all last evening and most of last night—she had slept only in fits and starts—and much of this morning too. But she had indeed forgotten and would not have remembered now if she had not suddenly noticed him standing, or rather, slouching in the doorway, one shoulder propping up the frame, one booted foot crossed over the other ankle, his arms folded over his chest, a smirk on his face.

She stopped barking abruptly and the music faltered and children went prancing off in all directions.

"Oh," she said. "Oh goodness. Children. Artists. It is time for your painting lesson."

She was horribly aware of her appearance, and of his. Since when had shabby men started to look impossibly attractive when immaculately tailored ones merely looked . . . well, immaculately tailored? Though it was not shabby *men* exactly—was it?—but a certain shabby *man*. It was really very puzzling.

There were sounds of protest from the art pupils, even, surprisingly, the boys. Joel held up one hand, palm out, and pushed himself away from the doorframe.

"Dancing?" he said. "It has not been taught here since Miss Rutledge's days. Most of you will not even remember her. But everyone should know how to dance. Among other things, it is an art form. A dancing lesson can conceivably be considered an art class. Let it proceed, then, and I will lend my support to Miss Westcott."

The children cheered and Camille wished she had realized before she started that knowing how to dance was somewhat different from knowing how to teach dancing. There was so much to teach. There were the steps and the figures, of course, but there were also things like daintiness and grace and the correct positioning of one's head and hands to consider, and even the expression upon one's face. And it was different for boys and girls. This could well be her biggest failure in two weeks of dubious successes—except that the children were obviously enjoying themselves enough to want to continue. And younger children and housemothers and even Roger and Miss Ford kept poking their heads about the door, smiles on their faces.

After Joel had explained that when he learned to dance they had all moved about with great enthusiasm and a bounce in their steps and no regard for style or grace, the process became easier and far more fun. He taught the boys the steps. Camille taught the girls. Together they pushed and prodded and led and coaxed and bullied and applauded the class into performing a dance that had some sort of resemblance to the Roger de Coverley. And since everyone ended up flushed and bright eyed and clamoring for more lessons and different dances another day, Camille supposed they had achieved some success after all.

She dismissed school early rather than herd everyone back to the schoolroom for a mere half hour. She thanked Ursula for playing the pianoforte and went back to the schoolroom to tidy up. Joel followed her there.

"Is this not the final day of your two-week trial?" he asked.

"It is." She half grimaced. "Miss Ford told me during luncheon that if I wish to stay for the next twenty years or so she will put no obstacle in my way. Is it because no one else has applied for the position, do you suppose?"

"What I suppose," he said, "is that it is because you are an excellent teacher and the children love you."

"I cannot imagine why," she said, straightening the books in the bookcase. "I seem to have brought nothing but chaos to the schoolroom. And I have no idea what I am doing."

He grinned at her. "Have you heard of the waltz?" he asked.

"The waltz?" She frowned. "Of course."

"Have you danced it?" he asked.

"Of course."

"It is said to be both risqué and hopelessly romantic," he said. "Which is it, in your estimation? Or is it both?"

She had never considered it particularly romantic. But then, she had never found anything romantic. Romance was not for the likes of people like Lady Camille Westcott. She had never found it risqué either. If it was danced properly, with the emphasis upon grace and elegance, then it was a perfectly unexceptionable dance. Her partners had always been chosen with great care, of course. She had waltzed a number of times with Viscount Uxbury, and no one was more proper than he—until, that was, he had begun calling her a doxy. Was that what he had called her, she wondered, when Avery and Alexander had chucked him out of the ball in London?

"Or is it neither?" Joel asked when she did not immediately reply.

"I believe," she said, "it could be the most romantic dance ever conceived."

"Could?" he said. "But it never has been in your experience?"

"I did not look for romance on the ballroom floor," she told him.

"Or anywhere else?" He was leaning back against the teacher's desk, his arms crossed. He was almost always relaxed and leaning, arms crossed. Was that part of his appeal—his total lack of formality and studied elegance?

"Or anywhere else," she said severely. "You have never seen the waltz performed?"

"I had never even heard of it until recently," he said. "Teach me."

What?

"Here?" she said. "Now? But there is no music and there are desks everywhere. Besides . . ."

"The desks are easily disposed of," he said, and to Camille's dismay he started to push them aside to create something of a space in the center of the room. "The music should be easy to provide. You have a voice, do you not?"

"I do," she said. "But no one, having once heard it, has ever pressed me to favor any gathering with a solo."

"A fair warning," he said. "But there is no gathering of people here. You must know a tune that would fit the waltz."

"Must I?" He was not going to let this go, was he?

He strode to her side, took the book she was holding from her hands, replaced it any-old-where on a shelf, and held out a hand for hers. "Madam," he said, "will you do me the great honor of waltzing with me?" And he made her a tolerably elegant leg, scuffed boots and all—*boots* for waltzing?—and bowed with a flourish.

"You sound like something out of the last century," she told him. "I expect to see lace and frills and a powdered wig and buckled shoes." But she set her hand in his, and with the greatest reluctance allowed herself to be led onto the cleared space.

"All that remains," he said, flashing his grin at her again, "is for you to teach me how to do it."

"It is relatively easy," she said doubtfully, "but first you have to know how to . . . hold me." She took his right hand and set it against the back of her waist before placing her left hand on his shoulder. She set her other hand within his and raised them to shoulder height. "There must always be space between us, not too much or we cannot move together with any symmetry, but not so little that we touch anywhere but where we are already touching." She moved half a step closer to him, arching her spine slightly so that she could look up at him.

Good heavens, why had she not simply said a firm no? She suddenly remembered his telling her yesterday afternoon that he would never abandon a woman he had impregnated—or their child. She did not believe she had ever heard that word spoken aloud before—*impregnated*. She had been shocked right down to her toes, and she was shocked again now. She glared at him as though the words had only just come out of his mouth.

"I like this dance," he said.

She pressed her lips together. This was not going to work. "And then there are the steps," she said severely. And there were all the variations on the steps that made the dance exhilarating and graceful and could, she supposed, make it hopelessly romantic if one were romantically inclined.

"One-two-three, one-two-three," she counted, and they moved off together as though they did not have a single leg between the two of them that was not made of wood.

"This is as exciting as waiting for oil paint to dry," he said.

"One normally dances the steps on one's toes and at a faster pace and with rhythm and grace and elegance," she told him, "and to music. And one does not always take three steps to one side and three back again. One moves about the floor, and sometimes one twirls about as well."

"The secret being, I suppose," he said, "never to get so dizzy that one topples over and never to tread upon one's partners toes, especially if one is the man."

"The man leads," she said, "and the woman follows."

"It all sounds easy enough," he said, spreading his hand more firmly against the back of her waist. "Provide the music, madam, and I shall endeavor to lead you into the grand romance of the waltz."

It was awkward; it was clumsy; it was impossible. Where he led, without any signal to provide her with a clue, she could not always follow. They seemed to possess more than the requisite number of feet, and the extra ones were very large. They danced apart until their arms were almost not long enough. They danced close enough to bang together, chest against bosom, before bouncing hastily apart. Camille la-la-la-ed until she was breathless, protested that he was quickening the pace instead of keeping to the steady beat she had set, and la-la-la-ed again. He laughed.

And then suddenly they got it. They were dancing as a couple. They had the steps and the rhythm. They were waltzing. And smiling into each other's eyes with a certain delighted triumph. But Camille was running out of breath again, and she lost it altogether when he twirled her into a sweeping spin. She shrieked, though they completed the spin successfully, all feet and toes accounted for and unstepped upon and unsquashed. She laughed up at him with sheer exhilaration, and he laughed back.

And then, suddenly, they were not laughing any longer.

She was not singing either.

Nor were they dancing.

Nor was the requisite space between them.

They were bosom to chest, his hand spread against her

back, her hand half on his shoulder, half behind his neck, fingertips touching bare flesh, their other hands clasped against his heart. They were gazing into each other's eyes, mere inches apart, both slightly breathless, both with fast-beating hearts, both . . .

And that was the precise moment at which the schoolroom door opened abruptly to admit Miss Ford, closely followed by Cousin Elizabeth—Lady Overfield, Alexander's sister—and Anastasia, Duchess of Netherby.

Thirteen

There was a moment when all five persons paused, startled. Then—

"I have been teaching Mr. Cunningham the steps of the waltz."

"Miss Westcott has been teaching me to waltz."

They spoke simultaneously before moving hastily apart, and it registered more fully upon Joel's mind who these ladies were—two of them anyway. He had never seen the third before.

"Anna!" he exclaimed, and strode toward her, both hands outstretched. "You are here already." He had received one of her long letters yesterday morning, and in it she informed him that she and Netherby were expecting to be in Bath by the beginning of next week for her grandmother's birthday celebrations. But *not* today.

"Joel!" She met him halfway, set her hands in his, and

squeezed them as tightly as he was squeezing hers. "We could see that my grandparents were suddenly homesick and decided to leave a few days earlier than planned."

Joel's first coherent thought was that marriage agreed with her. She was dressed with simple yet obviously expensive elegance, as the change in her status had made inevitable, but the most noticeable change since she had last stood in this room as a teacher was the glow of health and vitality she seemed to exude. Her face seemed fuller and her slight figure less thin. Yet another change was in himself. He did not feel immediately heartsick and resentful over the fact that another man must be at least partly responsible for the improvement in her looks. It was a bit of a startling realization. Was he getting over her at last, then?

Camille meanwhile was greeting the other lady, who was holding one of her hands in both her own and smiling warmly at her. She was noticeably older than both Camille and Anna, but she was elegant and had an amiable, good-looking face. He could hazard a guess at who she was since Anna had written a great deal about Cousin Elizabeth, Lady Overfield, in the early days.

"We arrived late this morning," Anna was explaining, "after taking my grandparents home to Wensbury. We expected that we would be the first of the family to arrive, but it was not so. After luncheon we all went to call upon Mrs. Kingsley. We left Cousin Althea, Aunt Louise, and Jessica there with her and Abigail while Elizabeth and I came here to see Camille, and Avery and Alexander walked back to the hotel. Do let me make the introductions. Lizzie, this is my dear friend Joel Cunningham, who grew up here with me and teaches art here a couple of afternoons a week. Elizabeth is Lady Overfield, Joel, Alexander's sister—he is the Earl of Riverdale, you may recall."

He had not been mistaken, then. "You are the lady who went to live with Anna in London until she married," he said as he shook hands with her.

"And you, Mr. Cunningham," she said, "are the friend to whom she wrote long, long letters every day. I am delighted to meet you."

"And I you, ma'am," he assured her.

Miss Ford left the room quietly and closed the door after her while Joel and Lady Overfield exchanged pleasantries and Camille and Anna eyed each other. Part of his attention was on them, these half sisters who had grown up unaware of each other's existence. Anna had been delighted to discover that she had three half siblings and had wanted to love them and share her inherited fortune with them in equal measures. But of course the situation was far less rosy from their point of view, for the discovery of her existence had come simultaneously with the knowledge of their own illegitimacy. It had stripped them of their titles and their homes and fortunes.

"Camille," Anna said as she turned from him and Lady Overfield. Joel was aware of her hesitation over whether to stretch out her hands, as she had done to him, or to step up closer to Camille and hug her. But she hesitated too long and ended up doing neither. Poor Anna.

"Anastasia." Camille, he was aware, was enacting one of her less appealing roles—stiff, cold, dignified lady—as she clasped her hands at her waist and inclined her head, the language of her body setting a shield about herself that firmly discouraged either a handshake or a hug. Poor Camille.

It surprised Joel that he could see both points of view, whereas until recently he had been able to see only Anna's and had been predisposed to dislike Camille.

"Abigail wrote to Jessica and told her you had come here," Anna said, "first to teach and then to live as well. I have been longing to come and see you here. Just now, Miss Ford has been telling Lizzie and me that she has offered you the job for at least the next twenty years and hopes you do not think she was joking." She smiled brightly, but Joel could see the strain, the wariness she was feeling.

"I believe," Camille said, "that is because no one else has applied for the position."

"I believe rather," Anna told her, still smiling, "it is because you have endeared yourself to the children with innovative and imaginative teaching."

"It is kind of you to say so," Camille said stiffly, and though she did not curtsy, she came dashed close to it, Joel thought. He could have shaken her—and Anna too, for while Anna was trying hard to say something kind and generous to her sister, she was coming very close to sounding condescending. Their relationship was not going to improve if they continued this way.

Lady Overfield must have had the same thought. "It is just like you, Camille," she said, "to take on something so very challenging and to do it well. I applaud you, though you may find the rest of the family more disapproving. You were learning to waltz, Mr. Cunningham?"

"It was one dance Anna had to learn when she went

to London," he said. "I had a full account of the lessons in her letters, including your part in them, ma'am. I believe you demonstrated the dance with your brother."

"Oh goodness, yes," she said, her eyes twinkling. "Anna's dancing master was ridiculously pompous. He would still be teaching her how to position herself correctly if Alex and I had not stepped in to demonstrate how it is actually done—with some enjoyment as well as a little bit of grace."

"And if Avery had not arrived to insist I waltz with him instead of with Mr. Robertson, the dancing instructor," Anna said. "I had not even heard of the waltz before I went to London."

"I had never heard of it until you went to London either," Joel said. "But Miss Westcott was teaching the children a country dance this afternoon, and after they had been dismissed I begged her to teach me the waltz. I account both her instruction and my efforts an unqualified success. I did not tread on her toes even once."

They all laughed except Camille, who was impersonating a straight-backed, tight-lipped marble statue. Good God, if they had not been interrupted, he would have ended up kissing her—and she him if he was not very much mistaken. The air between them and all about them had been fairly crackling. Had it been noticeable? But how could it not have been?

"Avery has reserved a private dining room for the family at the Royal York Hotel," Anna said, addressing Camille. "Grandmama and Aunt Matilda will not be here until next week, but Aunt Mildred and Uncle Thomas are probably on the way and may even arrive tomorrow.

Abigail has agreed to dine with us tomorrow evening. Mrs. Kingsley unfortunately has another engagement. Will you come too, Camille? We would like it above all things."

Camille's demeanor did not change, but she hesitated for only a moment. "Thank you," she said. "I will."

"Oh splendid." Anna looked again as though she might rush forward to take her half sister's hands in her own, but she did not do so. Joel wondered if they would ever be comfortable with each other. Not that Camille was even trying, though she had accepted the invitation. Anna turned toward him. "And will you come too, Joel? Abigail told us that you are to paint her portrait and Camille's and have already been to her grandmother's house several times to make some preliminary sketches. I want to hear all your news. It must be almost two weeks since I last heard from you."

It was to be a family dinner, Joel thought. He would be an outsider. He glanced at Camille, who was looking steadily back at him, her expression giving him no indication of whether she would welcome his presence there or resent it. But did her approval matter?

"Abigail told us something of your methods as a portrait painter, Mr. Cunningham," Lady Overfield said. "They sound very different from the norm. I too would love to hear more. Do please come."

"Very well," Joel said. "Thank you."

"Avery will send the carriage for you, Camille," Anna said. "And there is no point in protesting, as I can see you are about to do. I would agree with you that the distance from here to the Royal York Hotel is not a great one. But he told me to inform you—did he not, Lizzie?—that he would send the carriage, and you know him well enough to understand that he will not take no for an answer. If I were to carry a refusal back to him, he would be sure to say, looking infinitely bored, that you may choose to walk if you wish, but that the carriage will be moving along beside you anyway."

For the first time Camille's lips quirked into what was almost a smile. "Thank you," she said.

"Seven o'clock, then?" Anna said. "Seven o'clock, Joel?"

"I will be there," he promised.

The ladies made their farewells soon after, and Joel strode to the door to hold it open for them.

"It has been a pleasure, Mr. Cunningham," Lady Overfield said, extending her hand to him again as she paused in the doorway. "I shall beg Anna to seat me beside you tomorrow evening."

Anna was at last extending her hands to Camille, who took them awkwardly. "I am so glad you will come," Anna said. "Everyone would have been disappointed if you had not."

Joel closed the door after them.

"Oh, that was uncomfortable," Anna said with a sigh as they set out in the carriage for the Royal York Hotel on George Street. "But what do you think, Lizzie?"

"I think she must have been wearing the plainest, drabbest dress she possesses," Elizabeth said, "that her hair was untidier than I have ever seen it, that her face is thinner than it used to be, and that she was a bit flushed and uncomfortable with our sudden appearance. I also think we interrupted a waltz lesson that was about to culminate in an embrace."

"I was not the only one who thought so, then," Anna said. "But really, Lizzie—Joel and Camille?"

"You think it an odd pairing?" Elizabeth asked.

"*Odd* does not even begin to describe it," Anna said.

"Could you possibly be a little jealous?" Elizabeth asked. "No, pardon me. *Jealous* is quite the wrong word, for if anyone has ever been more totally besotted with her husband than you are with Avery, I would be surprised to hear it. Protective, then. That is a better word. Are you a little protective of him, Anna?"

"Oh, perhaps." Anna admitted after thinking a moment. "I long to love Camille, Lizzie, but I find it so difficult to *like* her. Does that even make sense? Joel surely deserves better. And now I feel disloyal to my sister for saying so. No, it is not jealousy, Lizzie. I never loved Joel in that way. But I did and do love him nevertheless."

"I do not believe anyone really likes Camille," Elizabeth said as the carriage slowed on the uphill climb to the hotel, "except, I would hope, Abigail and probably Harry and their mother. But . . . when Miss Ford was describing her as a teacher, I could scarcely believe she was describing the Camille I know. Dancing with the children? Singing with them? Getting them to knit a purple rope? Becoming emotionally attached to an abandoned baby? Is it possible she is becoming human?"

"I have not known her for long," Anna said unhappily. "Indeed, I have met her only a few times in all. She does not like me, and that is quite understandable. But I admire her immensely for what she is doing. It must be very difficult for her. Yet she is doing it well. Oh, Lizzie, I long to like her as well as love her. Will it ever be possible? But Camille and Joel? I cannot for the life of me see them as a couple."

"He really is rather gorgeous, is he not?" Elizabeth said, smiling sidelong at her companion.

"Joel?" Anna looked at her in surprise.

"You grew up with him, "Elizabeth said. "To you he is a sort of brother. It took me a while to realize how devastatingly handsome Alex is in the eyes of other women. To me he was always just my tall, good-looking young brother."

"Joel is *gorgeous*?" Anna frowned. "Is he really?"

"And Camille would be remarkably handsome," Elizabeth said, "if she would not always be so intent upon looking like a prune."

"Perhaps she is not always so," Anna said. "She is doing well as a teacher. The children like her. I know just how demanding a job teaching is, Lizzie, and how difficult it is to earn the liking and respect of one's pupils. They must have seen aspects of her you and I have not. And that baby lights up with joy when she sees Camille, according to Miss Ford. Perhaps Joel has seen these other sides of her too."

"For a brief moment after Miss Ford opened the door," Elizabeth said as they arrived at the hotel, "I did not recognize the woman as Camille."

"Oh," Anna said, "neither did I."

Camille hastened over to the bookcase to finish straightening the books. Except that the task had already been completed and there was nothing left to do.

"I must look a fright," she said.

"In contrast with your cousin and your sister?" he said. "That is because you have been too deeply involved in your day's work to worry about your appearance. A look of slight dishevelment does not necessarily make a person look a fright, though."

Slight dishevelment. His words were not reassuring. "*Half* sister," she said, frowning. "Does it hurt you to see her looking so happy?"

"No," he said. "Does it hurt you?"

Happiness—a deep sort of contentment—had surrounded Anastasia with a glow that was almost visible, and Camille did not believe it was just the acquisition of property and fortune that had caused it. Avery had had something to do with it. Whatever could she see in Avery except bored affectation? Except that he had felled Viscount Uxbury with his bare feet—in defense of *her,* Camille's honor. There must be something terribly wrong with her, Camille thought, that she could neither feel nor attract love. Was it possible that her quest for perfection had somehow deadened an essential part of herself?

"No," she said, switching the positions of two books for no other reason than that it gave her something to do. "Why should it?"

He had been going to kiss her. She had been going to kiss him back. But they had been interrupted. Now she was resentful. Or relieved. And horribly embarrassed. Why did he not just leave? He was over there by the door. All he had to do was open it and step through—and leave her to move the desks and chairs back where they belonged. She looked up at him. He was leaning back against the door, his arms crossed, staring broodingly at her.

"I cannot bring myself to look at it," he said abruptly.

She stared blankly at him for a moment before realizing his thoughts had not been moving along the same lines as her own.

"I could not bring myself to unwrap it in the carriage yesterday. I thought I needed to be alone. But I was alone all evening and all night and this morning until I went up to the Royal Crescent to make more sketches of your sister. I did not once even glance its way. Now I cannot bear the thought of going home alone and knowing it is there and that I do not have the courage to deal with it. There must be something wrong with me."

What if she had never known her own mother? What if now suddenly and unexpectedly she had been presented with a portrait of her, all neatly wrapped up? She would surely be all fingers and thumbs in her eagerness to tear off the wraps that kept that image from her view. Or would she? Would she too be afraid to look? To see the face she had never looked upon in real life and never would now? To see the face of a stranger she could not quite believe was her mother? To come face-to-face with the loneliness she had spent a lifetime denying? She thought of her own mother, of her resentment that she had gone, leaving her two daughters behind in Bath. But at least Mama was alive. At least Camille could bring her image to mind, complete with voice and touch and characteristic gestures and fragrance.

"Do you think there is?" he asked. "It is only a painting, after all, and probably not even a good one, if Cox-Phillips was right about my father's talent."

"Do you want me open the package with you?" she asked.

He did not immediately answer but continued to frown at her. "I cannot ask it of you," he said.

But he had not said no. He wanted her—no, he needed to have her with him. She was a bit shaken by the rush of . . . joy she felt. When had anyone ever needed her?

"You did not ask," she said. "I offered."

"Then yes," he said. But he smiled suddenly. "What if I then discover that I need to be alone?"

"Then I will come back here." She shrugged. "I need the exercise anyway."

"After all the dancing?" He was still smiling.

"I will fetch my bonnet and shawl," she said, and left the room.

He had not told Anastasia about his discovery of his identity. He had not told her about the portrait of his mother. He had not asked her to go with him to give him the courage to look at it. Not that he had asked *her*, Camille, exactly, but she knew he wanted her to be with him. Oh, she wished, wished, *wished* she did not hate Anastasia. In her head she did not, but her heart would not seem to soften. She must make a determined effort to be civil tomorrow evening and during the coming week. But she already was civil. She must go beyond civility, then. She must initiate some conversation with Anastasia, show some interest in her, find some common ground they might share—the school, perhaps, and the pupils they had both taught. She *would* learn to like the woman if it was the last thing she ever did. Perhaps in time she would even be able to call her *sister* without always having to add the word *half* in order to set the proper distance between them.

They did not talk during the walk to Grove Street or while he unlocked the door of the house and she started on her way upstairs ahead of him. Unlike the other two times she had been here, though, a door on the first floor opened abruptly as she rounded the newel post to continue upward, and a man's head appeared around the door.

"Is that you, Joel?" he asked. "I wonder if you— Oh, pardon me." And his head disappeared back inside and the door clicked shut before either Camille or Joel could say a word.

"Marvin Silver, my neighbor," Joel said. "I am so sorry, Camille. I did not expect he would be home yet. I would not have had that happen to you for worlds, especially when you are doing me such a favor."

"It does not matter," she said. "And I offered to come, if you will remember." She waited for him to unlock the door to his rooms and then hung up her bonnet and went into the living room.

"I will have a word with him," he said. "He will not tell anyone."

"It does not matter, Joel," she said again. "I am sick and tired of the rigid rules of propriety that have always governed my behavior. What have they ever done for me?"

"Well," he said, "if you can be so brave and decisive, then so can I. It is in the studio. *It*. You see? I cannot even name it. I fervently wish Cox-Phillips had not even thought of it yesterday."

"Bring it out here, then," she said, "and I will look at it

with you. Or I will turn my back and look out through the window while you do so alone, if you would prefer."

"No," he said. "In there."

She raised her eyebrows. Into the studio? Was it not his holy of holies? The one place he took no one?

He turned to her outside the closed door and extended a hand for hers. "Come in with me. Please," he said.

Fourteen

J oel took Camille's hand in his and took her into his
studio. It was an incredibly difficult thing to do. He
had never before invited anyone into his work space, even
when it was just his crowded bedchamber.

His almost-completed portrait of Mrs. Wasserman was
on the easel, the eighteen charcoal sketches he had done
of her strewn on the table beside it. It was an odd moment
for him to realize what had been nagging at him for days,
the missing detail that would allow him to complete the
portrait and sign his name to it, satisfied that it was the
best he could possibly do. Although she was always carefully, elaborately coiffed, there was invariably one slender
lock of hair that escaped the rest and curled across her
forehead just beyond the outer edge of her left eyebrow.
It was surely in every one of the sketches, but it was
absent from the portrait. She did not look quite herself

without it. And such a very small omission made all the difference.

But this was not why he had come in here and brought Camille with him. He took Mrs. Wasserman's portrait off the easel and set it on the table beside the sketches. Then he strode over to the corner of the room behind the door and picked up the clothbound package he had propped against the wall there yesterday and stood it on the easel instead.

"Come and see," he said as he removed the cloth carefully and dropped it to the floor. She came to stand silently beside him.

His first reaction—perhaps it was a defensive one—was purely critical. She had been formally posed on a gilt-backed, gilt-armed chair, one elbow resting on a small cloth-covered table beside her, her hand dangling gracefully over her lap, holding a closed ivory fan. Her other hand rested on the back of a tiny dog in her lap, its eyes all but invisible beneath its long hair. She was half smiling at the beholder with a carefully contrived expression. There was a certain stiffness about it and about her pose generally, and Joel knew that she had been painted from life, and that she had sat still, probably for hours at a time, while the artist painted her. She was pretty, dainty, graceful—and totally unreal. Looking at her, one saw only the prettiness, the daintiness, the grace, the perfection of hair and complexion and dress and expression, and nothing of the person herself. The eyes looked outward but did nothing to draw the beholder inward. There was no hint of character, of mood, of vitality, of individuality. One could see this young woman, even admire her beauty and the care with which she and her props and surroundings had been arranged and painted. But one could not know her.

His second reaction was that outside the painting, where he was standing now, was the invisible figure of the painter. There was no hint, either in the facial expression and posture of the woman or in the way she had been painted, of any connection of tenderness, of intimacy, of passion, of love between painter and subject. Had he expected there would be? Had he feared there would not?

His third reaction—the one he had been holding back— was that this was his mother. She was blond, blue eyed, apparently small and dainty, pretty in a fresh, youthful way without any individuality to set her apart from hundreds of other young ladies her age. She was *his mother.* She had died giving birth to him. He wondered how old she had been. She looked no older than eighteen in the portrait, probably younger. And the hand that had painted her—the invisible hand though it had touched this canvas numerous times—was his father's.

His fourth reaction was that the painting had not been signed. He had not even realized that he had been hoping for some clue, however small, to his father's identity.

He became aware again of Camille standing beside him, looking at the painting with him, but not speaking, for which fact he was grateful.

"Cox-Phillips was right about one thing," he said, surprised to hear his voice sounding quite normal. "The painter was not particularly talented." Why had he chosen that of all things to say? The painter was his *father*—at least, in all probability he was. "He left the beholder with no clue as to who she was. I do not mean her identity.

That must be undisputed. I mean *her,* her character and personality. I see a pretty girl. That is all. I do not feel—"

"The connection of son to mother?" she said softly after he had circled one hand ineffectually in the air without finding the words he needed.

"Did I expect to?" he said. "Did I expect to know her as soon as I saw her? To recognize her as part of myself? It is not the painter's fault, is it, that she is just a pretty stranger, a decade younger than I. I wonder if the dog was hers or the painter's. Or was it a figment of his imagination? But there is no other evidence that he had an imagination or could paint something that was not before his eyes. He painted her as she sat there before him. She had to sit still for a long time and probably over several sessions."

His hand reached out to touch the paint, but he rested his fingertips on the top of the frame instead.

"There is no evidence," he said, "that he loved her or felt anything for her. Did I expect that there would be? A grand passion transmitted onto the canvas by a painter deeply enamored of his subject, to be transmitted to the beholder more than a quarter of a century later?" He closed his eyes and lowered his head. "It is a pretty picture."

All his life there had been an emptiness, a blank, where his parents ought to have been. He had never dwelled upon it. He had got on with his life, and he had little of which to complain. On the whole, life had been good to him. But the emptiness had always been there, a sort of hollow at the center of his being. Now there was something to fit into that hollow, and it brought pain with it. So close, he thought. Ah, so close. They were so close to him, those two, painter and painted, father and mother, yet so eternally unattainable.

"Joel." Her voice was a whisper of sound from beside him.

Why the devil was he going all to pieces over a mere painting, and not a very skilled one at that? He could have lived the whole of the rest of his life knowing no more than he had ever known about himself without feeling any pain greater than that certain emptiness. Why should knowing a little feel worse than knowing nothing? Because knowing a little made him greedy for more when there was no more?

He would find a place to hang the painting, he decided, somewhere prominent, where he would see it every day, where it would no longer be something almost to fear but on the contrary, an everyday part of his surroundings. It must hang somewhere where other people would see it too, and he would point it out to any of his friends who came here—*Ah yes, that is my mother when she was very young. Pretty, was she not? The painter was my father. He was Italian. He returned to Italy before he knew I was on the way and she never did let him know. A bit tragic, yes. I suppose there was a reason. A lovers' quarrel, perhaps. She died giving birth to me, you know. Perhaps she intended to write to him afterward. Perhaps he waited to hear from her and assumed she had forgotten him and was too proud to come back.* A comfortable myth would grow around the few facts he knew.

He turned to look at Camille. "I will not paint you with a contrived smile on your face," he told her, "or with a fan in one hand that has no function but to be decorative. I will not set a little toy of a dog on your lap to arouse sentiment in the beholder. I will not paint you with flat eyes and an unnatural perfection of feature and coloring."

"They would have to be very unnatural," she said. "And I do not like little dogs. They yap."

He smiled at her and then laughed—and then reached for her and drew her against him with such force that he felt the air whoosh out of her lungs. He did not loosen his hold but clasped her as though she were his only anchor in a turbulent sea. She let herself be held and set her arms about him. Her face was turned in against his neck. For long moments he buried his own face against her hair and breathed in the blessed safety of her.

"I am sorry," he said then. "I am behaving as though I were the only person ever to suffer. And how can I call this suffering? I ought to be rejoicing."

"There are some things worse than not knowing your parents," she said. "Sometimes knowing them is worse." She sighed, her breath warm against his throat, and lifted her head. "But that is not really true, of course. How can I know what it would have been like not to know my father? How can you know what it would have been like to know yours? We cannot choose our lives, can we? We have some freedom in how we live them, but none whatsoever over the circumstances in which we find ourselves when we are born. And I do not suppose *that* is a very original observation."

"Camille," he said, smiling at her.

"But here we both are," she said, half smiling back, "on our feet and somehow living our lives. Why are we so gloomy? Must we wallow in the tragedies of the past? When I stepped out of my grandmother's house just over two weeks ago and set out for the orphanage and Miss

Ford's office, I had decided that for me at least the answer was no. Definitely not. Never again."

"I have identity at last," he said. "All is well."

He cupped her face in both hands, and they gazed into each other's eyes, both half smiling, for long moments. She closed her own briefly when he traced the line of her brows with his thumbs and ran one of them along the length of her nose, and opened them again when he feathered both thumbs along her lips, pausing at the outer corners. Her fingertips came to rest lightly against his wrists. He smiled more fully at her, drew breath to speak, changed his mind, and then spoke anyway.

"Come to bed with me," he said.

He regretted the words immediately, for her hands tightened about his wrists, and he guessed he had ruined the fragile connection he had felt between them. She did not step away from him, however, or pull his hands away from her face. And when she spoke, it was not with either indignation or outrage.

"Yes," she said.

They left the portrait of his mother on the easel, uncovered, and crossed the hall to enter his bedchamber, not touching each other.

"I am not the tidiest of mortals," he said as Camille heard the door close behind her.

The bed had been made up, but the blankets hung lower on one side than on the other, and one pillow still bore the imprint of his head, presumably from last night. A book lay open and facedown on a table beside the bed. Camille itched to mark the page, close the book, and check to see that the spine had not been damaged. A few other books were strewn on the floor with a scrunched-up garment, probably his nightshirt. But at least there was no noticeable sign of dust.

"I never had to be tidy until recently," she said. "I always had servants to do everything for me except breathe." Her hair had given her particular trouble in the last couple of weeks. She was unaccustomed to brushing and styling it herself. And why did dresses almost invariably have to open and close down the back, when one's elbows did not bend that way and one had no eyes in the back of one's head?

But why were they talking and thinking of such things, allowing awkwardness and self-consciousness to enter the room with them? She had made a decision, a very spur-of-the-moment one, it was true, for his suggestion had been totally unexpected, but she had no wish to go back on it. She had come to believe that for twenty-two years she had been only half alive, perhaps not even that much, that she had deliberately suppressed everything in herself that made her human. Now suddenly she wanted to *live*. And she wanted to love, even if that word was a mere euphemism for desire. She would live, then, and she would enjoy. She would not stop to think, to doubt, to feel awkward.

She turned toward him. He was looking steadily back as though giving her the chance to change her mind if she so wished. How could she ever have thought him anything less than gorgeous? His hair, very dark, like his eyes, had surely grown in just the two weeks since she had known him. His facial features were all suggestive of firmness and strength. His Italian lineage was very obvious in his looks, but so was his English lineage, though he looked nothing like the young woman in the portrait. It was not just his looks, though. Mild-mannered and soft-spoken though he was, and seemingly uninterested in male pursuits and vices, there was nevertheless something very solid about him and very male. She could not quite explain to herself what it was exactly and did not even try. She just felt it.

He was gorgeous and she wanted him. It was really as simple—and as shocking—as that. She did not care about the shocking part. She wanted to be free. She wanted to experience life.

"Camille," he said, "if you are having second thoughts . . ."

"I am not," she assured him, and took one step closer to him even as he took one toward her. "I want to go to bed with you."

He set his hands lightly on her shoulders and moved them down her arms. For a moment she regretted not being as slender and delicately feminine as Abby was—and as Anastasia was. But she brushed aside such foolish, self-doubting thoughts. She was a woman no matter what she looked like, and it was she he had asked to go to bed with him, not either of the other two. She slid her hands beneath his coat to rest on either side of his waist. His body was firm and warm.

He began to remove her hairpins, slowly and methodically, setting them down on the table beside the open book. She could have done it faster herself. So, probably, could he. But this was not about speed, she realized, or efficiency. This was about enjoying desire and building it—her first lesson in sensuality. Oh, she knew nothing about sensuality, and she wanted to know everything. All of it. She leaned into him, setting her bosom to the firm muscles of his chest, and holding his eyes with her own while his hands worked. She half smiled at him. Tension built in the room almost like a tangible thing.

"I am guessing," she said, "that you have some experience in all this. I hope so, because one of us needs to know what to do."

His hands stilled in her hair, and his eyes smiled back into hers while the rest of his face did not. It was a quite devastating expression, one that surely would only ever be appropriate in the bedchamber. It made her knees feel weak and the room seem a bit deficient in breathable air.

"I am not a virgin, Camille," he told her, and as he removed one more pin her hair came cascading down her back and over her shoulders. "My God. Your hair is beautiful."

She had not worn it down outside of her dressing room since she was twelve, but sometimes, in rare moments of vanity, she had thought that a pity. She had always thought her hair was her finest feature. It was thick and heavy and slightly wavy.

"*You* are beautiful," he said, his fingers playing through her hair, his eyes on hers.

She did not contradict him. She said something foolish instead, though she meant it and would not unsay it even if she could. "So are you," she said.

He cupped her face with his hands while she grasped his elbows, and he kissed her, his lips parted, his mouth lingering on hers, his tongue probing her lips and the flesh behind, entering her mouth, circling her own tongue, feathering over the roof of her mouth so that she felt a raw, purely physical ache of desire between her thighs and up inside her. He moved his hands behind her waist, pressed them lower to cup her buttocks, and drew her hard against him so that she could feel the shocking maleness of him, the physical evidence of his desire for her. Her own hands flailed to the sides for a moment and then settled on his upper arms.

"Mmm." He drew back a little and leaned beyond her to draw back the bedcovers. "Let me unclothe you."

She let him do it, did not try to help him, and did not allow herself to feel embarrassed as garments were peeled away one by one with tantalizing slowness. He was looking at her, drinking her in with eyes that grew heavier with desire. He had called her beautiful when all her clothes were on. She felt beautiful as they came off— beautiful in his eyes, anyway, and for now that was all that mattered. Her heart hammered in her chest and her body hummed with anticipation and her blood pulsed with desire.

Who would have thought it? Oh, who would? Not her, certainly. Not until . . . when? A few hours ago when she waltzed with him? A few days ago when she dashed laughing through the rain with him? A short while ago when she watched him look on his mother's face for the first time?

"Lie down," he said when she was wearing nothing at all and he was turning his attention to removing his own clothes.

She did not offer to unclothe him. She would not have known how to go about it. She lay on the bed instead, one knee bent, her foot flat on the mattress, one arm beneath her head. It did not even occur to her to pull the bedcovers over herself to hide her nakedness. He watched her as he undressed, his eyes roving over her, and she watched him.

His shoulders and arms were firmly muscled. So was his chest. It was lightly dusted with dark hair. He was narrow waisted, slim hipped, long legged. If he was imperfect, as she was, she was unaware of it and it would not have mattered anyway. He was Joel, and it was Joel she looked at, not any romantic ideal of the perfect male physique. She drew a slow breath when she saw the evidence of his desire for her, and for the first time she was afraid, though not with the sort of fear that might have had her leaping off the bed to grab up her clothes and bolt from the room. Rather, it was the sort of fear of the unknown that might just as accurately be described as an aching yearning for what she had never experienced before and was about to experience now.

She had never seen a picture of a Greek or Roman statue, because of course they had been sculpted nude, a shocking thing indeed and to be kept far from a lady's eyes. But he looked as she imagined those statues must look, except that he was a bronzed, living, breathing man while they would be cold white marble with sightless eyes, like those busts in the hall of Mr. Cox-Phillips's house. Perhaps he was perfect after all. His eyes, those eyes that could not possibly belong to any statue, were dark and hot upon her.

And then he lay down beside her, gathered her into his arms, and turned her against him. She felt all the shock of his warm, masculine nakedness against her own, but she was not about to shrink away from it now when the long, slow building of desire was at an end, and the urgent heat of passion and carnality was about to begin, and their hands began to explore and arouse, and their mouths met, open and hot and demanding. She was not going be a passive recipient either. All the longings and passions of her suppressed femininity welled up in her and spilled over as she made love with a fierce eagerness to match his own.

But ultimately she was shocked into stillness when his body covered hers, his weight bearing her down, his knees pressing between her thighs and spreading her legs, his hands coming beneath her buttocks. She twined her legs about his as he pressed against her entrance and came into her, slowly but firmly and not stopping until she felt stretched, until she feared there could be no deeper for him to come without terrible pain, until the pain happened, sudden and sharp, and there was indeed somewhere deeper for him to come and he came there, hard and thick, and her virginity was gone.

He slid his hands from beneath her and found her own hands and laced his fingers with hers on either side of her head. He raised his head to gaze into her eyes, his own heavy lidded and beautiful, his weight full on her. And he kissed her while her body adjusted to the unfamiliarity and she tightened inner muscles about him to own him and what was happening between them. She would never regret this, she thought quite deliberately. She would not no matter what conscience and common sense told her afterward. She felt as though she were awakening from a lifelong sleep during which she had dreamed but never been an active participant in her own life.

She thought he was leaving her body and almost cried out with protest and regret. But he withdrew only to return—of course. And it happened again and again and again until it settled into a firm, steady rhythm in which a slight soreness and a pounding sort of pleasure and the sucking sounds of wetness combined into an experience like no other, but one she did not want ever to end. And it did not for what might have been several minutes or only just two or three. But finally the rhythm became faster and deeper, and he released her hands in order to slide his own beneath her once more to hold her firm and still. Pleasure swirled from her core to fill her being, though she willed him not to stop yet, ah, not yet. She did not want the world to resume its plodding course with this behind her, all over, to be lived again only in memory.

He held firm and deep and strained against her so that almost, for a moment, oh, almost . . . But she did not find out what almost happened, for he sighed something wordless against the side of her head, and she felt a gush of heat deep within, and he relaxed down onto her. She wrapped her arms about him and closed her eyes and let herself relax too. *Almost* was good enough. Oh, very much good enough.

After a few all-too-short minutes he moved off her to lie beside her, one bare arm beneath her head, the other bent at the elbow and resting across his eyes. The late-afternoon air felt pleasantly cool against Camille's damp body. There was a soreness inside, though it was not unpleasant. He smelled faintly of sweat and more markedly and enticingly of something unmistakably male. She could sleep, she thought, if the bedcovers were over them, but she did not want to move to pull them up and perhaps disturb the lovely aftermath of passion.

"And I will not even be able to answer with righteous indignation," he said, "when Marvin waggles his eyebrows and makes suggestive remarks about this afternoon, as he surely will."

Camille felt suddenly chilled at the suggestion of sor-
didness.

"I am so sorry, Camille," he continued. "I ought to
have known I was feeling too needy today to risk asking
you to come here with me. You must not blame yourself.
You have been kindness itself. Promise me you will not
blame yourself?"

He removed his arm from his eyes and turned his head
to look at her. He was frowning and looking unhappy—
and guilty?—far different from the way she had been
feeling mere moments ago.

"Of course I will not blame myself," she said, sitting
up and swinging her legs over the far side of the bed. "Or
you either. It is something we did by mutual consent. I
wanted the experience and now I have had it. There is no
question of blame. I must be getting back home."

"Yes, you must," he said. "But thank you."

She felt self-conscious this time, pulling on her clothes
while he sat on the side of the bed and began to dress
himself. Self-conscious and chilly and suddenly unhappy.
If her education as a lady had taught her anything, it was
surely that men and women were vastly different from
one another, that men had needs that must be satisfied
with some frequency but did not in any way involve their
emotions.

What had she thought while they were making love—
Oh, that *was* a foolish, inappropriate phrase after all. But
what had she thought? That they were embarking upon
the great passion of the century? That they were in love?
She did not even believe in romantic love. And he certainly was not in love with her.

Neither of them spoke again until they were both out

in the hall, she tying the ribbons of her bonnet while he watched, and arranging her shawl about her shoulders and turning to the door. He reached past her to open it, but he did not do so immediately.

"I can see that I have upset you," he said. "I really am very sorry, Camille."

And she did something that was totally unplanned and totally without reason. She raised a hand and cracked him across the face with her open ungloved palm. And then she hurried from the room and down the stairs without a backward glance and without any clear idea of *why*.

Except that by apologizing and saying it ought not to have happened he had cheapened what for her had been perhaps the most beautiful experience of her life.

Oh, what an idiot she was! What a *naïve* idiot.

Fifteen

❧

Before the morning was half over Joel had tidied and cleaned his rooms, hung the portrait of his mother in what he thought the best spot on the living room wall, completed the painting of Mrs. Wasserman, walked to the market and back to replenish his supply of food, and decided that he was the world's worst sort of blackguard.

It had not been seduction—she had said herself that it was consensual. But it had felt uneasily like seduction after she left, for he had been needy and she had comforted him. Then she had slapped his face and rushed away before he could ask *why*. It was obvious why, though. She had regretted what she had done as soon as it was over and rational thought returned, and she had blamed him. It was not entirely fair, perhaps, but oh, he felt guilty.

He felt like the blackest hearted of villains.

Worse, he had remembered after she left that he had

promised to dine at Edwina's and spend the evening with her. He had gone there and stood in the small hallway inside her front door and ended it all with her, rather suddenly, rather abruptly, and without either sensitivity or tact. There had never been any real commitment between them and never any emotional tie stronger than friendship and a mutual enjoyment of sex, but he had felt horribly guilty anyway. She had had a meal ready for him, and she had been dressed prettily and smiling brightly. And she had behaved well and with dignity after he had delivered his brief, blunt, unrehearsed speech and made no attempt to keep him or demand that he explain himself. She had not slammed the door behind him.

Had there ever been a worse villain than he?

To end a perfectly delightful evening—though it had still been early—on his return he had run into Marvin Silver on the stairs and been grinned and leered at as he brushed past. He had felt . . . dirty.

It had not been the best day of his life.

Joel stood and brooded before his mother's portrait, wondering what he was supposed to do with himself for the rest of the day. Of course, there was that dinner engagement at the Royal York this evening. He grimaced at the very thought. He could go to the orphanage to apologize again to Camille, but he did not know quite what he would say, and he did not imagine she would be thrilled to see him. In other words, he could add abject cowardice to his other shortcomings. He could stay at home and sketch her—flushed and flustered and animated as she taught the children the Roger de Coverley; flushed and martial of spirit as she taught him the steps of the waltz; flushed and vividly triumphant a few minutes later after he had spun her recklessly through a turn. But when he tried to bring the images into focus, he could see her only as she had looked on his bed—gloriously, voluptuously naked and feminine with her hair down.

Make some stew?

That old man was dying. He could have no wish to set eyes upon Joel again, and he certainly would not want to be pestered with more questions. If Uxbury was still at the house—and he probably was—he would undoubtedly do all in his power to keep Joel out, and there might well be two other equally hostile family members there by now. Even the butler would be difficult to get past. Going back there, then, would be a pointless waste of time and money.

He went anyway.

He was certainly right about one thing, though. He did not see Mr. Cox-Phillips.

As the hired carriage drew up at the front of the house, the door was opening, coincidentally as it turned out, and a gangly young servant stepped outside, an armful of what looked like black crepe in his arms. The butler came after him and stood on the threshold, watching as the young man twined the black strips about the door knocker, presumably to muffle the sound of it. When Joel stepped down from the carriage, the butler looked up at him, his eyes bleak and quite noticeably reddened. Joel took two steps toward him and stopped.

"I am so sorry," he said.

The butler said nothing.

"When?" Joel asked.

"An hour ago," the butler told him.

"Did he suffer?" Joel's lips felt stiff.

"He was in the library," the butler told him, "where he insisted upon being brought every day. I was pouring his morning coffee when he told me not to bother if all I could bring him was swill that smelled like dirty dishwater. He scolded Mr. Orville for forgetting to wrap his blanket about his legs. When Mr. Orville informed him that it was already wrapped about him warm and tight, he looked at it, and then he looked surprised, and then he was gone. Just like that." He looked bewildered, and tears welled in his eyes.

"I am so sorry," Joel said again. If he had come yesterday . . . But he had not. He felt a curious sense of loss even though Mr. Cox-Phillips had been no more than a stranger who happened to be related to him. He had also told Joel his mother's name and given him a small portrait of her, and both were, Joel realized for the first time, priceless gifts. "I am sorry for your grief. Have you been with him long?"

"Fifty-four years," the butler said. "Mr. Orville is laying him out on his bed."

Joel nodded and turned back to the carriage. He was stopped, however, by another voice, haughty and imperious.

"You again, fellow?" Viscount Uxbury asked. "You have come begging again, I suppose, but you are too late, I am happy to inform you. Take yourself off before I have you thrown off my property."

Joel turned back to look curiously at him and wondered briefly who would do the throwing. The butler? The thin young man who had finished with the strips of black crepe and was ducking back into the house behind the butler? Uxbury himself? And *my property*? It had taken him less than an hour to claim it for himself, had it? Joel wondered what the other two claimants would have to say about that.

"You left your doxy behind today, did you?" Uxbury said.

"You have just suffered a family bereavement," Joel told him. "Out of respect for the late Mr. Cox-Phillips and his faithful servants, I will let that gross insult to a lady pass by me, Uxbury. But take care never to repeat it or anything like it in my hearing again. I might feel obliged to rearrange the features on your face. You may proceed," he added to the grinning coachman as he turned back to the carriage and climbed inside.

It would surely be false self-indulgence to feel bereaved over the death of a stranger. He felt bereaved anyway.

Camille rearranged her room. She hung the Madonna-and-child sketch over the table and stood looking at it for a few minutes. She toyed with her breakfast and ate it only because she would not waste food in such a place. She played the pianoforte in the playroom and sang with the handful of children who clustered about her, four girls and two boys.

She took Sarah out into the garden and sat on a blanket with her, playing with her, tickling her to make her laugh, rubbing noses with her, talking nonsense to her, and otherwise making an idiot of herself. Winifred joined them and earnestly informed her how important it was for babies to be played with and touched and held even if they would not remember it when they grew older.

After Sarah had fallen asleep and been taken indoors,

Camille turned one handle of a long skipping rope while a succession of girls and one boy jumped through it. She even joined in the strange chant that was the accompaniment to the jumping. Winifred informed her that she was a good sport.

When several of the children asked her what they were going to knit now that the purple rope was completed, she suggested a baby blanket made of squares, and, after a visit to Miss Ford's office, she went off to the wool shop with one boy and two girls to purchase supplies. Winifred, who was inevitably one of them, informed her she included Miss Westcott in her nightly prayers because she was a good and caring person.

The child was getting on Camille's nerves with her everlasting righteousness. She was not exactly unpopular with the other children, though she had no particular friend. But Camille had been somewhat horrified to recognize something of herself in the girl, and she wondered *why* she was as she was. Was she trying to be very good, even perfect, so that someone would love her? And having the opposite effect upon people than she hoped for? The thought somehow hurt Camille's heart.

She did a thousand and one other things during the course of the day, including one quiet half hour of reading in her room, during which time she did not turn a single page. She wrote to Abby, remembered that she would be seeing her this evening, and tore the letter up.

And all through her busy, restless day, her mind was plagued by two things. *Yesterday*—she tried not to let her thoughts stray beyond that one word. And *tonight*. She had not seen most of her father's family since that disastrous day that had changed her life forever. She dreaded seeing them again. Yet all day she resisted the temptation to hurry up to the Royal Crescent to choose something more elegant to wear than anything she had with her in her room—and to beg her grandmother's personal maid to dress her hair becomingly.

Her heart was pounding by a little before seven o'clock, when she was ushered into the private dining room at the Royal York Hotel, for which reason she held herself stiffly erect, her chin raised, her features schooled into a mask of gentility. The room was already full of people, most of whom got to their feet and greeted her with hearty enthusiasm. But Camille saw only one of them.

"Camille." Her mother was hurrying toward her, both hands outstretched.

"Mother!" There was a moment when they might have hugged each other, but her mother's arms were stretched to the front rather than to the sides and they clasped hands instead. Rather than a joyful embrace, there was a strange awkwardness. And Camille heard the word she had used—*Mother*—as though there were an echo in the room. Not *Mama*. "You came."

"I did," her mother said, squeezing her hands tightly while her eyes searched Camille's face. "It seemed like a good idea to see my daughters again and celebrate your grandmama's birthday at the same time. I arrived this afternoon."

"Can you believe it?" Abigail, eyes shining with happiness, hugged Camille. "I was never more surprised in my life."

But Camille had no chance to respond except to hug her sister in return. Others were crowding about and telling her how well she looked and how delighted they were to see her, and everyone was hearty and smiling and probably as uncomfortable as Camille.

Aunt Mildred and Uncle Thomas—Lord and Lady Molenor—had arrived earlier in the day. They were a placid, good-natured couple, except when their boys got into one of their not-infrequent scrapes, and showed no outward sign of fatigue after the long journey from the north of England. They soon appropriated Camille's mother and sat conversing with her. Aunt Mildred was holding her hand, Camille could see. The former sisters-in-law had once enjoyed a close friendship. Aunt Louise, the Dowager Duchess of Netherby, and Cousin Jessica, her daughter, had been here since the day before yesterday, having left Morland Abbey at the same time as Avery and Anastasia and the latter's grandparents. Jessica and Abigail were soon sitting happily next to each other, their heads nearly touching as they talked. It looked quite like old times.

And oh, it *was* good to see them all again, Camille thought. Despite everything, they were family.

Cousin Althea had arrived yesterday morning with Alexander, the Earl of Riverdale, her son, and Cousin Elizabeth, Lady Overfield, her daughter. Aunt Louise and Cousin Elizabeth, Anastasia and Avery settled into conversation with one another while Alexander drew out a chair from the table for Camille, though dinner was apparently not to be served for another fifteen or twenty minutes yet.

"I hope," he said as he seated himself beside her, "you do not bear any lasting grudge against me, Camille."

"Why should I?" she asked him, though the answer was, of course, obvious.

"I took the title away from Harry," he said.

"No," she assured him, "you did no such thing. My father did that when he wed Mama while he was still married to Anastasia's mother. Nothing that has happened was your fault, Alexander."

"You must know," he said, "that I never, ever coveted the title and looked forward to the day when young Harry married and produced a dozen sons and removed me far from the awkward position of being the heir. I wish a simple refusal could have solved everything." His smile was a bit rueful.

Cousin Alexander was an extremely handsome man, and tall and dark too—the three requirements for the quintessential prince of fairy tales. He was also a thoroughly likable person. Perhaps it was that fact that had stopped Camille from resenting him as she had Anastasia, who was equally blameless. Not that she had ever given her half sister the opportunity to be likable or not.

"Even if I could have refused the title, though," he said, "it would not have remained with Harry. I understand he was wounded in the Peninsula but is making a swift recovery?"

"So he claims," she said. "We have heard nothing from any official source—which is probably good news in itself."

"Camille," he said earnestly, "I think I can understand how badly you have been hurt, though it may seem presumptuous of me to say so. I daresay I do not know the half of it, but I admire what you are doing, standing on your own feet, earning your own living, even going to do it at the very place where Anna grew up. But . . . may I make a suggestion?"

"If I were to say no," she said somewhat stiffly, "I would wonder for the rest of the night what it was you wished to suggest."

He smiled. "You are much loved by your grandmother and aunts," he said, "and by the rest of us too. You always have been. You cannot be cast out of the family now at this late date just because circumstances have changed. You cannot suddenly become unloved. Your own personal way forward, as well as Harry's and Abigail's, is more difficult than it was, of course. No one can deny that much has changed forever in your lives. But will you not draw some comfort from the fact that you are still loved, that your position as granddaughter and niece and cousin in this family has in no way been diminished, that we are all here to support you in every way we are able? Individually we all wield power and influence. Together we are quite formidable, and I would not envy anyone who attempted to thwart our will. Let yourself be loved, Camille. Let . . . No, I will leave it at that, for really that does say everything. Let yourself be loved."

"I was unaware," she said, "that I had told anyone to stop loving me, Alexander. But enough of me. What difference to your life has being the Earl of Riverdale made? Have you made Brambledean your home?"

Although it was the earl's principal seat, Brambledean Court had never been a favorite of Camille's father. Neither he nor they had spent much time there, and he had not spent a great deal of money on its upkeep either. Both house and park had fallen into somewhat of a dilapidated state and all but the barest minimum of servants had been let go. There was a steward, but he had never been diligent in his duties. Camille had heard that the farms were not prospering as they ought and that there was discontent among the tenant farmers and actual hardship and suffering among the laborers. Alexander had inherited it with the title, while Papa's fortune, which might have helped him run it, had gone to Anastasia with everything else that was not entailed.

"Not yet," he said, "though I have spent some time there. Somehow I am going to have to find a way to—"

But he was prevented from saying more by the arrival of Joel and the attention Anastasia drew to him when she exclaimed with delight, jumped to her feet, and hurried toward him to take his arm and introduce him to those who had not already met him. He was looking distinctly uncomfortable, Camille thought, at having been forced to walk into a roomful of aristocratic strangers only to have everyone's attention focused upon him. He was dressed suitably for an evening occasion, though he looked only slightly less shabby than he normally did.

Unconsciously Camille flexed her right hand beneath the table. She could still feel the sting of the slap she had dealt him yesterday. She had probably hurt her hand at least as much as she had his face. She had hit him because he had apologized again, because he had assumed that there was something to apologize for. And thus he had ruined her memories of what had happened, had made it seem like a sordid mistake, for which he had assumed the entire blame. He had hurt her far more deeply than her slap could have hurt him, though she had despised herself ever since for allowing herself to be hurt. He was neither as handsome as Alexander nor as magnificent as Avery nor as amiable as Uncle Thomas. How could she *possibly* have allowed him to hurt her?

She gazed at him, hot cheeked and tight lipped, and paradoxically a bit cold in the head as though she were in danger of fainting. *Nonsense,* she thought, pulling herself together. *Absolute nonsense!*

Anastasia presented him to Alexander.

"Riverdale," he said, and inclined his head in acknowledgment of the introduction before turning his eyes upon Camille. They were grave and very dark. He looked as if perhaps he had not slept well last night. Good. She was glad. "Camille."

"Joel." But there was something else. She could sense it as soon as their eyes met. There was more than embarrassment and remorse in his eyes. *What is the matter?* She almost asked the question aloud.

Dinner was served soon after his arrival, and the conversation while they ate was lively and general. Aunt Mildred spoke of the exploits of her boys through the summer; Jessica talked about her debut Season next year and Avery remarked with a sigh that he supposed she expected that he and Anastasia would arrange a grand ball for her at Archer House; Mama told a few stories about her life with Uncle Michael at the vicarage in Dorsetshire; Aunt Louise commented upon what perfect dears the Reverend and Mrs. Snow, Anastasia's maternal grandparents, were and how she had enjoyed their company at Morland Abbey during the past couple of months; Camille recounted a few anecdotes from the schoolroom; Abigail described the sittings she had had with Joel while he sketched her and prepared to paint her portrait; and Joel, in answer to Elizabeth's questions, described the process by which he produced portraits of his subjects.

It was only after the covers had been removed from

the table and coffee and port served that they all sat back, more at their ease, and divided into smaller conversational groups. After a few minutes, during which Uncle Thomas had been expressing his hope to Camille and Cousin Althea that he and Aunt Mildred could remain at home for at least a year after they returned there in two weeks' time, Camille heard Anastasia ask the question that had been bothering her all evening.

"What is it, Joel?" she asked. "Something is troubling you."

"Do I look as if something is?" he asked in return.

"Yes, indeed," she said. "I know you well, remember."

Camille felt annoyed with herself for feeling stabbed to the heart—and for shamelessly listening while Uncle Thomas continued to talk to Cousin Althea.

"I must admit to having been a bit shaken this morning," Joel said. "I went to call on a very sick old man of my acquaintance, only to discover that he had died an hour before I got there. Ever since I have been berating myself for not going yesterday."

"Oh, Joel!" Camille's words, from several places down the table, were startled out of her. "Mr. Cox-Phillips has died?"

"Yes," he said, glancing bleakly her way. "An hour before I got there. His butler was upset. He had tears in his eyes. I beg your pardon," he added, looking about at everyone else, obviously uncomfortable with having become the focus of attention again. "This is not a topic for such an occasion."

"But how very distressing that must have been for you," Elizabeth said. "Was he a particular friend of yours, Mr. Cunningham?"

"He was my great-uncle," he said after a brief hesitation. "My grandmother's brother."

"Joel?" Anastasia leaned closer to him across the table, her eyes wide. "Your *great-uncle*? Your *grandmother*?"

"He invited me to call," Joel explained. "I assumed he wished to discuss some painting commission with me, but when I went earlier this week, he told me it was his now-deceased sister who took me to the orphanage as a baby after my mother died in childbed. So you see, Anna, you are not the only one to have discovered your parentage this year."

"Cox-Phillips." Aunt Louise frowned in thought. "He used to be in the government in some capacity, did he not? Netherby—my husband—had an acquaintance with him. I had assumed him to be long deceased. Not that I have spared a thought for him in years, I must confess. If memory serves me correctly, though, he was some connection of Viscount Uxbury's. I remember hearing it when Uxbury began to show an interest in Camille."

It seemed to Camille that everyone—except Avery—determinedly did not look her way.

Avery, unapologetically resplendent in satin and lace long after they had passed out of fashion with most other gentlemen, sat at his elegant ease, a glass of port in one hand, a jeweled quizzing glass in the other, his smooth blond hair like a shining halo about his head. His heavy-lidded eyes were fixed upon Camille.

"Yes, he was," Joel said. "Uxbury is there at the house now."

"The less said about him, the better," Aunt Mildred said. "I do not feel at all kindly toward that young man."

"He must be Cox-Phillips's heir, then," Avery said.

"That could be unwelcome news to you, Camille, though I do not suppose he will spend any great amount of time here as your near neighbor. He does not strike me as the sort to make his permanent home in Bath."

"Perhaps," Camille said, "he will be discouraged by the possibility that you will come to my defense again, Avery, with your bare feet."

His eyes gleamed with appreciation, and his hand closed about the handle of his quizzing glass. "Ah, you have heard about that slight episode, have you?" he said.

"What is this about bare feet?" Aunt Louise asked sharply.

"You would not wish to know, Louise," Uncle Thomas said firmly. "More to the point, you would not wish Jessica or Abigail to know."

"Know what?" Jessica cried, leaning forward across the table to fix her eager gaze upon her half brother. "What did you do to Viscount Uxbury, Avery? I hope you punched him in the nose without first removing any of your rings. I hope you ran him through the ribs with the point of your sword. I hope you shot him—"

"That is quite enough, Jessica," Aunt Louise said sternly.

"He is a thoroughly nasty man, Aunt Louise," Anastasia said, "and I can only applaud Jessica's bloodthirsty wishes for his fate. He was horrid to me at my first ball and he was horrid about Camille—worse, in fact, because he had been betrothed to her. I am so *glad,* Camille, that you escaped his clutches in time, though I daresay you were unhappy at the time. Avery avenged you, and I do not care how many ladies know how he did it and are shocked. And if Avery had not avenged you, then Alex would have. They love you."

There was a brief silence about the table as Anastasia looked at Camille and Camille frowned back at her. She blinked, feeling that hotness behind her eyes that sometimes presaged tears. She nodded curtly.

"I am not shocked," her mother said. "I am enchanted."

"But . . . bare feet, Avery?" Abigail said.

"You see," he said softly, raising his glass to his eye to survey her through it and sounding horribly bored in that annoying way of his, "I had no choice. I had removed my boots. And my stockings."

"Mr. Cunningham," Aunt Mildred said, "accept my congratulations at having discovered your identity at last and my commiserations at your loss of your great-uncle so soon after you found him."

And everyone's attention returned to Joel.

"Thank you, ma'am," he said.

Sixteen

After having felt a great deal of nervous apprehension about walking in upon a family gathering of such illustrious persons, most of whom he had not met before, Joel had found his welcome gracious, even warm. He might have almost enjoyed the evening if Camille had not been there, looking a bit like a regal Amazon, to make it impossible for him to put aside his great sense of guilt, at least for a few hours. Fortunately, perhaps, dinner was served soon after his arrival, and he had found himself seated between Lady Overfield and Lady Molenor, with Anna across from him and Camille farther along the table on the same side as he, where he need not be constantly looking at her.

But he did need to talk to her, to apologize again, to try to clear the air between them if at all possible. They still had to share a schoolroom occasionally, after all, and he had to paint her portrait. Besides, yesterday might have had consequences, and he would not close his mind to the possibility, just as he had not—to his shame—even yesterday. He knew a great deal about illegitimate, unwanted children, and neither of those adjectives would ever apply to any child of his.

His chance came when the former Countess of Riverdale, Camille's mother, decided that it was time she and her younger daughter returned home and Netherby raised a hand—actually it was one languid forefinger—to summon a servant and instruct him to have the ducal carriage brought around.

"It will deliver Camille to Northumberland Place first, if that meets with your approval, Aunt Viola," he said, "before taking you and Abigail up to the Royal Crescent."

"It really is not far for me to walk," Camille said.

"Nevertheless," Netherby said with a sort of haughty weariness, clearly expecting that the one word was enough to settle the matter. It never ceased to amaze Joel that Anna had married him. He was all splendor and affectation. However, Joel knew there was a great deal more to the Duke of Netherby than met the eye. There were those Far Eastern martial arts he had perfected, for example, which apparently made him into a lethal human weapon. And there was the fact that he loved Anna, though that was not something that had particularly endeared him to Joel at first.

"I will be passing Northumberland Place on my way home," Joel said. "I will happily give you my escort to your door, Camille, unless you prefer to ride."

Anna beamed across the table at him, and Lady Overfield

turned her head toward him and smiled too for no apparent reason.

"I will walk home with Joel, Avery," Camille said stiffly.

Joel stood exchanging pleasantries with Lord Molenor while she took her leave of her relatives and promised her mother that she would walk up to the Royal Crescent tomorrow afternoon.

"I shall probably see you there, Camille," Anna said. "I know that Aunt Louise and Aunt Mildred want to call upon Aunt Viola. There is something I wish to tell you."

Camille gave a brief, chilly nod, Joel saw.

The outside air had cooled with the descent of darkness, but it was still almost warm. The stars were bright. There was not a breath of wind. The silence of the street seemed loud after the clamor of voices in the dining room.

"You were not expecting to see your mother?" Joel asked, clasping his hands behind his back as they walked.

"I was not," she said. "I did not believe she would come at all. She gave no hint of it in the letter she wrote me this week. She feels herself to be an outsider."

"Yet she must have been a close member of the West-cott family for more than twenty years," he said. "She still is in the minds of the others. That was clear to see. So are you and your sister."

"Alexander said a strange thing to me before dinner," she told him, "and before you arrived. It was in the nature of a suggestion—that I allow myself to be loved. I have never thought before about the difference between loving and being loved, though I learned early in my schooling the distinction between the active and passive voices of verbs. I think I have always behaved in the active voice. It is easier to do something oneself than wait for someone else to do it. One might wait forever, and even if one did not, the thing might not be done as well as one could do it oneself. I have always liked to be in control. It is easier to love than wait to be loved—or to trust that love even if it is offered."

"You love your Westcott relatives, then?" he said.

"Yes, of course," she said, shrugging. "Though I tend to avoid using the word *love,* for it is used to cover a multitude of different emotions and attitudes, is it not? They are my family. The fact that I will no longer allow myself to be dependent upon them does not alter that."

"Was the Earl of Riverdale suggesting that you do not allow them to love you in return even though they wish to do so?" he asked.

"I do not know what that *means,*" she said.

He remembered her telling him that throughout her girlhood she had craved her father's love, that she had tried to shape herself into the sort of perfect lady he would love. She had been far more damaged by that man than she realized. The fact that he had knowingly made her illegitimate was the least of his sins against her.

"It was clear to me tonight," he said, "perhaps because I am indeed an outsider and could judge dispassionately, that your family members have been hurt by what has happened to you and your mother and sister and brother. The pain they feel is perhaps the deeper for the fact that they feel largely helpless to lessen your burden. They want to cherish you and make your lives easier again, less painful, but there are limits to what they can do. They can and do love you, however. Your sister seems willing to accept that. You and your mother hold yourselves more aloof, and it hurts both yourselves and them."

She did not immediately reply, and he listened to their footsteps on the silent, deserted street.

"Not that it is any of my business," he said belatedly.

"I must do this alone," she said. "I *need* to do it alone."

"I know," he said, and he unclasped his hands and reached out without conscious thought to take one of hers. "But perhaps you can find some sort of middle ground. Perhaps you are already doing it, in fact. You went to spend the evening with them tonight. Tomorrow you are going to see some of them again at your grandmother's house. Then afterward you will return to your room at the orphanage, and on Monday you will teach again. Independence and an acceptance of love offered need not be mutually exclusive."

She did not snatch her hand away as he half expected she would. Her fingers curled about his instead.

"But what on earth am I doing, talking about myself?" she said suddenly. "What about you, Joel? You went back up to that house again today? I am so sorry you were too late. You must have felt wretched. Strange as it may sound, I rather liked Mr. Cox-Phillips. I think you did too even though you had good reason not to. You must be feeling some grief. I saw in your face as soon as you arrived this evening that something had happened."

Just as Anna had. He squeezed her hand. "With my head I cannot grieve," he said. "But the head does not always rule the heart, does it? His stiff, impassive butler was shedding tears, Camille, and a younger servant was wrapping the door knocker in black crepe. Someone had died—someone related to me when all my life I have assumed I would never discover anyone of my own. Crusty as he was, he gave me what I believe will always remain the most precious gift I have ever received. He gave me the portrait of my mother. And he was a . . . person. Yes, I feel bereaved and bereft and foolish."

"Oh, not foolish," she said, turning her head to look at him. "He sent for you before it was too late. He even admitted you a second time though you had rejected his plan for a new will the first time. He answered your questions even though he was very ill. And yes, he remembered your mother's portrait and gave it to you."

But they were close to the orphanage, and he must speak about what was surely uppermost in both their minds. He stopped walking and took her other hand in his. "Camille," he asked her, "why did you slap my face? What happened was not seduction . . . was it?"

She drew a sharp breath and snatched her hands away. "No, it was not," she said, enunciating each word clearly. "But when you apologized, you made it seem that *you* thought it was. It cheapened what had happened. And it made me feel that I must have seemed frigid or been totally inadequate if you could have so misunderstood. I was upset. More than that, I was angry."

Good God, he *had* misunderstood, but not for either of the reasons she had suggested.

"I thought you generous and giving and kind," he said. "You once asked me to hold you, but I asked much more of you. I feared I had taken advantage of you and you might regret and resent that I had demanded so much.

Camille, you might be *with child*. I might have done that to you. I might have forced you into a marriage you would not dream of entering into of your own free will."

She had clasped her hands at her waist and was staring at him. He could not see in the darkness whether she had turned pale, but he would wager she had.

"You did not even think of that, did you?" he asked her. "That you might be with child."

"Of course—" she began, but she did not finish what she had started to say.

"No," he said. "I did not think you had."

"Of course I did," she protested. "Oh, of course I did. How could I not?"

She turned to walk onward, and he fell into step beside her. What had their lovemaking meant to her? She had slapped him because his apologies had cheapened what had happened. Cheapened what? She surely could not have had any deeper feelings for him than sympathy and the desire to comfort. Could she?

And what had their lovemaking meant to him? Had he merely reached blindly for someone to hold him—in the ultimate embrace? Blindly? Would any woman have done, then? And if the answer was no, as it assuredly was, then what did that mean? What did it say about his feelings for her?

"You will let me know immediately if you discover there are consequences?" he said, his voice low. "We have both suffered illegitimacy though in different ways. We both know how it can devastate a life. We will neither of us condemn a child of ours to that, Camille. Promise me?"

They were outside the door of the orphanage, and she

turned to him, her face expressionless, her manner devoid of any of the roles she adopted to fit various circumstances. The silence stretched for several moments.

"I promise," she said. "I am tired, Joel, and you must be too. Thank you for walking home with me."

He nodded, but before he could turn away she raised both hands and cupped his face and kissed him softly on the lips.

"You have nothing about which to feel guilty, Joel," she said, her voice suddenly fierce. "*Nothing.* You are a decent man and I am more sorry than I can say that Mr. Cox-Phillips died before you could know him better. But at least you did know him, and through him you know more about your parents and grandparents and yourself. You are less alone than you have always felt even if none of them are still alive. Take comfort. There *is* comfort. I think I began to learn that for myself this evening. There *is* comfort."

And she turned without another word, opened the door with her key, and stepped inside before closing the door quietly behind her.

Joel was left standing on the pavement with—the devil!—tears burning his eyes.

There is *comfort.*

Camille awoke early the following morning and was immediately surprised that she had slept at all. The last thing she remembered from last night was putting her head down on the pillow. All the events of the last couple of days that might have teemed through her mind and kept her tossing and turning all night must have actually exhausted her to the point of rendering her almost comatose instead.

She got up filled with energy, washed and dressed, and went to an early church service. When she returned she spent a while in the schoolroom preparing a reading lesson that could be adapted to each age group tomorrow morning. And then she had breakfast in the dining room. There she learned that Sarah had had a restless night as two teeth pushed up on her lower gums and made them red and swollen. Her housemother was pacing one of the visitor parlors with her when Camille found them. The child was thrashing about in her arms, wailing and refusing to be consoled. She turned her head when Camille appeared, and held out her arms.

Camille had no idea how to comfort a baby who was feverish and cross and in pain and probably desperately tired too. But she must do something. She took the blanket in which the child had become entangled, shook it out and spread it on the sofa, and took Sarah from Hannah's arms to lay her on it before wrapping it tightly about her.

"She won't keep it on her," Hannah warned. "She will tire you out in no time, Miss Westcott."

"Perhaps," Camille agreed. "But you look exhausted. Go and have some breakfast and relax for a while."

Hannah hurried away as though fearful Camille would change her mind. Camille picked up the baby, smiling into her eyes as she did so, and proceeded to rock her with vigorous swings of her arms. Sarah stopped crying, though her face was still drawn into a frown.

"Shhh." Camille lifted her a little higher in her arms and smiled at her again. "Hush now, sweetheart." She searched her mind for a lullaby, could not think of a single one—perhaps she had never known any—and hummed instead the waltz tune to which she and Joel had danced a couple of days ago, an hour or two before they made love.

Sarah gazed fixedly at her until her eyelids began to droop and finally closed altogether and remained closed. Camille rocked her for a while longer before lowering herself gingerly onto a chair. She held the soft, warm, sleeping bundle to her bosom and swallowed against what felt very like a lump in her throat.

Let yourself be loved.

Sarah, who was growing more responsive to the other people at the orphanage, was nevertheless a quiet baby who did not smile or gurgle a great deal, even when she was not cutting teeth, and did not demand attention. Yet whenever Camille appeared in the playroom, her face lit up with recognition, and she either smiled broadly or held out her arms, or both.

Sarah loved her. It was not just that Camille had grown fond of the child to such a degree that she looked forward each day to seeing her, to holding her and talking to her. No, it was not just a one-way sort of affection. *Sarah loved her.*

Joel had mentioned something last night that she had quickly pushed from her mind, just as she had when it occurred to her after they had been to bed together. She had even promised last night that she would tell him without delay if she discovered that there was a need for them to marry. She did not believe it would be necessary. What were the odds that during one lovemaking she had conceived? They were slim to none. Well, perhaps not none. But they were slim nevertheless. But what if . . .

What if within a year—within nine months—she had a child of her own to hold like this? Her own and Joel's. No, she could not possibly wish for it, could she? She was not the maternal sort.

Yet now she longed, she yearned . . .

But would a child of her own replace Sarah in her heart? Could one love replace another? Or did love expand to encompass another person, and another, and on and on without end? She had never thought about love. She had always dismissed it as part of the uncertain chaos that threatened from just beyond the boundaries of her ordered, disciplined, very correct existence. There was love of mother and siblings and other family members, of course. There was love of *father.* But those loves, or *that love*—was love ever plural? Or was it only and ever singular? Those loves had been all tied up with duty in her mind and had never been allowed the freedom to touch her heart.

Would her life have been different if Papa had loved her? Papa had never allowed himself to be loved, and his life had been hugely impoverished as a result. How much was she her father's daughter?

Let yourself be loved, Alexander had said.

There was a tap on the door and it opened to reveal Abigail and their mother. Camille's eyes widened as they stepped inside the room.

"Camille?" her mother said softly. "We were told you were in here with a feverish baby."

Abigail had come hurrying across the room to peer down at the baby, a soft smile of delight on her face. "Oh, Cam," she said, "she is adorable. Just look at those plump cheeks."

"She is teething," Camille explained, "and kept her housemother up most of the night. I have just rocked her to sleep."

Her mother had come closer too to look at the baby and then to gaze steadily at Camille. "And you felt obliged to give her caregiver a chance to have some breakfast and relaxation, Camille?" she said.

"She has taken a fancy to me," Camille told them almost apologetically. "Sarah, that is—the baby. And I must confess I have taken a fancy to her. I was not expecting you. I was to come up to Grandmama's this afternoon to call on you."

"And I beg you to come anyway," her mother said, seating herself on the sofa. "But there will be other visitors, and I wanted you—both of you—to myself for a while."

Abigail went to sit beside her.

"You resent my coming back here," their mother said. She was still speaking softly in deference to the sleeping baby.

"Oh no, Mama," Abigail protested.

Her mother reached out to cover her clasped hands with one of her own. "I was referring to Camille," she said. "You were not entirely happy to see me last evening, Camille."

Oh, she had been, had she not? She had been happy, but also . . . resentful? Her mother had always been perfect in her eyes, the person above all others she had tried to emulate. But there was no such thing as perfection in human nature. Her mother had become human to her in the last few months, and it was something of a jolt to the sensibilities. Parents were not supposed to be human.

They were supposed to be . . . one's parents. What a foolish thought.

"Abby was and is eighteen, Mama," she said. "Only just out of the schoolroom, not yet launched upon society. She had recently lost Papa and had just learned the terrible truth about herself. She had just seen Harry lose everything and go off to war. And I—" She swallowed. "I had just been spurned by the man I had expected to marry."

"And I went away," her mother said, "and left you both here alone with only your grandmother to comfort you."

"Oh, Mama," Abigail said. "Grandmama has been wonderful to us. And you explained why you must leave. You did it for us, so that we would not so obviously be seen as the daughters of someone who had never actually been married. I still do not believe people would have judged you so harshly, but you did it for our sakes."

Their mother squeezed Abigail's hands and gazed at Camille. "That is what I told you," she said. "It is what I told myself too. I am not sure, however, that even at the time I deceived myself into believing I spoke the truth. The truth was that I had to get away, not quite to be alone, perhaps, since I went to your uncle Michael's, but away from . . . you. I could not bear the burden of being your mother and seeing your worlds come crashing about your ears. I could not bear to see your suffering. I had too much of my own to deal with. So I left you in order to nurse my own misery. It was terribly selfish of me."

"No, Mama," Abigail protested.

Camille looked down at Sarah, who was fussing slightly though she was still sleeping. "Have you come back to stay?" she asked.

"But Uncle Michael needs you," Abigail said.

"No." Her mother smiled. "He was doing very well without me, and he is launched, I believe, on a very gentle, very gradual courtship of a lady who is currently employed as a governess. My presence at the vicarage has probably slowed its course, and that is a great pity, for I believe they are truly fond of each other."

"You are here to stay, then," Camille said, "because you feel you ought to leave there." Her tone was more bitter than she had intended.

Her mother sighed. "I am not as penniless as I thought," she said. "I have heard from Mr. Brumford—your father's solicitor, if you will recall, and Harry's after him. It would seem that the dowry I took to my wedding is to be returned to me since the wedding never actually took place, not in any legal form anyway. It was a sizable sum, and it has gained considerable interest in almost a quarter of a century. It is not a vast fortune, but it is certainly enough to enable me to live independently with my daughters, either here in Bath or elsewhere."

"Is this part of the money that went to Anastasia a few months ago?" Camille asked sharply.

Her mother hesitated. "Yes," she said. "But it has been judged to be mine, not hers. She certainly will not miss it. She still has the bulk of your father's fortune. And she is married to Avery."

"Did you protest the will?" Camille asked.

"No," her mother said. "The news came as a surprise to me."

Camille stared at her. The money had come from Anastasia, then. She had found a way to give them some of her fortune without making them feel beholden to her.

She had found a way to give some of her fortune *to Mama*. At first she had wanted to divide her entire fortune four ways to include Camille and Abigail and Harry—they had all refused—but had made no mention of Mama beyond suggesting that she and they continue to live at Hinsford Manor, which she now owned.

Her mother cut her eyes to Abigail without moving her head and then looked pointedly back at Camille. She had thought of it too, then. But she had decided to accept the money anyway, so that she could provide a home again for herself and her daughters. And perhaps she was right to accept. It seemed just. The dowry had been paid by Grandpapa Kingsley on Mama's wedding to Papa. But there had been no real wedding. Papa had not been entitled to that money. Therefore, Anastasia was not entitled to it either or the interest it had gained over the years.

"We are going to live together again, Mama?" Abigail asked, her voice painful with hope.

"Would you like that?" their mother asked. "It would be nothing as grand as the house on the Royal Crescent."

Two tears trickled down Abigail's cheeks. "I would like it," she said. "If it is what *you* want, Mama."

Mama smiled at her and squeezed her hands again.

"I will remain here," Camille said, smoothing a hand over Sarah's head as she fussed quietly again.

"I understand," their mother said. "I honor you and what you are doing, Camille."

Camille lifted her head and looked at her. "I am glad you have come," she said. It would take a shift in her thinking to see her mother as a person rather than just as her mother and Abby's and Harry's. But everything in her life these days was causing a shift in her thinking. She wondered if life would ever be a stable thing again.

Sarah opened her eyes and gathered herself to express her displeasure vocally. But her gaze focused upon Camille and she smiled broadly instead.

"Hello, sweetheart," Camille said, and bent her head to kiss her cheek.

Her mother and sister gazed in silence.

Seventeen

※

Aunt Louise had gone with Aunt Mildred and Uncle Thomas to call upon an old acquaintance they had met at church during the morning, Camille was informed when she arrived at the house on the Royal Crescent during the afternoon. Alexander had taken Grandmama and Mama and his own mother for a drive out to Beechen Cliff with the argument that the weather was too fine to be wasted indoors. Elizabeth, Jessica, Anastasia, and Avery were at the house with Abigail.

Avery soon maneuvered Elizabeth over to the drawing room window—by design?—and the two of them stood there, talking and looking out and pointing to various things outside. Abigail and Jessica were seated side by side on the sofa. Camille took a chair close to them and Anastasia joined them. It was brave of her, Camille had to admit silently to herself. She and Abigail were the half sisters who had spurned her advances of sibling affection, and even Jessica, who was her sister-in-law and lived with her and Avery as well as Aunt Louise, had resented her at first and perhaps still did.

It was all unfair, of course. Although Anastasia now dressed expensively, she certainly made no parade of her wealth. She dressed with simple, understated elegance. And she behaved with quiet dignity. She was also looking pretty and happy if a little uncertain at the moment. It was increasingly difficult to dislike her. And a bit impossible not to.

"I hoped I would have the opportunity of a private word with my sisters this afternoon," she said, first glancing Avery's way and then looking at them each in turn. "We will be making some sort of announcement to the whole family this week, but I wanted the three of you to be first to know that Avery and I are expecting a child and that we are ecstatically happy about it. We do hope you will be pleased too at the prospect of being aunts."

They all stared at her as though transfixed by shock. But it was really not so surprising. Anastasia and Avery had been married for a few months, and there was a certain look about Anastasia, a glow of contentment and physical well-being that should have spoken for itself. Such an announcement from one sister to three others should surely be eliciting squeals of excited delight, but Jessica looked rather as though she had been punched on the chin, Camille felt like a mere observer, and Abigail—ah, dear Abby!—was recovering herself. She set her hands prayer fashion against her lips and smiled slowly and radiantly around her fingers until even her eyes sparkled.

"Oh, Anastasia," she said with quiet warmth, "how absolutely wonderful! I am so pleased for you. And thank you for telling us first. That was terribly sweet of you. Goodness, I am going to be Aunt Abigail. But that makes me sound quite elderly. I shall insist upon Aunt Abby. Oh, do tell us—do you hope for a boy or a girl? But of course you must wish for a boy, an heir to the dukedom."

"Avery says he does not care which it is provided only that it *is*," Anastasia said, and Camille could see now the bubbling excitement she had been keeping at bay. "If it is a girl this time, she will be loved every bit as dearly as an heir would be. And really, you know, Abigail, I would not think of a boy as *the heir,* but only as my son and Avery's."

Jessica had caught some of Abby's enthusiasm and was leaning forward on the sofa. "Is *that* why you were being lazy and sleeping late every morning a while ago?" she asked.

"Laziness. Is that how Avery excused my lateness?" Anastasia asked, grimacing and then laughing.

"Oh goodness," Jessica continued. "I am going to be an aunt too, Abby. Or a half aunt, anyway. Is there such a thing as a *half* aunt?"

Across the room Camille met Avery's lazy glance. She looked away before he turned back to the window.

"I am delighted for you, Anastasia," she said, and she was jolted by the look of naked yearning her half sister cast upon her before masking it with a simple smile.

"Are you, Camille?" she said. "Thank you. After the baby is born, you and Abigail must come and stay for a while at Morland Abbey if Miss Ford can be persuaded to do without you at the school—and if you can be persuaded to do without it. I want my children to know all their relatives and to see them frequently, especially their aunts and their uncle. Family is such a precious thing."

Camille did not think she was being preached at. Anastasia was merely speaking from the heart and from the lonely experience of having grown up in an orphanage unaware that she had any family at all. Camille's own heart was heavy. She knew how precious a baby felt in her arms even when it was not her own. Sarah was not her own, and Anastasia's would not be. Oh, how wonderful it must be . . . But the force of her maternal longing startled her.

Abigail and Jessica were laughing merrily—quite like old times. They were suggesting names for the baby and getting more outrageous by the moment. Anastasia was laughing with them. Avery was saying something to Elizabeth and pointing off to the west. The splendor of his appearance contrasted markedly with the simplicity of Anastasia's. He was wearing a ring on almost every finger, while her only jewelry was her wedding ring. Wise Anastasia. She had chosen not to compete with him. Or perhaps it had been an unconscious choice.

Camille decided to leave before her mother and grandmother returned from their excursion. If she stayed, there would be tea and at least an hour of conversation, and then like as not either Alexander or Avery would insist upon conveying her home. She had made the decision to spend some of her time with her family in the coming week, but she did not wish to be sucked back into the fold at the expense of her newly won independence. She was not to escape entirely, however. Avery turned away from his conversation with Elizabeth when Camille got to her feet.

"I shall do myself the honor of escorting you, Camille," he announced in the languid manner that characterized him. "I shall leave the carriage for you and Jessica, Anna."

"There is really no need," Camille said sharply. "I am quite accustomed to walking about Bath unaccompanied. I have not yet encountered even one wolf."

"Ah," he said, raising his quizzing glass halfway to his eye, "but it was not a question, Camille. And in my experience there is very little one *needs* to do. One shudders at the thought of ordering one's life about such a notion of duty."

She knew Avery well enough to realize that there was never any point in arguing with him. She took her leave of everyone else.

"I wonder," she said tartly when they were on the pavement outside the house and the door had closed behind them, "if you told Anastasia that she was going to marry you and, when she refused, informed her that you had not been asking."

"I am wounded to the heart," he said, offering her his arm, "that you would think me so lacking in charm and personal appeal that Anna would not have said yes on the instant when I told her she was to marry me."

She took his arm and looked at him, quelling the urge to laugh. "How did you persuade her?" she asked.

"Well, it was like this, you see," he said, leading her toward Brock Street and, presumably, toward the steepness of Gay Street down into the town, a route she normally avoided. "The dowager countess and the aunts and the cousins, with one or two exceptions, were trying to convince her that the most sensible thing she could do was marry Riverdale."

"Alexander?" she said, astonished. But it would indeed have made sense. A marriage between the two of them would have reunited the entailed property and the fortune to sustain it.

"I offered her an alternative," Avery said. "I informed her that she could be the Duchess of Netherby instead if she wished."

"Just like that?" she asked him. "In front of everyone?"

"I did not drop to one knee or otherwise make a spectacle of myself," he said. "But now that you have put a dent in my self-esteem, Camille, I must consider the fact that my title outranked Riverdale's and my fortune very far surpassed his. Do you suppose those facts weighed heavily with Anna?" He was looking sideways at her with lazy eyes.

"Not for a moment," she said.

"You do not consider her mercenary or calculating, then?" he asked her.

"No," she said.

"Ah," he said. "You know, Camille, it is just as well that Bath boasts hot springs that are said to effect miracle cures whether the waters are imbibed or immersed in. Otherwise it would surely be a ghost of a city or would never have existed at all. These hills are an abomination, are they not? I am not even sure it is safe for you to hold my arm. I fear that at any moment I will lose control and hurtle downward in a desperate attempt to keep my boots moving at the same pace as the rest of my person."

"Sometimes you are very absurd, Avery," she said.

He turned his head toward her again. "You are in agreement with your sister upon that subject," he said. "It is what she frequently says of me."

"Half sister," she said sharply.

He did not reply as they made their way down Gay Street. Camille had to admit in the privacy of her own mind that it felt good to have the support of a man's arm again. And Avery's felt surprisingly firm and strong when she considered the fact that he was scarcely an inch taller than she and was slight and graceful of build. But . . . he had felled Viscount Uxbury with his bare feet.

"Avery," she asked him, "why did you insist upon coming with me?"

"The fact that I am your brother-in-law is not reason enough?" he asked. Strangely, she never thought of him in terms of that relationship. "Ah, I beg your pardon—*half* brother-in-law. But that makes me sound smaller than I am, and I really am quite sensitive about my height, you know."

She smiled but did not turn her face his way or answer his question. They were almost down the steepest part of the descent.

"The thing is, you see, Camille," he said, his voice softer than it had been, "that though my father married your aunt years ago and so made us into sort-of cousins, and I have felt a certain cousinly affection ever since for you and Abigail and Harry; and although I have known Anna for only a few months and it may seem unfair that I do not feel less for her accordingly, in reality, my dear, I am quite desperately fond of her. If you will forgive the vulgarity—the former Lady Camille Westcott might not have done so, but the present Camille possibly might—I would even go further and say that I am quite head-over-heels besotted with her. But that is only if you will indeed forgive the vulgarity. If you will not, then I will keep such an embarrassing admission to myself."

Camille smiled again, though she felt a bit shaken. It made a certain sense, however, she thought, that the cool, aloof, cynical, inscrutable, totally self-sufficient Duke of Netherby would fall as hard as a ton of bricks if ever he did fall. Who, though, could have predicted that it would happen with someone like Anastasia—*who had looked as shabby as Joel did now when she first appeared in London*. That last thought left her feeling even more shaken.

"What are you trying to say, Avery?" she asked him.

"Dear me," he said, "I hope I am doing more than *trying,* Camille, when I have braved the perils of such a suicidal hill. What I am saying is that Anna understands. I believe her understanding and patience and love will be endless if they must be, just as her heartache will be. She loves me as dearly as I love her—of that I have no doubt. She is as exuberantly happy about the impending birth of our child as I am terrified. She loves and is loved by a largish circle of family members on both her mother's side and her father's. Her maternal grandparents adore her and are adored in return. She has everything that only her wildest dreams were able to deliver through most of her life. No, correction. *Almost* everything."

"Avery," she said as they reached flat land. "I was courteous when you and she called at my grandmother's house on your return from your wedding journey. I was courteous last evening. I wished her well this afternoon. I told her I was delighted for her, and I meant it. Why would I not? How could I wish her ill? It would be monstrous of me. And why single out me? Will Abby and Jessica and Harry be recipients of this admonition?"

He winced theatrically. "My dear Camille," he said, "I hope I never *admonish* anyone. It sounds as if it would require a great expenditure of energy. Anna craves the love—the full, unconditional love—of all four of you, but yours in particular. You are stronger, more forceful than the others. She admires you more and loves you more—though she scolds me when I say such a thing and reminds me that love cannot be measured by degree. One might have expected that she would be chagrined or contemptuous or any number of other negative things when she heard that you were teaching where she had taught and then that you were living where she had lived. Instead she wept, Camille—not with vexation, but with pride and admiration and love and a conviction that you would succeed and prove all your critics wrong."

Camille could not recall any other occasion when Avery had said so much, and most of it without his customary bored affectation.

"Avery," she said, "there is a difference between what one knows and determines with one's head and what one feels with one's heart. I was taught and have always endeavored to live according to the former. I have always believed that the heart is wild and untrustworthy, that emotion is best quelled in the name of sense and dignity. I am as new to my present life as Anastasia is to hers.

And I am not at all sure that the first twenty-two years of my life were worth anything at all. In many ways I feel like a helpless infant. But while infants are discovering fingers and toes and mouths, I am discovering heart and feelings. Give me time."

What on earth was she saying? And to whom was she saying it? *Avery* of all people? She had always despised his indolent splendor.

"Time is not mine to give, Camille," he said as they turned onto Northumberland Place. "Or to take. But I wonder if the advent of Anna into your life was in its way as much of a blessing as her advent into mine has been. It is enough to make one almost believe in fate, is it not? And if that is not a wild, chaotic thought, I shudder to think what is."

Camille, what happened to you must surely have been the very best thing that could possibly have happened.

. . . I wonder if the advent of Anna into your life was in its way as much of a blessing as her advent into mine has been.

Two very different men, saying essentially the same thing—that the greatest catastrophe of her life was perhaps also its greatest blessing.

"Ah," Avery said, "the lovelorn swain if I am not mistaken."

She glanced up at him inquiringly and then ahead to where he was looking. Joel was outside the orphanage.

"The *what*?" she said, frowning.

But Joel had spotted her and was striding toward her along the pavement. He looked a bit disheveled as well as shabby.

"There you are," he said when he was still some distance away. "At last."

Joel had been to an early church service but had decided to spend the rest of the day at home. He felt the urge to work despite the fact that it was Sunday. He was ready to paint Abigail Westcott. He could not literally do that, of course, because first he would have to pose her in the right clothes and with the right hairstyle and in the right light and setting. He would do that one day in the coming week if her time was not too much taken up with the visit of her family. But he could and would work on a preliminary sketch.

This was different from all the other sketches he did of his subjects. They were fleeting impressions, often capturing only one facet of character or mood that had struck him. In them he made no attempt to achieve a comprehensive impression of who that person was. The preliminary sketch was far closer to what the final sketch and then the portrait would be. In it he attempted to put those fleeting, myriad impressions together to form something that captured the whole person. Before he could do it, however, he had to decide what the predominating character trait was and how much of each of the others would be included—and, more significantly, *how*. He had to decide too how best to pose his subject in order to capture character. It was a tricky and crucial stage of the process and needed a fine balance of rational thought and intuition—and total concentration.

He started it on Sunday morning rather than observe the day of rest because he was sick of the fractured, tumbling thoughts brought on by the various events in the last couple of weeks and wanted to recapture his familiar quiet routine. And soon enough he was absorbed in the sketch.

He wanted to paint her seated, straight backed but leaning slightly forward, gazing directly out at the viewer as though she were about to speak or laugh at any moment. He wanted her face slightly flushed, her lips slightly parted, her eyes bright with eagerness and . . . Ah, the eyes were to be the key to the whole thing, as they often were in his portraits, but more than ever with her. For everything about her suggested light and cheerfulness and the joyful expectation that life would bring her good things and an eagerness to give happiness in return. Even the eyes must suggest those things, though they must do a great deal more than that. For he must not give the impression that she was just a pretty, basically shallow girl who knew nothing about life and its often harsh realities. In the eyes there must be the vulnerability he had sensed in her, the wistfulness, the bewilderment, even the pain, but the essential strength of hope in the power of goodness to overcome evil—or, if perhaps those words were too strong for what he sensed in so young a girl, then the power of light to overcome darkness.

Had he sensed correctly? Were there the depths of character in her that he thought there were? Or was she just a sweet girl who had suffered some sadness in the past few months? He had talked with her for a number of hours. He had made numerous sketches. He had observed her last evening at dinner. He knew a lot of facts. But ultimately, as always, he must sketch and paint from intuition and trust that it was more true than all the facts he had amassed. Facts missed a great deal. Facts missed what lay beneath the facts. Facts missed spirit.

He felt a great tenderness for Abigail Westcott—as he did for all his subjects. For there was nothing like the process of painting someone's portrait to help one know the person from the inside, and knowing, one could not help but feel empathy.

He had just finished the sketch and taken a step back from his easel in order to look upon it with a little more objectivity when a knock sounded upon the door and startled him back to reality. He had no idea what time it was, but he did know that when he became immersed in his work, hours disappeared without a trace and left him feeling that surely he had started only minutes ago. His stomach felt hollow, a sure sign that he must have missed a meal by more than an hour or two. Perhaps it was Marvin or Edgar, come to rescue him and drag him off to eat somewhere.

It was neither. The man who was standing outside his door was a stranger, an older man of firm, upright bearing and severe, handsome countenance. He carried his hat in his hand. His dark hair was silvered at the temples.

"Mr. Joel Cunningham?" he asked.

"Yes." Joel raised his eyebrows.

"Your neighbor below answered the door to my knock," the man explained, "and suggested that I come up."

What Edgar ought to have done, Joel thought, was call him down. Obviously he had judged the man to be respectable enough to let in.

"I explained," the man said as though reading his thoughts, "that I am a solicitor and have personal business of some importance with you."

"On a Sunday?" Joel said.

"The matter is something of a delicate one," the man said. "May I come in? I am Lowell Crabtree of the legal firm of Henley, Parsons, and Crabtree."

Joel stood to one side and gestured the man in. He led the way to the living room and offered him a seat. He began to have a horrible premonition.

"I am the solicitor in charge of the estate of the late Mr. Adrian Cox-Phillips," Crabtree said. "I understand that you have already been apprised of his sad passing yesterday morning."

"I have," Joel said, sitting opposite him.

"It is my usual practice," the solicitor said, "to read a will to the family after the deceased person has been laid to rest—on Tuesday in this particular case."

So soon? Joel frowned. He had decided last night that he would try to find out when the funeral was to be and attend, though he would not make himself known to any other mourners. He did not imagine that Viscount Uxbury would take any notice of him.

"It was Mr. Cox-Phillips's wish," Crabtree explained, "that he be laid to rest as quickly as possible and with as little fuss as possible. He has . . . three surviving relatives, all of whom are currently staying at his house. Two of them have been particularly insistent that I not wait until after the funeral to read the will. They need to return to their busy lives as soon as they have paid homage to their relative."

Joel read some disapproval into the stiffness of the man's manner.

"They have insisted that I read the will tomorrow morning," Crabtree said. "My senior partners have seen fit to persuade me to agree, though Monday—especially Monday *morning*—is an inconvenient time, coming as it does after Sunday, which I have always observed quite strictly as the Sabbath with Mrs. Crabtree and our children. However, Monday morning it is to be. Mr. Cox-Phillips extracted a promise from me when I conducted business with him a few days ago. He instructed me to find and speak to you privately before I read the will to his relatives."

Joel's sense of foreboding grew stronger. "To what end?" he asked, though the question was doubtless unnecessary. Having said so much, the solicitor was hardly about to stop right there and take his leave. "Although related to Mr. Cox-Phillips, I am merely the bastard son of his niece."

Crabtree drew some papers out of a leather case he had with him, rustled them in his hands, and looked with solemn severity at Joel. "According to his will," he said, "generous pensions are to be paid to certain of his servants who have been with him for many years, and similarly generous payments are to be made to the others. A sizable sum has been left to an orphanage on Northumberland Place to which he has made large annual donations for almost thirty years past. The rest of his property and fortune, Mr. Cunningham, including his home in the hills above Bath and another in London, which is currently leased out, has been left to you."

There was a buzzing in Joel's ears. It had never occurred to him . . . Good God.

"But I refused," he said. "When he offered to change his will in my favor, I refused."

"But he changed it anyway," Crabtree said. "I cannot put an exact monetary value on your inheritance at the moment, Mr. Cunningham. This has all been rather sudden and I will need to work upon the matter. I suggest you come into my office one day this week and I can at least give you some idea of where your investments lie and what their approximate worth is likely to be. But it is a sizable fortune, sir."

"But my great-uncle's relatives?" Joel asked, his eyebrows raised.

"I believe," the solicitor said, a certain note of satisfaction in his voice, "that Viscount Uxbury, Mr. Martin Cox-Phillips, and Mr. Blake Norton will be disappointed. It is altogether possible that one or more of them will contest the will. However, they will be further disappointed if they do. Mr. Cox-Phillips was careful to choose six highly respectable men to witness the signing of his new will. They included his physician, the vicar of his parish church, and two of his closest neighbors, one of whom is a prominent Member of Parliament, while the other is a baronet, the sixth of his line. Yet another is a judge whose word not even the boldest of lawyers would dream of questioning."

Mr. Crabtree did not linger. Having delivered his message, he rose, shook Joel by the hand, expressed the hope of seeing him soon at his office, wished him a good day, and was gone.

Joel locked the door behind him, went back into the living room, and stood at the window looking out but seeing nothing, not even the departure of the solicitor along the street. No, it had not once occurred to him that his great-uncle would go ahead with his plan to cut his legitimate relatives out of his will even after he, Joel, had told him in no uncertain terms that he had no wish to be used as a pawn in a game of spite.

He had done it anyway.

His great-uncle had been contributing to the orphanage for almost thirty years. Twenty-seven to be exact? That was Joel's age. Why? His grandmother had always supported him there.

Was it just spite against those other three that had determined him to change his will in Joel's favor?

Why had he not made himself known a long time ago? Shame?

Why had he summoned Joel to tell him about the planned change? And had he just made up that story of wanting to thumb his nose so to speak to three men who had never shown any affection for him apart from his money? Had his real reason been a wish to leave everything to a closer relative, grandson, albeit an illegitimate one, of his sister, of whom he had clearly been fond? At the very end had he not been able to resist taking a look at Joel just once before he died? Joel remembered standing for what had seemed a long time in that shaft of sunlight while the old man's eyes moved over him from head to foot, perhaps looking for some likeness to his sister or his niece.

It was too late to ask the questions. There was the soreness of unshed tears in Joel's throat.

His first instinct had been to repudiate the will, to tell Crabtree that he still did not want anything, that he would not accept what he had been left. Would it have been possible? The answer did not matter, though, for he had found on more honest reflection that after all he did not want to refuse.

That house was his. Apparently there was another in London. He did not know the extent of the fortune he had inherited, but the solicitor had said it was sizable. Joel had no idea what sort of amount comprised a sizable fortune, but even a few hundred pounds would seem vast to him. He suspected there would be more than that. Thousands, perhaps?

He was rich.

And who did not, in his heart of hearts, wish for a windfall to come his way just once in his lifetime? Who did not secretly dream of all he could have and all he could do with an unexpected fortune?

He and Anna—and the other children too—had played the game numerous times during their growing years. What would you do if someone gave you ten pounds, a hundred pounds, a thousand pounds, a million pounds . . .

And thinking of Anna led him to thinking of Camille. And suddenly he felt the overwhelming, almost panicked need to see her, to tell her, to . . . He did not stop to analyze. He grabbed his hat and his key and left his rooms without looking back. He remembered when he was crossing the bridge that she had been going up to the Royal Crescent this afternoon to visit her mother. Would she be back yet? Would she stay there for dinner? Perhaps for the night?

She was nowhere in the orphanage, and no one knew with any certainty when she would be back, though she had said nothing about not returning tonight. He paced the pavement outside for a few minutes, wondering if he should go up to the Crescent to speak with her there or just go home. It would be thought most peculiar if he went up there, and he might miss her if she came home by a different route from the one he took. He was still undecided when she turned onto the street. Joel hurried toward her, not even noticing that she was not alone.

"There you are," he said, his whole being flooded with relief. "At last."

Eighteen

❧

"He took no notice of what I said," Joel said, grabbing both of Camille's hands and squeezing tightly. "He did it anyway."

Camille looked her inquiry while she returned the pressure of his hands. But, strangely, she knew exactly what he was talking about.

"He has left everything to me," he blurted, "apart from a few bequests to faithful servants and *to the orphanage*, Camille, to which he has been donating annual sums my whole life. Good God, he has left me everything." At which moment he became aware of Avery, who was standing quietly beside her. "I beg your pardon. I did not see you there."

"Dear me," Avery said faintly. "Am I to understand that you have just inherited Cox-Phillips's fortune? Allow me to felicitate you."

"You do not understand," Joel said, his hands sliding away from Camille's. "When he informed me at our first meeting a few days ago that he intended changing his will in my favor, I refused the offer quite adamantly."

"Cox-Phillips *informed* you? You refused his *offer*?" Avery said. Inevitably his quizzing glass had found its way into his hand, though he had not raised it quite to his eye. "Rich and powerful men do far more telling than asking, my dear fellow. In many cases it is *why* they are rich and powerful."

"It did not occur to me," Joel said, "that he would not take me at my word."

"Joel," Camille said, "I am so sorry."

Avery's quizzing glass swung in her direction, all the way to his eye this time. "Extraordinary," he said. "It must run in the family. You refused a share of your father's fortune a few months ago, Camille, as did Harry and Abigail; Anna would have refused the whole of it if she had been able; now you are commiserating with this poor man because he has just inherited a fortune. It is enough to make me quite rejoice that no Westcott blood runs in my veins—though some will in my children's veins, I recall."

"I beg your pardon," Joel said again. "Had I seen you, Netherby, I would not have blurted my news as I did."

"And I have the distinct impression that my continued presence here as my stepcousin's escort would be decidedly de trop," Avery said. "I shall assume she has been delivered safely home and take myself off." He proceeded to do just that without another word, returning the way they had come.

"It must seem peculiar," Joel said, frowning after him, "that I did not even notice he was with you."

"I am flattered," Camille told him. "Avery usually draws all eyes wherever he goes. It is that extraordinary sense of *presence* he has cultivated. Everyone else might as well be invisible. But that's not what's important now. Joel, how do you know about the will?"

"Those three kinsmen of my great-uncle's have insisted that the will be read tomorrow morning," he told her, "even before the funeral on Tuesday. But he left specific instructions that his solicitor seek me out beforehand and inform me privately of the contents of the will rather than summon me to the official reading. Perhaps he hoped to spare me any unpleasantness my presence might arouse."

"One could only wish," Camille said, "that my father's solicitor had exercised similar discretion."

"Mr. Crabtree—my great-uncle's solicitor, that is—came to my rooms this afternoon," Joel told her, "even though it is Sunday."

"So the other three will not know until tomorrow morning," she said.

"No." He frowned. "I do not imagine they will be thrilled. But Crabtree assured me that if they try to contest the will, they will not succeed."

"I do wish I could be hidden somewhere in that room tomorrow," she said, "as Anastasia was hidden in the branches of a tree in Hyde Park on the morning of the duel. I *wish* I could see Viscount Uxbury's face when the will is read. Are you very unhappy about inheriting?"

He hesitated for a few moments. "I am almost ashamed to admit it," he said, "but I do not believe I am."

Anastasia grew up at this orphanage, Camille thought, glancing ahead at it, and had recently discovered that she was sole heiress to great wealth. Joel grew up here and had just discovered that he was sole heir to a fortune. What were the odds? They must be millions to one— perhaps billions. Or perhaps not. It was, after all, an orphanage at which a number of the children were supported by rich benefactors, mothers, fathers, or other relatives. It had happened, anyway. She, on the other hand, had gone in quite the opposite direction. But she was not about to sink into self-pity.

"Then I am happy for you," she said, even as she realized that everything would change now, that she was probably about to lose this newfound friend whom she had only just begun to think of as such.

His eyes searched her face. "It has turned into a lovely day after all," he said, glancing upward at blue sky, from which all the morning's clouds had disappeared. "Shall we go for a walk? Or have you walked enough already? You have just come from the Royal Crescent, I suppose. But . . . along by the river? It is not far and there are some seats there."

"Very well," she said, and they made their way past the orphanage. But instead of crossing the Pulteney Bridge when they came to it, they turned down onto the footpath to stroll beside the river, past the weir, which was like a great arrowhead across much of its width, in the direction of Bath Abbey. The sun sparkled off the water and beamed warmly down upon them. A few ducks bobbed on the surface of the river. Children darted and whooped along the path, their accompanying adults coming along behind them at a more sedate pace. A couple of children on the other side were pulling a toy boat on a string parallel to the bank. Two elderly men occupied the first seat they passed. One of them was tossing bread crumbs to the ducks. A middle-aged couple vacated the next seat just before they reached it, and they sat down.

"You really are quite happy with what has happened, then?" Camille asked, almost the first words either of them had spoken since they had started to walk.

"It is very base of me, is it not?" he said. "I rejected what I thought was an offer a few days ago because I did not want to be used as a pawn in a game of Cox-Phillips's devising and because I abhorred the idea of allowing my affections to be bought when I would have given them freely and gladly all through my boyhood. He left everything to me anyway. I do not know why, and I never will know now. My first reaction this afternoon was horror and denial. But I must confess it was only a momentary reaction. Then reality struck me—I was rich. I *am* rich. At least, I believe I am. Crabtree could not tell me how large the fortune is, but he assured me it is sizable, and it includes that mansion on the hill and even a house in London. How could anyone resist a fortune when it is thrust upon him? I keep thinking of how it might change my life—of how it *will* change my life."

He was leaning forward on the seat, his forearms resting on his thighs, his hands dangling between, gazing at the river, his expression intent. Camille could sense his leashed excitement and felt somehow chilled despite the heat of the sun. Yes, his life would change, and he would change. There was no doubt about it.

"I could live in that house if I chose," he said, "with servants. And with a carriage of my own. I could go to

London. I have a house there, though it is leased at the moment. *London*. I could see it at last. I could go to Wales or Scotland. I could go to Wales *and* Scotland, and all over the world. I could cut back on portrait painting and paint more landscapes just for myself."

"You could buy yourself a new coat and new boots," she said.

He turned his head sharply toward her as though he had just remembered she was there. "*You* resisted a fortune," he said. "Or one quarter of a fortune at least. How did you do it, Camille, when the alternative was penury?"

It would not really have been taking charity, would it? Her father had made a will after Anastasia's birth but had neglected to make another during the twenty-five years that followed. He had always acted as though *they* were his legitimate family, Mama and she and Harry and Abby, though he had never displayed any real love for any of them. Perhaps he had come to believe it. Surely he had intended to see them well provided for. Perhaps he had forgotten the earlier will. Or perhaps he had always meant to make another but had never got around to doing it. Or . . . perhaps he had deliberately enjoyed the joke of what was bound to happen after his death. Who knew? But surely Anastasia was being fair, not merely charitable, in her belief that the four of them should share the part of his property and fortune that was not entailed. They might have accepted without feeling unduly beholden to her.

"I was not the only one concerned, you see," she said. "Harry lost far more than I. He was the Earl of Riverdale, Joel. He was fabulously wealthy. He had been brought up to just the sort of life he had begun to live. He would have lived up to his responsibilities even though he was still sowing some rather wild oats. Everything, the very foundation of his life, was snatched away. And my mother lost far more than we did. She had married well and fulfilled her duties as countess and wife and mother for more than twenty years before everything, even her name, was taken away. And, quite unfairly, she had to bear the guilt of having given birth to three illegitimate children. She was left with nothing, though she did tell us today that the dowry my grandfather gave my father when she married has been returned with all the interest it has accrued. She will be able to live independently, though modestly, after all. I suspect it was Anastasia rather than her solicitor who thought of that way of helping us. Even Abby lost more than I. She was to make her come-out in society next spring with all the bright prospects that would have offered for her future. Instead she has had her youth taken from her and all her hopes."

"Hope is something that lights her eyes from within," he told her. "She has not given it up, Camille. Perhaps she is fortunate to be so young. She will adjust her hopes to her circumstances. And youth has not been taken from her. She exudes youthfulness."

He was looking very directly at her, his head turned back over his shoulder. She was going to miss him, she thought, and berated herself for having allowed herself to become attached to him in so short a time. Was she that needy? Of course, there was the complication that she had lain with him and that she had enjoyed the experience and that he was powerfully attractive.

"You are an incredibly strong person, Camille," he said. "But sometimes you build a wall about yourself. You are doing it now. Is that the only way you can hold yourself together?"

She was about to utter an angry retort. But she was feeling weary. Her feet were sore. "Yes," she said.

His eyes continued to search her face. "Yet behind the wall," he said, "you are amazingly tenderhearted. And *loyal* hearted."

A little boy dashed past at that moment, bowling a metal hoop and making a great deal of noise. A woman—his governess? his mother?—called to him from some distance behind to slow down.

Camille felt a bit like crying. It was becoming an increasingly familiar feeling, as though the tears she had not shed from the age of seven until a week or so ago were determined to make up for lost time.

Joel sat back so that his shoulder was touching hers, and looked out toward the river. "Or," he said, "I could sell the houses, invest all the money somewhere, and forget about it. Would it be possible? Would it always be there, beckoning and tempting me? Or I could give it all away. But would I then forever regret having done so? What do you think, Camille? Do you ever regret having said no?"

Did she? She had never allowed herself to think about it. But the thought had seeped in anyway, specifically the realization that she had turned her back on more than just the money. She would not easily forget that fleeting look of yearning on Anastasia's face earlier when Camille had congratulated her on being with child. And she would not forget Avery's scold as they walked down the hill on the way home—and that was what it had been. And she would not forget Alexander's suggestion that she allow herself to be loved. Was that what the money meant to Anastasia? Love? Was that what she, Camille, had rejected?

Joel turned his head again when she did not immediately answer. Their faces were very close—uncomfortably close. His eyes looked intensely dark beneath the brim of his hat. "An honest answer?" he said.

"I do not regret this road of self-discovery I am on," she said, "though it is incredibly painful."

"Is it?" His eyes dropped to her lips.

"You will feel pain too," she told him. "Being forced out of the life one has always led without any great deal of introspection is painful. Most people never have to do it. Most people never really know themselves."

"And you know yourself now?" His eyes smiled suddenly beneath the brim of his hat. "You did not on the day we went to Sally Lunn's. You told me so."

She knew something then with mind-shattering clarity, and it was something that would have shocked Lady Camille Westcott to the core. She wanted him to kiss her even though they were in a horribly public place. She wanted to go to bed with him again. Was this self-knowledge? Was she promiscuous? But no. She had never wanted any such thing with any other man and could not imagine ever doing so. And what did *that* tell her about herself?

"I am learning," she said.

His gaze did not shift. It was most disconcerting, but

she would not lean away from him or look away either. She was no longer that prim, oh-so-correct aristocrat. It was a beautiful day and she was sitting by the river on a public path with a man she desired in a most shocking way, but she would not feel either shocked or ashamed. Even though he was going to change and move into a world where she could not follow. She had guarded her feelings all her life, and where had it got her?

His lips touched hers very briefly before he seemed to remember where they were and sat back again, his shoulder against hers. The boy with the hoop came roaring back along the path, the same female calling plaintively to him from behind. A mother duck was gliding across the river, five ducklings coming along behind her in a slightly crooked line. An infant squealed with delight and pointed at them while she bounced astride her father's shoulders and her mother held a hand behind her lest she pitch backward.

"Joel," Camille said, "take me home with you."

He ought not to have done it, of course, but how could he have said no when it had been what he wanted too? Joel had no idea if her comings and goings had been noted by any of the neighbors on the street, but certainly this time they were fortunate inside the house. Either his fellow tenants were out, or they were occupying themselves quietly in their own rooms.

Camille made no pretense of having come with him for any other reason than the obvious one. Having removed and hung up her bonnet and shawl, she turned into the bedchamber and looked around. He was glad he had cleaned and tidied yesterday. He had even changed the bed linen.

She undressed herself today, methodically and efficiently, her back to him. They had scarcely exchanged a word since leaving that seat by the river. Her hair came down last. She drew out the pins, set them on the table beside his book, and shook her head. Her hair was dark and thick and shining and fell in waves almost to her waist. Despite the fullness of her figure evident through her clothes, one would never guess that she was so voluptuously beautiful. And young. In most of the personas she adopted for the outside world, she looked ageless, but certainly not youthful. Now she looked her age—she must be all of five years younger than he—and youthful and vibrant and so desirable that the blood seemed to be singing through his veins and filling him with an almost painful desire.

She drew back the bedcovers and lay down, apparently without self-consciousness as he finished undressing and joined her on the bed. She turned onto her side and reached for him. She had been a virgin the first time, of course, and somewhat passive, though not by any means cold or shrinking. Today she made love with a fierce abandon that he soon matched, her hands, her mouth, even her teeth, all over him while he set about the wholly unnecessary task of arousing her. He rolled onto her and thrust into her far sooner than proper finesse would have dictated, but not too soon, by God. She was hot and wet and eager, and she matched him stroke for stroke with rolling hips and inner muscles and straining hands and twined legs until she cried out her release a moment before he spilled into her.

"Camille." He disengaged from her, moved to her side without taking his arms from about her, settled her hot, damp body against his own, and smiled as she sighed and slid into a deep, totally relaxed sleep.

He had enjoyed regular sex with Edwina for two years or longer without ever feeling the need to examine his feelings or wonder about hers or consider his obligations. He did all three as he lay there, comfortable and sated and teetering on the brink of sleep but not quite falling asleep. She smelled of that faint fragrant soap he had noticed before—and of sweat and woman. She smelled wonderful.

She woke up sometime later and moved her head back far enough to gaze at him. He wondered if he was in for another stinging slap across the face, but no—she was the one who had asked to be brought here for just what had happened between them. Besides, she had explained that she slapped him that other time because he had apologized and thus cheapened what for her had been a lovely experience.

"I am *not* about to apologize," he said.

She smiled slowly. It began in her eyes and spread down to her mouth—a lazy, amused, happy smile. And oh, God, when had that ghastly Amazonian woman he remembered from a couple of weeks ago metamorphosed into this infinitely desirable woman in his arms and in his bed?

"A pity," she said. "I could have slapped your other cheek and evened things up a bit."

Camille Westcott *making jokes*?

He kissed her, moving his lips warmly, lazily over

hers, and by unspoken consent they made love again, slowly this time, in no hurry to get where they were going, taking their time, enjoying every moment, every touch and caress along the way. And when it came time to join their bodies, he took her on top of him, drawing her knees up to hug his hips, and penetrated her before they rode together for long minutes of pure pleasure until desire turned the ride into something more urgent and they reached the climax together. He stayed deep and she clenched tightly about him and then opened as he spilled his seed into her once more.

He walked her home in the middle of the evening after they had eaten and talked and laughed and he had sketched her and she had pulled gargoyle faces—which he had drawn—and they had laughed more, like a couple of children, and they had made love once more, fully clothed except for essential places, on the sofa.

They would marry, he thought as they walked. They almost certainly would even apart from the fact that three separate times he had made it more likely that he had impregnated her. But he did not ask. He was not certain of her answer. And—foolishly—he did not know how to go about it. There was a great deal of turmoil facing him in the coming days. She had her family to be concerned about for the next week. He would wait. And there was no great hurry anyway. A baby took nine months to be born, did it not?

They said good night when they reached the orphanage, and she let herself in with her key and closed the door behind her without looking back at him. He ought to have asked anyway. But it was too late now.

Did all men feel gauche and slightly clammy with panic when it came time to propose marriage?

He walked home with his head down and found himself longing illogically for his old life, just a couple of weeks or so ago, when the only complications to be dealt with were a leftover love he could not quite shake off and not enough hours in the day to paint all the portraits people wanted.

Nineteen

❧

Viola Kingsley, formerly Countess of Riverdale, Camille's mother, chose to accompany her own mother
and Abigail to the Pump Room on Tuesday morning. It
was a courageous move, since it was the first time she
had appeared to Bath society, many of whose members
knew her well, since the scandal of her invalid marriage
had supplied enough gossip to keep polite drawing rooms
abuzz almost to the exclusion of all else for a week and
more just a few months ago.

She went because she could not hide forever and
because her mother and her younger daughter had faced
down the gossip before her and made her feel cowardly,
and because her elder daughter had stepped out into the
new world with incredible courage and determination to
make it her own. She wondered how she could have given
birth to such admirable children—Harry was on the Peninsula, fighting the forces of Napoleon Bonaparte and

risking his life every day—and be so abjectly timorous herself, cowering in her brother's vicarage, where she was not really needed and where she was impeding his path to happiness with a lady who deserved him.

She was not received in the Pump Room with the flattering deference she had once commanded as a countess, but neither was she given the cut direct. A few of her mother's friends greeted her kindly and a few others nodded politely, while some simply pretended not to have seen her. Soon, however, her former mother-in-law, the Dowager Countess of Riverdale, arrived with Matilda and Louise and Jessica. The dowager countess, having received Abigail's bright smile and curtsy with a smile of her own, a hand beneath her chin, and a comment that she was looking as pretty as ever, linked an arm through Viola's, leaned upon it, and joined the morning promenade about the room with her, nodding graciously from side to side as they went. Matilda and Louise came behind them, all nodding feathered bonnets and benevolent hauteur.

Abigail, who had no young friends in Bath yet, Viola had learned since her arrival, happily made the promenade with Jessica, their arms linked, their heads bent toward each other, their smiles bright and genuine.

When Avery and Anastasia arrived a short time later, a buzz of excitement raised the noise level in the room. Avery was not only a duke, something that would have caused a stir in itself, but he was also . . . well, he was the Duke of Netherby, and no one played the part of bored, haughty, glittering aristocrat better than he. And everyone present knew the story of his duchess, who had grown up and taught at an orphanage little more than a stone's throw from the Pump Room until it had been discovered earlier this spring that she was the legitimate daughter of an earl and wealthy beyond belief. Her story quite cast Cinderella into the shade.

They became the focus of everyone's admiring attention, though good manners prompted most people to keep their distance and content themselves with deferential bows and deep curtsies and warm smiles.

"How he does it, I do not know," the dowager countess said, nodding in Avery's direction, "since he makes no attempt to win the adulation of all around him but indeed looks as though he is almost too bored to live. Yet he has that incredible *presence*."

"He does," Viola agreed. "But I will always love him, Mother. He saved Harry from a dreadful fate after the poor boy rushed out to enlist as a private soldier. And he purchased Harry's commission for him. I think it was the best solution for my boy under the circumstances even though I suffer daily anxiety for his safety, as I daresay thousands of other mothers throughout the land do. Is he happy? Avery, I mean."

The dowager looked sharply her way. "I believe he is, Viola," she said. "He annoyed us all considerably, of course, when we were in the midst of making elaborate plans for their wedding and he simply bore her off one morning without a word to any of us and married her by special license in an insignificant church no one had ever heard of with only Elizabeth and his secretary for witnesses. But . . . well, if Louise is to be believed, and I daresay she is since she lives with them, they adore each other. Yes, he is happy, Viola, and so is she."

Viola nodded, and they proceeded on the their slow course about the room, nodding to people as they went, occasionally stopping to exchange a few words. When they had completed the circuit once, however, they came face-to-face with Avery and his bride, and Anastasia surprised Viola.

"Will you take a turn about the room with me . . . Aunt Viola?" she asked.

Aunt Viola. Viola was no such thing, but Matilda and Mildred and Louise, her former sisters-in-law, certainly were Anastasia's aunts. The young woman had chosen to call her that, Viola supposed, albeit hesitantly, rather than address her by the only alternative, Miss Kingsley.

"Of course," Viola said, and they set off side by side. It was hard, so very hard, not to resent the girl, of whose existence Viola had been aware for years when she had assumed the girl was a by-blow of her husband's. She had even arranged for a generous settlement to be made on her after her husband's death, a gesture that had probably precipitated the discovery of the truth.

"I believe," she said stiffly, beginning the conversation, "I have you to thank, Anastasia, for the fact that my dowry has been returned with interest, enabling me to set up a home for myself and my daughters where we may live independently."

"You must know," Anastasia said, "that you are entitled to at least that much. What happened to you was insufferable."

"I will accept," Viola said, "because I agree that the dowry money ought to be mine. However, I doubt Mr. Brumford was the one to think of it. I believe that was you, and I thank you."

They were interrupted by two ladies who wished to pay their respects to the Duchess of Netherby . . . and of course to Miss Kingsley. The Duchess of Netherby returned their greetings amiably but showed no inclination to engage the two ladies in conversation. They moved on.

"I live at Morland Abbey with Avery," Anastasia said. "I will continue do so for the rest of my life, or at one of his other numerous homes, including Archer House in London. Yet I am the owner of Hinsford Manor and of Westcott House in London. I believe I have persuaded Alex that it would be appropriate for him to stay at Westcott House whenever he is in town since he is the holder of the title. But Hinsford, which is extremely pretty, is uninhabited, and the people who live in the neighborhood are unhappy about it. They look back with nostalgia to the years when you and your family lived there."

Viola stiffened. "They would hardly be delighted to see the return there of Miss Kingsley and the Misses Westcott," she said.

"I do believe you are wrong," Anastasia said, nodding to a couple who would have detained them with the smallest encouragement. "Forgive me, but I understood from my one visit there that my father was never well liked. I equally understood that you were. Sympathy and understanding are very heavily on your side. Some of those I spoke with were cool toward me, a fact from which I took comfort rather than offense. Their loyalty lies with you, regardless of the change in your status, which they quite firmly attribute to my father."

"They are kind," Viola said, almost overcome with a great surge of nostalgia for home, or what had been her home for more than twenty years. And for her friends and neighbors there.

"Aunt Viola," Anastasia said, and then paused. "Oh, do you find it offensive when I call you that? I do not know what else to call you. I cannot address you as Miss Kingsley."

"I am not offended," Viola told her.

"Thank you," Anastasia said. "Aunt Viola, *will* you go back home? *Please?* It would mean so much to me. I do not suppose that argument will weigh a great deal with you, but . . . for Abigail's sake? I met some of her friends there, and they were genuinely melancholy about her absence and the reason for it. One of them even shed tears and dashed from the room while her mama tried to convince me that she was suffering a head cold. For Camille's sake too, though it would not surprise me if she chose to remain here rather than go with you."

Viola frowned and shook her head. "You will have children, Anastasia," she said. "Your eldest son will, of course, inherit from Avery eventually. But the younger ones will have to be provided for too."

"Avery will provide for them all, no matter how many children we have," Anastasia said. "He is quite adamant about it. He warned me you would be sure to use that argument. He told me to tell you to think of a more convincing one—if you could." She smiled, but there was anxiety in her eyes. "Please will you go home and consider it your own? I have drawn up a will, Avery having insisted that what I brought to the marriage remain mine to be done with as I choose. I am leaving Hinsford to Harry and his descendants. There will be no point in his arguing against it. It is done and it will remain so. So if you go home, you will be merely keeping your son's future home in good order for him."

Viola drew breath to speak, let the breath out, and drew it in again. "You have made it nearly impossible for me to say no," she said.

"You must say no, though," Anastasia said, looking stricken, "if you truly do not want to live there. But, please, do not refuse for any other reason. Do not punish me to that degree."

"Punish you?" Viola frowned. "Is that what I would be doing? But I suppose you are right. I wish you were not such a . . . pleasant young lady, Anastasia. It would be a great deal easier to dislike you if you were not."

For some reason they both laughed.

"Yet the offer is made for selfish reasons," Anastasia said. "I want to feel happy about everything in my life, but at the moment I feel happy only about *almost* everything. I cannot close that gap unless I can somehow make amends for what I know was neither my fault nor yours. Think about it, Aunt Viola. Talk to Camille and Abigail about it, and to Mrs. Kingsley, if you will. Talk to Avery and all the others. It is your right to live in the home my father provided for you. It is *not* right that it be taken from you because of his wickedness. He *was* wicked, sad as I am to say it."

Viola sighed. "He was my husband, Anastasia," she said. "And though I know now that he never truly was, it is nevertheless hard for me to be disloyal to the vows I made him when I married him. He was as he was, and he did *something* right, at least. He fathered four fine young people."

"Four? You include me?" Anastasia glanced at her, her eyes suspiciously bright. But they had completed the circuit of the room and Avery was stepping forward to meet them, his lazy eyes taking in his wife's unshed tears. Viola felt a wave of envy for the sort of love she had known fleetingly once upon a time, before her father presented her with the perfect marriage partner.

"I will think about your suggestion, Anastasia," she said. "Avery, do I have you to thank for Harry's promotion to lieutenant?"

"Me, Aunt?" He looked astonished. "Harry made it perfectly clear at the start that he would allow me to purchase his commission but nothing else. I understood that he meant it, that he would be mortally offended if I were to intervene to purchase promotions for him. I took him at his word. And *has* he been promoted?"

"A letter arrived yesterday addressed to Camille and Abigail," she said. "He sounded quite excited. And thank you for not interfering. It is more important that he acquire a sense of self-worth than that he achieve high rank in his regiment."

"It is to be hoped that he will acquire both," he said. "I have great faith in young Harry."

Joel kept himself busy during the first half of the week in an attempt not to be overwhelmed by the new fact in his life. He did not want to be the sort who would dash out and squander a fortune on riotous living and ruin his own character in the process. And it would be quite easy to do, he had realized in alarm down by the river on Sunday. Money held immediate and almost overwhelming temptation.

He also did not want to think too much about Camille— or, rather, what he owed Camille. He owed her marriage.

Having an affair with her was somehow quite different from having an affair with Edwina had been. With Edwina it had been like a game in which they both knew the rules and had no wish to change them. With Camille it was no game. He knew she had slept with him not just for the simple enjoyment of sex. And it had not been just that with him either. The trouble was that he did not know quite what it *had* been. Love? But frequently she annoyed him enormously, and, to be fair, he believed he annoyed her too at times. Regardless of what it was between them, of course, he did owe her marriage. He just did not want to think about it yet. His head felt a bit as though it had been invaded by wasps or hornets.

But good God, the sex had been enormously enjoyable.

He spent most of Monday working. He was at the house on the Royal Crescent during the morning, explaining to Abigail Westcott how he planned to pose and paint her. He sent her off to change into her favorite dress, not necessarily the most fashionable or the finest or the most admired or even the prettiest, but the one in which she felt most herself. In the meanwhile he chose a chair and its correct positioning with relation to the light and the other aspects of the room. Her mother was there, taking the place of the maid who usually sat silently in a corner as chaperon.

Abigail returned wearing a light blue cotton frock, which looked well-worn and slightly faded. Her mother looked at her somewhat askance, but Joel knew immediately that it was perfect. Her hair was dressed simply and took nothing away from the pure youthful prettiness of her face. He had had some doubt about the cheerful floral upholstery of the chair he had chosen, but when she sat in it, leaning slightly forward, and gazed at him with her happy, eager face and her sparkling, slightly wounded eyes, he knew that the painting he wanted was before his eyes and merely needed to be melded with the sketch he had made yesterday and then transferred to canvas in his studio.

"No, ma'am," he explained when Miss Kingsley asked him if he would be painting here at the house. "When I paint from life, my mind becomes too caught up in getting every fine detail correct and my spirit is silenced. And my subject becomes stiff and wooden from holding a pose and an expression. No, I will sketch what I see now as quickly as I can and then paint in my studio. If I need to see the original again, as I probably will, then we will set up this scene again."

He spent all afternoon on the painting and the evening too until the light became too poor. He was a bit uneasy that it was all happening so fast. Each step of the process usually took him a great deal longer. But inspiration was something that must be trusted above all else. He had learned that over the past ten years or so. And he was inspired now. He saw the girl as she was and as she must appear on his canvas, and he could not paint fast enough so that he would not lose that spark in himself that would do her justice. How did one capture light and hope and vulnerability on canvas without losing the fine balance among the three and without giving in to the temptation to paint the merely mundane—a very pretty girl in her case?

A notice of the death appeared in the Bath papers on Tuesday morning and identified Joel by name as both the great-nephew of the deceased and the principal beneficiary of his will. Mr. Cox-Phillips was described in the notice as one of the wealthiest men in Somerset and, indeed, the whole of western England.

Joel went to the funeral. It was at a church in a village north of Bath, where apparently his great-uncle had worshipped regularly until the last six months or so, when deteriorating health had kept him at home. Joel was a bit surprised at how well attended the funeral was. He sat alone in a pew at the back, and he stayed behind the small crowd that gathered around the grave in the churchyard afterward for the burial. Uxbury was there, making a show of dignified grief, as were the two men with him. Joel did not think Uxbury had seen him until, just as Joel turned away at the end to return to his waiting carriage, the man leveled a steady look at him. Joel had not made any display of grief during the ceremonies, though he felt some. Perhaps, he thought in the carriage on the way back to Bath, it was the grief of regret for what might have been. If he had learned the truth a year ago, even six months ago, perhaps he could have had some sort of relationship with the man in whose house his grandparents and his mother had lived. Now it was too late.

He went to the offices of Henley, Parsons, and Crabtree in the afternoon. Mr. Crabtree seemed to take satisfaction in informing him that Mr. Cox-Phillips's relatives did indeed intend to contest the will with all the vigor of their combined influence. They would not succeed, he told Joel again. They had remained in Bath, however, though they had removed from the house. In the meantime, the solicitor produced some papers and spread them upon his desk, went into a lengthy explanation that Joel would have liked to have translated into intelligible

English, and concluded with a rough estimate of the total fortune, which might have had Joel's jaw hanging if he had not been clenching his teeth so hard.

He would have painted himself into oblivion for the rest of the day if his door had not been almost constantly knocked upon from the moment he returned home. Everyone he had ever called friend, and a few who were mere acquaintances, came to commiserate with him at his loss and congratulate him upon his good fortune. Even Miss Ford came from the orphanage, accompanied for propriety's sake by Roger, the porter. She had closed the school for the rest of the week, she informed him. She supposed he would have more important things to do on Wednesday and Friday than teach his art pupils, and Miss Westcott certainly did. The Dowager Countess of Riverdale had arrived in Bath with her eldest daughter, Lady Matilda Westcott, and the family was busy celebrating and wished to include Miss Westcott in their activities. Miss Ford herself had been invited to join the family at the public tea in the Upper Assembly Rooms on Thursday afternoon and to attend a private assembly there on Saturday evening.

Anna and Netherby called at Joel's rooms too not long after Miss Ford left—the first time Anna had ever been there. She hugged him tightly while Netherby looked on complacently, exclaimed with delight at the size of his rooms, examined closely the portrait of his mother, and sat beside him on the sofa, patting his hand and assuring him that if her experiences were anything to judge by, he would soon recover from his bewilderment and reconcile his life to the new reality without losing himself in the process.

"For that is one's greatest fear," she said, echoing what

he had been feeling. "One starts to believe that one does not know oneself at all. It is a terrifying feeling. But of course you are who you have always been, and you will get through to the other side more or less intact."

"It is the *less* part that worries me," he said, and they both laughed.

Netherby informed him that he had better attend the public tea in the Upper Assembly Rooms on Thursday so that they could all boast of an acquaintance with the man who had become the sensation of Bath.

"There is nothing like the background of an orphanage upbringing to lend an irresistible aura of romance to a story like yours," he said with a weary-sounding sigh.

Anna laughed at her husband. "And you must come to the assembly on Saturday too," she said to Joel. "Camille has taught you to waltz, and I simply must see for myself how apt a pupil you have been."

"I can go up and see the house whenever I wish," Joel said impulsively. "I believe I would rather not go alone." But, no, it would not do to invite Anna to accompany him—or even Anna and Netherby. "The gardens seem extensive and well tended, and the view is spectacular. Perhaps some of your family would like to come up there with me—for a picnic, maybe, which I will provide, of course. On Friday afternoon?"

He was struck by the dizzying fact that he could afford such an extravagance.

"Oh, Joel," Anna said. "That would be wonderful. Would it not, Avery?"

"I can confidently predict," Netherby said, "that your newly acquired property will be mobbed by Westcotts on Friday, Cunningham."

That was settled, then, it seemed.

Camille did not come to his rooms. But of course she did not. Had he expected she would? It seemed to Joel far longer than two days since he had seen her. Now, with school canceled for the rest of week, he would not see her until Thursday afternoon. It seemed like an eternity away.

He did not go to her either. He did not know why. He felt a bit . . . shy? That was not at all the right word. But something had happened on Sunday to change everything, and he was feeling a bit—well, panicked. And he was feeling too overwhelmed by everything else to sort out his feelings for her and do what must be done. Except that it was not just what *must* be done, was it? Surely, it was what he wanted to do. Quite frankly, he did not know anything any longer, least of all the meaning of love. And his obligation to Camille was not only about love, anyway. She might be with child by him. And even if she was not . . .

And so his thoughts chased one another about in his head.

On Wednesday morning, not in the finest of moods, he took himself off with firm step and gritted teeth to a tailor and a bootmaker and a haberdasher.

Twenty

※

Camille half expected to see Joel on Monday while telling herself she did not expect him at all. She more than half expected him on Tuesday after her attention was drawn to the death notice in the morning paper. It was also the day of the funeral, she knew. He did not come, even though Miss Ford told her she had been to call upon him and that she had seen the Duke and Duchess of Netherby's carriage approaching the house as she left. Miss Ford also told her that she had canceled school for the rest of the week so that Camille could spend time with her family during their brief visit to Bath.

He would not need to come on Wednesday, then, with the school closed. And, indeed, he did not come. Camille tried to tell herself that she was not disappointed. She tried, in fact, not to think of disappointment as a possibility. Why should he have come at any time during those three days, after all? Just because she had invited him to take her to bed and he had obliged her?

Ah, but it had not felt as sordid as that at the time. And at the time—or, at least, between times—they had talked and laughed and even been silly and had behaved like the best of friends.

Oh, she knew *nothing*! He did not come.

She was busy during those days. She taught on Monday and Tuesday. The main focus of attention was the knitted blanket, which had fired the children's imaginations. Some of the girls wanted to learn to crochet so that they could help weave the squares together eventually and make a pretty border about the finished product. A few wanted to learn to embroider so that they could implement the idea one of the boys had to stitch the name of each knitter across the relevant square. A few of the boys dashed away to measure the babies' cots and work out the size of each square and how many they would need to knit in order to make a blanket of the right size. Another of the boys made a design for the blanket, using the four colors of wool they were working with. During their knitting sessions the children took turns reading stories to the others.

Camille played with Sarah as often as she was able and gave some attention to Winifred, having realized that that was what the girl craved. She walked to the Royal York Hotel on Monday afternoon, having received a note from Aunt Louise to inform her that her grandmother and Aunt Matilda had arrived. She went to a reception her maternal grandmother gave Tuesday evening and surprised herself by almost enjoying it. It felt treacherously like old times to mingle and make polite conversation with Grandmama's carefully selected guests.

Her mother took her aside late in the evening, and they sat together on a love seat while her mother told her she was going to return to Hinsford.

"To live?" Camille frowned.

"Yes," her mother said. "Anastasia has begged me to do so, and in that clever, tactful way she has, she has made it appear that I will be doing her a favor by going. She will never live there herself now that she is married to Avery, yet she hates to see it empty and to know how its emptiness affects the morale of the people who work there and the social spirit of the neighborhood. Our neighbors and friends have spoken kindly of us to her, and . . . Well, Camille, she has willed Hinsford Manor to Harry after her time and has pointed out that if I go there to live, I will be keeping it lived in for my own family. I told her I would think about it, but really it has not taken a great deal of thought. I am going home."

Camille felt a bit like weeping, but she found herself reverting to the old Camille, stiff and reserved and showing nothing of her feelings.

"Abigail is coming with me," her mother continued. "She needs me and she needs her home. We will go there and . . . see what happens. Nothing will be the same, of course, and it may not be easy to be living the old life, when the old life cannot be fully recaptured. We will be Miss Kingsley and Miss Abigail Westcott instead of the Countess of Riverdale and Lady Abigail. But . . . Well . . ." She shrugged and smiled ruefully. "Will you come too, Camille? Or do you prefer your life here?"

Home. Camille felt suddenly awash in nostalgia. And temptation. But, as her mother had just said, there was no real going back.

"I do not know, Mama," she said. "I will have to think about it."

And she dropped, like a rock in a pond, into the murky depths of depression. She was living in a dreary little room in a building where she did not belong. She was teaching from instinct alone with very little idea of what she was doing or plan for how she would proceed in the weeks and months—and years?—ahead. She was in love with a man whose absence in the last couple of days suggested that she meant nothing to him apart from a casual lover, and a man who would almost inevitably move on to a new life of his own now that he was wealthy. She adored a baby who was not her own. She had cut herself off quite deliberately from everyone who would love her if she gave them the chance because she did not know who she was and did not want to be smothered by a protective love that would prevent her from finding out. The future yawned ahead with frightening emptiness and uncertainty. And she hated herself. She hated the fact that she could no longer hold herself together as she had done all her life, not realizing that what she held together was an empty core of nothing. She hated her own self-pity. She hated the fact that she was abjectly in love with a man who had made love to her three separate times just two days ago and had made no attempt to see her since. She hated . . .

"I will have to think about it," she said again when she realized her mother's eyes were fixed upon her. "But I am glad you and Abby are going home, Mama. And I am glad for Harry. Do you hate her?"

"Anastasia?" Her mother shook her head slowly. "No, I do not, Camille. She is your sister, and as I told her this morning, your father left behind something of far greater value than a large fortune. He sired four fine children."

"Four." Camille drew a slow breath. "How can you be so forgiving?"

"Because the alternative will only harm me," her mother told her.

Cousin Althea and Mrs. Dance came to join them at that moment and they said no more on the subject.

On Wednesday morning, Camille joined her family for breakfast at the hotel. They did not linger over the meal, as several of their number were to make an excursion to Bathampton a few miles away, where they would enjoy a late luncheon before returning. Camille stayed to wave the three carriages on their way and then turned to Anastasia, who was standing out on the pavement too, listening to something Avery was saying to her.

"Anastasia," Camille said before she could change her mind, "would you care to come and look in the shops along Milsom Street with me?"

Avery raised his eyebrows and pursed his lips. Anastasia looked at her with wide surprised eyes. "Oh, I would indeed, Camille," she said. "Just give me a moment to fetch my bonnet and reticule."

Avery looked steadily at Camille and then conversed for several minutes about the weather. "For the weather will always offer an endless supply of fascinating conversation," he said, "especially when one is fortunate enough to live in England. Or unfortunate, as the case is more likely to be."

The two ladies set off downhill toward Milsom Street, the most fashionable shopping street in Bath, a few minutes later. They walked side by side, talking about . . . the weather when they spoke at all. It was only as they turned onto Milsom Street that Camille changed the subject.

"Do you prefer to be called Anna rather than Anastasia?" she asked abruptly.

"Anna seems more like me," Anastasia said. "I did not even know until a few months ago that it is not my full name. I prefer Anna, but I do not resent Anastasia. It is my name, after all."

"I shall call you Anna from now on," Camille said. "And, since it is less of a mouthful to call you sister rather than *half* sister, I shall do that too."

Oh, this was difficult. This was very difficult. If her lips felt any stiffer, she would not be able to move them at all.

Anna turned her head and smiled at her. "Thank you, Camille," she said. "You are very kind. I used to walk along this street occasionally for the pure pleasure of looking in the windows and dreaming of what I would buy if only I had limitless money. Once I saved for several months to buy a pair of black leather gloves that were so soft they felt more like fine velvet. I used to come and gaze at them every week. But—"

"Let me guess," Camille said. "When you had finally saved enough and came to buy the gloves, they were gone."

"Oh, they were still there," Anna said. "I tried them on and they fit like . . . well, like a glove. I felt a few moments of glad triumph and utter joy—and then discovered that I could not justify such an extravagance. I left them on the counter with an unhappy shopgirl and went on my way."

"Oh, but you had killed a dream," Camille protested.

"I believe I had merely proved," Anna said, "that having a dream and being on the journey to fulfilling it sometimes brings more happiness than actually achieving it. We have a habit, do we not, of thinking happiness is a future state if only this and that condition can be met? And so much of life passes us by without our realizing how happy we can be in this present moment, or how nearly happy. I had a good life as a girl and young adult despite what I was missing. And I had a dream."

They had been gazing at bonnets in a window and had now moved on to a bookshop.

"Are you not happy now, then?" Camille asked.

"Oh, I am," Anna assured her. "Happier than I have been my whole life. But it is not unalloyed happiness, Camille. Nothing is. This is human life in which there is no such thing as perfection. But I *am* happy. Today you have made me happier. It seems absurd, does it not, when all you have done is invite me to walk here with you and inform me that from today on you will call me Anna and sister? Camille, we are *sisters*. That is unbelievably precious to me."

Camille felt guilty, for she could not say quite the same. She had been determined to reach out, though, to act as though Anna were her sister in the hope that in time she would also feel the truth of it.

"I have been very *unhappy*, Anna—for all the obvious reasons," she said. "But in a strange way, that very fact is encouraging, for before all this happened I had dedicated my life to achieving perfection. I wanted to be the perfect lady above all else. Happiness meant nothing to me. Nor did love. They frightened me, for they suggested chaos and the impossibility of achieving perfection. Now that I have been desperately unhappy, I understand that I can be happy too and that I can love and be loved, and that unless I allow these things to happen to me, I will be only half alive. Oh, why are we gazing at books and talking about such strange things?"

"Because we are sisters," Anna said. "This was always my very favorite shop in Bath. I *did* spend money here when I had some to spare. I have always loved books and the fact that I can read them and ponder them and keep them and see them and smell them—and reread them. What a treasure they are."

"There is a coffee shop a little farther along the street," Camille said. "Shall we go there?"

A few minutes later they were seated opposite each other at a small table, smelling the wonderful aroma of the two cups of coffee that had been set before them.

"Anna," Camille said as she stirred in a spoonful of sugar, her eyes upon what she did. "I am happy about the baby. I shall enjoy being an aunt. There is a baby at the orphanage. She makes my heart ache. I believe I love all the children there, but there is something about her . . . Well." She looked up. "I wish my father had confessed the truth after your mother's passing. I wish he had married my mother properly after that and brought you into their home. I would have had an elder sister. I would not have been the eldest myself, and perhaps I would not have felt compelled to earn my father's forgiveness for not being a son. I think I would have liked being a younger sister, and I think I might have enjoyed looking up to you. Perhaps not, though. Perhaps we would have squabbled incessantly."

"I wish it too," Anna said, "or that he had admitted the truth and acknowledged me and left me with my grand-parents. I wish he had made another will. I wish he had married your mother properly so that Harry could have kept the earl's title. I do not feel disloyal to Alex in saying so, for even he—perhaps *especially* he—wishes it were so. But it is not so, none of it, and we have to take life as it is. Camille—" She leaned forward across the table. "Do you love him? Does he love you?"

Camille stared at her. She knew Anna was not refer-ring to Alexander. "Joel?" she said. And she heard a gurgle in her throat and felt her eyes grow hot and said what she doubted she would have said to another soul in the world, even Abby. "Yes. And no. Yes, I think I do, but no, he does not. We spent some time together on Sunday after Avery walked me home, and . . . I do not believe I have ever been happier. But I have not set eyes on him since. All sorts of momentous things are going on in his life, and lately he has been turning to me when he needs a friend in whom to confide, but I have not seen him since Sunday."

It felt more horrible, more ominous put into words—not to mention abject.

"Then he must be in love," Anna said. "I always knew he was an idiot. This proves it."

There was no logic, no comfort in her words. Camille

frowned, drew a deep breath, and turned her cup on its saucer without lifting it. She must get to the point of this contrived meeting. "I wanted to talk to you about something in particular," she said.

Anna sat back in her chair.

"I am glad I have lived at the orphanage," Camille said. "I am glad I have taught there. I have already learned a great deal—about you, about myself, about where I belong and do not belong. About being poor. I may well continue, for I have always been stubborn and do not give up a challenge easily. But there is an alternative, and I am at least considering it. My mother wants me to go home to Hinsford with her and Abigail. She will not press me, and I will not make a hasty decision. But . . ."

She looked up at last and met her sister's eyes. It was going to be incredibly difficult to go on. But Alexander had advised her to allow herself to be loved. Avery had suggested something similar.

"Whether I go or stay," she said, "will you—? Are you still willing to share the fortune you inherited from Papa?"

"Oh." Anna expelled her breath on a long sigh. "You must know I am, Camille. If your mother has told you I will be leaving Hinsford to Harry, you must surely have guessed that I will also be leaving three-quarters of my fortune to my brother and sisters. It is not charity, Camille. It is not my attempt to buy your love. It is *fair*. We are all equally our father's children."

"Then I will take my share," Camille said after drawing a ragged breath. "Not because I need it or necessarily intend to use it, but because—" She swallowed awkwardly. "Because you are offering it."

Anna's eyes filled with tears, and Camille could see that she was biting down on her upper lip. "Thank you." Her lips mouthed the words, though very little sound came out. "It will be done immediately. Never mind the will. Wills can be changed. I shall write to Mr. Brumford. I wonder if Abigail . . . But it does not matter. Oh, I am so very happy." She glanced downward. "And I would be even happier if we had not both allowed our coffee to grow cold."

"Ugh," Camille said, and they both laughed rather shakily.

It was not easy to allow oneself to be loved, Camille thought, to make oneself vulnerable. She really, really had not wanted to take the money—because her father had not left it, or anything else either, to her and she might never forgive him, though she remembered what her mother had said on that subject last night. But now the money was Anna's, and sharing it with her sisters and brother was important to her. And accepting Anna with more than just her head had become necessary. She must somehow find a way of opening her heart too, but this was at least a start. If one could give love only by receiving it, then so be it.

And however was she to continue with her new life if she had riches in a bank account somewhere to tempt her? But perhaps she *would* go back home with Mama and Abby. There she would be far away from Joel. Oh, and the life would be familiar to her. She could give up the struggle . . .

Was she a coward after all, then?

"I suppose," Anna said, frowning, "we could have

these cups taken away and two fresh ones brought. They will think us strange, but what of that? I am a duchess, after all. And I have something to celebrate with one of my sisters."

She raised an arm to summon the waitress, and they both laughed again.

Joel had never been inside the Upper Assembly Rooms, since they were largely the preserve of the upper classes. Afternoon teas there were open to anybody who had paid the subscription and, as in his case on that Thursday, to anyone who had been specifically invited. He donned the new coat he had bought yesterday, one that was ready-made and therefore not quite as formfitting as an obsequi-ous tailor assured him he would make the other two Joel had ordered. The tailor's manner indicated to Joel that he had read the paper on Tuesday morning and had recog-nized the name of his new client. Joel was pleased with the coat anyway and decided that he would at least not disgrace himself when he walked into those hallowed and dreaded rooms. Now if only there had been a readymade pair of boots to fit him . . .

He was feeling ridiculously nervous. He was also wish-ing he had sought out Camille before today. It was going to be awkward meeting her for the first time since Sunday in a public setting and surrounded by all of her family. Sunday! It seemed like a bit of a dream. Why the devil had he not gone to see her since then? He was behaving like a gauche schoolboy with his first infatuation.

He arrived five or six minutes later than the time appointed

for fear of being early and so, of course, had to make something of a grand entrance, or what felt like one. The Upper
Rooms were crowded and humming with conversation.
He stood upon the threshold of the tearoom and looked
about for familiar faces. He spotted Miss Ford first and
could see that she was sitting among a group of tables
occupied by the Westcotts. Anna had raised her arm to
attract his attention and was smiling broadly. He made
his way toward them.

The Dowager Duchess of Netherby took it upon herself
to introduce him to her mother and sister, the Dowager
Countess of Riverdale and Lady Matilda Westcott. Joel
made his bow to both ladies, greeted everyone else, and
took a seat at a table with Lady Overfield, her brother the
earl, and Camille's mother. It was only as he did so that
he saw Camille for the first time. She was sitting almost
back-to-back with him at the next table with Mrs. Kingsley and Mr. and Mrs. Dance. He glanced at her and opened
his mouth to speak, but she was impersonating her former self today, all stiff, aristocratic formality as she
inclined her head to him with haughty condescension and
turned her back.

She was annoyed with him, was she? Because she
regretted last Sunday? Because she wished him to know
that that was then and this was now and never the twain
should meet? Because he had not been to see her? Because
he had not spotted her immediately when he had entered
the room?

He gave his attention to the conversation at his own
table and strained his ears to listen to that at the next.

It was a while later when Riverdale uttered a muffled

exclamation, a frown on his face, his eyes fixed on the doorway. Joel turned his head to look. Viscount Uxbury was standing there with the two men who had been at the funeral with him. They were looking about the room for an empty table. Suddenly Uxbury's eyes alit upon Camille, or so it seemed to Joel, and remained on her as he moved away from the other two and strolled toward her table. Other members of the family were beginning to notice him and were falling silent one by one, but he seemed not to be aware of them. He had but the one object in his sights. He stopped by Camille's table, raised a quizzing glass to his eyes, and regarded her insolently through it.

"I wonder," he said, "if your companions and the other respectable citizens of Bath here present realize that they are rubbing shoulders with a bastard, *Miss* Westcott."

What? What the devil? Had the man been so offended by the setdown she had given him a few days ago that he was willing to breach all semblance of good manners in order to get back at her?

Uxbury had not spoken loudly, Joel realized afterward. He had not drawn a great deal of attention his way. Conversation at all but the tables occupied by their group continued as usual while cutlery tinkled cheerfully against china and white-aproned waiters bearing trays wove their way among tables. Nonetheless, Riverdale rose from his place and set his linen napkin on the table. Netherby was doing likewise at his table. So was Lord Molenor. In another minute they would have ushered the viscount outside and dealt with him there in a perfectly well-bred manner for as long as it was likely they might be observed by people arriving or leaving or passing on the street. They also, very probably, would have made an appointment to meet him privately, as Netherby had done once before in London.

Joel was not well-bred. He knew nothing of the rules that governed a gentleman's behavior, especially in the presence of ladies. He got to his feet, took two strides forward, and smashed his fist into Uxbury's mouth.

The viscount, taken by surprise, went down heavily in a shower of blood, grasping with one flailing hand at the tablecloth of the table behind him as he went in a vain attempt to save himself. His fall was followed by a noisy shower of crockery and cutlery and smashing glassware and cream cakes and tea. One of the cakes landed upside down on the bridge of his nose.

There were screams, shouts, general mayhem. Everyone was standing. Some were trying to escape danger. Most were craning their necks to see what had happened. Others were moving closer to get a better look. Joel flexed his stinging knuckles.

"Oh, bravo," Riverdale said quietly beneath the hubbub.

"Very well-done," Lady Overfield agreed.

"Dear me," the Duke of Netherby said, and somehow—how did the man do it?—all around him fell silent and those farther back shushed others so that they could hear. "New boots, my dear fellow? They can be embarrassingly slippery for a while, I have found. Too bad that you have made such a spectacle of yourself, though I daresay you are among friends here who will make every effort to forget the whole thing and never remind you of it. Allow me to help you to your feet."

"He must have caught his mouth on the edge of a table on his way down, Netherby," the Earl of Riverdale said, "and knocked out a tooth. Ah, Viscount Uxbury, is it not?"

Uxbury was not unconscious. He scrambled to his feet without assistance, brushing aside Netherby's hand as he did so. He pulled a large handkerchief out of his pocket and held it to his bleeding mouth. His face was chalky white. His two relatives had come up to him and were taking an arm each to lead him out. He went quietly after glaring at Joel and speaking to him, his voice muffled by the handkerchief.

"You will be hearing from my lawyer," he said.

"I shall look forward to it," Joel told him.

He was standing, he realized, almost shoulder to shoulder with Camille. He turned his head toward her, and she turned hers to him.

"Thank you," she murmured before turning back to resume her seat. She was not the haughty aristocrat now. She was the marble lady with the complexion to match the title.

The three men left without further incident, everyone sat down again, conversation buzzed, waiters rushed about clearing debris, making up the table again with fresh linen and bringing fresh tea and food, and within minutes anyone arriving at the Upper Rooms would not have known that something very ungenteel had just happened there. Indeed, it seemed probable to Joel that many people who had been there the whole time did not realize it either. A number of conversations were probably on the topic of how dangerous new boots and shoes could be before the soles had become properly scuffed by use.

Perhaps it was as well he had been unable to purchase a ready-made pair yesterday.

"I owe you a debt of gratitude, Mr. Cunningham,"

Camille's mother said to him. "I am deeply ashamed that I once approved that young man's courtship of my daughter."

"I understand we are to go picnicking tomorrow, Mr. Cunningham," Lady Overfield said. "I look forward to it enormously. I confess to a great curiosity to see your new home."

Twenty-one

Camille was basking in the sunshine out in the garden the following morning. She was seated on a stone bench while Sarah sat at her feet, grasping blades of grass and pulling them out before looking up at Camille, thoroughly proud of herself. Winifred was sitting cross-legged on the ground, watching her. Several other children were outside, involved in various games. Everyone was enjoying the brief holiday from school, though most of the children had greeted Camille cheerfully.

She had not been invited. The family was going up to Mr. Cox-Phillips's house, now Joel's, this afternoon for a picnic and probably a tour of the house.

She had not been invited.

Yesterday, on her first full appearance in public, she had been called a bastard. She hugged her elbows with both hands and smiled down at the baby, whose triumphant smile displayed her two new bottom teeth. Joel, like a knight errant, had punched Viscount Uxbury in her defense. And somehow Avery's words had covered up the whole potential scandal, at least temporarily. It was too much to hope, of course, that absolutely no one outside their family group had seen what happened or heard the fatal words. Joel was the one who had acted, and he had drawn blood and possibly a tooth.

And then he had sat down again with Mama and Elizabeth and Alexander and continued with his tea and conversation as though nothing had happened. He had not spoken a word to her.

He had not invited her to today's picnic.

If he had taken a horn up onto a rooftop and bellowed through it, his message could not be louder than his silence was. Well, then. She squared her shoulders and wished the bench was not quite so hard.

"I prayed every night that Sarah's teeth would come through," Winifred said as the baby held up her arms and Camille picked her up and set her on her lap, "and they did."

Winifred's occasional piety could be even more annoying than her general righteousness. But Camille smiled. "It is good to know," she said, "that prayers are answered. She is a good deal more contented now."

And then, suddenly, he was there, standing in front of the bench in his old coat and scuffed boots, looking down at them, a smile in his eyes. His head blocked the sun and made Camille feel chilly. And Sarah, the treacherous child, gurgled and reached up her arms again. He swung her up, held her above his head while she chuckled and drooled onto his neckcloth, and lowered her to sit on one arm.

"Good morning, ladies," he said.

"Sarah has two teeth," Winifred told him. "I prayed that they would come through and they did."

"That's the girl," he said, patting her shoulder with his free hand. But Hannah was coming for Sarah. It was time for her feed. Winifred went inside with them. Joel stayed where he was, his eyes fixed upon Camille. "I had a note from Anna this morning. She told me you are not coming to the picnic."

Damn Anna, Camille thought, using a shocking word in her mind she would not dream of speaking aloud. "No," she said. "I have other things to do."

He folded his arms and stared down at her. "I am sorry, Camille," he said. "I have been behaving like an ass. It is just that— Well, the earth moved on Sunday. It moved more than it always does, that is. I—"

"That is quite all right," she said. "You do not need to explain or apologize if that was your intention. Sunday was my suggestion, if you will recall, and I do not regret it in any way. It was very enjoyable. But that was the past, and it is always wise to let the past go and concentrate upon the present and as much of the future as can be reasonably planned for."

"Damn it," he said, "I have hurt you."

"I would be obliged if you would watch your language," she said, ignoring the fact that her mind had quite consciously used the same word a mere minute or so ago.

"Why will you not come?" he asked.

She looked hard at him. "I have not been invited," she said. "In my world—in my former world that is, one does not attend events to which one has not been invited."

He scratched his head, leaving his hair untidy. It was growing, she noticed. "Good God, Camille," he said, "you were so central to the whole plan that it did not occur to me that you would need an invitation."

Indignation warred with something else. She was *central to the whole plan*? Whatever did that mean?

"I want you to see it," he said. "I went up there on Wednesday and saw the house and the garden. *Garden* is actually a misleading word. It is more like a park. And *house* is the wrong word too. It is huge and terribly impressive. My great-uncle may have been elderly, but nothing has been neglected and allowed to grow shabby. I still cannot believe it is mine. I still cannot imagine myself living there. But ideas went teeming through my head while I was there and I wished you were with me."

"Not Anna?" she said stiffly.

He sighed aloud. "I did not think of her even once while I was there," he said. "I wanted you."

"I plan to be busy today." She looked down sharply at her hands.

"Doing what?" he asked.

"That is not your concern," she told him.

"Yes, it is," he said. "There is no school today and no family. You are planning to be busy doing nothing merely to punish me. I deserve to be punished. I have been shy about coming to see you since Sunday, but I ought to have done so, especially as I wanted to come. And if I am sounding horribly confused and contradictory and idiotic, that is because I am all those things. Camille, please come." He had stooped down on his haunches before her and reached for her hands before apparently remembering the playing, shrieking children all about them and setting his hands on his knees instead. "Please?"

He had been *shy about coming*?

She looked at him for long moments. "I am going home," she said abruptly. "My mother is going back to Hinsford Manor to live—Anna has persuaded her. Abby is going with her. And so am I." She had no idea if she spoke the truth. Surely not. But how could she stay . . .

He frowned as his eyes searched her face. "Come this afternoon anyway," he said. "Come with your family. You have only a few days left here with them, and it is a lovely spot for a picnic. It looks as if it is going to remain a beautiful day too. Come, Camille, if not for my sake, then for theirs and yours."

She frowned back at him and he suddenly smiled.

"But come for my sake too," he said. "The earth really did move on Sunday. I think it did for you too."

"I will come," she said stiffly. "I will ask someone from the family to take me up in one of the carriages."

He stood up. "Thank you," he said.

But she noticed something suddenly and grabbed his right hand with both of hers. His knuckles, if not quite raw, were red enough to look sore.

"I would guess," he said, "that his mouth looks and feels considerably worse."

"I hope," she said, "he really did lose a tooth."

Judge Fanshawe had called upon Joel on Wednesday just after he returned from being measured for new clothes and boots. The judge was an elderly gentleman much bent by age and had sent his servant to summon Joel down to the street, where he stood waiting outside his carriage. He had told Joel that he had never been more offended in his life than when he discovered that Viscount Uxbury,

Mr. Martin Cox-Phillips, and Mr. Blake Norton were contesting the will.

"I look forward with great glee to crushing them to powder beneath my bootheel, should they persist, which, alas, I fear they will not do when they take a closer look at the list of witnesses," he had said. "I was one of them, and even the others are formidable. You may safely consider your inheritance your own, Mr. Cunningham."

He had shaken Joel's hand with a surprisingly strong grip before climbing back inside the carriage with his servant's help and going on his way.

So, on impulse, Joel had gone up to see his new property, which he would probably sell as soon as all the business of the will had been settled. He had spoken with the butler—Mr. Nibbs—and assured him that all the servants might remain until further notice and that Mr. Crabtree would be directed to pay their salaries. Nibbs had shown him about the house before summoning the head gardener to take him through the gardens. Afterward Joel had spent another hour wandering about the house on his own. It was all far larger and more imposing than he had realized, and intimidating too. But something had happened when he had stood at last in the library behind the chair where his great-uncle had sat, his hands resting on the high back. He had felt . . . a connection, a longing, though he could put neither feeling into clear words in his mind.

His mother had grown up here. His grandparents had lived here as well as his great-uncle. He had not felt the presence of ghosts exactly, but he had felt . . . well, a connection. It was the one thing that had always been absent from his life. Not that he was complaining. His life so far had been remarkably blessed, even if he omitted the happenings of the last couple of weeks. But . . .

Well, he had fallen in love. And, perhaps by an association of thought, he had wished Camille were with him. He had been fairly bursting with thoughts, ideas, needs . . .

He had informed Mr. Nibbs of Friday's picnic and warned him that the guests would wish a tour of the house. He had asked that some chairs and blankets be carried out to the front lawn, weather permitting, and that arrangements be made for horses and carriages. He had assured the butler, however, that he had engaged the services of a caterer in Bath so that the cook and kitchen staff need not be thrown into consternation. He had not been sure they would be up to catering to a large party of aristocrats after having worked for some time with an ailing old gentleman who probably had not entertained a great deal. He had given only one other direction before he left.

"If you could arrange to have those blind-eyed busts removed from the hall as soon as humanly possible, Mr. Nibbs," he had said, "I would be much obliged to you."

The butler was too well-bred to smirk, but Joel would have sworn he was doing it inwardly. "I shall give the order, sir," he had said. "They were a wedding gift to Mr. and Mrs. Cunningham, but Mr. Cox-Phillips was never overfond of them."

And now Joel was back, pacing the terrace before the house, noting that the lawns had been freshly scythed, that five chairs had been set out in a semicircle on the lawn so that no one would have to face away from the view. There was a neat pile of blankets to one side of them. And what the devil was he doing? Joel wondered.

He had no idea how to host anything more grand than an evening gathering of his male friends in his rooms. When the caterer had asked him what specifically he wanted for food and drink, he had gaped—he hoped he had not literally done so—and asked for advice. He had had enough money to pay for the picnic, but only just. His meager savings were wiped out, and he could only hope that Judge Fanshawe was correct.

He would have a tailor's bill and a bootmaker's bill to pay within the next week or two.

Fortunately, he did not have long to brood. One carriage was crunching over the gravel of the driveway and another was coming right behind it. Joel moved onto the steps outside the front door and stood with his hands clasped behind him, trying to pretend that he was the grand master of all he surveyed. He wished his boots were not quite so scuffed.

Everything proceeded remarkably well after that. Everyone was in high spirits, and they all admired the house and the view and the garden. The housekeeper gave them a tour of the house, though the Dowager Countess of Riverdale decided to remain in the drawing room after they had arrived there, and Lady Matilda Westcott chose to stay too to ply her with smelling salts despite her mother's vociferous protests. Everyone went their separate ways after the tour was over, most of the family strolling outdoors across lawns, through the rose arbor, down onto the steeply sloping rock garden, behind the house to the woods through which a carefully cultivated path ran.

"Joel," Anna said, linking an arm through his just before they all gathered on the main lawn for the picnic tea, "this is a quite exquisite jewel of a place, is it not? And to think that we grew up down there within sight of it and were never aware of it. Do you regret . . . Oh, never mind."

"Yes, I do," he said. "If only one could reach back in time and *know*. But it cannot be done, and it was their choice to remain unknown to me. I do, however, owe the decency of my upbringing to them—it might have been very much worse. And I owe my grandmother my career. It would not have happened if I had not been able to go to art school."

"You were always very talented," she said. "But you are probably right. What are you going to do? Are you going to live here?"

"Rattle about alone in such a vast mansion?" he said. "It is hard to imagine."

"Alone, Joel?" she said, and he was aware that her eyes were resting upon Camille, who was looking remarkably pretty in a light muslin dress and straw bonnet Joel had not seen before—and who had scarcely glanced his way since her initial stiff greeting when she had arrived with her maternal grandmother and her mother and sister.

"I have not decided what to do about the house," he said. "I was determined to sell it, but . . . Well, my mother grew up here, and . . ."

She squeezed his arm. "Take your time to decide," she said. "All will be well. I promise."

"Oh, you do, do you?" he said.

"I do." She laughed and released him in order to join two of her aunts.

The picnic fare seemed like perfection itself to Joel, and everyone appeared to agree with him. Everyone complimented him, and he laughed and told the truth.

"I left everything in the hands of the caterer," he said. "When I was shown a list of possibilities, I did not even know what most of the items were. They all had fancy names. So I had to leave the choice to the experts and have been relieved to discover that I recognize the foods even if not the names."

Everyone laughed with him and it was time for his little surprise. Servants came from the house with trays of champagne and Joel proposed a toast to the dowager countess, who was sitting upon one of the chairs beneath the shade of a tree, though Lady Matilda had made several attempts also to hold a parasol over her head.

"I do not know the exact date of your birthday, ma'am," he said. "But I wish you a happy birthday week." And everyone clinked glasses and echoed the toast.

"My birthday is today, young man," the dowager said, "and so far it has been perfect. I cannot imagine a more delightful setting for my birthday tea or more delicious food or more congenial company. Thank you."

The toast and her words signaled the end of the visit. The carriages were summoned and everyone gathered on the terrace waiting for them, talking cheerfully among themselves, thanking Joel again and complimenting him on his new home.

And still he and Camille had exchanged no more than that initial greeting. She had avoided him all afternoon. Or perhaps he had avoided her.

"Camille," he said, "can I persuade you to stay a little longer? There are some things I would like to show you. You may return home with me later."

He had not spoken loudly. He had not expected anyone else but her to hear. But it seemed everyone did, and a general hush fell on the gathering as everyone, it seemed, looked first at him, then at Camille, and then back at him.

"It is hardly the thing, Mr. Cunningham," Lady Matilda said, "for a single lady—"

"I believe my granddaughter is quite capable of making her own decisions, Matilda," the dowager countess said.

"Of course she is," Lady Molenor agreed. "If she—"

"Perhaps, Mr. Cunningham," Elizabeth, Lady Overfield, said, "you will permit me to stay too. I would love to spend a quiet hour in the library looking at all those books. If, that is, Camille chooses to stay."

All eyes swung her way. The color was high in her cheeks. That stubborn jaw of hers was in full evidence, as were the lips set in a thin line. "Yes, certainly," she said.

They stood on the terrace, the three of them, watching the carriages move off down the driveway. Lady Overfield turned a smiling face to Joel. Her eyes were twinkling.

"I shall make myself scarce," she said. "I daresay I could spend a week in that library without running out of books to look at, so you must not feel rushed. And I know the way." She turned her smile upon Camille, picked up her skirts, climbed the steps, and disappeared into the house.

"I suppose I scandalized everyone," he said. "I do not know how to behave like a gentleman, do I?"

He heard her draw a breath and release it. "Why did you want me to stay?" she asked him.

Because he was the world's worst coward. And because *he did not want her to go home to Hinsford Manor with her mother and sister.*

He closed the short distance between them and took her determinedly by the hand. "I told you I came here on Wednesday," he said, setting out with her along the terrace and around the side of the house, "and wished you were with me. Today you have been here with me and a dozen or so other people and I almost let you go with them. My mind is like a hornets' nest, Camille. There is so much bubbling up inside it. Is that a mixing of images? That will tell you the state of my mind, perhaps. Did you walk through the woods back here earlier? The path rises rather steeply, but it is well worth the climb. There are all sorts of places to sit and relax and simply enjoy the views."

"I did not come this far," she said as they climbed.

They arrived at the part that had particularly struck him on Wednesday—a clearing among the trees that had been made into a little flower garden with a wrought iron seat in the middle. From here one could see down between a framework of tree branches over the roof of the house to the dazzling white elegance of the Georgian buildings of Bath. He led her to the seat and they sat down side by side.

"I thought that perhaps I would sell this place," he said, "but I cannot bring myself to do it, Camille. It is the only real connection I have to my family. I cannot see myself living alone here, but I can see all sorts of possibilities, none of which I have thought through to know if they are possible or practicable or anything else. I picture an art school here, or a place for art retreats, perhaps. Possibly for some of the children from the orphanage, perhaps for other children too, perhaps for adults. I picture a music school—or retreat house—for various instruments and for voice. Even for dancing. Or a writing retreat. I picture bringing distinguished experts here to give courses of instruction upon a variety of different subjects and to offer demonstrations and concerts. More than anything, though, I see and hear children dashing about down there on the lawns, up here playing hide-and-seek among the trees, running through the house making noise and tracking dirt. Happy, free."

"Your own children?" she asked, and he knew as soon as he turned his head to look at her that she was wishing she could bite out her tongue. Her cheeks were flushed.

"Among others," he said. "I would like to have children of my own. I would like to give them what I never knew— a father and a mother. But I see other children here too, enjoying a holiday and a chance to kick up their heels in a place where there is so much space to run."

She did not say anything.

"Of course," he said, "it is a considerable distance from Bath, and I have never been anywhere else but there. It seems a bit isolated up here. Wide-open. Beautiful too, though. Close to heaven."

"You would not be isolated," she said, "if there was always something going on here and people constantly coming and going. And, Joel, you could afford your own carriage to take you back and forth to the city."

"So I could," he said, though it was not the first time he had thought of it. "I could have horses. And perhaps a dog or two and a cat or three. Maybe rabbits. As a boy, I believe I longed for a pet almost as much as I longed for a family. They have never been allowed in the orphanage, for very obvious reasons. But I have always thought that the presence of pets would be so very good for the children. Dogs and cats, I have heard, will always love you even when no humans seem to. Pets can be cuddled with and read to. They do not judge. They . . . simply love. Do you think I could talk Miss Ford into allowing some of the children to come here to stay for a few days at a time for lessons and music and romping and riding on horses and playing with cats and dogs and rabbits? Am I being very naïve? Building castles in the air? Sand castles? Am I being a fool?"

"Would you consider having a small orphanage of your own up here?" she asked.

He thought about it for a while. "No," he said. "If there were to be children here permanently, they would have to belong to me."

"Your own children," she said.

"Or adopted." He was on new ground here. He had not thought of this before. "Perhaps . . . Sarah," he said.

Their eyes met and held. He saw her swallow and he watched her eyes fill with tears before she turned her head away.

"And Winifred," she said.

"Winifred?" He frowned.

"She is not a terribly likable child, is she?" she said. "She is righteous and pious and neat and judgmental. I recognize myself in her, Joel, to the point of pain. She wants desperately to be loved and believes love must be earned with good behavior. She does not understand that her efforts are pushing love away rather than gathering it in."

"You would like to *adopt* her?" he asked.

She looked back at him with blank eyes. "You were the one speaking of adoption," she said, "and of bringing children here as your own. I was merely speaking hypothetically. I just wish she could know herself loved. More than loved. *Chosen.*" She blinked her eyes and stood up abruptly. "Elizabeth will be running out of books with which to amuse herself. Let us go back down."

And the moment, the edge upon which he had been teetering, had passed. It was just as well. Ideas had been spilling out of his mind and he was really quite unsure of any of them. He was not sure of *anything*.

No, that wasn't true. He was very, very sure of one thing. He was desperately in love with her. And he just as desperately wanted to marry her.

But still the moment did not feel quite right. He did not want a marriage proposal to sound as if it had just stumbled out of his mind into his mouth and out through his lips.

He stood up beside her and took her hand again. "Thank you for staying," he said. "Thank you for listening."

They made their way back to the house in near silence.

Twenty-two

※

After returning from taking Sarah and Winifred and two other young children to see the ducks down by the river and feed them bread crumbs the following morning, Camille sat beside Miss Ford and the nurse for luncheon.

"Are any of these children ever adopted?" she asked during a lull in the conversation. She had never heard of it happening, but then, she had not been here long.

"Occasionally," Miss Ford said. "The babies, that is. People looking for adoptive children rarely look for any above a few months old. This is not the sort of orphanage upon which unscrupulous employers cast their sights for cheap labor."

"What is the procedure for adoption?" Camille asked.

"In most cases," Miss Ford told her, "the real parent or whoever it is who is supporting the child here is consulted and grants or withholds permission. If the answer is yes, the legal details are handled by our solicitor, but the governing board is very careful to investigate the prospective parents. We offer love here and safety and a good quality of care, as you know. We try to make sure it is to the child's advantage to become part of a family."

"And if the real parents are unknown?" Camille asked.

"We follow the same careful investigative procedure," Miss Ford said. "Having our children adopted feels a little like giving up our own children, you know. We will do it gladly if it is for the child's benefit, but it is never easy to say goodbye. Understandably, most adoptive parents do not want to come back here for visits."

"Do you remember Sammy and his golden curls?" the nurse asked, and she and Miss Ford were off into reminiscences of babies they had lost to adoption.

Camille returned to her room and wrote to Harry to congratulate him upon his promotion. It was the first time she had written directly to him. It was painful. Harry had been the Earl of Riverdale. She had been forever annoyed with him because he was having the time of his life, surrounded by companions who numbered more sycophants than real friends, merely wearing a black armband in deference to their father's passing while Mama, Abby, and she were swathed in funereal black. But he had been a good-hearted boy, cheerful, intelligent, affectionate. She had loved him dearly without fully realizing it. And she loved him now and felt the pain of what had happened to him. His letters were always high spirited, but what was the reality? Would he even be alive to read her letter? Her fear for him was always there, deeply suppressed but very real.

The price of love, she thought, was pain. Was it worth it? Was it better not to love at all?

In the middle of the afternoon she walked up to the Royal Crescent, as she had done yesterday before the picnic, to raid her wardrobe for something more suitable to wear to the evening's ball than any of the few garments that hung in her room at the orphanage. It felt a little like digging into a past life she had left behind longer ago than a few months, but there was something undeniably enticing about it. What woman did not like to dress up and look her best at least once in a while?

She chose a gown of silver lace over blue satin, its waistline high beneath her bosom, its neckline low, the sleeves short and puffed. The hem was deeply scalloped and embroidered with silver thread. She donned long silver gloves and silver slippers and would carry a delicate fan that opened to reveal a brightly colored painting of fat winged cherubs hovering above a romantically handsome, languishing young man who looked as though he had been badly wounded by one of Cupid's darts. It amused Camille—though she had never thought of it before—to imagine that the holder of the fan perhaps held the fate of a young man's love literally in the palm of her hand. Her only jewelry was the pearl necklace her father had given her on her come-out—actually it was his secretary who had delivered it to her—and the matching earrings that had been her mother's gift. Her grandmother's dresser styled her hair high on her head with intricate twists and curls and some waved tendrils to lie along her neck and over her ears.

For a moment, looking at herself in her mirror, she felt

a wave of nostalgia for that familiar world she had left behind so abruptly. But it surprised her to realize that she would not go back now even if she could. She did not believe she particularly liked the person she had been then, and she certainly did not like the person to whom she had been betrothed. She turned away and went to Abigail's room, where she found her sister looking like a relic of springtime in a pretty pale yellow gown Camille had not seen before. She was in a fever of excitement and anxiety.

"Will it be like a *real* ball, do you think?" she asked. "Oh, you do look lovely, Cam. I always wish I had grown as tall as you." Abby had attended a few local assemblies in the country, but no formal balls. She had never had a coming-out Season.

"It will not be like a London squeeze, I suppose," Camille said, "but I understand the whole of Bath polite society has been invited, and I would imagine it is being touted as the grandest event of the summer. The Westcotts have more than their fair share of titles among them, after all. It will be well attended."

"Do you think—" Abigail stopped and fussed over donning her shawl and picking up her fan. "Do you think we may have a few partners, Cam? Apart from Uncle Thomas and Alexander, that is?"

"I think," Camille said, "our aunts will take their duties as hostesses seriously, Abby. A hostess does not like to see wallflowers decorating her ballroom. It reflects badly upon her."

"They will find us partners, then?" Abigail wrinkled her nose.

"It is the way things are arranged," Camille told her.

"And sometimes gentlemen will ask to be presented. It is not done, you know, for them to rush up and ask for a dance when there has been no introduction."

She hoped she was speaking the truth. She hoped her sister would have dancing partners and that they would not be just older married men who had been coerced into it or had taken pity on her. She did not care for herself. She would be quite content merely to watch the festivities and spend a little more time with her family before they returned home. And, as Abby had just said, Uncle Thomas and Alexander and even Avery would no doubt dance with her. And . . .

Joel?

She had tried very hard all day not to think about yesterday. What exactly had he been saying? He probably did not even know himself, though—he had compared his mind to a hornets' nest. But—*I would like to have children of my own. I would like to give them what I never knew, a father and a mother.* And he had spoken of adopting children. He had mentioned Sarah. And then, after seeming to be building to something, he had thanked her for coming and for listening and led the way down the hill.

Oh, she was going to go home to Hinsford with Mama and Abby. She was simply going to give up the struggle and be abject. No, she was not. She was going to remain at the school. She was going to stay firm and . . . Perhaps she would set up her own establishment somewhere and live independently. She could do it with the money she was taking from Anna. She could live very well on it, in fact. She was sure even a quarter of her father's fortune was a very handsome sum. Yes, perhaps she would do just that or. . . .

Oh, Joel.

Abigail was ready to go downstairs, and soon they were in the carriage with their mother and grandmother on the way to the Upper Assembly Rooms even though the distance was a very short one. Mama held Abby's hand tightly, Camille noticed. She herself opened and closed her fan on her lap and wondered if there would be any waltzes.

Joel had become something of a local celebrity. He was already known by some people, of course, as a portrait painter, and those people were able to point him out to everyone else as the penniless orphan who had turned out to be the long-lost great-nephew—some even said grandson—of the very wealthy Mr. Cox-Phillips, who had lived in one of the mansions up in the hills. The elderly gentleman had discovered the truth in the very nick of time, or so the story ran, and left every last penny of his millions to the young man, whom he had been able to clasp to his bosom for the first and last time almost with his dying breath.

Joel's celebrity had been enhanced rather than diminished when the story began to circulate and then ignite fashionable drawing rooms that he had punched Viscount Uxbury in the face during a tea at the Upper Rooms, knocking all his teeth down his throat in the process, for insulting a lady.

It was with a great deal of trepidation, then, that Joel approached those same Upper Rooms on Saturday evening, uncomfortable in new evening clothes and shoes and wondering if it was imperative for a man to dance at such an event when he had only ever danced at the orphanage. And wondering too if there would be enough dark corners in which to hide. And wondering if it was too late to turn around and go back home. But he was mortally tired of his own cowardice. One thing was certain. He could not return to his old, comfortable life. Very well, then. He would move on with the new.

Besides, Camille might well take herself off to Hinsford Manor tomorrow with her mother and sister, and he was not going to allow it to happen without a fight—or without at least talking to her first.

He walked purposefully up to the door of the rooms, gave his name to the bruiser of a uniformed man who half filled the doorway—at least one person in Bath, it seemed, did not know him by sight—and stepped inside.

Every citizen of Bath except the bruiser at the door must have been invited, he thought over the next few minutes. The tearoom was crammed, the ballroom was full, and if he was not drawing attention wherever he went, then his imagination was far more vivid than he had realized. An orchestra on a raised platform was tuning its instruments, though the dancing had not begun. The place hummed with conversation and laughter, and if someone would just open a trapdoor in the floor Joel would gladly disappear through it without even checking for steps first.

And then Lady Molenor claimed him, all sparkling jewels and nodding hair plumes and gracious manners, and she was closely followed by the Dowager Duchess of Netherby, formidable in a royal blue gown and matching turban with a jewel the size of a robin's egg pinned to the front of it. They bore him off between them to greet the

Dowager Countess of Riverdale, who was seated in the ballroom on a chair that resembled a throne, happily receiving the homage and birthday greetings of all and sundry while Lady Matilda Westcott, her daughter, plied a fan in the vicinity of her face, all solicitous concern for her mother's comfort. Anna, looking very lovely indeed in deep rose pink, came to hug him, and Lady Jessica Archer and Miss Abigail Westcott fluttered their fans at him and smiled brightly before walking off arm-in-arm to display their prettiness before the gathered multitudes. And . . . Camille was there, standing for the moment a little off to one side of her grandmother, alone.

"I do not believe," he said, stepping closer to her, "I have ever seen a more beautiful woman."

She stared at him for a moment and he realized how very extravagant and silly his words must have sounded. But then she smiled slowly, an expression that began with dancing eyes. "Or I a more handsome man," she said. "Joel, you have been shopping. Was it very painful?"

"Excruciatingly so," he said, grinning at her. "But I walked all the way up here and my shoes have still not blistered all my toes. Or my heels. Nor has my cravat rubbed my neck raw."

"You do look very splendid," she said.

"Camille," he said, sobering, "are you really going to go home with your mother and sister?"

She did not answer immediately. "No," she said then. "It would be an admission of defeat, and I refuse to be defeated."

"Good girl," he said, as though he were speaking to one of the pupils at the school.

"But, Joel," she said, unfurling her fan and immediately adding a flourish of gorgeous color to the delicate blues and silver of her garments. "I have accepted Anna's offer of one-quarter of my father's fortune. I am not sure yet what I will do with it, if anything."

"Ah," he said, and he did not know if he was glad or sorry. "What made you change your mind?"

"I am trying to make my heart follow the lead my head has set," she said. "I am trying to love her, Joel. I am trying to think of her as my sister, not just as my half sister. Sharing her fortune is crucial to her happiness."

He had no chance to answer. There was an increase of movement all about them, and he realized that the orchestra had fallen silent and couples were gathering on the dance floor.

"My set, I believe, Camille," the Earl of Riverdale said, nodding genially at Joel and extending a hand toward his cousin.

"Yes, Alexander. Thank you," she said.

And Joel was left alone again until Lady Overfield stepped up beside him. "I remember Anna telling me about the dances that were held at the orphanage when her old teacher was still there," she said. "She knew the steps of everything except the waltz. I suppose you do too, Mr. Cunningham. At the risk of sounding unpardonably forward, would you care to try this one with me? The floor is very crowded. I daresay we will be lost among the masses and absolutely no one will even see us."

And if Camille was the most beautiful woman he had ever seen, Joel thought—and he might, of course, be partial—then surely Lady Overfield was the kindest.

"I shall do my very best not to shame you, ma'am," he said, smiling ruefully at her as he offered his arm.

"I was delighted to learn yesterday," Alexander said after leading Camille onto the floor, "that Cousin Viola is returning to Hinsford to live and that Abigail is going with her. Will you go too, Camille?"

"No," she said, "except for the occasional visit. But I do not disapprove. I am glad for them too."

"Your future lies here?" he asked her, looking beyond her shoulder to where Joel was leading Elizabeth out.

"For now, yes," she said. "I actually enjoy teaching, though it is the most chaotic, alarming activity I have ever been involved in and I sometimes wonder what on earth I am doing."

He looked back at her and smiled. "Apparently Miss Ford has offered you the job for at least the next twenty years," he said. "I believe that is a high recommendation."

"And what about you, Alexander?" she asked him. "However will you restore the fortunes of Brambledean Court? Or, like Papa, will you not even try?"

"Oh, I shall try," he told her. "It is my duty, after all. I shall have to marry a rich wife."

The dancing was about to begin, and it was an intricate country dance during which there would be little opportunity for private conversation. He was still smiling. His eyes were even twinkling, as though he had made a joke. Camille hoped it *was* a joke. Alexander had always been an honorable, kindly man. Although she had never believed in romantic love herself, she had always expected that when he married it would be for love with a lady who

matched him in temperament and amiability—and looks.
It chilled her that he might put his duty to the people at
Brambledean her father had so shamefully neglected
before his own happiness. The old Camille would have
understood and applauded. The new Camille wanted to
cry out in protest.

But the music began.

Abby, she saw, was dancing with Avery. And it had all
been very carefully calculated, she realized as the evening progressed. A duke and an earl danced the opening
set with the two illegitimate daughters of the earl's predecessor and thus displayed to the company that they
were perfectly respectable, that a slight to them might
well result in a snub from both noblemen and their families. Neither Camille nor Abigail lacked for partners all
evening, and while Camille danced with both Avery and
Uncle Thomas, Abigail danced every set except the first
with men who were not part of the family, most of them
young and unmarried. Abby might well remember this
evening as the happiest of her life.

This, of course, was Bath, not London, and Abby could
not always expect the sort of family support that was
behind her tonight. But even so . . . Well, perhaps there
was some hope after all. Perhaps what had happened was
not the unalloyed disaster it had seemed at the time and
until very recently.

Joel disappeared from the ballroom after dancing the
opening set quite creditably with Elizabeth. Camille
thought he must have left until she went into the tearoom
later on Uncle Thomas's arm and saw that he was sitting
with Miss Ford and a group of ladies who appeared to be
hanging upon his every word. His eyes met hers across

the room. She sat with her back to him and joined in the conversation at her own table. Ten minutes or so passed before she felt a hand upon her shoulder.

"I believe the next set is to be a waltz," Joel said, addressing her after nodding a greeting to the other occupants of the table. "Will you dance it with me, Camille?"

"Yes." She got to her feet and set her napkin down on the table. "Thank you."

"Or perhaps," he said as they walked in the direction of the ballroom, "you would feel safer if we merely promenaded about the perimeter of the room. I notice that is a favorite activity of a number of people."

"Have you turned craven, Mr. Cunningham?" she asked, unfurling her fan and wafting it before her face.

"Not at all, Miss Westcott," he said. "I have turned chivalrous. I do not want to make a spectacle of you on the dance floor. Not to mention endangering your toes."

"Are you saying, by any chance," she asked him, "that you do not trust my teaching skills, Mr. Cunningham?"

"I believe it is more my learning skills I doubt," he said. "But I am willing to give it a go if you are."

"Give it a go?" She frowned at him. "What sort of language is that, Mr. Cunningham?"

"The gutter?" he suggested.

And they dissolved into laughter, which was not at all a genteel thing to do, and Camille slid an arm through his.

"As Lady Overfield remarked earlier," he said, "the floor will doubtless be so crowded that no one will even notice us or any imperfections in our dancing prowess."

That proved less true than either of them could have wished. The waltz, it seemed, was not yet as fashionable in Bath as it was in London, and most of the guests preferred to watch or else remain in the tearoom. A number of couples took to the floor, but there was plenty of room for them all to dance freely without fear of collisions—and plenty of room for them all to be observed.

"This," Joel said as the music began, "was not the most brilliant idea I have ever had."

"Yes," she said, looking very directly into his face, "it was."

His hand was warm against the back of her waist, his shoulder firm beneath her own hand. His other hand, clasping her own, felt large and reassuring, and he smelled good of something indefinable—shaving soap, perhaps, new linen and coat fabric, perhaps. And of Joel. She was sure she could have been led here blindfolded and known exactly who held her in waltz position. His body heat enveloped her and she remembered last Sunday with an ache of longing. She so loved his lovemaking.

His gaze was intense, and she wondered if he was having similar thoughts. *Oh, Joel,* she asked him silently, *what did you mean yesterday?*

They waltzed with wooden legs again when the music began—one two three, one two three, three to one side, three back again—and Camille watched a flush begin to creep up his neck from beneath his cravat and something like panic gather in his eyes. She smiled at him and laughed softly.

And suddenly they were waltzing again as they had begun to do in the schoolroom, but without the inhibitions of space and the limits of her breath as she both sang and danced. This time a full orchestra and the ballroom at the Upper Rooms swept them onward, and they danced and twirled in a world that was theirs and theirs alone, their eyes on each other, smiles on their lips.

It was strange being both aware of one's surroundings and all alone within them at the same time. She knew that Anna was dancing with Avery, Alexander and Elizabeth and Abby and Jessica with unknown partners—even though Abby and Jessica had not even made their official come-outs yet and would not be allowed even then to waltz in London until they had been given the nod of approval by one of the hostesses of Almack's Club. She was aware of other dancers and the swirl of color from gowns and the flash of jewels in the candlelight. She was aware of the older members of her family and other people standing about watching. She was aware of the smell of candles and perfumes, of the sounds of dancing feet and swishing silks and satins beneath the beat of the music. She was even aware that she and Joel were attracting more than their fair share of attention, perhaps because of who she was, more probably because of whom Joel had just become. And yet all of these impressions merely formed a distant background to the world of music and movement and, yes, of *romance*, in which they danced.

The most wonderful, wonderful feeling in the world, she thought without trying to analyze the thought or distrust it or be made fearful by it—the most wonderful feeling in the world was being in love.

When the music ended, the two worlds came together, and Camille removed her hand from Joel's shoulder, slipped her other hand free of his, and smiled regretfully at him.

"I believe, Mr. Cunningham," she said, "I must be the world's best teacher."

"Only, Miss Westcott," he said, "because you have the world's best pupil."

They grinned inelegantly at each other.

"There is nowhere here to be even remotely private, is there?" he said. "Come for a stroll outside with me, Camille?"

In the late evening, when it was dark out there? Without a chaperon? Without—

"I'll fetch my shawl," she said.

The sounds of music and voices and laughter dimmed as soon as they stepped outdoors. There was the mere sliver of a new moon overhead. But the sky was cloudless and there was more than enough starlight to see by. The air had lost the heat of the day but was on the warm side of cool. There was no discernible wind.

"It is lovely out here," she said, lifting her face to the sky.

"It is," he agreed as they strolled the short distance along Bennett Street to the Circus. They crossed the road to the great circular garden at the center of it and strolled inside the rails. All around them rose the three massive curved segments of the circle of houses with their elegant, classical design. There were very few lights behind any of the windows. It was late.

"I painted all day," he told her. "I painted furiously and without a break and achieved that total focus I always aim for when I am creating. I painted your sister—from the sketches I made, from memory, and from that part of myself I can never describe in words. The portrait is not by any means finished, but I am terribly pleased with it. There is something so . . . delicate about her being that I have very much feared I would never quite capture it either in thought or in vision or on canvas. But I think I have caught her beauty, her joy in living, her vulnerability, her sadness, her unquenchable hope. Oh, I could pile word upon word and still not express what it is about her I sense. I have never painted anything so quickly. But it is not slipshod or shallow or . . ." His voice trailed away.

"I shall look forward to seeing it when it is finished," she said, her voice prim. They were strolling about the inner perimeter of the garden.

He sighed. "What I was trying to do," he said, "was focus my mind upon one thing so that all the thoughts that have been teeming through it and tormenting me for days would be silenced. I was more successful than I expected. But the thing is, Camille, that somewhere behind my concentration upon the one thing, my thoughts were being tamed and sorted so that when I finally stepped back from the canvas, I knew one thing with perfect clarity . . . well, two things, actually."

She turned her head to look at him. She was using both hands to hold together the edges of her shawl, but he took one of her hands in his and laced their fingers. She grasped both edges of the shawl with the other hand. She did not say anything. But what did he expect her to say? She would think he had brought her out here to tell her about his day of painting.

"One thing I knew, the lesser thing," he said, "was that I am indeed going to keep that house and use my money to do something with it that will share the bounty and the beauty, something that will lift people's spirits and feed their souls. Particularly children, though not exclusively. I do not know either the what or the how yet, but I will. And I will live there to give it the warmth of home as well as everything else. I will have animals there and . . . people."

Good God, he was a coward. He had not known that about himself until recently. He drew her arm beneath his own, their hands still clasped. He stopped walking and they faced outward, looking toward the steep descent of Gay Street.

"The other thing I knew with perfect clarity," he said, "was that I love you, that I want you in my life whatever that turns out to be, that I want to marry you and have children with you and make a family with you in that house—with children of our own bodies and adopted children and dogs and cats and . . . well, snakes and mice too, perhaps, if we have sons or intrepid daughters. I am not sure I can ask it of you. You have lived a very different life. You have grown up the daughter of an earl in an aristocratic household. You are a lady through and through. When I saw you tonight I thought you the most beautiful woman I had ever seen—I did not exaggerate that. I also thought you the grandest, the most remote, the most unattainable. It felt presumptuous to love you."

"Joel," she said, cutting his eloquence short. "You *can* be sure."

He looked at her blankly in the near darkness. He could be sure? He heard the echo of his own words—*I am not sure I can ask it of you.*

"Can I?" he asked.

"You will need a lady to run that house of yours while your head is among the clouds," she said. "One thing I can do with my eyes blindfolded and my hands tied behind my back is run a household. I may find it hair-raising to have shrieking children and barking dogs and squeaking mice and absentminded artists underfoot, but if I can walk into an orphanage and start teaching a schoolroom full of children of all ages and ability levels; if I can get them to knit a purple rope as a collective project and march them all about Bath clinging to it; if I can teach a certain absent-minded artist to waltz, I can do anything."

"But . . ." He was squeezing her fingers and her hand very tightly, he realized before relaxing his grip. "Would you want to, Camille?"

She sighed, a sound of exaggerated long-suffering. "The thing is, Joel," she said, "that I really am a lady by upbringing and cannot shrug off the training of a lifetime in a few brief months. I did it once, shockingly, almost a week ago when I asked you to take me home with you. I do not believe I could do it again. I could not possibly ask *you* to marry *me*. A lady does not, you know. That is a gentleman's task."

He gazed at her. Darkness or no darkness, there was no mistaking the expression on her face.

"I am not a gentleman," he said, his eyes settling on her lips.

"I think it is a man's task, Joel," she said, "even if he is not also gentle or genteel. You are very definitely a man. It was the first impression I had of you when we met in the schoolroom, and it offended me, for I had never consciously thought it of any other man, even Viscount Uxbury. It struck me that you were very . . . male."

He wondered if she was blushing. It was impossible to know in the darkness. But if she was, her eyes were certainly not wavering from his.

"It must be my Italian heritage," he said. "Do you suppose we have any sort of audience behind any of those darkened windows all about us?"

"I neither know nor care," she told him.

"Very well, then." And since he was apparently a man and very male even if not a gentleman—and half Italian to boot—he had better do the thing properly. He lowered himself to one knee and held her hand in both of his. He felt silly . . . and then he did not. He gazed up at her. "Camille, will you marry me? Because I love you with all my heart and really, *really* do not want to live the rest of my life without you? Because I hope you feel that same way about me? I wish I had composed and memorized some polished sort of speech you might have quoted to our grandchildren—if your answer is yes, that is. Though I daresay I would have forgotten every word of it by now. Dash it, Camille, *will* you?"

She was laughing softly. He loved her laughter. Actually, he loved the Amazon and the military sergeant and the brisk schoolteacher and the Madonna and child and this aristocratic goddess in her sliver-and-blue ball gown and elaborately piled hair. He loved the woman with whom he had made love in his rooms and the woman who had begged to be held when she was feeling upset.

"Well, I will," she said, freeing her hand and bending over him to cup his face in her hands and kiss him softly on the lips. "But do get up. You will be ruining your splendid new evening clothes."

"You will?" He scrambled to his feet and caught her by the waist.

"I will," she said, "but only because I love you and cannot bear the thought of living without you. Not for any other reason."

"You will." He gazed at her for a moment and then tipped his face up to the sky. *"She will."* He lifted her from the ground and spun twice about with her while she laughed down at him. *"She will."*

He did not think he had spoken loudly. Part of his mind was aware that there might be sleepers in the houses all about the Circus, and they might not appreciate being woken by voices from the central garden. But from somewhere—in the darkness it was impossible to know exactly where or even in which direction—came the sound of someone clapping slowly.

They looked at each other, he and Camille, as he set her feet on the ground, their eyes widening with shock and then filling with amusement. He drew her close and held her against him while she wound her arms about his neck, and they laughed softly.

Twenty-three

❧

The wedding of Miss Camille Westcott to Mr. Joel Cunningham was set for a date in early September, six weeks after the birthday ball in the Upper Assembly Rooms. It was to take place at Bath Abbey, a somewhat surprising choice, perhaps, when the bride was an earl's illegitimate daughter and the groom was the illegitimate son of a lady of no great social significance and an Italian artist whom few people remembered and none could identify by name. But the bride was acknowledged and held in high esteem by the powerful Westcott family and the formidable Duke of Netherby, who was married to one of their number, and by Mrs. Kingsley, widow of one of Bath's wealthiest and most prominent citizens and the bride's maternal grandmother. And the groom was the great-nephew of the late Mr. Cox-Phillips, a prominent politician in his time and wealthy citizen of Bath, who had acknowledged the groom in his will by leaving him his two homes and his fortune. Joel's story, and, by association, Camille's, had captured the imagination of Bath, at least temporarily, and invitations to their wedding were coveted.

The whole of the Westcott family was to return to Bath for the occasion. So was the Reverend Michael Kingsley, whom many people remembered from his boyhood, and his affianced bride, granddaughter of a baronet, with her sister. Other Kingsley relatives were expected too. Miss Ford, enjoying some fame of her own as matron of the orphanage where the Duchess of Netherby and Mr. Cunningham had both grown up and where Miss Westcott had taught until very recently, had also been invited, as had the whole staff of the orphanage and all the children. Many people recalled that they had seen a number of those children quite frequently through the summer walking out on various excursions in an orderly line as they clung to a rope of startling purple hue. Rumor had it that the bride and groom were in the process of adopting two of the orphans as their own children.

The groom had also invited a number of personal friends as well as the staff of a certain butcher's shop and all the lecturers and many of the former students of the art school he had attended ten years or so ago. And invitations went out to numerous citizens, including friends of Mrs. Kingsley and people for whom the groom had painted portraits.

One person of real importance would not be in attendance. Lieutenant Harry Westcott was in the Peninsula with his regiment and would not have been able to travel home in time even if he could have been granted leave or had wanted to. A letter arrived for Camille a few days before the wedding, however, in which he expressed his very best wishes for his sister's happiness and his trust in her choice of mate, though it had surprised him. He also mentioned the fact that he had recently been in a great pitched battle, which had been a touch-and-go thing before the inevitable rout of the enemy. He had sustained an assortment of cuts and bruises during the hostilities, but the regimental sawbones, who was a good sort, had patched him up and assured him that in no time at all he would be as good as new with the addition of a few interesting scars to appeal to the ladies. He sent his love to his mother and Abby and anyone else who might like to have it.

Strangely, Camille thought as she folded the letter, Harry was the only one who seemed a little dubious about her choice—it had surprised him. No one else did. Indeed, everyone seemed happy for her. Perhaps they recognized that she had changed—and perhaps they saw that the changes were for the better. Perhaps they could see that she was in love, just as it was perfectly obvious that Anna was in love with Avery. Perhaps, she thought with a smile and a soft laugh, everyone loved a lover. She raised Harry's letter to her lips and said a silent prayer for his safety.

Joel had given notice to his landlord—he would move to the house on the hill after his marriage. He had finished Abigail's portrait, to the delight and even awe of all who saw it, though her grandmother would not display it until Camille's had been painted too. Joel left that until after his wedding. He was not sure if his intimate relationship with her would make her portrait easier or harder to paint, but he always welcomed a challenge, and this would surely be the biggest yet.

Camille gave her notice to Miss Ford but did assure

her she would teach right up until her wedding day if
necessary. She was cheered to discover that there had been
two other very promising applications after the position
had been offered to her, and that one of those applicants
was still available and eager for the job. Camille met her
and approved of her sunny nature and sensible disposition
and enthusiastic knowledge on all sorts of subjects, academic and otherwise, and obvious love of children. Even
so, Camille felt a pang of regret for having to leave so
soon. She would see the children again, though. She would
visit, and a number of them would come up to the house
on the hill for various reasons. Joel was already concoct-
ing an ambitious scheme for gathering them all there over
Christmas for feasts and parties and games and gifts and
the celebration of the birth of a baby.

The legal arrangements for the adoption of Sarah and
Winifred were well under way. Sarah did not need to be
consulted, of course, being too young to express an opinion. However, that she loved Camille above anyone else
was acknowledged by all, as was the fact that Camille
adored the baby quite as much as she could possibly love
any child of her own.

There was to be no child of her own yet. She had discovered that a week after her betrothal.

Winifred, at nine years old, was old enough to be consulted. Indeed, it was imperative that her wishes be known.
She had lived at the orphanage all her life. It was the only
home she had ever known, the people there the only family. It might well be that she would choose to stay rather
than launch into the unknown several years before it
would be necessary for her to do so anyway. Camille took

her into one of the visitor rooms a week after her betrothal and closed the door.

"Winifred," she said when they were both seated, "you have probably heard that Mr. Cunningham and I are to be married."

"I have, Miss Westcott," Winifred said, seated primly on the edge of her sofa cushion, her hands folded in her lap. "I am very happy for you."

"Thank you," Camille said. "You probably do not also know that after we are married and move to our house up in the hills we will be taking Sarah with us as our adopted daughter."

The girl's thin hands tightened about each other. "I am very happy for her," she said. "I have prayed for her, and my prayers are to be answered."

"We have asked Miss Ford," Camille said, "and Miss Ford has asked the members of the board of governors if it is also possible for us to adopt you. They have granted permission, but since you are old enough to have a say in the matter, I have undertaken to be the one to speak privately with you. The choice will be yours, Winifred. You may remain here where you have always belonged and where you are safe and comfortable, or you may come with us and be our daughter and Sarah's elder sister. We would give you a home and love you and care for you and provide for you when you grow up. No matter what you decide to do when that time comes, you would always be our daughter, and our home would always be yours. We would always love you."

Winifred's eyes stared out at her from a thin pasty face. "But why have you chosen me?" she asked in a voice that was higher pitched than usual. "I always try to be good and to learn my lessons and be tidy and help others and say my prayers, but other people do not always like me because I am still a sinner. I am not worthy of such an honor, Miss Westcott. Sarah—"

"Winifred." Camille went to sit beside her and set a hand over the two clasped ones. They were icy cold. "Let me tell you something about love. It is unconditional. Do you know what that is?"

The child nodded. She had not taken her eyes off Camille's face.

"Love does not have to be earned," Camille told her. "You are indeed a good girl and conscientious and pious. Those are admirable qualities and have won my approbation. They alone would not necessarily win my love, however. Love is not the reward for good behavior. Love just is. I want you to know that if you choose to be my daughter and Mr. Cunningham's, we will love you no matter what. You would not have to feel you must be on your best behavior every moment. You would not have to feel you must prove yourself worthy or fear that we would send you back here if you did not live up to our expectations. We *have* no expectations, Winifred. We just love you and want you to be part of a family with us and Sarah and any other children we may have in the future. We want you to be happy. We want you to be able to run and play and talk and laugh and do whatever you wish to do, provided only that it is not dangerous to yourself or others. We want you to be the person you choose to be. I do love you, Winifred."

The eyes still stared. The complexion was still pasty. "I am not pretty," she half whispered.

Her brown hair fell in two braids over her ears and shoulders. Her forehead was broad, her eyes and other facial features unremarkable. It was a small face and had not yet grown into her permanent teeth. She was thin, even a bit gangly. She was indeed not a pretty child.

"Most girls and women are not," Camille said, resisting the temptation to protest and perhaps lose all chance of winning the child's trust. "Many are beautiful, however. Have you noticed that? Some women are plain, even bordering upon the ugly, but no one ever notices except perhaps upon a first encounter. There is so much goodness and light and kindness and happiness and vitality welling up from inside them that their outer appearance is transformed into beauty."

"Can I be beautiful?" Winifred asked.

"Yes, of course," Camille said. And perhaps even pretty in time, with an elfin, dainty sort of look. "You are already well on the way."

"Would I be Winifred Cunningham?" the child asked.

"I believe we would like that," Camille told her, "though the choice would be yours. Hamlin may seem too much a part of your identity to be abandoned."

"Winifred Cunningham," the girl whispered. "Would I call you Mama?"

"I would like that above all things," Camille said—though she was only thirteen years older. "Do you wish to think about it, Winifred? It is a huge decision for you and I do not want to press anything upon you that you may regret later. I do want you to know, however, that you will be loved regardless."

"I do not need time." Winifred was back to clasping her hands very tightly in her lap, and Camille withdrew her own. "When I heard you were going to marry Mr. Cunningham and leave here so soon after Miss Snow left and married the Duke of Netherby, I cried a bit and prayed for the strength to be glad for you. But I could not feel quite glad. It was selfish of me, but I am being rewarded anyway. Miss Westcott . . . I am going to have *a mama and a papa? And a sister?* I am going to be Winifred Cunningham, part of the Cunningham family?"

"And the Duke and Duchess of Netherby will be your aunt and uncle," Camille said. "And there are others too."

Winifred's face looked even more pasty, if anything.

"Would you like to be held?" Camille asked her. "Would you like me to hug you?"

The child nodded and squirmed into Camille's arms and clung tightly. She ended up somehow on Camille's lap, all gangly legs and thin body and urgent arms. Camille kissed the very white, very straight parting along the top of her head and rested her cheek there. She would do what her father had never done, she thought, closing her eyes. And because he had been the loser in his inability to love or accept love, she forgave him for all the pain he had caused her and loved him anyway.

Joel was familiar with Bath Abbey, inside and out. He had always admired its beauty and studied its architecture and intricate decoration with great attention and awe. He had wandered inside, and had often sat there for long minutes, absorbing the atmosphere of peace and exaltation he had not felt anywhere else, even in other churches. He had been to a few services there, but had always sat as close to the back as possible, more an observer than a participant.

In his wildest imaginings he could not have pictured himself being married there, the pews almost filled with people both humble and fashionable who had come to witness the event and share his joy and his bride's. Several rows were occupied by children close to bursting with excitement but on their best behavior under the eagle eyes of Miss Ford and their housemothers and the new teacher. Even so, a few of them bounced in their seats and waggled their fingers at Joel and smiled broadly at him as he walked to the front with Martin Silver, his best man, to take his seat and await the arrival of his bride.

Winifred and Sarah, in crisp new dresses, sat on the other side of the aisle from him, Sarah on Abigail's lap, sucking on two fingers and looking as if she was about to fall asleep, though she did remove the fingers and beam a wide smile at Joel when she saw him. Winifred, her braids wound in a coronet about the crown of her head, gazed at him with wide eyes and looked taut with anxiety. He felt a bit the same himself and winked at her before sitting down.

He thought with longing of his faithful old coat and boots and the old cravats, which had never been starched to death as this one had been. Everything had changed since he had put himself under the care of Mr. Orville, his great-uncle's erstwhile valet, now his own. He might never know comfort in his clothes ever again unless he learned to put his foot down, something he was finding virtually impossible under the fond, reproving eyes of the professional gentleman's gentleman. He had to admit, though, that the smart young gentleman who frowned back at him from the looking glass these days looked really quite dashing. Today, he thought with an inner grimace of discomfort, he appeared nothing short of magnificent. And he could check that impression anytime he wished by gazing down into the high gloss of his new Hessian boots. He carefully did not look down.

"She is here," Marvin murmured to him, leaning a little closer, and sure enough the two clergymen—one was the Reverend Michael Kingsley, Camille's uncle—both magnificent in clerical robes, had arrived at the front, the congregation was rising, and the organ was launching into something solemn and thrilling. Joel stood and turned.

She was approaching along the nave on the arm of the Earl of Riverdale. She was dressed with simple elegance in an ivory-colored dress and a small-brimmed straw bonnet with flowers about the crown. As she drew closer Joel could see that the bodice and hem of her dress were encrusted with pearls. She wore slippers and gloves of dull gold. In truth, though, he did not spare much attention for her appearance. He saw only Camille. She was wearing none of her recognizable personas today. Today she was without masks, without defenses, or so it appeared to him. Today she was simply herself. Today she was a bride, *his* bride. Her eyes singled him out and focused upon him as she approached, and she smiled.

Someone must have lit a dozen candelabra overhead. The fanciful thought banished his terror, and he smiled back at her. He was in Bath Abbey, surrounded by people of great importance and people who were simply important to him. His daughters were across the aisle from him and his bride was almost at his side, and there really were no words . . .

They turned together and the church and congregation were behind them and only the clergymen and the altar and the great solemnity of the occasion before them.

"Dearly beloved." They were two of the most solemn, most awe-inspiring, most joyful words in the English language when spoken together and at the beginning of the nuptial service. They had been spoken now, and the service was *for him and Camille*.

Joel spoke only to her when he made his vows, and she spoke only to him. But there were moments in life—their waltz in the Upper Rooms had been one and this was another—when one was aware simultaneously of the two realities of being alone or at least alone with one other person and yet surrounded by other people, all in one harmony of belonging to friends, family, community, the human race. They were precious moments, to be lived to the full and cherished in memory for the rest of a lifetime.

And then they were man and wife and no one was to put them asunder. They signed the register in the vestry and waited while their signatures were witnessed, and came out again, her arm drawn through his, to look about at their friends and family and well-wishers and pass along the nave and out into the spacious yard Bath Abbey shared with the Roman baths and the Pump Room.

He saw faces in the congregation this time, all smiling warmly, a few—Camille's mother and both grandmothers, Anna—with tears in their eyes. Sarah was still looking on the verge of sleep, but she held out her arms as they approached and Joel took her from Abigail and held her nestled against his shoulder. Winifred gazed up at them with longing eyes, and Camille bent over her to kiss her cheek and then took her by the hand. And they walked along the nave, the four of them, a patched-together family united by the powerful glue of love and hope.

Joel smiled at his wife—good God, she was *his wife*—and held her arm more tightly to his side.

"Camille," he said beneath the sound of the joyful anthem the organ was playing, "my wife."

"Oh yes," she said, breathless as they passed through the great doors into sunshine. "Yes, I am."

A flower-decked open carriage would be waiting for them on the other side of the classical columns at the end of the yard to take them up to the wedding breakfast in the Upper Rooms, but first they would have to run the gauntlet of guests who had slipped outside ahead of them armed with flower petals to pelt at them and of curious bystanders who had gathered to watch the show.

"They will be horribly disappointed if we do not make a run for it," Joel said, releasing Camille's arm and grasping her hand instead. Sarah was snug and secure on his other arm. He leaned forward and grinned at Winifred. "Ready?"

"Yes, Papa," she said, smiling sunnily back at him.

"Hold tight," Camille said.

And they were off, running the gauntlet, laughing helplessly. Winifred's giggles were high pitched and utterly joyful. Even Sarah was chuckling as though the game had been designed for her exclusive amusement.

"Happy?" Joel cried as petals rained about them and clung to their clothes.

"Happy," his wife said.

"Happy," their elder daughter screeched.

There were no other words beyond that obvious one.

But why did there need to be when there were feelings in overabundance that were shared by one's nearest and dearest?

The abbey bells were pealing out the glad tidings of a couple newly married.

Yes, this was indeed happiness.

READ ON FOR AN EXCERPT FROM THE THIRD BOOK
IN MARY BALOGH'S WESTCOTT SERIES,

Someone to Wed

AVAILABLE FROM PIATKUS IN NOVEMBER 2017.

"The Earl of Riverdale," the butler announced after opening wide the double doors of the drawing room as though to admit a regiment and then standing to one side so that the gentleman named could stride past him.

The announcement was not strictly necessary. Wren had heard the arrival of his vehicle, and guessed it was a curricle rather than a traveling carriage, although she had not got to her feet to look. And he was almost exactly on time. She liked that. The two gentlemen who had come before him had been late, one by all of half an hour. Those two had been sent on their way as soon as was decently possible, though not only because of their tardiness. Mr. Sweeney, who had come a week ago, had had bad teeth and a way of stretching his mouth to expose them at disconcertingly frequent intervals even when he was not actually smiling. Mr. Richman, who had come four days ago, had had no discernible personality, a fact that had been quite as disconcerting as Mr. Sweeney's teeth. Now here came the third.

He strode forward a few paces before coming to an abrupt halt as the butler closed the doors behind him. He looked about the room with apparent surprise at the discovery that it was occupied only by two women, one of whom—Maude, Wren's maid—was seated off in a corner, her head bent over some needlework, in the role of chaperon. His eyes came to rest upon Wren and he bowed.

"Miss Heyden?" It was a question.

Her first reaction after her initial approval of his punctuality was acute dismay. One glance told her he was not at all what she wanted.

He was tall, well formed, immaculately and elegantly tailored, dark haired, and impossibly handsome. And young—in his late twenties or early thirties, at a guess. If she were to dream up the perfect hero for the perfect romantic fairy tale, she could not do better than the very real man standing halfway across the room, waiting for her to confirm that she was indeed the lady who had invited him to take tea at Withington House.

But this was no fairy tale, and the sheer perfection of him alarmed her and caused her to lean back farther in her chair and deeper into the shade provided by the curtains drawn across the window on her side of the fireplace. She had not wanted a handsome man or even a particularly young man. She had hoped for someone older, more ordinary, perhaps balding or acquiring a bit of a paunch, pleasant-looking but basically . . . well, ordinary. With decent teeth and at least *something* of a personality. But she could hardly deny her identity and dismiss him without further ado.

"Yes," she said. "How do you do, Lord Riverdale? Do

have a seat." She gestured to the chair across the hearth from her own. She knew something of social manners and ought to have risen to greet him, of course, but she had good reason to keep to the shadows, at least for now.

He eyed the chair as he approached it and sat with obvious reluctance. "I do beg your pardon," he said. "I appear to be early. Punctuality is one of my besetting sins, I am afraid. I always make the mistake of assuming that when I am invited somewhere for half past two, I am expected to arrive at half past two. I hope some of your other guests will be here soon, including a few ladies."

She was further alarmed when he smiled. If it was possible to look more handsome than handsome, he was looking it. He had perfect teeth, and his eyes crinkled attractively at the corners when he smiled. And his eyes were very blue. Oh, this was wretched. Who was number four on her list?

"Punctuality is a virtue as far as I am concerned, Lord Riverdale," she said. "I am a businesswoman, as perhaps you are aware. To run a successful business, one must respect other people's time as well as one's own. You are on time. You see?" She swept one hand toward the clock ticking on the mantel. "It is twenty-five minutes to three. And I am not expecting any other guests."

His smile disappeared and he glanced at Maude before looking back at Wren. "I see," he said. "Perhaps you had not realized, Miss Heyden, that neither my mother nor my sister came into the country with me. Or perhaps you did not realize I have no wife to accompany me. I beg your pardon. I have no wish to cause you any embarrassment or to compromise you in any way." His hands closed about the arms of his chair in a signal that he was about to rise.

"But my invitation was addressed to you alone," she

said. "I am no young girl who needs to be hedged about with relatives to protect me from the dangerous company of single gentlemen. And I do have Maude for propriety's sake. We are neighbors of sorts, Lord Riverdale, though more than eight miles separate Withington House from Brambledean Court and I am not always here and you are not always there. Nevertheless, now that I am the owner of Withington and have completed my year of mourning for my aunt and uncle, I have taken it upon myself to become acquainted with some of my neighbors. I entertained Mr. Sweeney here last week and Mr. Richman a few days after. Do you know them?"

He was frowning, and he had not removed his hands from the arms of his chair. He still looked uncomfortable and ready to spring to his feet at the earliest excuse. "I have an acquaintance with both gentlemen," he said, "though I cannot claim to *know* either one. I have been in possession of my title and property for only a year and have not spent much time here yet."

"Then I am fortunate you are here now," she said as the drawing room doors opened and the tea tray was carried in and set before her. She moved to the edge of her chair, turning slightly to her left without conscious intent as she did so, and poured the tea. Maude came silently across the room to hand the earl his cup and saucer and then to offer the plate of cakes.

"I did not know Mr. and Mrs. Heyden, your aunt and uncle," he said, nodding his thanks to Maude. "I am sorry for your loss. I understand they died within a very short while of each other."

"Yes," she said. "My aunt died a few days after taking to her bed with a severe headache, and my uncle died less than a week later. His health had been failing for some time, and I believe he simply gave up the struggle after she had gone. He doted upon her." And Aunt Megan upon him despite the thirty-year gap in their ages and the hurried nature of their marriage almost twenty years ago.

"I am sorry," he said again. "They raised you?"

"Yes," she said. "They could not have done better by me if they had been my parents. Your predecessor did not live at Brambledean, I understand, or visit often. I speak of the late Earl of Riverdale, not his unfortunate son. Do you intend to take up permanent residence there?"

The unfortunate son, Wren had learned, had succeeded to the title until it was discovered that his father had contracted a secret marriage as a very young man and that the secret wife had still been alive when he married the mother of his three children. Those children, already adults, had suddenly found themselves to be illegitimate, and the new earl had lost the title to the man now seated on the other side of the hearth. The late earl's first marriage had produced one legitimate child, a daughter, who had grown up in an orphanage in Bath, knowing nothing of her identity. All this and more Wren had learned before adding the earl to her list. The story had been sensational news last year and kept the gossip mills grinding for weeks. The details had not been difficult to unearth when there were servants and tradespeople only too eager to share what came their way.

One never knew quite where truth ended and exaggeration or misunderstanding or speculation or downright falsehood began, of course, but Wren did know a surprising amount about her neighbors, considering the fact that she had absolutely no social dealings with them. She knew, for example, that both Mr. Sweeney and Mr. Richman were respectable but impoverished gentlemen. And she knew that Brambledean had been almost totally neglected by the late earl, who had left it to be mismanaged almost to the point of total ruin by a lazy steward who had graced the taproom of his local inn more often than his office. By now the house and estate needed the infusion of a vast sum of money.

Wren had heard that the new earl was a conscientious gentleman of comfortable means, but that he was not nearly wealthy enough to cope with the enormity of the disaster he had inherited so unexpectedly. The late earl had not been a poor man. Far from it, in fact. But his fortune had gone to his legitimate daughter. She might have saved the day by marrying the new earl and so reuniting the entailed property with the fortune, but she had married the Duke of Netherby instead. Wren could well understand why the many-faceted story had so dominated conversation both above and below stairs last year.

"I do intend to live at Brambledean," the Earl of Riverdale said. He was frowning into his cup. "I have another home in Kent, of which I am dearly fond, but I am needed here, and an absentee landlord is rarely a good landlord. The people dependent upon me here deserve better."

He looked every bit as handsome when he was frowning as he did when he smiled. Wren hesitated. It was not too late to send him on his way, as she had done with his two predecessors. She had given a plausible reason for inviting him and had plied him with tea and cakes. He would doubtless go away thinking her eccentric. He would probably disapprove of her inviting him alone when she was a single lady with only the flimsy chaperonage of a maid. But he would shrug off the encounter soon enough and forget about her. And she did not really care what he might think or say about her anyway.

But now she remembered that number four on her list—a man in his late fifties—had always professed himself to be a confirmed bachelor, and number five was reputed to complain almost constantly of ailments both real and imagined. She had added them only because the list had looked pathetically short with just three names.

"I understand, Lord Riverdale," she said, "that you are not a wealthy man." Perhaps it was too late—or very nearly so. If she sent him away now, he would think her vulgar as well as eccentric and careless of her reputation.

He took his time about setting his cup and saucer down on the table beside him before turning his eyes upon her. Only the slight flaring of his nostrils warned her that she had angered him. "Do you indeed?" he said, a distinct note of hauteur in his voice. "I thank you for the tea, Miss Heyden. I will take no more of your time." He stood up.

"I could offer a solution," she said, and now it was very definitely too late to retreat. "To your relatively impoverished state, that is. You need money to undo the neglect of years at Brambledean and to fulfill your duty to the people dependent upon you there. It might take you years, perhaps even the rest of your life, if you do it only through careful management. It is unfortunately necessary to put a great deal of money into a business before one can get money out of it. Perhaps you are considering taking out a loan or a mortgage if the property is not already mortgaged. Or perhaps you intend to marry a rich wife."

He stood very straight and tall, and his jaw had set into a hard line. His nostrils were still flared. He looked magnificent and even slightly menacing, and for a moment

Wren regretted the words she had already spoken. But it was too late now to unsay them.

"I beg to inform you, Miss Heyden," he said curtly, "that I find your curiosity offensive. Good day to you."

"You are perhaps aware," she said, "that my uncle was enormously rich, much of his wealth deriving from the glassworks he owned in Staffordshire. He left everything to me, my aunt having predeceased him. He taught me a great deal about the business, which I helped him run during his last years and now run myself. The business has lost none of its momentum in the last year, and is, indeed, gradually expanding. And there are properties and investments even apart from that. I am a very wealthy woman, Lord Riverdale. But my life lacks something, just as yours lacks ready money. I am twenty-nine years old, very nearly thirty, and I would like . . . someone to wed. In my own person, I am not marriageable, but I do have money. And you do not."

She paused to see if he had something to say, but he looked as though he were rooted to the spot, his eyes fixed upon her, his jaw like granite. She was suddenly very glad Maude was in the room, though her presence was also embarrassing. Maude did not approve of any of this and did not scruple to say so when they were alone.

"Perhaps we could combine forces and each acquire what we want," Wren said.

"You are offering me . . . *marriage*?" he asked.

Had she not made herself clear? "Yes," she said. He continued to stare at her, and she became uncomfortably aware of the ticking of the clock.

"Miss Heyden," he said at last, "I have not even seen your face."

Do you love historical fiction?

Want the chance to hear news about your favourite authors (and the chance to win free books)?

Mary Balogh
Charlotte Betts
Jessica Blair
Frances Brody
Gaelen Foley
Elizabeth Hoyt
Eloisa James
Lisa Kleypas
Stephanie Laurens
Claire Lorrimer
Sarah MacLean
Amanda Quick
Julia Quinn

Then visit the Piatkus website and blog
www.piatkus.co.uk | www.piatkusbooks.net

And follow us on Facebook and Twitter
www.facebook.com/piatkusfiction | www.twitter.com/piatkusbooks

piatkus